Augustus Row

Masonic Biography and Dictionary

Augustus Row

Masonic Biography and Dictionary

Reprint of the original, first published in 1868.

1st Edition 2022 | ISBN: 978-3-37504-754-2

Verlag (Publisher): Salzwasser Verlag GmbH, Zeilweg 44, 60439 Frankfurt, Deutschland
Vertretungsberechtigt (Authorized to represent): E. Roepke, Zeilweg 44, 60439 Frankfurt, Deutschland
Druck (Print): Books on Demand GmbH, In de Tarpen 42, 22848 Norderstedt, Deutschland

MASONIC

BIOGRAPHY AND DICTIONARY

COMPRISING

THE HISTORY OF ANCIENT MASONRY, ANTIQUITY OF
MASONRY, WRITTEN AND UNWRITTEN LAW,
DERIVATION AND DEFINITION OF
MASONIC TERMS,
BIOGRAPHIES OF EMINENT MASONS,
STATISTICS,

LIST OF ALL LODGES IN THE UNITED STATES, ETC.

COMPILED BY

AUGUSTUS ROW, K.T.

"Let there be Light."

PHILADELPHIA:
J. B. LIPPINCOTT & CO.
1868.

Entered, according to the Act of Congress, in the year 1868, by

AUGUSTUS ROW,

In the Clerk's Office of the District Court of the United States for the Western District of Pennsylvania.

TO

ALFRED CREIGH, LL.D.,

WASHINGTON, PA.

M. P. GRAND MASTER OF CRYPTIC MASONS OF PENNSYLVANIA, GRAND
RECORDER OF KNIGHTS TEMPLAR OF PENNSYLVANIA, AND
PAST PROVINCIAL DEPUTY GRAND COMMANDER
AND GRAND PRIOR OF KNIGHTS TEM-
PLAR OF CANADA, ETC.

BROTHER CREIGH:

As a memorial of esteem and respect, and on account of the friendly relations existing between us, I dedicate this work to you.

THE AUTHOR.

(iii)

PREFACE.

THE advantages of a comprehensive Masonic Cyclopedia must be so apparent to every member of the craft, that there is no necessity to speculate upon the merits of such a work. The design in the execution of the present volume has been to compile facts, free from useless verbiage, so as to meet the want of a work for ready reference. This has been the result of much labor and expense, and we tender it to the craft, with the full assurance of many intelligent brethren of the United States and Europe, that this want has been supplied in this volume. Everything that has any connection with, or has been in any manner the offspring of Freemasonry, or systemed after it, with or without merit, political, civil, religious, or charitable, has been introduced; together with full and complete lists of all Lodges in the United States. It is sincerely hoped that the work will prove an honor to the fraternity, and lead to a correct understanding of the truths of Freemasonry, as exhibited by an enlightened Christian system of strict morality, religion, and charity.

THE AUTHOR.

CONTENTS.

	PAGES
BIOGRAPHY AND DICTIONARY	9–298
LIST OF LODGES IN THE UNITED STATES AND CANADA	299–354
LIST OF GRAND CHAPTERS IN THE UNITED STATES AND CANADA	355–362
SUBORDINATE ENCAMPMENTS ORGANIZED UNDER AUTHORITY OF THE GRAND ENCAMPMENT OF THE UNITED STATES, OR RECOGNIZED BY IT	363–365

(vii)

MASONIC

BIOGRAPHY AND DICTIONARY.

A.

Aaron's Rod.—A symbol in the H. R. A. C., constituting one of the Holy things that were preserved in the Tabernacle, referring to the rebellion of Korah and his friends. Twelve rods were directed to be brought in—one for each tribe—by Moses. It being an honor to compete with Aaron for the priesthood, the princes obeyed the command. When the rods were produced before the people, eleven of them remained as they were, without change, but the twelfth rod budded, blossomed, and bare fruit. This was Aaron's rod.

Aaron.—The oldest son of Annam, of the tribe of Levi, and brother of Moses. He assisted in bringing the Israelites from Egypt. As the priesthood was hereditary among the Levites, he became the High Priest of the Hebrews. He died at Mt. Hor, aged 123 years.

Abaciscus.—Checkered blocks from which the pavement of Solomon's Temple was paved.

Abacus.—As used by the Knights Templars, is a circle with a Maltese Cross in red. On the circle is inscribed *In hoc signo vinces.* It is also used as the name of the Staff Officer of the Grand Commander of K. T.

(9)

ABBREVIATIONS.

Abbreviations.—The following are masonic abbreviations in general use:

A∴ D∴ (*Anno Depositionis.*) In the Year of Deposit. Used by Royal and Select Masters. To find this date, add 1000 to vulgar era.

A∴ L∴ (*Anno Lucis.*) In the Year of Light. Used by ancient craft Masons. Add 4000 to the vulgar era.

A∴ H∴ (*Anno Hebraico.*) In the Hebrew Year. Used by Masons of the Scottish Rite. The year begins 17th September, the first of Tisri. Add 3760 to vulgar era.

A∴ I∴ (*Anno Inventionis.*) In the Year of the Discovery. Used by Royal Arch Masons. Add 530 to vulgar era.

A∴ M∴ (*Anno Mundi.*) In the Year of the World. Used in Scottish Rite.

A∴ O∴ (*Anno Ordinis.*) In the Year of the Order. Used by Knights Templar. Subtract 1118 from vulgar era to find the year of the order.

A∴ D∴ (*Anno Domini.*) In the Year of our Lord.

A∴ C∴ (*Ante Christum.*) Before Christ.

J∴ N∴ R∴ J∴ (*Jesus Nazarenus Rex Judæorum.*) Jesus of Nazareth, King of the Jews. Knights Templar will understand.

J∴ H∴ S∴ (*Jesus Hominum Salvator.*) Jesus, Saviour of men.

A∴ L∴ G∴ D∴ G∴ A∴ D∴ l'U∴ (French—*A la gloire du Grand Architecte de l'Univers.*) To the glory of the Grand Architect of the Universe. All French masonic writings have this caption.

A∴ l'O∴ (French—*A l'Orient.*) At the East. Seat of the Lodge.

F∴ or FF∴ (French—*Frère ou Frères.*) Brother or Brothers.

G∴ M∴ Grand Master.

J∴ W∴ Junior Warden.

ABBREVIATIONS.

M∴ M∴ (French—*Mois Maçonnique.*) Masonic Month. The French masonic year begins with March. Ours ought also to begin at same time.

M∴ W∴ Most Worshipful.

R∴ □ (French.) Respectable Lodge. Worshipful Lodge.

R∴ W∴ Right Worshipful.

S∴ S∴ S∴ (French—*Trois fois salut.*) Thrice Greeting. Common on French masonic certificates.

S∴ W∴ Senior Warden.

V∴ (French—*Vénérable.*) Worshipful.

V∴ L∴ (French—*Vraie Lumière.*) True Light.

V∴ W∴ Very Worshipful.

W∴ M∴ Worshipful Master.

P∴ M∴ Past Master.

S∴ SS∴ Saint or Saints.

U∴ D∴ Under Dispensation.

T∴ I∴ Thrice Illustrious.

D∴ I∴ Deputy Illustrious.

P∴ C∴ W∴ Principal Conductor of Work.

C∴ G∴ Captain of the Guards. These last four are officers of the Council of Royal and Select Masters.

S∴ D∴ Senior Deacon.

J∴ D∴ Junior Deacon.

G∴ C∴ Grand Commander.

G∴ Generalissimo.

C∴ G∴ Captain-General.

P∴ Prelate.

W∴ Warden.

S∴ B∴ Standard or Sword Bearer.

G∴ M∴ A∴ (French—*Grand Maître Architect.*) Grand Master Architect—12th degree Ancient Scottish Rite.

C∴ D∴ S∴ A∴ (French—*Chevalier du Serpent d'airain.*) Knight of the Brazen Serpent—25th degree Ancient Scotch Rite.

ABBREVIATIONS.

K∴ C∴ M∴ Knight of the Christian Mark.

K∴ C∴ Knight of Constantinople.

C∴ d'O∴ (French — *Chevalier d'Orient.*) Knight of the East.

C∴ d'O∴ d'O∴ (French — *Chevalier d'Orient et d'Occident.*) Knight of the East and West—17th degree Ancient Scotch Rite.

K∴ H∴ S∴ Knight of the Holy Sepulcher.

S∴ M∴ Sovereign Master.

C∴ Chancellor.

M∴ P∴ Master of the Palace.

P∴ d'L∴ (*Prince du Liban.*) Prince of Libanus—22d degree Ancient Scotch Rite.

C∴ d'S∴ (*Chevalier du Soliel.*) Knight of the Sun— 28th Scotch Rite.

S∴ P∴ R∴ (*Souverain Prince Rose-Croix.*) Prince of Rose Croix—18th Scotch Rite.

P∴ J∴ (*Prévôt et Juge.*) Provost and Judge—7th Scotch Rite.

R∴ A∴ and H∴ R∴ A∴ Royal Arch and Holy Royal Arch.

A∴ and A∴ R∴ Ancient and Accepted Rite.

B∴ B∴ Burning Bush.

C∴ C∴ Celestial Company.

D∴ G∴ M∴ Deputy Grand Master.

D∴ D∴ G∴ M∴ District Deputy Grand Master.

E∴ A∴ Entered Apprentice.

F∴ C∴ Fellow Craft.

G∴ Com∴ Grand Commandery.

G∴ E∴ Grand East; Grand Encampment.

GG∴ L∴ (*Grandes Loges.*) Grand Lodges.

G∴ O∴ Grand Orient.

G∴ R∴ A∴ C∴ Grand Royal Arch Chapter.

I∴ T∴ N∴ O∴ T∴ G∴ A∴ O∴ T∴ U∴ In the name of the Grand Architect of the Universe.

Knt∴ T∴ Knight Templar.
M∴ E∴ G∴ H∴ P∴ Most Excellent Grand High Priest.
R∴ †∴ Rose Cross.
R∴ E∴ A∴ et A∴ (*Rite Ecossais Ancien et Accepté.*) Ancient and Accepted Scotch Rite.
R∴ E∴ G∴ C∴ Right Eminent Grand Commander.
S∴ S∴ Sanctum Sanctorum.
S∴ G∴ I∴ G∴ Sovereign Grand Inspector General.
S∴ P∴ R∴ S∴ Sublime Prince of the Royal Secret.
Surv∴ 1er, Surveillant 1er. Senior Warden.
Surv∴ 2e, Surveillant 2e. Junior Warden.
T∴ S∴ (French—*Très Sage.*) Wisest.

Abelites.—A sect mentioned by St. Augustine in Africa. An order in Germany in 1746 of Christian principles. Its motto: "Sincerity, Friendship, and Hope."

Abiram.—A son of Eliole, the Reubenite. He with others conspired to divest Moses and Aaron of the power conferred upon them by God, and on account thereof was, with his family, swallowed up in the earth. Referred to in the Elect of Nine.

Ablution (a symbol in the ancient S. Rite).—Washing and purification.

Abracadabra.—The name of the Almighty was secreted by the Basilidians under this word, and written

```
          A
         A B
        A B R
       A B R A
      A B R A C
     A B R A C A
    A B R A C A D
   A B R A C A D A
  A B R A C A D A B
 A B R A C A D A B R
A B R A C A D A B R A
```

Abney, Asbury Arnold.—Was born in South Carolina in 1818, and died at Bellevue, Louisiana, November 4th, 1866. He received his degrees in Minden Lodge, No. 51, and was a Past Master of Fillmore Lodge, No. 154, and W. M. of Bellevue Lodge, No. 95, and was its Master at

14 ABRAXAS—ACCEPTED.

the time of his death. He was District Deputy Grand of the G. L. He was buried at Bossier Point, November 5th, 1866.

Abraxas.—A Basilidian intelligence, from the name Abraham, and bestowed upon the Sun. The Basilidians held that the seven planets made up the Universe, and as such to be God.

Acacia.—A kind of decondria momogynia class of plants. Its flower is composed of five petals arranged in a circular form. It is found in the East and America. The fragrant Cassia was one of the sweet spices from which the oil for anointing was extracted. A Jewish custom prevailed of planting it upon the graves of the departed. It is held by Masons to have been the color of the aprons worn by the brethren who searched under King Solomon.

Academie des Illumines d'Avignon.—Established at Avignon, in 1785, and admitted both sexes, and taught Philosophy.

Academy of Antiquities.—Originated in Rome, in the sixteenth century. Opened in Warsaw in 1763. Its secrets were Alchemy with masonic forms.

Academy of Sages.—Established in France in 1776, and aimed at the introduction of the high degrees of the Philosophic Rite.

Academy of Sublime Masters of the Luminous Ring.— A degree introduced by Baron Grout, of Blairsfindic, into Douay Lodge, France, in 1815. The studies of Freemasonry occupied a prominent place in the institute.

Academy of True Masons.—Established at Montpellier, France, 1778. The degrees, six, to wit: True Mason, True Masonic the Right, Knight of Golden Key, Knight of Iris, Knight of Argonautus, and Knight of Golden Fleece.

Accepted.—A term acquired by Masons at the building of the second Temple. Solomon declared the fraternity

ACELDAMA — ADAMS. 15

free, and at the completion of the work were given a medal with the word *free* upon it. That portion who aided in building the Temple, settled in Judea, and afterward taken into captivity by the Jews, were released from bondage by Cyrus, and freed from taxes and duties, and declared *free and accepted*.

Aceldama.—A field near Jerusalem, used to bury the dead of the Crusaders and pilgrims. Reference is made to it in K. T.

Acting G. Master.—When Kings honored the order in accepting the office. of Grand Master, it was conceded that they should act thus during life. In 1782 the Grand Lodge ordered that when a prince of royal blood accepted the position, they should have power to appoint an Acting Grand Master.

Adams, William H.—The late Right Worshipful Grand Secretary of the Right Worshipful Grand Lodge of Pennsylvania, was born in Philadelphia, August 27th, 1809. His father, William Adams, came to this country in 1798, in the same vessel which bore the infant form of him whose presence as one of the Grand Chaplains of this Grand Lodge at all its communications is looked for and expected as regularly as that of the Right Worshipful Grand Master himself. William Adams, the father, was an active Mason; he resided in Philadelphia, and for many years was Tyler of a number of the subordinate Lodges, and among others of Washington Lodge, No. 59, where he held the office for fourteen successive years, from 1825 to 1839, during which time his son, the subject of these remarks, was a member of, and passed through all the Chairs of the same Lodge. The father was at one time a member of Philadelphia Lodge, No. 72, and at the date of his death, which took place about the year 1848, was a member of Solomon's Lodge, No. 114.

In September, 1828, the petition of William H. Adams

16

ADAMS.

for initiation and membership was presented to Lafayette Lodge, No. 71, in Philadelphia; and upon the 24th of the following month, he was approved, and by virtue of a dispensation from the Right Worshipful Grand Master, initiated into the mysteries of Freemasonry, being then but little over nineteen years of age. The degrees of Fellow Craft and Master Mason he took in due course in the months of November and December respectively, of the same year. In January, 1829, he resigned from membership in Lodge No. 71, and in April of the same year was elected a member of Washington Lodge, No. 59, in Philadelphia, a connection which he maintained uninterruptedly for a period of not quite the full measure of thirty-seven years, and which terminated only with his death.

Upon the 14th of December, 1830, Brother Adams was elected Junior Warden of this Lodge; in December of the following year Senior Warden ; and December 11th, 1832, he was elected to the Oriental Chair. He was installed in this office at a special meeting, held December 19th, 1832, by Brother Samuel H. Perkins, now one of the Past Grand Masters of the Grand Lodge, acting as Worshipful Master, *pro tem.*

After serving one term as Worshipful Master, Brother Adams was elected, December 10th, 1833, Secretary of his Lodge; this office he held for twenty-seven years, by successive re-elections, up to December, 1860.

It was during this period that the Anti-Masonic storm arose and raged in all its fury and violence. Many bent before the blast, and, yielding to the force of the tempest, were driven from the altars of the fraternity, and openly forswore their allegiance, or sought safety and repose by a tacit denial of their faith. Not so Brother Adams : he remained firm, faithful and true, amid all the blasts of that most malignant and unrighteous persecution.

A Grand Visitation was made in the fall of 1836 to Washington Lodge, No. 59, by the then Right Worshipful Grand Master, Tristram B. Freeman, Esq., accompanied by his Grand Officers. The storm of opposition to the fraternity which had culminated in the attempt, so nobly and happily frustrated, to extract the secrets of Freemasonry through an Inquisitorial Committee of the Legislature of Pennsylvania, had scarcely then begun to subside, and the attendance at the meetings of the Lodges was still small. On the occasion of the Grand Visitation, Brother Adams attended to his duties as Secretary, and at the same time filled the Oriental Chair. At a subsequent Grand Visitation, in June, 1842, the report of the Right Worshipful Grand Secretary, which is spread upon the minutes, states that for the three preceding years, the average attendance upon the meetings of the Lodge had been but six; but that the circumstances of the Lodge were then improving; and that its then present "flourishing condition was mainly owing to the zeal and devotion" of four of its Past Masters, Brother Adams being one of those mentioned by name.

For many years he served upon the Committee of Charity of the Lodge; in 1853, his name was returned to this Grand Lodge as the Past Master upon whom the choice of the Lodge had fallen to be recommended to the Right Worshipful Grand Master for appointment as one of the Building Committee of the new Hall; for one year he acted as the representative of his Lodge on the Board of Almoners of the Grand Lodge Charity Fund, and declined a reappointment. On December 13th, 1864, he was unanimously elected a Life and Honorary member of the Lodge, a well-deserved tribute to his long and faithful services.

Brother Adams's connection with Royal Arch Masonry commenced in June, 1842, when he had the honorary degree of Mark Master conferred upon him, was received and accepted Most Excellent Master, and exalted to the supreme

18   *ADONAI—ADONIS.*

degree of the Royal Arch, in Jerusalem Chapter, No. 3, Philadelphia. In December of the same year he was elected Scribe of the Chapter; and filled the offices of King and High Priest in regular succession by election in the two following years. For sixteen successive years, from 1848 to 1864, he was elected Secretary of his Chapter, declining a re-election in December of the latter year.

For some years Brother Adams was a member of St. John's Commandery, No. 4, of Knights Templar, Philadelphia. The movement which resulted in placing the Commandery under the jurisdiction of the General Grand Encampment of the United States, did not meet his approval; and at or about the time when this measure was consummated he resigned from the Commandery, and thenceforth took no active part in Templar Masonry.

Michael Nisbet, Esq., the then Right Worshipful Grand Secretary, having died in 1842, Brother Adams was appointed on the 6th of June in that year, by the Right Worshipful Grand Master, Joseph R. Chandler, Esq., to fill the vacancy. This office he continued to occupy and discharge the duties of, up to the time of his death: having been elected by the Grand Lodge at the annual election in December succeeding his appointment, and been re-elected annually.*

Adonai.—One of the names of God. It signifies my Lords' as *Adoni* does in the singular.

Adoniran.—The principal receiver of Solomon, and director of the 30,000 sent to cut timber in Lebanon for building the Temple. They were divided into Lodges of 300. He was Chief of the Provosts and Judges and Seven Grand Superintendents.

Adonis.—In mythology, a beautiful youth, son of Cinyras, King of Cyprus, beloved by Venus, and killed by a

---

* He died 11th Feb , 1866, aged 57 years.

ADOPTIVE—AFRICA. 19

wild boar. The name also of a river in Phœnicia, which in certain seasons of the year acquire a deep color by the rains washing up the red earth. Adonis is thought to be identical with Osiris of the Egyptians. Adonis was killed by a wild boar, and Osiris by a Typhon. It was a contest between Truth and Error, in the latter case. In Syria the Adonis mysteries were celebrated, and the Syrian architects practiced a portion of them, who afterward introduced it into Judea. They represented the grief of Venus, and the death and resurrection Adonis. The devotees depicted a deep mourning, and at the end of the proper time, the priest announced the resurrection of Adonis, which occasioned much joy.

Adoptive Masonry.—These degrees originated in France, and were for the benefit of ladies who had claims upon Freemasonry. It consisted of four degrees: Apprentice, Companion, Mistress, Perfect Mistress. The jewel is a ladder, with five rounds, on the left breast. The American Rite has five degrees: Jephtha's Daughter; Ruth, or Mason's Widow; Esther, or Mason's Wife; Martha, or Mason's Sister. It is known as the "Eastern Star."

Advanced.—A term in Mark Lodges applied to a candidate after having received the degree of Mark Master, being advanced toward the Royal Arch.

Adytum.—The pillars Wisdom, Strength, and Beauty, representing the Triad of Deity. In the British mysteries the Lodges are supported by three pillars of Stone, and held to regenerate the accepted. In the Hindoo mysteries the pillars were crowned with human skulls, and referred to origin of the work in Wisdom, executed in Strength, and crowned in Beauty.

Affiliation or Affiliated.—Reception of a profane into Freemasonry. A Mason in masonic standing and a member of a warranted Lodge.

Africa.—Freemasonry was introduced here in 1736. The

20   AFRICAN — AHIMAN.

numerous Lodges have been chartered by the Grand Lodges of England, France, Scotland, and Netherlands. There are a number of Lodges, convened by the colored people in Liberia, working under a Grand Lodge of their own. In Monrovia a large and active Lodge of colored Masons meet regularly.

African Master Builders. — Organized in 1756, and copied after the masonic system. Its creed promoting truth and virtue, and had five degrees: Apprentice, or Egytian Secret, Instructions in the Egyptian Secrets, Cosmopolite, Christian Philosopher, and Love of Truth. The higher degrees had chapters. Of these degrees there were three.

Agape (*Love*).—Love feasts were common among the primitive Christians. After the celebration of the communion, the oblations, which were made in the Temple, consisted of meat and bread, which were brought by the wealthy, and consumed at a common table. It was instituted by Clemens of Rome, and patterned after the masonic form. It is also held that from this Agape sprang the Table-Lodges of the Freemasons.

Agathapodes.—Instituted in Brussels in 1600. It was a conservative course between the Protestants and the Catholics. It ceased to be a society in 1837. Schages revived it under the name of New Agatha in 1846. The chief of the order is named *Hog*, and its members receive the name of some wild animals.

Aged Patriarch. — Found in the Odd Fellows ceremonies.

Agenda (*Things to be done*).

Agnus Dei.—Seal of the old Knights Templar.

Ahiezer (*Brother of Help*).—A prince of the tribe of Dan.

Ahiman Rezon.—The Book of Constitutions adopted by the Seceding in 1740.

AHOLIAB — ALCHEMY. 21

Aholiab.—In order that Bezoleel might not be lifted up in conceit, God chose Aholiab from the lowest tribe in Dan. One of this tribe is said to have been the most skillful workman in the building of the Temple. Yet it is not to be supposed that any excelled those especially chosen for that work.

Akirop.—An assassin at the building of King Solomon's .Temple.

Alabama.—The exact date of the introduction of Freemasonry into Alabama is not known. Charters for Lodges were granted by the Grand Lodges of S. Carolina and Tennessee. The Grand Lodge organized 14th June, 1821. The Grand Chapter, 2d June, 1827. The Grand Council of Select Masters, 9th June, 1827. The Knights Templar, 29th Nov. 1860. During the late rebellion of the Southern States, Morris Lodge, at Pollard, was broken into, and robbed of its jewels and charter, etc. The jewels fell into the hands of a Federal soldier not a Mason. While the army was on its march to Montgomery, they were discovered by a fellow-soldier and a Mason, who purchased them from his comrade, and on his arrival at Montgomery, placed them in the hands of Bro. Strenna, to be returned to Morris Lodge. This instance of fidelity and zeal for the craft, although then arrayed against one another, is but one of the many instances of brotherly love that occurred during that dark period.

Alcantra, Order of.—The order of Alcantra or St. Julian's, or Peortria, was instituted 1156, at Alcantra, a town of Estramadura, by Hadrion II. King of Leon. The King of Spain is Sovereign of this order of Knighthood.

Alchemy.—An imaginary art once introduced among the modern nations. The name is a mixture of the Greek and Arabian. Some suppose the art to have originated among the Arabs of Colifita. The object was the production of gold and silver. The principle was that all metals are convertible into these precious substances. **To** this they added an infinity of fantastic imaginations respecting the planets, in hastening and retarding the work. The instrument by which this was to be effected was a certain mineral to be produced by these processes, which being mixed by the base metals would transmute it, and this was termed the philosophic stone. Hence the term *adept adeptus*, for him who was supposed to have obtained the secret of alchemy. Dr. Price, of Guildford, England, is said to have been the last person who proposed to turn stone into gold. The Egyptian Hermes is also claimed as the author of the system. It has also been denominated a Hermetic art. It had a connection with Freemasonry in the last century. In Freemasonry one of the degrees is styled "Adepts."

Alcoran.—The Mohammedan Bible or Sacred Book. It occupies the place of a Bible in a Mohammedan Lodge of Masons.

Aldworth, Elizabeth (*The Female Mason*).—Elizabeth Aldworth, of New Market, Cork County, Ireland, was of the St. Leger family, and a daughter of Lord Viscount Doneraile, whose ancestor, Arthur St. Leger, was Lord-Lieutenant of Ireland, under Henry VIII. Elizabeth died at New Market, Dec. 1810, aged 80 years. Her father, Lord Doneraile, held a Lodge at Doneraile House, County of Cork. The Lodge warrant was No. 150, and several of the lord's family were members. Mrs. Aldworth, then single, was in a room undergoing repairs, and adjoining the Lodge-room, and hearing voices she listened, and with her scissors made a hole through the plaster, and thus witnessed the masonic ceremonies of opening and initiation. Attempting to escape she met the Tyler, who, giving an alarm, seized her and took her into the Lodge, where she confessed what she had learned. She expressed her desire to be made a Mason, and, taking the obligation, was made

ALISON — ALMANACS.

a Mason on the spot. She was faithful to her vows, spent much of her life in charity, founded masonic schools, and at the procession of the schools, appeared in masonic regalia.

Alison, Sir Archibald.—This illustrious Mason of Scotland was made a Mason in Glasgow, Kilwinning Lodge, No. 4, in 1837. In 1847, June 1st, he was elected Prov. Grand Master. His first public act was laying the corner-stone of Borrony Parish Poor-house. In 1851 he laid the corner-stone of Victoria Bridge, Glasgow. On the 31st July, 1856, he laid the corner-stone of the Court-house, Market-house, and Railway station, at Wisha. In June, 1861, the 24th, and on the 546th anniversary of the battle of Bannockburn, he assisted in laying the foundation-stone of the Wallace Monument. In 1861 he laid the foundation-stone of Hamilton and Rutherglen. When the death of the Duke of Athol, Grand Master of Scotland, occurred, on the 16th Jan. 1864, he held a funeral or sorrow Lodge in his memory. In 1865 he laid the corner-stone of a new school and hall at Renfrew. He was a man of great literary talent, a polished scholar, and was termed the "Historian of Europe." He was justly revered, and died universally lamented, the 25th July, 1867.

Allah.—The name of the Arabian God.

All-Seeing Eye.—Whom the Sun, Moon, and Stars obey, and under whose care even Comets perform their stupendous revolutions, pervades the innermost recesses of the heart, and rewards us according to our faithfulness and merit.

Almanacs, Masonic.—A system of finding the year, etc. The masonic year commences with the creation of the world: 4000 years intervene between the creation and the birth of Christ. So to find the masonic year we add 4000 to the Anno Domini date. The Rite of Misraim adds 4 years to the common era. The Scotch Rite uses the Hebrew chronology. The York Rite commences with the

24 ALMOND — AMERICAN.

1st January. The Royal Arch, from 530 B.C., the time of building the second Temple. The Royal and Select Masters, 1000 B.C., from the completion of Solomon's Temple. The Knights Templar, A.D. 1118, the founding of the order. The Strict Observance, 1314, the destruction of the Knights Templar.

Almond Tree.—From this tree Aaron's rod, that budded, blossomed, and bore fruit, was taken.

Almoner.—An officer of the K. T.

Aloadine.—An Assyrian prince of a Syrian tribe that professed the Mohammedan creed, and is known as the Order of Israelites. The term assassin is said to have originated with this plundering tribe.

Amalthea-Horn.—The Steward's Jewels.

Amenthes.—In Egyptian mythology, the kingdom of the dead, or Tartarus of the ancient Egyptians.

American Military Lodges. — The following are the military lodges that were instituted in the American army during the revolutionary war.

1. *St. John's Regimental Lodge*, in the U. S. Battalion, warranted by the G. L. of New York, Feb. 24th, 1775.

2. *American Union Lodge*, in the Connecticut Line, warranted by the G. L. of Massachusetts, Feb. 15th, 1776.

3. *No.* 19, in 1st Regiment Pennsylvania Artillery, warranted by G. L. of Pennsylvania, May 18th, 1779.

4. *Washington Lodge*, in the Massachusetts Line, warranted by the Massachusetts G. L., Oct. 6th, 1779.

5. *No.* 20, in North Carolina Regiment, warranted by G. L. of Pennsylvania, —— 1779.

6. *No.* 27, in Maryland Line, warranted by G. L. of Pennsylvania, April 4th, 1780.

7. *No.* 28, in Pennsylvania Line, warranted by G. L. of Pennsylvania, —— 1780.

8. *No.* 29, in Pennsylvania Line, warranted by G. L. of Pennsylvania, July 27th, 1780.

AMMI — ANCIENT. 25

9. *No.* 31, in New Jersey Line, warranted by G. L. of Pennsylvania, March 26th, 1781.

10. *No.* 36, in New Jersey Line, warranted by G. L. of Pennsylvania, Sept. 2d, 1782.

Ammi.—The general corruption among the Israelites in Hosea's time was alarming, but among those who had not bowed down to Baal were Ammi and Ruhamah, who remained as faithful servants of the true God.

Ample Form.—Where the G. M. opens a Lodge or performs masonic ceremonies, it is said to have been done *in ample form*.

Anchor and Ark.—Emblems of well-grounded *hope* and that divine *ark* that wafts us over this world of troubles and *anchors* safe in a peaceful harbor, where the weary cease from trouble and shall find rest.

Ancient Archive Depository.—The main pillars of King Solomon's Temple were hollowed out and so constructed as to serve as a depository of the Sacred Rolls of the Hebrews, their inspired and Prophetic writings, and the ancient charges and documents of Freemasonry.

Ancient Correspondence.—The following letters passed between the King of Israel and the King of Tyre:

SOLOMON TO KING HIRAM.

"Know thou, that my father would have built a temple to God, but was hindered by wars, and continual expeditions, for he did not leave off to overthrow his enemies till he made them all subject to tribute; but I give thanks to God for the peace I at present enjoy; and on that account I am at leisure, and design to build an house to God; for God foretold to my father that such an house should be built by me; wherefore I desire thee to send some of thy subjects, with mine, to Mount Lebanon, to cut down timber, for the Sidonians are more skillful than our people in

3

26 ANCIENT.

cutting of wood; I will pay whatsoever price thou shalt determine."

HIRAM TO KING SOLOMON.

"It is fit to bless God that he hath committed thy father's government to thee, who art a wise man, and endowed with all virtues. As for myself, I rejoice at the condition thou art in, and will be subservient to thee in all that thou sendest to me about; for when by my subjects, I have cut down many, and large trees of cedar and cypress wood, I will send them to the sea, and will order my subjects to make floats of them, and to sail to what place soever of thy country thou shalt desire, and leave them there; after which thy subjects may carry them to Jerusalem; but do thou take care to procure us corn for this timber, which we stand in need of, because we inhabit in an island."— *Josephus's History of Antiquities of Jews.*

Ancient Freemasonry.—After the Grand Architect of the Universe had created man in the image of himself, he stamped the great principles of Freemasonry upon his heart as a Divine gift from heaven. Preston tells us truly "that from the commencement of the world, we may trace the foundation of Freemasonry. In the dark ages of antiquity, while literature was in a low state, Masonry diffused its influence. Science, thus unveiled, arts arose, and civilization took place. Governments being settled, authority given to laws, the assemblies of the fraternity acquired the patronage of the great and good." Freemasonry is a science confined to no particular spot, but extends its wings over the entire globe. It becomes a universal language to the fraternity by its secret signs, carefully preserved and handed down orally. All religions teach morality, and hence the private opinions of the adept are left to God and himself, and to God he must answer how the talents intrusted to his care have been employed. It

ANCIENT.

unites in a bond of indissoluble affection, men of all climes and tenets. Thus it is truly said, that in every nation the true Freemason finds a friend and a home.

The principles of geometry were well known to Adam, as after his expulsion from the Garden of Eden he built an habitation for himself and family, and no doubt instructed his descendants in that art. Cain and his adherents being instructed in the principles of geometry and architecture, built a city, and called it Dedicate, or Consecrate, after the name of his eldest son, Enoch. The descendants of Seth were not in the background in this noble science. This patriarch profited by the instruction of Adam, with whom he had lived 930 years, and succeeded in direction of the craft. Seth, seeing the destruction and desolation that would happen by fire and water, and deprive mankind of those arts and sciences then existing, raised two pillars of stone, and inscribed thereon the principles of the arts and sciences, and more particularly geometry and Masonry, in order to withstand the overthrow of the flood. Josephus states that in his time these pillars were to be seen in the land of *Siriad*, and known as Seth's or Enoch's pillars. Methuselah, Lamech, and Noah preserved the religion of the Messiah in its purity, and also the art of Masonry till the flood. After the flood, Noah and his sons being all of one language, they journeyed from the *East* to the *West* and found the land of Shinar, and there dwelt together as *Noachidæ*, the first name of Masons. The Scriptures tell us that at the building of the Tower of Babel, God in his wise providence confounded the language of the builders for his own purposes. These people all dispersed and carried with them the knowledge of Masonry into different portions of the world. Nimrod kept possession of the plains and founded the great city of the Babylonish Empire. From Shinar the arts and sciences were carried to distant parts of the world, and

28   ANCIENT.

thus it was, notwithstanding the different dialects, that the
practice of conversing by means of tokens and signs came
into general usage. Mizraim, the second son of Ham,
carried the skill into Egypt. The Pyramids remain to this
day as evidences of the cultivated art. Mizraim's succes-
sors carried the art down to the last of their race, King
Amasis. The offspring of Shem carried the science as far
as China and Japan. Abraham had learned the science,
and he communicated it to the Canaanites, for which they
honored him as a prince. Isaac, Ishmael, and Jacob, no
doubt, were all taught the science and arts. Joseph was
well instructed in them by his father, as he excelled the
Egyptians in knowledge, and was appointed as a ruler over
the people by Pharaoh. The Israelites were "trained up"
to build cities with stone and brick for the Egyptians. On
the voyage to the promised land, it pleased God to give
Moses the Decalogue written on tables of stone. When
Moses, after a sojourn of forty days in Mount Sinai, came
down with the laws, he entered his tent and explained the
laws to Aaron. After that, Aaron placed himself at the
right hand of Moses, and Aaron's sons were admitted to
hear the laws. Moses afterwards declared the laws to the
seventy Elders of the Sanhedrim, and reduced the law to
writing, except the explanation, which was intrusted to
the memory, with the injunction to teach them to their
children. The most skillful, Moses ordered to meet him in
the Lodge or Tabernacle, and gave them charges from
which they were not to deviate. Joshua succeeded Moses,
with Caleb, Eleazar, and Phineas. After the settlement
of the promised land, the Israelites made further progress
in the arts and sciences. The City of Tyre was built by a
body of Siebonian Masons from *Gabala*, under a Grand
Master and a number of princes. In after-times, Ahibal,
King of Tyre, and Hiram, his son, also a Mason, repaired
and beautified the city. Thus we have traced Ancient

Masonry down to the period when Hiram, King of Tyre, entered into a league with King Solomon to build the Temple at Jerusalem. The reader of the Bible will find this compilation a true settlement of Ancient Masonry by a reference to that great source of light.

Ancient Order of Foresters.—Composed of mechanics in England and United States, with masonic forms.

Anderson, Rev. James.—Was born in Scotland, at Edinburgh, 5th August, 1662, and died about 1738. He was a highly educated gentleman of refined taste, and published several works. In 1705 he issued a work, "Showing that the Crown of Scotland is Imperial and Independent," in reply to Mr. Atwood, who held the Superiority of the Crown of England over that of Scotland.

Shortly after this the Scottish Parliament authorized him to publish a work, "The Ancient Charters of Scotland, with Seals of the Scottish Kings." In 1727, he published collections relating to the history of Mary Queen of Scots. About this time he also published a work, "The Rise and Progress of Freemasonry," in defense of the order. About 1705, he removed to London, and became minister of Scots Presbyterian Church. In 1714, he published a volume of sermons. Dr. Anderson had been made a Mason early in life, but no record is left of the date or the Lodge wherein he received the honor. In 1721, 29th September, the Grand Lodge, then in session, were dissatisfied with the copies of the old Gothic Constitution, which were accessible, and "Brother Jas. Anderson, A. M., was ordered to digest them in a new and better method." This work was however contemplated by G. M. Geo. Payne, who was elected June 24th, 1718, and at that time requested the brethren to bring to the G. L. any old writings and records concerning Masonry in order to show the ancient usages, and from these documents Dr. Anderson

3*

30 ANDREW—ANDROGYNOUS.

compiled the Book of Constitutions the following 27th December. Fourteen brothers were appointed a committee to examine the work, and, after a rigid examination, they found it good, and approved it. The Grand Lodge met 25th March, 1722, and received the work. At this session, Dr. Anderson was elected one of the Grand Wardens. On the 17th of January, 1723, a special meeting of the Grand Lodge was held to approve some additions which were added to the work. At an assembly of the Grand Lodge in February, 1735, Dr. Anderson presented a new edition of the Book of Constitutions, which the Grand Lodge, on 25th January, 1738, ordered him to publish. In April, 1738, he was again a member of the Grand Lodge. He died shortly after this period.

Andrew Masonry.—A degree instituted by the Pretender, and introduced into Germany and France about 1735. In the Swede system, the 4th is formed by "St. Andrew's Apprentice" and "St. Andrew's Companion." The 5th degree is styled "Master of St. Andrew." The 9th degree includes "Favorite Brothers of St. Andrew" and "Knights of Purple and Red."

Andrew's Day.—The day on which Scottish Lodges hold their feasts. It is the 30th November.

Andrew, St.—One of Christ's Apostles and brother of St. Peter. He is a patron of Freemasonry.

Andrognal.—A term similar to that of adoptive, and explained in Adoptive Masonry.

Androgynous.—This theory of Adoptive Masonry affords to certain classes of females, entitled by masonic constitutions to the protection of the order, means whereby they may be *known* and *made known* to the craft. As females cannot lawfully be intrusted with the secrets of Freemasonry, these means are originated for their especial

ANGEL — ANTI. 31

benefit. The system is almost as old as that of Capitular Masonry.

Angel of Jehovah.—Was supposed to have been Michael the leader of the Host of Heaven, who appeared at the Burning Bush to Moses, but there is no doubt that it was Jehovah himself. Moses was commanded to approach with naked feet, as it was Holy Ground.

Angel's Alphabet.—In the Scottish Rite allusion is made to this alphabet. The Jews assert in their mysteries the knowledge of such an alphabet.

Angerona.—Goddess of Silence; worshiped by the Egyptians and Romans.

Annuities are granted to poor and indigent Masons, and widows of deceased brothers.

Anti-Masonry.—In 1826 a great cry was raised by the political tricksters of the country against Freemasonry. To insure success, the party had recourse to every stratagem, and among the most popular was the story hatched out of the so-called and supposed abduction of an individual named Morgan, at Batavia, New York, in 1826, for exposing the secrets of the order. This fellow, finding no doubt his enterprise a failure, secreted himself, and circulated the story in order to meet a ready sale of his work, which was but a republication of "Jachin and Boaz," published in Albany, in 1790, from an English work. The frenzy with which politicians hashed and rehashed this story, obtained for them about 100,000 supporters in New York. In Pennsylvania, where the Hon. Judge Gillis was arrested for complicity in the affair, the party succeeded in dividing the vote. In Vermont, the party, fired with unceasing efforts, succeeded for a time. But this was not to last. The party had grown so rapidly, swollen so hugely with broken-down politicians, and presented such an empty hollowness of principle, that it exploded with the contempt of all good citizens. In Pennsylvania, the

32 *ANTIQUITY.*

Legislature inaugurated a series of persecutions, and the hero Thaddeus Stevens, Esq., of Lancaster, *a rejected applicant* of Good Samaritan Lodge, Gettysburg, Pa., was not able to force the secrets from the order. The principles of the order having become known and found their way to the people, the sentiment was soon changed, and the ill-shaped Anti-Masonic party, having no other aim than power and corruption, came to an end. But the power behind the throne has again shown its huge-footed plans and the resurrection of its skeleton is now proposed. Whether the new effort will succeed, remains for the future to disclose, but it matters little, as the truths of a genuine Christian system of charity and benevolence, as produced by Freemasonry, are engrafted in the minds of the people, not to be rooted out by persecution. (See U. S. "Anti-Masonic Convention.")

Antiquity of Freemasonry.—Under this head we propose to compile the history of the order as derived from modern writers. In Britain the Freemason Society has been attributed to the difficulty of procuring workmen in building churches, monasteries, castles, and religious asylums. In order to increase their number they were much favored by the popes and princes. The Italians, Greek refugees, French, German, and Flemings, joined in a fraternity of architects, and procured papal bulls for their particular privileges. These adherents styled themselves Freemasons, and wandered from one nation to another in search of labor. Wherever they found buildings to erect, they cast their tents in order to be near the work. A surveyor governed in chief, and a *warden* was established over every nine workmen. In Britain this order arose about 674, and styled themselves free because they had liberty to go and come in the nation at pleasure. Again, a combination was formed not to work without advance of wages, when Edward III. directed his sheriffs to gather them to-

ANTIQUITY. 33

gether to build and enlarge the Church of St. George at Windsor. It is stated that the Masons at this time fixed certain signs and tokens to assist each other from impressment, and not to work unless *free* and on their own terms. We may here state that we do not intend to trace the order from King Solomon's time, but simply that of modern date, as we recognize the doctrine "that the order has ever had an existence since symmetry began, and harmony displayed her charms." Wm. Preston, in 1792, holds that Freemasonry was introduced into England prior to the Roman invasion, as stupendous edifices existed then. The Druids also had customs derived from Pythagoras, similar in their workings. Cæsar favored the system, as also did the Roman generals. The progress of the system was much obstructed by the wars, and did not revive until the time of Caranseus, who protected it. This general, who endeavored to found the British empire, encouraged the arts, and collected together artificers and masons, and appointed Albanus, his steward, the particular overseer of their assemblies. Albanus obtained a charter for them from the king to hold general assemblies. This man was the noted St. Albanus who suffered martyrdom for his Christian faith. After the departure of the Romans, Masonry declined on account of interruptions by the Scots and Picts. After the introduction of Christianity the order began to flourish, but to no degree of importance. In 557, St. Austin, with 40 monks, came into England and introduced the Gothic style. He headed the fraternity in the building of the old Canterbury cathedral in 600; that of Rochester, in 602; St. Paul's, London, 604; St. Peter's, Westminster, 605; and others. In 640, some French experts arrived and formed a Lodge under Rennet, Abbot of Winal, whom Kened, King of Mercia, appointed Inspector of Lodges and Superintendent of Masons. In 856, it was further advanced by St. Swithin, whom Ethelwolf employed. From

34 ANTIQUITY.

this time to 872 it maintained its advance, when Alfred the Great became its protector. Under Edward, Alfred's successor, the Masons held their Lodges under the sanction of Ethred, husband of the king's sister, and Ethelword, his brother, to whom the care of the order was given. Ethelword founded the University of Cambridge. The true re-establishment of Freemasonry in England, however, dates from the reign of King Athelstane, grandson of King Alfred. (Athelstane is said to have been the first King of England who translated the Scriptures into the Saxon tongue, A.D. 930.) Edward, the brother of the king, obtained a charter from Athelstane and founded a lodge at York, in 926, of which he became the Grand Master. By virtue of this charter all Masons in the kingdom assembled at York, where they established a general Grand Lodge for their future government. As York was thus the original seat of masonic government, the appellation *Ancient York Masons* thus obtained its establishment. At this convention at York, all the Latin, Greek, and French writings of the order were brought, and from them were framed Constitution and Charges of the Ancient English Lodge. After Edwin's death, Athelstane patronized the order; but after his death the Masons were dispersed, until the reign of Edgar in 960, when St. Austin employed them; but as no permanent encouragement was given them, they declined for about 50 years. In 1041, under Edward the Confessor Masonry again revived. Leofrick, Earl of Coventry, being appointed Superintendent of Masons, he rebuilt Westminster Abbey. After the Conquest in 1066, Gundulph, Bishop of Rochester, and Roger de Montmorency, Earl of Shrewsbury, became joint patrons of the Masons, and began the Tower of London, which was completed in the reign of William Rufus, who built the Palace and Hall of Westminster. From this time the Masons were successively patronized by the kings of England. In the reign of

ANTIQUITY. 35

Henry I. and Stephen, the society built several works, among them Westminster, now House of Commons,—the President of the order now being Gilbert de Clare. During Henry the Second's reign, the Lodges were superintended by the S. M. of Knights Templar, who employed them in building their temple in Fleet Street in 1155. Masonry continued under this order till 1199, when John succeeded Richard I., and Peter de Colechurch was appointed G. M. He commenced building the London Bridge with stone, which was finished by Wm. Alcmoin in 1209. Peter de Rupibus succeeded Colechurch, and Geoffrey Fitz-Peter acted as his deputy. In 1272, during the reign of Edward I., the superintendence of Masons was intrusted to Walter Gifford, Archbishop of York, Gilbert de Clare, Earl of Gloucester, and Ralph, Lord of Mt. Hermen. During the reign of Edward II., Exeter and Oriel Colleges, Oxford, Clerepoll in Cambridge, etc., were built by the fraternity under Walter Stapleton, Bishop of Exeter, G. M., appointed in 1307. Edward III. patronized, revised, and ameliorated the ancient charges, and added useful regulations to the order. William Wykeham was continued G. M. on accession of Richard II., and by him the new College, Oxford, and Winchester College were founded at his own expense. On the accession of Henry IV., Thomas Fitz-Allen was appointed G. M. He founded Battle-Abbey and Fotheringay, and built Guildhall, London. On accession of Henry V., Henry Chichely, Archb. of Canterbury, was G. M. In 1425, during the reign of Henry VI., Masonry was interdicted, and the act was passed by the *Bat Parliament* forbidding the assemblage of Masons. The servants and followers of the peers came to Parliament with clubs and stones, and hence the above name. In 1442, after the difficulties which brought about the interdiction, the king joined the Masons, and presided over the Lodge in person and nominated Wm. Wonefleet, Bishop of

36 ANTIQUITY.

Winchester, G. M. About this time, James I. of Scotland encouraged the order and became a zealous supporter. Masonry was interrupted by the wars between the houses of York and Lancaster, but in 1471 it revived under Robert Beauchamp, Bishop of Sorn, who was appointed G. M. by Edward VI., and honored with the title *Chancellor of the Garter* for repairing Windsor Castle. During the reign of Edward V. and Richard III. it declined; but in 1485 it again took its stand under Henry VII. The Master and Fellows of St. John of Malta, who chose Henry for their Prelector in 1500, patronized the order. On the 24th June, 1502, a Lodge of Masters was formed in the Palace, at which the king presided as G. M., and proceeded to Westminster Abbey, when the corner-stone of Henry the Seventh's Chapel was laid. On the accession of Henry VIII., Cardinal Wolsey was made G. M., who was succeeded by Thomas Cromwell, Earl of Essex, and built St. James's Palace, etc. John Touchel succeeded Cromwell as G. M. In 1547, the Duke of Somerset became G. M. After the death of Somerset, John Poynel, Bishop of Winchester, presided over the Lodges until the death of the king in 1553. During the reign of Elizabeth, Sir Thomas Lockville became G. M. In 1567, Francis Russell, Earl of Bedford, succeeded Lockville, and Sir Thomas Gesham, Russell, who erected the Royal Exchange in 1566-7. Charles Howard, Earl of Effingham, succeeded Gesham as G. M., and presided until 1588, when George Hastings, Earl of Huntingdon, was chosen. On the accession of James I., Inigo Jones became G. M. In 1618, the Earl of Pembroke became G. M. After the accession of Charles I., Henry Donver, Earl of Danby, became G. M., and in 1633, Thomas Howard, Earl of Arundale, succeeded him, and in 1635, he by Francis Russell, Earl of Bedford. On 27th December, 1663, Henry Innigo, Earl of St. Albans, was elected G. M., and succeeded in 1666 by Earl Rivers.

ANTIQUITY. 37

In 1674, George Villars, Duke of Buckingham, became G. M., and 1679, Henry Bennet, Earl of Arlington, and in 1685, Sir Christopher Wren succeeded to the G. Mastership. In 1695, King William having been initiated, the order regained a new impetus. In 1697, Charles, Duke of Richmond, became G. M., and in 1698 he was succeeded by Sir Christopher Wren. During the reign of Queen Anne Masonry made but little progress. Sir Christopher's age drew off his attention from the office, and the number of Masons began to diminish. It was therefore determined that the privileges of Masonry should not be confined to operatives, but that all persons regularly approved should be initiated into the order. Thus the society once more rose to esteem, and on accession of George I. to the throne, the four Lodges at London met at Apple Tavern, Covent Garden, and having voted the oldest Master present to the chair, constituted themselves a Grand Lodge *pro-tempore.* On the 24th June, same year, they met again and elected Anthony Sayer G. M. Up to this time a certain number of Masons could meet together and make Masons, but they now resolved that such privilege must be invested in Lodges warranted by them. In 1718 Geo. Payne succeeded Sayer. In 1719, 24th June, De Desaguliers was elected G. M. In 1720 a great loss was occasioned by the burning of the old manuscripts by some of the brethren, who were alarmed at the publication of the Constitutions. The General Assembly at York still met regularly, and harmony subsisted between the two Grand bodies. The northern Lodge was called "Grand Lodge of all England," and the other "Grand Lodge of England." In course of time innovations having crept into the order, and troubles arising, it was deemed expedient to unite both these Grand bodies, which was accomplished in 1813 by a complete reconciliation of differences, and the union was made under the title of "United Grand

APIS—ARCHÆOLOGY.

Lodge of Ancient Free and Accepted Masons of England." From this period the order has progressed without any interruptions, and the Grand Lodge of England has bright record of carrying the usefulness of Freemasonry into all sections of the globe.

Apis.—In mythology, a bull to which divine honors were paid by the Egyptians, especially at Memphis. He was required to be black, with peculiar spots and marks. One of this description was not allowed to live over twenty-five years. He was buried with great solemnity.

Apostate Masons.—Those Masons who have violated their pledges and renounced the masonic faith and law.

Apostles' Creed.—A confession of faith, supposed anciently to have been drawn up by the Apostles themselves, and deriving the title Creed from the word with which it begins in Latin, *credo* *(I believe)*. It is taught and practiced by all orthodox churches, and is used in the K. T. system.

Appeal.—The Grand Lodge is the supreme authority of the order, and the representative of every individual member of the order, and has the power of finally adjusting the interests of the craft.

Apprentice.—The Entered Apprentice is the first degree in Masonry. An apprentice is represented in the Lodge as a brother, and is instructed in the work of the degree, and hence receives the title.

Apron.—An operative mason wears the apron as a necessary article of clothing, while the Freemason as symbolic.

Arcade de la Pelleletria.—An epithet applied to the old Grand Lodge prior to the union with the Grand Lodge of France in 1799.

Archæology.—The science or study of antiquities, of those minor branches which are discarded from the general history ; *i.e.* genealogies, architecture, manners, and customs.

ARCH — ARK. 39

Arch.—An emblem of R. A. M.

Arch of Enoch.—Enoch was the son of Jared. He built a ninefold temple under the ground and dedicated it to God. He was assisted in the work of making this subterranean passage or temple by his father and son.

Arch of Heaven.—Allegorical of the degree of Royal Arch in Masonry. The heavens are said to be an arch supported by two pillars. They are emblemized masonically as Wisdom and Strength,—the first signifying the Wisdom of God, the second the Stability of the Universe.

Arch of Steel.—In the order of Knights Templar, an arch is formed of steel with swords, by the Sir Knights raising and interlocking their swords.

Archimagus.—High Priest of Chaldean mysteries.

Areopagus.—The chief court of judicature at Athens. So called because it met in a hall on the eminence called the Hill of Mars. It had cognizance of capital crimes, and from it was an appeal to the people. In Belgium and France the name is applied to the council of the 30th degree.

Argonautes.—5th degree of Hermetic Masonry.

Argonauts.—The name given to the chieftains who accompanied Jason, in the ship Argo, on the fabled expedition to Colchis, after the Golden Fleece of Phryxus. This expedition was supposed to have been a commercial one. In Adoptive Masonry, a society founded by the order of Strict Observance, in Germany, 1775. The place of holding their meetings was in a vessel. Its seal, a silver anchor, and the motto, *So live our friends.*

Ark.—The sacred ark, which stood in the Most Holy Place of the Tabernacle and Temple, was a small chest made of shittim-wood, overlaid with gold. Its lid was called the Mercy-seat, because above it hovered the Shechinah, or symbol of Divine presence, was of pure gold, and out at the two ends of this lid were two cherubim of gold,

40 ARK.

which, with their extended wings, covered the whole Mercy-seat above, and with their faces seemed to hover over it. Within this ark was deposited the two tables of the law, and the golden pot of manna; Aaron's rod, that budded, bloomed, and bore fruit; and a copy of the five books of Moses. This ark had two rings, for receiving the staves of shittim-wood, by which the Levites bore it. This vessel was so sacred that it was death for any one but the priest to look at it; hence it was carried under a canopy. This ark being consecrated by the sprinkling of blood and anointing of oil, was carried about by the Hebrews in the desert. On its being borne by the priests into the channel of Jordan, the waters divided and opened a clear passage for the Israelites. It was thence transferred to Gilgal. It was carried thirteen times in seven days around the City of Jericho, and on the seventh day the walls of that city fell down before it. After the conquest of Canaan it was fixed in the tabernacle of Shiloh, and there continued about three hundred years. Just before the death of Eli, the Israelites, probably remembering its miraculous virtues at Jericho, carried it to the field of battle. The Philistines gained the victory, and seized upon the ark; they placed it in their temple of Dagon, and their idols were broken to pieces before it; and wherever they placed it a plague of emerods came on the people, and perhaps another of mice upon the land attended it. The Philistines were glad to return it with presents. It halted at Bethshemeth, where a multitude of Hebrews were divinely struck dead for their looking into it. It was thence removed to the house of Abinadab, at Gibeath, on the hill of Kirjath-jearim, where, except when Saul brought it to the camp at Gibeath, it remained fifty, if not ninety years; thence David attempted to bring it to Jerusalem, not on the shoulders of the Levites, but upon a cart. The punishment of Uzziah for touching it made him leave it in the home of Abedom.

ARK — ASTRONOMY. 41

But hearing soon after that Abedom's house was blessed by it, David, with great solemnity, carried it to Jerusalem. Forty years afterward Solomon caused it to be transplanted in the innermost part of the Temple. When the Temple was destroyed by the Chaldeans, account was lost of it. This, being the symbol of Divine presence, did not occur until after the building of the second Temple. The ark takes a prominent part in the ceremonies of the Royal Arch degree.

Ark and Dove. — A degree in American Adoptive Masonry.

Ark Mariner.—In the Royal Arch, a speculative degree, founded on account of the Deluge.

Arkansas. — The early records of this State were destroyed by fire, when the hall at ——— was burned, in December, 1864. The Grand Lodge was organized 14th June, 1821. The Grand Chapter, 2d June, 1827. The Grand Council of R. and S. Masters, June, 1827. The Grand Commandery of Knights Templar, 29th November, 1860.

Asia.—The Grand Lodge of England granted a warrant for a Lodge in Asia, in 1728, at Calcutta, by Sir George Pomfret.

Asiatic Masonry.—This sect organized in Germany, in 1850. They had seven degrees. They explained the symbols on rites in a visionary style.

Astrea. — Mythology states that Goddess of Justice was dissatisfied with the vices of the mortals with whom she dwelt, and returned to heaven. However, being satisfied with the justice of Freemasonry, she embraced it in her sanctuary. She is now said to have commenced a constellation of stars.

Astrology.—Similar to Alchemy, and practiced in Hermetic Masonry.

Astronomy.—The science which teaches the knowledge

4*

42 ASYLUM—AUSTRIA.

of heavenly bodies. The pillars of the Lodge are likened by some, *Wisdom* personifying the first person in the Egyptian trinity; the second person, Osiris; the Sun, the Maker of the World, representing *Strength;* and the Moon, Isis, the third person, held as *Beauty.*

Asylum.—An edifice erected in Croydon, in Surrey, on a liberal plan, is used for aged Freemasons. The originator and endower was Dr. Crucifix. It is now under the jurisdiction of the G. L. of England.

Atheist (*Without God*).—One who denies the existence of God. Such an individual cannot become a Freemason, as a belief in God is an essential rule of the order.

Athelstane.—King of England, succeeded his father, Edward the Elder, in 925. He patronized the order of Masons, and, under his reign, they built many fine edifices. He granted a warrant for his brother Edwin to open a Lodge at York, in 926; from whence sprang the Ancient York Masons.

Athersda (*Strong Hand*).—The name was given to the Persian governors, who went with Zerubbabel to Jerusalem. It is the title of the Chief of Honor in the order of Herodeus of Kilwinning.

Athol Masonry.—A term applied to that body of Masons that separated from the Lodge of England in 1739. They assumed to themselves the name of Ancient Masons. In the organization, the Duke of Athol was elected Grand Master of Scotland. (See Ant. of Masonry.)

Australia.—The Grand Lodge of England, France, and Scotland chartered the first Lodge. It is now in a flourishing condition.

Austria.—Freemasonry was introduced into Austria by a warrant from the Grand Lodge of Germany, in 1742, for holding a Lodge at Vienna. The Grand Lodge was organized in 1784, by the Lodges of Hungary, Bohemia, Transylvania, and Prague, at Vienna.

AXE—BAIN.

Axe.—Of the building of King Solomon's Temple, it is said the sound of the axe was not to be heard. The noise of the workmen was confined to the quarries, that harmony and peace might prevail in the building of the Temple.

Axe, Knights of the Royal.—A degree in the French system.

B.

Baal.—The god of the Phœnicians and Carthagenians, worshiped chiefly at Tyre. The term Baal signifies Lord or Master. It is probable that Baal of the Phœnicians and Belas of the Babylonians were one and the same divinity. The priests of Baal amounted to 450. The Phœnicians that went to Jerusalem introduced the mysteries of this deity represented in the Sun. The Sun was a symbol of the Druids, Tyrians, and the Freemasons.

Babel.—A tower undertaken to be built shortly after the flood by the posterity of Noah, and remarkable for the frustration of the attempt by confusion of tongues. This occurred 120 years after the flood. Nimrod was the leader.

Babylon.—The site where the Tower of Babel was built. It was founded by Nimrod. Nebuchadnezzar made this city famous.

Bærwanger, C.—The first Grand Standard Bearer of the M. P. G. Consistory S. P. R. S., 32d degree, of Kentucky, was born in the kingdom of Prussia, and died at Louisvile, Ky., January 18th, 1864.

Bain, Wm. I.—Born in Bladen County, North Carolina, November 11th, 1793. Donald, the father of William, came from Scotland in 1784. William was made a Mason in 1820, in Lodge No. 64, Kilwinning. He affiliated with No. 40, Hiram Lodge, of Raleigh, after his removal to that place, and served as Secretary a number of

44 BAIN.

terms. In 1836, he was elected Secretary of the Grand Lodge of North Carolina, and remained in the position until his death, in 1867. A true estimate of the esteem in which he was held by his brethren, is the fact that he was elected to serve twenty-seven times as Grand Secretary. The following extract from the address of Bro. Lassiter, before the G. L., gives a true estimate of his character :

"During this long period, through years of severe trial for Masonry, he gave undoubted evidence of his integrity, and stood as one of the landmarks to our order, exemplifying in his life and conduct the excellence of its tenets, and illustrating the beauty of that character which is adorned by the virtues of Masonry and the piety of the Christian.

"During the long period of his connection with this Grand Lodge, he received many testimonials of the esteem in which he was held by his brethren, and the appreciation of his services as Grand Secretary by the Grand Lodge. The most recent one was the presentation of a Grand Secretary's jewel, by a unanimous vote of the Grand Lodge, upon the recommendation of the 'Committee on the Grand Secretary's Books.'

" His address, upon accepting the same, is alike creditable to his heart and his understanding, and shows what strong fraternal regard he bore to his brethren, and what liberality of sentiment he maintained for his fellow-men.

" The highest degree in Masonry to which he attained was that of 'Select Master.'

" Though his zeal for Masonry was unsurpassed, he was far from being an enthusiast. The most striking feature in the character of our esteemed and lamented brother was philanthropy. He was a sincere friend, and his warm and loving temper imparted its warmth to those around. As by the brook freshness is given to the air and verdance to the fields, so by the love of one heart many others were inspired with love. They seemed to possess his ardor, to breathe his fervor, to become philanthropists themselves. The same sentiment is no less visible in the ardent and tender attachment shown to all the brethren. Masonry seemed to have attracted his attention, to have engaged his thoughts, and absorbed his soul.

BAHRDT'S—BANNER. 45

"Her interest was his; her prosperity or adversity was his joy or sorrow; he seemed to be glad or mournful, to weep and rejoice with her. The same happiness attended his private life. The cares of a family were made pleasures by love. Adversity in his public career was relieved by happiness in private life, and the joy of prosperity was heightened by domestic pleasures. The peace and quiet of home afforded a sweet interchange with the corroding cares and stirring scenes of public life—a rest from the troubles of the past, a refreshment for those of the future.

"There are few who can be useful in a large sphere. When the energies of man are concentrated upon one point, when one object is pursued unwaveringly through life, it is almost inevitably gained. Bro. Bain was a Mason nearly half a century, and during the larger portion of this time filled honorable positions, with credit to himself and profit to the craft. In zeal and knowledge perhaps no one in the State excelled him. Upon Masonry he expended his time and talents. Here he sowed abundantly, and bountiful harvests have been his reward. He had the confidence and esteem of his brethren, and was known and respected by many others."

Bahrdt's Rite.—Carl Frederick Bahrdt introduced a system of Freemasonry into Germany, consisting of six degrees.

Baldchin.—A covering placed over the Oriental chair of King Solomon.

Ballot.—A vote by balls of different colors into a box, the greater of one color predominating giving the result. For masonic usage, a ballot on admitting a person for membership is always taken. Some Lodges hold that it must be unanimous; some allow three dissenting balls to be the criterion. This latter view is scarcely in usage.

Banner.—A flag or standard under which men are united for some common purpose. In the march of the Israelites through the desert, the tribes were marshaled under the banner of Judah, Ephraim, Reuben, and Dan, respectively designated with a lion, an ox, a man, and an eagle.

BANNERET—BARRY.

Banneret.—A knight who in feudal times possessed a certain amount of fiefs, and had the right of carrying a banner. It was practiced in England. When a bachelor was made a baronet on the field of battle, the act was done by cutting off the tails of his pennon, thus converting it into a banner. In the system of Knights Templar, the officers that led all warlike in connection with the Chief Marshal.

Baphomet.—The imaginary idol or symbol which the Templars were accused of employing in their sacred and mysterious rites. It arose from a corruption from the word Mahomet, by the transcriber. It had a connection with the Arabian mysteries.

Barabbas.—A notorious robber, guilty of sedition and murder. He happened to be imprisoned when Christ's process was carried on. As it had been usual to release some prisoners to the Jews at their passion feast, Pilate put Jesus and Barabbas in the list, that the Jews might choose one of them to be released. Contrary to his expectations and wish, they strongly recommended the release of the latter, and the crucifixion of the former.

Barefooted.—An ancient Israelitish custom prevailed whereby a contract was sealed by placing upon the bare foot a slipper. It was also a mark of respect to appear in the naked feet. The priests performed their ministrations in their bare feet.

Barri, W. I.—Grand Secretary of the Grand Lodge of South Carolina, died February 1st, 1867, at Raleigh, aged 74 years. He was Grand Secretary for many years, and held the esteem of men and Masons wherever he was known.

Barry, Wm. T.—A distinguished statesman and Mason, died August 30th, 1835, at Liverpool, England. He was a member of Lexington Lodge, No. 1, of Kentucky. After having lain eighteen years in a foreign soil, his remains were ordered to be brought home and interred, by the Legislature of Kentucky. His remains were interred in the Frankfort Cemetery, November 8th, 1854.

Bavaria.—About 1744, Freemasonry was introduced, but almost ceased to exist in 1776, as the "Illuminati" had tried to connect itself with it. In 1806, the order took a new start, and soon gained ground, and ultimately established the Grand Lodge at Munich.

Beauseant.—The banner of the order of the Temple. It is black and white—protection to the faithful, terror to the foe.

Behind the Back.—Every Mason is to defend a brother when his character is wrongfully traduced behind his back, his cause being just.

Belgium.—Freemasonry was introduced into Belgium at Mavis, by the G. L. of England, by granting a warrant to open a Lodge at this place. In 1786 they had become strong and embraced all the sections of the kingdom. The same year the Emperor Joseph II. suspended all but three Lodges. While the French revolution was in progress, these Lodges were interdicted. In 1798 they were re-opened. In 1814 they dissolved their connection with the G. L. of France, and in 1815 organized the G. L. of Belgium and Netherlands. The O. and A. S. Rite was established at Brussels in 1817.

Belief.—The belief of a Freemason is often called into question by those not properly informed. A Freemason holds the true Christian belief and doctrine of the Trinity. His belief is such that of necessity he should become a true and faithful Christian.

Benai.—Fellow craftsmen at the building of the Temple employed as setters.

Benevolence Fund.—A fund established for the relief of the poor and distressed. The applications are monthly.

48 BENIAH — BIER.

The Lodge consists of all Grand Officers, Actual Masters of Lodges, and twelve Past Masters.

Beniah.—The commander of David's guards. His exploits were celebrated in Israel. He overthrew the Moabitish champions, slew an Egyptian giant with his spear, and went into an exhausted cistern and slew a lion that had fallen into it. The word is now used in the degree of the Elected Grand Master.

Benjamin.—Youngest son of Jacob. His mother dying in childbed, called him Benom, *son of my sorrow*. Jacob, to forget his grief, called him Benjamin, "son of my right hand." Referred to in the K. T. system.

Benton, Wm. Col.—Was born in Providence, R. I., in 1750. He was an officer of the Revolution, and effected the capture of Prescott, the British general, for which services Congress voted him a sword and a grant of land in Vermont. He was disabled at Bath's Hills, in August, 1778. He was entered a Mason in Providence, St. John's Lodge, 1779. He became involved in law, and was imprisoned for debt. In 1825, Gen. Lafayette, having heard of his incarceration, liquidated the debt and released him from prison. He died at Providence, in 1831, aged 84 years, respected and esteemed as a man and Mason.

Bezaleel.—One of the zealous workmen engaged in the building of the Temple.

Bible (*a Book*).—A Mason is taught to believe that the greatest light of the order is the Bible, because it is the infallible rule of our faith. No Lodge exists without the acknowledgment of a Bible, and would, without, be illegal and unwarrantable.

Bier, Henry.—Was a native of Baltimore, Md., and was born in July, 1804, and died at New Orleans, October 14th, 1866. For many years he was a citizen of New Orleans, residing there since 1832. He was raised to the sublime degree of Master Mason in Mount Moriah Lodge, No. 59.

BLACK—BOHEMIA. 49

He was an active member of many of the charitable associations of Louisiana.

Black Ball.—In balloting for a profane for membership, white and black balls are used. The white balls elect, and the black balls reject. In 1738, the Grand Masters allowed Lodges to admit members if not above *three* ballots were against them. The universal landmark that requires an unanimous election is now adhered to.

Blue Lodges.—The first three degrees of Masonry are clothed with blue, and from this arises the term Blue Lodges. During the time of William III., blue was adopted by the craft.

Board of General Purposes.—Twenty-five persons compose this board.

Boaz (*Strength*).—A noble and wealthy Jew, son of Salmon and Rahab, who dwelt in Bethlehem, and after much kindness to Ruth, married her, and had a son Obed. As about 360 years elapsed between the marriage of Salmon and the birth of David, some have supposed two or three by the name of Boaz, but a threefold genealogy concurs to overthrow such a supposition. Boaz might be born 60 years after the death of Moses. In the 100th year of his age he married Obed, and she bore him Jesse. Boaz was also the name of a pillar that stood on the north side of King Solomon's Temple. Hence the candidate for Masonry is to strengthen himself in the sciences, and receive the moral light of Masonry.

Bobbs, John.—One of the pioneer Masons of Kentucky. He was I. W. of Lexington L. No. 1, and elected Grand Tyler of the Grand Lodge in 1800. In October, 1801, he was J. G. D.; in October, 1802, he was P. M. of No.1; and in April, 1803, Grand Pursuivant; in September, 1805, he was appointed G. Tyler and G. Steward.

Bohemia.—Freemasonry was introduced into Bohemia

50

BOOK—BOWEN.

in 1749, by warrant for the opening of a Lodge in Prague, under the authority of the Grand Lodge of Scotland.

Book of Constitutions.—Containing the principles of Masonry, its rules and regulations, duties of officers, and charges, etc.

Book of the Law.—The Bible so called is to be found in every legally constituted Lodge of Masons, and should lie open upon the Altar. In the E. A. deg. at Ruth, iv. 7; in the F. C. deg. at Judges, xxii. 6; in the M. M. deg. at I. Kings, vii. 13, Psalms, cxxxiii., Amos, viii., and Ecclesiastes, xii.

Bond-Woman (*a Woman Slave*).—The Biblical account of Abraham's wife Sarah is, that at eighty years she conceived herself past bearing children, and gave Abraham her servant Hagar, who, on conceiving, was ill humored toward her mistress, and in order to escape the punishment so severely inflicted by Sarah, fled to the Wilderness. However, being promised that her posterity should never be blotted out, she returned to her bondage.

Bourbon, Duchess.—She was installed *Grande Maitresse* of the Adoptive Rite of Masonry in France, May 2d, 1775.

Bowen, Jabez.—Was born in Providence, R. I., in 1740. He was a graduate of Yale. He was chancellor of Providence College for 30 years. He was a stern patriot during the revolutionary struggle, and a member of the Board of War, Judge of Supreme Court, and Lt. Governor of R. I. No date can be found of his initiation into Masonry. In 1762 he acted as Junior Warden in St. John's Lodge, Providence. In 1778, July 15th, he was commissioned to open St. John's Lodge, which was closed during the war, from the Provincial G. M. of Mass. He acted as Master of this Lodge until 1791, when a Grand Lodge was constituted in the State, of which he was the Dep. Grand Master. In 1794 he was elected Grand Master. He died in 1815, May 7th, aged 75 years.

BOZRAH — BRANT. 51

Bozrah.—A city of the Edomite. Mention is made of it in the Knights of the Christian Mark.

Brahmins.—The first of the highest of the four castes of the Hindoos, said to have proceeded from the mouth of Brah (seat of wisdom). They form the sacerdotal class, and its priests have maintained a greater sway than those of any other nation. Their chief privileges consist in reading the Veda, the Sacred Book. The life of the Brahmin is divided into four periods: the first beginning at the age of seven, when he learns the Veda; the second, he marries; the third, his religious duties multiply, and are quite numerous; and in the fourth, he is admitted into personal communication with the Deity. Their origin is veiled in obscurity.

Brant, Joseph.—An Indian, born on the banks of the Ohio, about 1742. He was called *Thayendonegea* by his father, a chief among the Mohawks. He belonged to the Six Nations, and was one of its renowned chieftains. When Brant was thirteen years of age, he accompanied Sir William Johnson against the French, at Lake George. Molly Brant, Joseph's sister, was the wife of Sir William Johnson, whom he married after the ancient Indian style, but at a later day legitimized the children of Molly, with the ceremonies of the English church. During Brant's early life he resided with Sir William, at Johnsonville. In 1766, May 23d, Sir William organized a Lodge at that place, and became its Master. In 1775, Brant then being Chief of the Mohawks, visited England, where he was made a Mason. During the Revolution, Brant adhered to the British interests, and his bloody deeds were the terror of the frontier men. In 1776, Col. McKinistry was taken prisoner at the battle of the Cedars, and condemned to the stake, but Brant recognizing in him a brother, had him safely conducted to Quebec. In 1777, Brant gathered a large force of savages on the Susquehanna, at Unadilla, and Gen.

BRASSART—BRAZEN.

Heckmier was sent to hold a conference with him, and prevent his intended outrages. They were both old friends and Masons; but Heckmier was unable to enlist his sympathies for the colonies, and the conference was broken up. In 1779, at the battle of Minisiole, Major Wood was entrapped in an ambuscade by Brant, and having become possessed of the masonic appeal of distress, was not slow to avail himself of it. Brant instantly recognized and respected the appeal, but soon after found that the major was an impostor. However, he spared his life, and the major, while a prisoner at Niagara, was made a Mason in a British Military Lodge, at which Brant was present, and paid the fee. Another incident of Brant's masonic mercy is the case of Jno. Maynard, of Framingham, Mass. He was taken a captive and condemned to death. When he was divested of his clothing, Brant recognized the masonic emblems upon his arm, and immediately released him, and sent him a prisoner to Canada. In 1785, Brant visited England to settle his claims upon the British Government. He shortly afterward returned to the United States, and devoted his life to the elevation and education of his race.

Brassart.—In plate armor, the piece which protects the upper part of the arm from the elbow to the shoulder. It belongs to the Knights Templar armor.

Brazen Laver.—Used in the tabernacle for the ablution of the priests. In the higher degrees of Freemasonry it is used emblematically by the candidate to perform ablutions.

Brazen Pillars.—The two pillars at the entrance porch of King Solomon's Temple are represented on the masonic trestle-board. They were made between Succoth and Zeredatha, and composed of brass, and made hollow to preserve the records of Freemasonry.

Brazen Serpent.—To punish the idolatrous Israelites, God commanded Moses to make a Brazen Serpent, and if it came to pass that a serpent had bitten any one, and he looked upon the Brazen Serpent, he lived. In the course of time the Brazen Serpent was with other idolatrous things abolished by Hezekiah.

Brazil. — In 1816, Freemasonry was introduced into Brazil. The Grand Lodge was organized in 1822.

Breast.—All just secrets should be carefully preserved in a Mason's breast. A brother Mason's secrets should be as sacred in my keeping as though not intrusted to me.

Breastplate.—The pin or plate worn by the High Priest. It was set with twelve precious stones, bearing the name of each tribe, which it represented by its color.

Bridge.—The bridge is a symbol in the higher order of Freemasonry.

Brotherly Kiss.—This was a practice in the time of the primitive Christians. Hence it is now almost out of use except in some of the European Lodges. The newly made brother is then greeted with a kiss from the Master.

Brothers of the Bridge.—A charitable order in France in the middle ages. The members built bridges, roads, hospitals, and provided for the comforts of travelers. They built the bridge Bon Pas, near Avignon, and Pont St. Esprit, over the Rhine. This was commenced 21st August, 1265. Favors were granted them by Pope Clements III. The order had reciprocal relations with the Knights of St. John of Jerusalem, and the Roman builders. Several of the French degrees of Masonry are taken from this system. Its jewel was a pickaxe worn upon the breast.

Brothers of Kabend.—This order was organized in Germany in 1200. It was a religious and moral sect of some notoriety.

Bruce, Eli.—A native of Massachusetts, and born at Templeton, November 8th, 1792 or 1793. In 1825, being a resident of Niagara County, New York, he filled the office of Sheriff of Niagara. In 1827, he was brought before a

54   BRUCE.

justice in Lockport, and charged in aiding the abduction
of Wm. Morgan. The charge not being sustained, he was
dismissed. Shortly after this an effort was made to have
him removed from the office of Sheriff. The case came before the Court at Canandaigua, August 20th, 1828. The
indictment charged him with conspiring and abducting
one Wm. Morgan. Much excitement existed while the
case proceeded. When the verdict of guilty was rendered,
the Anti-Masons became jubilant over their victory. The
Hon. N. M. Howell, presiding Judge, sentenced Bruce to
imprisonment for twenty-eight months. From this sen-
tence an appeal was taken to the Supreme Court, and the
prisoner held in custody. On May 13th, 1829, the sen-
tence was executed. Bro. Bruce was an exemplary man
and citizen. A true Christian and honest man, he won
friends in every circle of life. He is styled the "Masonic
Martyr," in a valuable work by Bro. Robert. Morris.
Whether Bruce was justifiable or not in acceding to Morgan's desires in secreting and enabling him to reach Canada,
the reader may infer from the following extract from his
testimony given at the trial of Whitney :

"That on the evening of the 13th of September, 1826, he was
first apprised that William Morgan was coming on from Canandaigua, on the *ridge road*. He was told this by Burrage Smith
and another person, then living at Lockport. Some six or eight
days previous to this, he had been informed by a gentleman from
Batavia, that Morgan was willing to go away from Miller, and
the witness was requested to assist in his removal, which he declined. He, however, had been requested by another person to
prepare a cell for Morgan in the jail at Lockport, in contemplation
of Morgan's being directly carried across from Batavia to Lockport, and thence to Niagara. Smith and the person who came with
him told witness that Morgan had come voluntarily, and was willing to go into Canada; they said he had come peaceably, and
wanted witness to assist in getting him on. Witness declined at
first, but finally agreed to do so, and between nine and ten o'clock
went to the house of Solomon C. Wright, living on the ridge road,

BRUCE.

three miles north of Lockport, where he found the carriage and got into it. William Morgan, or a person called Morgan, was in it, one Hague, who is now dead, and himself, and no others, were in the carriage. It was driven by a person of his acquaintance. There were several persons at Wright's who did not belong to the house; and on his way there he met some strangers on foot going toward Lockport. He never saw Lawson until he saw him here in jail. He did not see Whitney, and did not know him. He afterward stated that he saw Whitney at the installation at Lewiston.

"He went in the carriage from Wright's to Lewiston, where another carriage and horses were procured; the same passengers got into that carriage and drove to the ferry near the fort. On their way they took in another passenger. The testimony of Corydon Fox is perfectly correct. Witness did not see Morgan until their arrival at Lewiston, when they came to the ferry and got out of the carriage. Morgan *locked arms* with the two who accompanied witness.

"Witness and his companions, four besides himself, crossed the river to Canada, having Morgan in the boat. Their object was to get Morgan away from Miller, into the interior of the country in Canada, and place him on a farm. The expected arrangement for the reception of Morgan in Canada had not been made, and it was thought best to wait a few days. Morgan was accordingly brought over to this side of the river, and was put into the magazine in Fort Niagara, to await the preparations on the other side to receive him. It was past midnight, and before daylight, when they put him into the magazine. He has never seen Morgan from that day to this.

"While with Morgan in the carriage, the conversation among them was that he (Morgan) was going among his friends; he appeared to be easy, and said nothing. At Lewiston witness took a sulky and horse that were there, and drove them to Lockport; they were to be forwarded on to the East somewhere; did not know where. Did not learn at Lewiston that Burrage Smith came on in a sulky; understood the horse he drove was owned on the ridge somewhere.

"When the carriage with Morgan drove up to Molyneux's, another person rode up on horseback. He did not stop there.

56

BRUCE—BURNS.

Witness does not know what became of him. He says that he supposes Morgan went voluntarily. On being again interrogated, whether upon the oath he had taken he still persisted in declaring his belief that Morgan went voluntarily, he said *he did.*"

Bruce, Robert.—He succeeded in defeating the English under Edward, at Bannockburn, and thus securing the independence of his crown, 24th June, 1314; was the author of the Royal Order of Herodem and Rosy Cross, which he established at Kilwinning. immediately after the battle of Bannockburn. He was acknowledged as a thorough Christian Mason. He died in 1329, universally beloved and lamented by his subjects.

Burial.—Masonic funerals are conducted at the request *only* of the deceased brother. In the ancient charges it states he must be advanced to the third degree.

Burning Bush.—As Moses led the flocks of Tethra to the northwest side of Sinai, the Lord appeared to him in a Burning Bush, but not consumed. Astonished, he drew near, when the Lord spoke to him out of the bush, and bade him put off his shoes, as it was sacred by his presence. God had made known to Moses how he would deliver the Israelites from bondage. It is used in the higher masonic degrees as a symbol.

Burns, Robert.—Born in Ayr, Scotland, January 25th, 1759, and died July 21st, 1796. This distinguished poet was made a Mason in Tarbolton Lodge, No. 178. He was entered 4th July, and passed and raised October 15th, 1781. His address of farewell to St. James Lodge was given in 1785. Burns felt and appreciated the benefits of Freemasonry. He visited Connough, Kilwinning Lodge, Edinburgh, in December, 1786, and became a warm friend of Past Master Erskine. During this year he was elected by this Lodge as Poet Laureate. In 1787, he was made a Royal Arch Mason, at St. Abbey Lodge, Weymouth. In

1820, a fine masonic monument was erected to perpetuate his memory, at Alloway.

By-Laws.—A code of laws to govern the Lodge. Every Lodge frames its own By-Laws, and are then submitted to the Grand Lodge for approval, and if not inconsistent with regulations of the Grand Lodge, are adopted.

C.

Caaba.—A sacred stone and object of veneration with the Mohammedan. The pilgrims, on their visit to Mecca, salute it with kisses as they gather around it. Its touch, they assert, imparts a divine influence, cures bodily infirmities, and purifies the heart.

Cabal.—A district given to Hiram, King of Tyre, by Solomon, in acknowledgment of the important service which he had rendered toward building the Temple. Hiram was by no means pleased with the gift, and the district received the name of Cabal (*unpleasant*). In the A. and A. S. R., in the Intimate Secretary, the history is fully given.

Cabbala.—A Hebrew word, signifying the oral tradition which the Rabbins conceive to complete the system of scriptural interpretations. They maintain that it was delivered in the first instance to Adam, and again to Abraham and Moses, by direct revelation, but that since the time of Esdras the memories of the elders and the priests have sufficed to preserve it. As the Masora details the literal explanations of the language of Scriptures, so the Cabbala reveals the hidden truths of which it is the symbol. The mysteries appear to have been an invention of philosophizing Jews, accommodating speculations of the Gnostics to the religion of the Old Testament.

Cabiri—In Pagan mythology, sacred priests or deified

58   CABLE — CANADA.

heroes, venerated by the Phœnicians as founders of religion. The order embraces the adjoining cities. Hiram, King of Tyre, embraced it, and through him it is said the legend of the third degree of Masonry has been perpetuated. The Essenes order is said to have been taken from the Cabiri.

Cable-Tow.—The length of an E. A. cable-tow is three miles. According to the ancient landmark a brother must attend to the Lodge if within his reach.

Caiaphas.—The High Priest of the Jews that adjudged Christ, by the living God, to declare whether he was the true Messiah. He attended the trial and helped deliver Christ to the Jews.

Calendar, Freemason.—In 1775, the Grand Lodge of England commenced the publication of the first Masonic Calendar. The proceeds are given to the poor.

California.—In 1849, the Grand Lodges of Missouri, Connecticut, District of Columbia, etc. granted warrants for opening Lodges in this State. In 1850, April 19th, the Grand Lodge was organized. In 1854, 10th August, the Grand Commandery was commenced. In 1854, the Grand Chapter was organized. The first Chapter in the State was in 1850.

Calling-Off.—A term used in masonic ceremonies, which "calls-off" the craft to refreshments from their labors.

Calling-On.—A term similar to calling-off. The craft are "called-on" from refreshments to labor.

Camp of Israel.—The station of the Israelites when resting from a journey. The Tabernacle was placed in the center of the camp. The food for these people came down from heaven in the shape of manna.

Canada.—The exact date of the introduction of Freemasonry into this Province is not known. The Grand Lodges of England, Ireland, and Scotland have the honor of granting the first warrants. In 1855, the Grand Lodge

CANCELLARIUS—CARPET. 59

was organized, and the Grand Chapter in 1818, 27th August.

Cancellarius.—An office of the Templar system.

Candidate.—Is a person who is applying to be admitted into a Lodge, and whose name is entered upon the record, that his character may be inquired into.

Candles.—The three luminaries or candles are placed in pillars. They are distinguished from the Sun, Moon, and Master, by the masonic brother.

Canopy.—On the Continent the Canopy is used in processions. The Grand Master is covered with a canopy of blue, purple, and crimson, borne upon staves, and the Masters of private lodges under blue.

Capitular Degrees.—The degrees of the Chapter.

Captain-General.—4th officer of Commandery of K. T.

Captain of the Host.—The 4th officer of the Chapter.

Captivity.—When God punished the rebellious Jews by using Nebuchadnezzar to force them into captivity, the Temple was burned, and the two pillars, Jachin and Boaz, were carried off.

Carbonari.—A political society formed after the masonic system, with four degrees. Baraca was the Lodge. Wood was the outside places; and Vendita the inside. They were for liberty of freedom of conscience. Its motto, "hatred to all tyrants."

Cardinal Points.—The East, the source of light—the place of the W. M., represents the Sun. The South, the pillar of Beauty, the J. W., marks the Sun at its meridian. The West, the pillar of Strength, the S. W., marks the setting Sun and closing day.

Carpet Knights.—In the 16th century a rich green cloth was spread before the Royal Throne of the English Sovereign, whence Knights dubbed upon it, at convocations, etc., were called Carpet Knights, to distinguish them from those made in the field.

60 CASS—CAURAUCIUS.

Cass, Lewis.—Born at Exeter, New Hampshire, October 9th, 1782, and died at Detroit, Michigan, June 17th, 1866. He was a distinguished American statesman, and occupies a prominent part in the history of the country. He was the first Grand Master of Masons in Ohio, in 1809, and presided as such until he removed to Detroit. He was also the first Grand Master of Masons in the Territory of Michigan. Up to the time of his death he manifested his sincere attachment to the mystic circle. After a long life of usefulness to his country, he was summoned by the Supreme Grand Architect of the universe to the Grand Lodge above.

Casswell, Richard.—Was born in Maryland, in 1729, August 2d. He went to North Carolina at an early age. In 1753, he was Deputy Surveyor and Clerk of Court at Orange. In 1754, he was a delegate to the Colonial Congress. In 1774, he was the delegate to the General Congress, at Philadelphia. In 1776, he was elected Governor of North Carolina. He entered the American army in 1779, as a brigadier-general. He was Speaker of the Senate of North Carolina in 1784. He was a delegate that helped frame the Federal Constitution in 1787. In 1789, he was again elected to the State Senate, and, while presiding, was struck with paralysis, and died on the 10th August, aged sixty years. He was made a Mason in North Carolina, but at what date is not known. He was the second Grand Master of the Independent Grand Lodge, and acting as such at the time of his death.

Catenarian Arch.—Is the form a Chapter Lodge. The semicircular arch will not sustain itself, but must have an abutment for support. The catenarian arch, bearing alike at all points of the curve, stands independent of any aid.

Cauraucius or Caraucius.—A Roman Emperor. In the year 800 he favored the Masons of Britain by conferring certain privileges upon them. Through the influence

CAUTION — CHAPITER.

of Altanus a charter was obtained from Cauraucius, and many reunions of the order took place.

Caution.—The Entered Apprentice, after his initiation, is particularly enjoined to be cautious in his words and actions that he may not give any one information who is an enemy of the order, and hence the name given him is *caution*.

Cave.—The ark and cherubim were placed by Solomon in a deep cave under the Temple, to guard it carefully in case the Temple should be destroyed, and to preserve it from falling into the hands of the heathen. It is even said that Josiah afterward used this same secret place for preserving the ark.

Cephas.—Used in the Royal Master's degree in connection with cubical stone. The word means rock or stone.

Cerde, Local.—A political order of France that took a prominent part in the French Revolution in 1791. Its object was to entrap the masonic influence into their support.

Chamber.—Solitude is the place to reflect. Here our thoughts dwell upon life and immortality. The skeleton forms of corruption and decay cannot terrify us when once mature reflection forms our judgment. Our duty then becomes plain and easily accomplished.

Chamber of Reflection.—A room set apart in the Knights Templar and Ac. and A. S. R. where the candidate reflects upon the responsibilities he is about taking upon himself. The room is peculiarly fitted with emblems of mortality, so as to lead an intelligent mind to reflect upon the uncertainties of life.

Chancellor.—Officer of Knights of Red Cross.

Chapiter.—The upper part of capital of a column pillar. In Solomon's Temple these chapiters are fully described in the Bible.

62   CHAPLAIN — CHASSIDES.

Chaplain.—An officer in all the Lodges. He offers up devotions to Almighty God for blessings and benefits.

Chapter.—A legal body of Royal Arch Masons. Its officers are King, Priest, Scribe, Secretary, and Treasurer.

Chapter.—The various bodies are distinguished as Grand Chapter, General Grand Chapter, and Chapter

Charges.—The ancient charges embrace God and Religion, Civil Magistrates, Lodges, Masters, Craft, and our duties. These charges were given under direction of the Grand Lodge of England, and compiled by Br. James Anderson in 1721.

Charity.—Commences at home, hence it is the duty of the brèthren to assist a needy brother if in their power to do so.

Charles XIII.—King of Sweden, was born 7th October, 1748. He came to the crown at a very critical period in the history of Sweden. The revolution of 1809 had hurled Gustavus Adolphus from the throne, and placed Charles at the head of the State as administrator of the realm. On the 20th June, 1809, he was crowned king. On the 27th May, 1811, he established the Order of Charles the XIII., which he founded. This order was conferred upon Freemasons of a high degree. He was the Grand Master of the order. He enjoyed the love of his people by his prudent government until his death, 5th Feb. 1818.

Charles XIII., Order of.—This order of knighthood was originated by Charles XIII., King of Sweden, 27th May, 1811. One of its statutes is that it shall only be communicated to Masons. It is limited to 27 secular and 3 ecclesiastical members. The reigning king is always the Grand Master. It is considered the highest degree of Swedish Masonry.

Charter.—An act warranting the assembling of Masons in the capacity of a Lodge, etc.

Chassides.—The name of the chief of the 75th and 76th

CHERUBIM — CHRIST. 63

degrees in the Rite of Misraim. Mention is made of this sect in the first book of Maccabees.

Cherubim.—Solomon's Temple was adorned with four cherubim. Two were made by Moses, and two by Solomon. The first were part of the Mercy-seat, and the latter were for the greater glory of the Temple.

Chili.—Freemasonry was introduced into Chili in 1841 under the authority of the Grand Lodge of France. The Grand Lodges of Massachusetts and California also granted charters for Lodges in 1850–1. In 1862, 20th April, the Grand Lodge was formed, and the Grand Chapter was organized about this same period. Several councils of the A. and A. R. are held under the authority of the Grand East of the United States, located at Charleston, S. C.

Chisel.—The chisel is a small instrument used by operative masons, and intended to make impressions on hard matter and fashion it into comely forms. Morally it is to carve our actions and virtues, and to display the beauties of a true upright character in its devotedness to truth and Christianity.

Chivalry.—From the French chevalier, *knight*. The customs pertaining to the order of knighthood. The system of manners and tone of sentiment which the institution of knighthood strictly pursued, produced in Europe, in the middle ages, the term chivalry. This imaginary institution of chivalry had no full existence at any period. It was the ideal perfection of a code of morals and pursuits.

Chivington, J. M.—First Grand Master of Masons of Colorado; is a minister of the M. E. Church. He was identified during the Kansas difficulties as the "Fighting Parson." He reached Colorado in 1860 as Presiding Elder. He also served as major and colonel of the First Colorado Cavalry.

Christ Jesus.—The Lord and Saviour of mankind. He

64   *CHRISTIANITY.*

is called Christ or Messiah, because he is anointed and sent by God to execute his mediatorial office ; and is called Jesus, because by his righteousness, power, and spirit he is qualified to save mankind. He is appointed by God for that end. He is the eternal son of God, equal with the Father. When the government was about departing from Judah, an angel appeared to the Virgin Mary, and stated that through the influence of the Holy Ghost, she would conceive and bear the promised Messiah. She was espoused to Joseph. He was the 32d in descent from David in the royal line of Solomon. Mary was the 34th from David by Nathan. The two lines of Solomon and Nathan met in the persons of Shelathiel and Zerubbabel. Christ was born in Bethlehem of Judea. He was accused of the Jews as an evil-doer, and delivered up by Pontius Pilate to be crucified. He was hurried to Golgotha, the place of execution, where he was nailed to the cross. Pilate caused a plate to be inscribed and placed on the top of the cross— *This is Jesus of Nazareth, King of the Jews.* At noon, just before he bowed his head and died, and gave up the ghost, he cried in Hebrew, *My God, my God, why hast thou forsaken me?* His body was taken by Joseph of Aramathea, and placed in a tomb. On the 3d day he arose. He showed himself to his disciples at various times after this. Forty days after his resurrection he took his disciples with him to the Mt. of Olives, near Bethany, and there blessed them, as he was conveyed by a multitude of angels up to heaven, and sitteth at the right hand of God, the Father Almighty, from whence he shall come to judge the quick and the dead.

Christianity.—The religion of Jesus Christ. From the period when the disciples were first called Christians at Antioch to the present day, the main doctrines of the gospel, and the principles it reveals and confirms, have been preserved by the church. If a Mason be a true and consistent believer in the doctrines he professes, he is in reality a true Christian.

Cincinnatus, Order of.—Instituted on the 13th November, 1783. This was a society that originated with masonic officers who were associated with Washington in the Revolution. It had long been their desire to see Washington placed and constituted the head of Masons in the United States. The object of the association was benevolence, relief, and to perpetuate the lasting friendship formed under trying circumstances and patriotism. Gen. Knox is the author of the system. Although Rev. Wm. Smith claims that he gave the name for the society, as in a sermon preached before the G. L. of Pennsylvania by him in 1777, at St. John the Evangelist's festival, he alluded to Washington, then present, as the "Cincinnatus of America." The descendants of the members of this society had the privilege of entering it. A golden medal was used as a badge. Provision was also made for its indigent members.

Circles.—There is a point within a circle in which Masons cannot err or go astray. It is formed north and south by two perpendicular lines; on the upper part rests the Bible, supporting Jacob's ladder reaching into the heavens. If a Mason keeps within these bounds and remembers his duties, he may safely rely upon reaching the point from whence all blessings and benefits flow.

Clandestine Lodge.—Unwarranted and illegal Lodges, formed by mercenary Masons, whose only design is to extort money from the credulous. They endeavor to conceal themselves as much as possible. Since Lodges have formed themselves under a grand head, these illegitimate concerns have almost died out.

Classes.—The builders of the Temple were divided into classes or divisions. Grand Master Adoniram commanded 30,000 Apprentices; Hiram Abiff, 80,000 Fellow Crafts; Stotkyn, 2000 Mark Men; Mohabin, 1000 Masters; Shib-

66

CLAY — CLINTON.

lein, 600 Mark Masters; Joubert, 24 Architects; Hiram Abiff, 45 Most Excellent Masters; Adoniram, 12 Grand Architects; Tite Zadok, 9 Super Excellent Masters.

Clay, Henry.—Born in Hanover County, Va., April 12th, 1777, and died at Washington, June 29th, 1852. In April, 1803, he was regularly reported as a member of Lexington Lodge, No 1, Lexington, until 1826, when he was demitted. In 1820–1, he was Past Grand Master of Grand Lodge of Kentucky. The corner-stone of the Clay Monument was laid at New Orleans, April 12th, 1856. He was a bright Mason, and often selected by the Grand Lodge to fill the important station of orator. In 1812 he was designated to deliver the address commemorative of the death of G. M. Jos. H. Daviess. His usefulness as a citizen, and his important services as a statesman, will ever endear him to the memory of Masons and citizens of the Union.

Cleft in the Rocks.—Caves and crevices produced by nature. The mountainous regions of Jerusalem were noted for these hiding-places.

Clermont.—A chapter of high degrees founded in 1754, at Paris, by De Bonneville.

Clesica Ordinis Templariorium.—A system of Masonry adopted at the close of seven years' war by the Order of Strict Observance.

Clinton, De Witt.—Was born at Little Britain, N. Y., 2d March, 1769, and died 11th February, 1828. He was made a Mason in Holland Lodge, N. Y., in 1793, and acted as Warden during the year. In December, 1794, he was elected Master of his Lodge. In 1795, he was elected Junior Warden of the G. L. In 1798, he was elected Grand Senior Warden of the G. L. In 1806, he was elected Grand Master of the G. L. He was a member of the Grand Chapter in 1799. In 1816, he was elected Grand Gen. High Priest of the Gen. G. Chapter of U. S. He was holding the position of Governor of N. Y. during the anti-masonic excitement of 1826–8, and was maliciously and foully accused of sheltering guilty parties. On 7th October, 1826, he issued a proclamation for the arrest of the offender of the law, and at a late date offered rewards for the conviction of the lawbreaker, etc. However, no clew could be obtained to the perpetrator of the alleged crime, and accordingly in 1827, he published officially that all efforts to find out the place where Morgan had secreted himself were unavailing, and offered $1000 for the arrest and conviction of the offender. He was determined if the guilty parties were Masons, that they should be punished, and the fraternity purged from such characters; but further developments showed that no Masons were engaged in the affair. On 18th June, 1814, he was elected thrice W. G. M. of Grand Encampment of N. Y. On the 2d June, 1816, he was elected G. G. Master of the G. G. Encampment of U. S.

Cloudy Pillar.—When Moses was commanded to take the Israelites from Egyptian bondage, Jehovah gave him a cloudy pillar as his guide by day. Thus when they had come to the sea, the Egyptians were frenzied with joy at the hope of compelling their bondsmen to return, but Moses having faith in the sign set before, pressed on, and the waters of the sea divided, and the Israelites passed over on dry land, while the Egyptian army, when once in the passage, were swallowed up by the returning element.

Cock, Oliver.—The first Grand Master of Grand Lodge of Iowa. He was a native of Miami County, Ohio; and an eminent Mason and Christian.

Collar.—An article of dress.

Collegia Artificum.—Alfred and Athelstane are said to have introduced the members of this college of Rome into England to build their palaces and fortresses. Afterwards they were united with the Greek colleges and protected by civil enactments. (See Ant.)

68   *COLOMBO—COMMANDMENTS.*

Colombo.—In 1820, Freemasonry was introduced into New Granada. In 1833, June 19th, the Grand Lodge was formed at Carthagena.

Colonial.—The G. L. delegated Dep. G. Masters to preside over the remote Lodges, and held them as Colonial.

Colorado.—The G. L. was organized August 2d, 1861, at Golden City. I. M. Chivington was elected first Grand Master. There are three Chapters in this State. No. 1, at Central City, established April 6th, 1863. No. 2, at Denver City, established —— —— The Colorado Commandery was established at Denver, —— —— Central City, No. 2, established Nov. 8th, 1866.

Columbia, District of.—The first warrants for holding Lodges in the District of Columbia were under the authority of the Grand Lodge of Maryland. On Dec. 11th, 1810, the Grand Lodge was organized. In 1825, the Knights Templar were organized, under warrant of the Grand Encampment of the United States.

Commander.—The title of the chief officer of the Commandery of Knights Templar.

Commandery.—An assembly of Knights with a warrant to confer degrees, etc. Commander, Generalissimo, Captain-General, Prelate, S. W., J. W., Treasurer, Recorder, Standard Bearer, Warden, Three Guards, and Sentinel, compose its officers.

Commandery, Grand.—Is formed of a number of subordinate Commanderies in a State or District. It has power over Councils, Red Cross, Knights Templar, and Knights of Malta.

Commandments.—The Ten Commandments given to Moses upon the Mount constitute the basis of masonic discipline. Masonry forbids paganism, image worship, blasphemy, murder, treason, adultery, perjury, theft, etc. Masonry requires observance of the Bible teachings, obedience to the laws of the land, etc.

COMMON--CONSERVATOR. 69

Common Gavel.—Is an instrument made use of by operative masons to fit the stone for the builder's use, but Masons are directed to use it for the purpose of diverting their minds and consciences from all vices and superfluities of life.

Companion.—Is the name addressed by R. A. Masons to each other when in the Lodge. When the Jews were in captivity they addressed each other with this title.

Compasses.—Teach us to limit our desires in every station, and is dedicated to the craft. It ought to keep us in bonds of union with all mankind, but especially with our brethren.

Conclave.—An assembly of Knights Templar.

Concord.—A masonic order founded by the Prince of Nassau in 1695. In 1718, Prince Swartzburg, Rudalstadt, organized a similar order, into which both sexes were admitted. In 175– a similar order was organized at Hamburg.

Congress.—The term is used for masonic conferences. The assemblies of these bodies took place, to wit: The Congress of Washington in 1822; of Baltimore, in 1843; the second at Baltimore in 1847; of Lexington, Ky., 1853; third Congress of Paris, 1855; North American Congress, Sept. 1st, 1859, at Chicago. These bodies met to institute reform in the order, and consult upon the general interests of Freemasonry.

Connecticut.—The Grand Lodge of Massachusetts granted a warrant for a Lodge, the 12th November, 1750, which was the first Lodge opened in the State. On the 8th July, 1789, the Grand Lodge was formed. The Grand Council was organized in 1819. The Grand Chapter, 17th May, 1798, and the Knights Templar, 13th September, 1827.

Consecration Elements.—Corn, oil, and wine.

Conservator, Grand.—An officer in the Grand Orient of France. The same name was given to the union of the

70   *CONSISTORY—CONVENTIONS.*

three Grand Conservators, when Grand Master Joseph Napoleon and Prince Corubaccies were called away in 1814.

Consistory.—In the Rite of Misraim and A. and A. Rite, the name of an assembly.

Consolidated Lodges.—The term applied to those Lodges of alchemy that united under the above appellation. In high Masonry, one of the degrees is taken from this consolidation.

Constituting.—To constitute a Lodge it is first duly formed, and after prayer and praise, the Grand Master has the petition, dispensation, and charter read, and having approved of the selection of officers, he then constitutes them the officers of the Lodge in due and ancient form.

Consumatum est.—The perfection of Freemasonry. The Rose Croix or 33d° is held to be the perfection of the order.

Conventions.—Below are principal masonic conventions that have been held for masonic reform:

The Convention of York, in 926, convoked by Prince Edwin, at the City of York, designated as the General Assembly.

The first Convention of Strasburg, in 1275, convoked by Edwin von Steinbough, in Strasburg.

The second Convention of Strasburg, in 1564, convoked by the Grand Lodge of Strasburg.

The first Convention of Ratisbon, in 1459, convoked by Lord Dotzinger. The second Convention, held in 1464, convoked by the Grand Lodge of Strasburg.

The Convention of Spier, in 1469, convoked by the Grand Lodge of Strasburg.

The Convention of Cologne, in 1535, convoked by the Bishop of Cologne.

The Convention of Basle, in 1563, convoked by the Grand Lodge of Strasburg.

The Convention of London, in 1717, convoked by the four Lodges of London, at the Appletree Tavern.

The Convention of Dublin, in 1730, convoked by the Lodges of Dublin.

The Convention of Edinburgh, in 1736, convoked by the four Lodges of Edinburgh.

The Convention of Hague, in 1756, convoked by the Royal Union Lodge.

The first Convention of Jena, in 1763, convoked by the Lodge of Strict Observance. The second Convention, in 1764, by Johnson, *alias* Becker.

The Convention of Altenberg, in 1765, convoked by Baron Hund.

The Convention of Brunswick, in 1775, convoked by Ferdinand, Duke of Brunswick.

The Convention of Lyons, in 1778, convoked by the Lodge of Chevaliers Bienfaisants.

The Convention of Lovers of Truth, in 1784, convoked by the Lodge of United Friends, in Paris.

The Convention of Wolfenbuttel, in 1778, convoked by the Duke of Brunswick.

The Convention of Wilhelmsbadt, in 1782.

But little good was derived to the order from these assemblies, and nothing of any moment was transacted. The York Convention made a radical reform. Those of Cologne and London also devised measures that were of benefit, but beyond these nothing was accomplished.

Convocations.—Is the name of the assemblies of Chapters, Councils, Commanderies, and Select Masters.

Copestone.—The Copestone is the binding or Keystone, last laid in the building. It is symbolical in the Most Excellent Master's degree.

Corn.—In the Master's degree this is duly appreciated, as it is a symbol of resurrection, and at its proper time rises to light and is clothed with life and beauty.

72 CORNUCOPIA — COUNCIL.

Cornucopia (*Horn of Plenty*).—The jewel of the Stewards.

Corwin, Thomas.—Born in Bourbon County, Kentucky, July 29th, 1794, and died in the City of Washington, December 18th, 1865. In 1798, he was removed with his father to Warren County, Ohio. He was made a Mason in Lebanon Lodge, No. 26, and in 1819, acted as Master of that Lodge. He received his Chapter degrees at Lebanon, and the honors of Christian Knighthood at Worthington, in the first Encampment organized in the West. In 1821 and 1826, he was Grand Orator of the G. L. of Ohio. In 1823 and 1827, he was Deputy Grand Master, and in 1828, the Grand Master of the Grand Lodge of Ohio. In early life he gave his attention to national affairs, and was noted as one of the most eloquent men of the age. As a Senator of the United States, Secretary of the U. S. Treasury, and as a foreign minister, he won a proud distinction. He was buried with masonic honors at Lebanon.

Coty.—The mysteries of this Goddess of Corinth and Chios were performed in the night-time.

Council.—An assembly of Royal and Select Masters, etc.

Council Degrees.—On the 20th February, 1783, the degrees of Royal and Select Master were organized in the City of Charleston, S. C., by Jos. Myers, M. Spitzer, and A. Frost, Deputy Inspector Generals of Frederick II., King of Prussia. They deposited certified copies of these degrees with the Grand Council of Princes of Jerusalem, and gave them under their control. Subsequently agents were appointed, and the degrees were soon scattered among the brethren of various States, but always counseled that their allegiance was due to the Council of A. and A. Rite. These agents granted charters to establish Councils of Royal and Select Masters to several States, and these Councils eventually formed Grand Councils, and severed their connection with the Supreme Council of A. and A. R., at Charleston.

Cousins.—Originated in France. Its mysteries included religious and mystical models of the mind.

Cowan.—The term *Cowan* has, among our brethren of the Free and Accepted Craft, a meaning and signification of its own, which is so well understood by every Mason, that there is no reason to speculate upon its masonic interpretation here; but there is a dearth of information among us as to whence the term is derived, and what was its original import, and a note on this part of the inquiry may, perhaps, be interesting to our readers.

In the sense understood by us, it will be sufficient if we quote one or two examples of the use of the word in question; thus in a song, " Once I was blind, and could not see," we have the following as part of the last verse:

> " Then round and round me he did tie
> A noble ancient charm,
> All future darkness to defy,
> And ward off *cowan's* harm."

And in another song we are told—

> " How happy are the ancient brave
> Whom no false *cowan* can deceive."

While another, entitled "We Brethren Freemasons," declares—

> " The name of a *cowan* we'll not ridicule,
> But pity his ign'rance, nor count him a fool."

This term, too, has not been without its difficulties to many of the writers on Freemasonry, whether charlatans or not, and without giving undue prominence to the catchpenny tribe, one of the most popular of these revelationmongers says, in a note: "the word *cowan* is a flash word peculiar to Masons. It signifies an enemy, but formerly

74

COWAN.

was expressive of kings and all those who had the power to persecute, and who did persecute the associated Masons."

In Preston's Illustrations, 13th edition, p. 80, is a note to the "Antient Charges," in which it is stated, "Twelvethly. That a master or fellow made not a mouldstone, square nor rule, to no lowan" (this no doubt should be *cowan*); "nor let no lowan worke within their Lodge, nor without to moulde stone." (See also *Freemasons' Magazine*, vol. iv. p. 352.) And in Dermott and Harper's *Ahiman Rezon*, 7th edition, 1807, among the ancient charges, No. V., entitled "Of the Management of the Craft in Working," p. 37, it says: "But Free and Accepted Masons shall not allow *cowans* to work with them, nor shall they be employed by *cowans* without an urgent necessity; and even in that case they must not teach *cowans*, but must have a separate communication: no laborer shall be employed in the proper work of Freemasons."

Now these two extracts positively refer to an operative class called *cowans;* and it occurred to me that as we symbolize many other matters connected with the handicraft of Masons, so we have treated the *cowans;* and as speculative Masonry long held its headquarters in Scotland, the word might possibly be of Scotch extraction. For this I had reference to a work published in two volumes folio, in Edinburgh, 1808, with a supplement of two volumes folio, published in 1825, and an abridgment in one volume 8vo., published in 1846, in all three of which the word *cowan* is given. And in that work we have the following definitions:

" COWAN, *s.* A fishing boat, etc.

" COWAN, *s.* 1. A term of contempt, applied to one who does the work of a mason, but has not been regularly bred. (Scottish.)

" 2. Also used to denote one who builds dry walls, otherwise denominated a *dry-diker*. (Scottish.)

COWAN. 75

"'A boat carpenter,' joiner, *cowan* (or builder of stone without mortar), gets 1*s.* at the minimum and good maintenance.' (P. Morven, Argylshire Statistical Account, x. p. 267.)

"'*Cowans*, masons who build dry stone dykes or walls.' (P. Halkirk, Caitness-shire, Statistical Account, xix. p. 24.)

"In the Suio-Gothic, or Ancient language of Sweden, it is *kujon* or *kughon*, a silly fellow, hominen imbellum, et cujus capiti omnes tuto illudunt, *kujon* appellare, moris est (Ihre, Glossarium Suido-Gothicum, 2 vols. fol., Upsal, 1769). French; *Coion*, or *coyon*, a coward, a base fellow (Cotgrave's French-English Dictionary, fol., Lond., 1650); Qui fait profession de lachetè, *ignavus* (Trevoux Dictionnaire, Universal François et Latin, de, 7 vols. fol., Paris, 1752). The editors of this dictionary deduce it from the Latin *quietus*. But the term is evidently Gothic. It has been imported by the Franks, and is derived from *kufw-a*, supprimere, insultare."

The supplement stating:

"Cowan, *s.* 2. Applied to one who does the work of a mason, *add;* Cowaner is the only term used in this sense in Lothian."

So, also, on referring to Dyker, Jamieson tells us:

"Dike, Dyk, *s.* 1. A wall, whether of turf or stone. (Derived from the Scottish.)

"3. A ditch; as in English, although now obsolete.

"Diker, Dyker, *s.* A person whose employment is to build inclosures of stone generally without lime; often called a *dry-diker*. (Derived from the Scottish.)

"The *dyker*, as he is called, gets from £2 to £3 sterling, and sometimes more, for three months in summer. (P. Tarland, Aberdeenshire Statistical Account, vi. p. 209.)"

From the foregoing it is presumed that *cowan* is derived in a twofold sense, the French application of the term suiting the speculative Mason, the Scottish the operative ma-

76 CRAFT—CREIGH.

son; and from the charges above quoted, equally applicable in both senses to the Free and Accepted Mason. The Scottish *cowan*, according to the operative craft, was a builder of walls of unhewn stone, and they were piled one on the other, either with or without mortar or mud, as is to be seen in Gloucestershire and the lower part of Oxfordshire at the present time; and the stringent law that ordered no master or fellow to set him a mould stone, was made for the purpose of guarding their art from the uninitiated, so that those who only could pile rough materials on each other should not invade the trade of a mason, or one that could both set and square the perfect ashlar.—*Ex.*

Craft.—A term applied to the members of the Lodge and Masons generally.

Crawford, Thomas.—A distinguished Mason of Maryland, died at Baltimore in 1813. He presided as Grand Master several terms. At the May session of 1813, he delivered his customary annual address as Grand Master, in a paternal and brotherly spirit. He then intimated to the Grand Lodge his earnest desire to retire from public life, and resigned the gavel to his deputy, and retired from the hall. At the door he grasped the hand of the aged Tyler, and observed that he would not live to pass by him again. The Grand Lodge re-elected him; but he died ere the close of the session. In 1814 a monument was directed by the Grand Lodge to be placed in the New Masonic Temple, commemorative of his virtues.

Created.—A term used in Knights Templar, Red Cross, and Knights of Malta.

Creigh, Alfred, LL.D. — Was born in Cumberland County, Pennsylvania. His ancestors residing in that part of Pennsylvania from the year 1725, hence we may regard him as a true type of the Keystone State.

Dr. Creigh was E. P. and raised in Waynesburg Lodge, 153, Greene County, Pennsylvania, in the months of

July, August, and September, respectively, of the year 1844.

In March, 1845, he was one of the petitioners for the resuscitation of Lodge 164, instituted at Washington, Pennsylvania. In August of the same year he was elected W. M. and served during the years 1845, 1846, 1847, and 1850, and for his valuable services was presented with a medal.

In March, 1846, Companion Creigh received the Capitular degree in Washington Chapter 150, of Washington, Pennsylvania, and has filled the office of High Priest during the years 1846, 1847, 1848, 1861, 1862, and 1864.

In November, 1847, Ill. Comp. Creigh passed the Circle of Perfection by receiving the degrees of Cryptic Masonry, and has presided over Washington Council during the years 1847, 1848, 1858, 1859, 1860, and 1861.

In April, 1849, Sir Alfred Creigh was created a Knight of the Red Cross, Knight Templar, and Knight of Malta in Pittsburg Commandery, No. 1, and was the first Eminent Commander of Jacques de Molay Commandery, No. 2, of Washington, Pennsylvania. He has been elected E. C. for seven different years.

In May, 1859, Ill. Bro. Creigh received the degrees of the Ancient and Accepted Scottish Rite (from the 4th to the 32d inclusive) in the Louisville Consistory, established at Louisville, Kentucky, and as a reward for his services in the cause of Masonry was made an honorary member of the 33d degree of Sovereign Grand Inspectors-General of the Northern Masqnic Jurisdiction of America, held at Boston, Massachusetts.

In December, 1854, Ill. Comp. Creigh was elected to the high and responsible office of the W. P. Grand Master of the Grand Council of Cryptic Masons of Pennsylvania, and by his untiring zeal and indefatigable perseverance has placed his Grand Council second to none in the United States.

7*

78

CRESCENT.

Thirty-one Councils are now subordinate to this Grand Council, and during his Grand Mastership for the last thirteen years he has added twenty-eight subordinate Councils.

In the orders of the Christian Knighthood he filled the office of the V. E. Deputy Grand Commander, and would have been elected the Grand Commander of the State, but at the request of the Sir Knights he consented to fill the office of Grand Recorder, and for the last twelve years has been fulfilling all its duties to the satisfaction of 'the entire body of Knights Templar.

Ill. Bro. Creigh has filled many important offices in the subordinate bodies of the Ancient and Accepted Rite as well as the Supreme Council.

In 1865, for his devotion to the history of Templarism—its ancient ritual, rites, and ceremonies—Sir Alfred Creigh received the appointment of Past Deputy Provincial Grand Commander and Grand Prior from the Grand Conclave of Canada, under the authority of the Grand Conclave of England and Wales.

I shall not advert to the Honorariums and medals and testimonials which from time to time he has received; suffice it to say that on no Pennsylvanian could they have been more appropriately bestowed.

I cannot close this sketch without stating that as a masonic author he stands second to none. Already has he written the following works: Masonry and Anti-Masonry; Book of the Council and the History of Knights Templar of Pennsylvania, the second volume of which is now in the press.

Bro. Creigh has identified himself more intimately with Freemasonry in Pennsylvania than any author which has preceded him.

Crescent.—In heraldry bearing in the form of a half moon. Crescent has been applied to three orders of knighthood. That instituted by Charles, King of Naples, in

1268. That by Rene, of Anjou, in 1448, and that by Sultan Selim in 1801. The latter is still in existence, and remarkable from the fact that none but Christians are eligible for admission

Cronne, Isaac.—First G. Treas. of M. P. G. C. S. N. R. S. 32d, was born at Dromore, County of Down, Ireland, May 9th, 1810. He died at Louisville, Ky., August 10th, 1865.

Cross.—A gibbet made of two pieces of wood laid upon each other at angles. It was used as a means of punishment. After Christ had suffered upon the cross for the transgression of mankind, it became the symbol of the Christian world, and has since been regarded with veneration.

A Cross Crosslet is one crossed on each arm. *A Cross Flory* has three points at each end. *A Maltese Cross* has arms increasing in breadth toward the ends, with double points. *A Patriarchal Cross* has two bars, the upper smaller than the lower.

Cross-legged Masons.—A term originating from the fact that the tombs of the ancient knights had the emblems of bow-legs engraved upon them, and after their connection with the masonic Lodge of Stirling, Scotland.

Crow.—An iron bar, used in Royal Arch Masonry as a symbol.

Crusades.—The Crusades were carried on by the Christian nations of the West against the Turks for the conquest of Palestine, from the 11th to the 13th century. The Christian nations were grieved that the Holy Land, where Jesus had lived and taught and died for mankind, should be in the hands of unbelievers. The pilgrims, on their return, related the dangers and hardships they encountered when paying homage at the tomb of their Saviour. The Caliph Hakem was described as a second Nero, and shed the blood of Christians without mercy. The zeal of the Chris-

80 CRUSADES.

tians was kindled into a flame, and they determined to deliver the sepulcher of Christ from the power of the infidel. The pope considered the invasion of Asia as the means of promoting Christianity among the infidels, and monarchs expected victory and increase of dominion. Peter of Amiens, or Peter the Hermit, was the immediate cause of the first Crusade. In 1093 he joined other Christians on a journey to Jerusalem, and on his return gave Pope Urban II. a description of the unhappy condition of Christians, and presented a petition from the Patriarch of Jerusalem, entreating assistance of their brethren. The pope disclosed to the council at Piacenza, in 1095, the message which Christ had sent through Peter the Hermit, and induced many to guarantee their assistance. He renewed the appeal in 1096 at the council at Clermont, where ambassadors of all nations were present. This appeal brought out numerous armies, which went forth in different divisions. This was the first Crusade. Many of these divisions, ignorant of military discipline, were destroyed before reaching Constantinople. A well-regulated army of 80,000 men, headed by Godfrey of Boulogne, Hugh, brother of Godfrey, Robert of Flanders, Raymond of Toulouse, Bohemond, and others. This army conquered Nice in 1097, Antioch and Edessa in 1098, and Jerusalem in 1099. Godfrey of Boulogne was chosen King of Jerusalem, but died in 1100. In 1102, an army of 260,000 men left Europe, however, perished partly on the march, and partly by sword of soldiers of Icomni. The second Crusade was occasioned by the loss of Edessa, which the Saracens conquered in 1142. This loss occasioned much alarm in Europe, and apprehensions as to the fall of Jerusalem. Pope Eugene III. induced Conrad III. of Germany and Louis VII. of France to defend the cross. These monarchs led their armies to the land in 1147, but were unsuccessful. In 1187, Sultan Saladin took Jerusalem; and Frederick of

CRUX — CUBICAL. 81

Germany, Philip Augustus, King of France, and Richard I., King of England, proceeded with forces in person in 1189, and the third Crusade. Frederick's enterprise was not successful, but the other monarchs seized Acre or Ptolemais. The fourth Crusade was conducted by Andrew II. of Hungary, in 1217, by sea. The Emperor Frederick II. undertook the fifth Crusade, and succeeded in regaining Jerusalem. In 1248, St. Louis, King of France, conducted the sixth Crusade. While Louis was still in Egypt, for he proposed conquering the Holy Land by invasion of Egypt, a revolution broke out which dethroned Saladin and established the dominion of the Mamelukes. They seized from the Christians Tripoli, Tyre, Barytus, and Acre, the last bulwark of the Christian empire on the Continent of Asia, and the end of the Crusades.

Crux Ausata.—A sign adopted by primitive Christians, signifying *life*.

Crypt.—A subterranean vault in the Mt. of Olives, constructed by Solomon.

Cryptic Masonry.—Cryptic, from the Latin word *crypticus*, signifying *concealed* or *subterraneous*. From the Greek *krupte*, signifying *subterranean vault* or *passage*. Hence the term "Cryptic Masonry," or, properly, "Masonry of Secret Vault."

Cuba.—In 1805 Freemasonry was introduced into Cuba under the authority of the Grand Lodge of France. In 1806, a Grand Consistory was formed. On Dec. 5th, 1859, the Grand Lodge was formed at Santiago. On account of the opposition from the authorities, the order does not exert a great influence.

Cubical Stone.—At the building of the Temple an event occurred which caused much disturbance among the masons. Hiram Abiff, the Grand Master, sent to the Craftsmen thirteen stones and instructed them to complete a work unfinished, near the copestone. These stones

82 CULDEES— DAIS.

consisted in all the fragments left from building. These stones or broken cubes were taken to Solomon, and, in connection with Hiram, King of Tyre, ordered that they be placed with the jewels of the craft on a cube stone in the center of the deep vault beneath the foundation of the Temple, and that the door be closed up that there might be no entrance thereto. When the Temple was rebuilt it was discovered by the Craftsmen, and they carried the stones to the king, who recognized in the form pieces of the cube. As a reward of esteem, the Craftsman was advanced.

Culdees (*Worshipers of the Sun*).—In 936, King Athelstane speaks of this society meeting in York. They flourished in England and Ireland, but being holy men, were much persecuted, and soon lost sight of.

Cyrus.—The restorer of the Temple at Jerusalem. He made a decree concerning the house of God at Jerusalem in the first year of his reign, which house is in Judah, and ordered all to go up to build the house of the Lord God of Israel.

D.

Dactyli.—In Phrygia, Priests of Cybele, so called, according to Sophocles, because they were five in number, corresponding with the number of the fingers of the hand, from which the name is derived. Their functions seem to have been similar to those of Coryboutes and Curates, other priests of the same goddess in Phrygia and Crete.

Dagger.—In the Elect, the 4th degree of the French Rite Knights of Kadash, and 30th degree A. and A. Rite. It is used as a portion of the armor.

Dais.—A raised floor. In the Blue Lodge, three steps are required, and in the Chapter, seven steps to reach it.

DALLAS. 83

Dallas, George M.—Vice-President of the United States, died 1864. aged 72 years, at Philadelphia. In the masonic life of Brother Dallas will be found incidents of a marked and striking character, and almost wholly unknown. To appreciate his masonic life, it is necessary to give a full account of the "Masonic Inquisition of Penna.," under the leadership of the Grand Inquisitor, Thaddeus Stevens, Esq., of Lancaster, Pa. We may here state, that Bro. Dallas was not the only one placed before this *legal auto da fe* There were other prominent men and Masons of the State that were summoned to testify before the Inquisition. Geo. Mifflin Dallas was born in Philadelphia, 11th July, 1792. His father, Hon. Alex. James Dallas, was Secretary of the U. S. Treasury under President Monroe. Geo. M. Dallas held at different times the offices of Mayor and Deputy Attorney-General at Phila., United States Senator from the State, Vice-President of U. S., and Minister Plenipotentiary to the Courts of St. Petersburg and St. James. In all of these, his duties were faithfully discharged. In his private life, he was a high-toned moral Christian gentleman and Mason. He was initiated in Franklin Lodge, No. 134, in March, 1818. In December, 1819, he was elected its Senior Warden, and in Dec. 1820, its Master, and re-elected Master in Dec. 1821. On the 21st June, 1821, he delivered an appropriate address on Masonry and its benefits to the members of his Lodge. On 18th August, he delivered another address upon the science and principles of Masonry; and again, in Oct. 20th, 1821, another lecture on the same subject On the 18th Jan. 1822, he was appointed on a committee from his Lodge to form a grand committee with representatives of other Lodges to consider the grievances of the subordinate Lodges. In 1832, No. 134 ceased its labors. On its reorganization, in Oct. 1846, he did not connect with it, being Vice-President of the U. S. at this time. While a

84 · DALLAS.

member of No. 134, he was elected Junior Grand Warden in Dec. 1828, and re-elected in 1829, of the G. L. In 1830, and 1831, he was elected Senior Grand Warden, but not installed until 3d Sept. 1832. He was elected Deputy Grand Master in 1832, and re-elected in 1833. At the Quarterly Communication, 16th June, 1834, it was resolved to celebrate St. John the Baptist's Day, and Bro. Dallas selected as the orator. On St. John's Day, he presided as R. W. Master, *pro tem.* At this meeting, the death of General Lafayette, which took place in Paris, 20th May, 1833, was announced, and Bro. Dallas prepared the Resolutions of Condolence. In his address, he alluded to Gen. Lafayette "as a man, the Guest of a Nation to whose services he had dedicated his early enthusiasm, fortune, and blood;" as a member of the Grand Lodge, Lafayette himself said: "a body of which Franklin was the Father, and Washington the associate;" he was an exalted Mason, whose virtues and exploits were alike in both hemispheres. Bro. Dallas was elected Grand Master 1st Dec. 1834. It was during the discharge of his duties as one of the Grand officers, that the Grand Lodge became the recipient of the "Stephen Girard Bequest." At the communication, in Dec. 28, 1835, he presided as Grand Master, and assisted in the dedication of the new Hall, which he labored hard to build. Prior to and while Bro. Dallas was Grand Master, the spirit of Anti-Masonry was gathering strength, and the order was persecuted and denounced. Grand Master, Bro. James Page, in his address upon the death of Bro. Dallas, says: "Some quailed before the storm, and veiling their Masonry, retired from and abjured its temple; but he, with other able and conspicuous brethren, continued steadfast in the faith, confronting its enemies, and braving its power. He was among the first members of the order summoned to Harrisburg, January, 1836, by a committee of the House of Representatives of the State,

DALLAS. 85

and there detained and threatened with imprisonment by the political party then in ascendency. Through this ordeal, he passed unscathed, never losing sight of his rights as a man, nor faltering in his duty as a Mason. He was as true to the one as he was firm to the other."

The spirited and dignified protest presented by him to the Inquisitors, was in the following words:

GENTLEMEN OF THE COMMITTEE:

I am a citizen of Pennsylvania by birth and constant residence. Having imbibed in early youth, I still retain a strong sense of the free spirit of her institutions; and am unconscious of ever having, directly or indirectly, intentionally or inadvertently, committed an act or uttered a sentiment repugnant to her Constitution, inconsistent with her laws, injurious to her morals, or derogatory to her character. My present purpose is to do that which, under existing circumstances, best harmonizes with my past life, and with an unabated devotion to her highest, purest, and most lasting interests.

I am a member of the society of Freemasons. It is more than twenty years since I became so. At that period the example of the wisest and truest patriots, of Dr. Franklin, Gen. Washington, of Gen. Warren, of Gen. Lafayette, and of many near and dear friends, were naturally alluring. Public opinion designated the association as alike virtuous, useful, and harmless; and legislation, which never discountenanced the connection, subsequently and expressly encouraged its continuance by signal marks of approval. In passing through the forms of admission, I voluntarily assumed obligations and duties in themselves perfectly compatible with the paramount obligations and duties of a citizen to his country, and tributary to the pursuits of enlarged philanthropy. If in the spheres of the institution beyond what is termed the Master's degree—spheres which I have not entered—or in other regions of its existence, there are, as I cannot believe, practices or ceremonies opposite in their tendencies, they are irreconcilable with its essential aims and true character. Certainly of any such I am entirely ignorant. It is, however, not my design or wish to eulogize or defend Freemasonry—I am neither authorized or required to do so—my only object is distinctly to explain and

8

86

DALLAS.

justify my own personal attitude and actions in regard to this committee.

The ninth article of the Constitution of Pennsylvania, entitled a *Declaration of Rights*, sets forth, and unalterably establishes, "the general, great, and essential principles of Liberty and Free Government." It was intended by this article to guarantee the citizen against the inroads of powers, exercised from whatever quarters, and under whatsoever pretext—and it is formally declared, "that everything in it is expected out of the general powers of Government, and shall forever remain inviolate." It is above the reach of legislation. We have no "omnipotence of parliament." Neither this committee, nor the House of Representatives, nor the General Assembly, nor all the organized Departments of the Government united, can touch, in order to evade or violate any one of its provisions. It is a sacred repository of the practical and substantial rights and liberties of the people, enumerated and reserved—inherent and indefeasible. When these shall be supinely yielded up, the freedom of which we now justly boast must become illusory and vapid.

As a private citizen of Pennsylvania, I claim, with especial reference to this article of her Constitution, to possess and to enjoy rights and liberties which no earthly power can abridge or destroy—nor will I consent, when mindful of the gratitude I owe to the community at large, to be, in the slightest degree, accessary to the mischiefs which a surrender or waiver of those rights and liberties, on an occasion so ostensible as this, might produce. I will not consent that human authority shall, "in any case whatever, control or interfere with the rights of conscience." I will not consent to discredit the declaration that "the free communication of thoughts and opinions is one of the inviolable rights of man." I will not consent to consider as idle and nugatory the emphatic precaution, that "the people shall be secure in their persons, houses, papers, and possessions, from unreasonable searches and seizures." I will not consent to the validity of any "ex post facto law." In a word, I will not consent to hold my rights and liberties of private intercourse, private sentiment, and private business, subject to the domiciliary visitations, the changeable majority, or the ideal policy of any body of men whatever.

DALLAS. 87

I understand this committee to be empowered by the House of Representatives to investigate what are called the evils of Freemasonry, and for that purpose to send for persons and papers; and I am summoned by subpœna, tested by Thaddeus Stevens, Esq., its Chairman, from my home, family, and professional pursuits, to attend here, in order to communicate, as a witness under oath, what I may know in relation to the subject of inquiry.

The society of Freemasons is, in this State, strictly of a private nature. It is not incorporated. Like other voluntary associations, it is neither formed nor forbidden by law. Without, therefore, pausing to illustrate and enforce the remark that it would be equally constitutional to investigate the evils of the Society of Friends, or other societies of religion, or societies of politicians, or societies of convivial gayety, or of any of the countless combinations of partnership by which men strive to realize calmness of conscience, the enjoyment of life and liberty, the acquisition and protection of property and reputation, and the pursuit of happiness, I respectfully affirm to this committee my absolute conviction, that the proceeding which attempts, under the forms of legislation and through my own agency, to pry into, expose, condemn, and ridicule my personal doings and relations with this body of citizens, is as utterly inconsistent with the tenor and terms of the constitution, as its expansion to similar cases would be fatal to freedom.

Superadded to the considerations at which I have thus glanced, it is impossible for me to be insensible to the just dictates of personal honor. Assuredly this sentiment should never restrain any one from denouncing what is criminal or dishonest, and were I acquainted with anything of that nature in the operation and tendencies of Freemasonry, nothing could bind me to silence. But I was received by this association into its own confidence, upon my own application. I have been allowed a knowledge of the modes in which its members identify each other, and avoid deceptions upon their benevolence. At a time when neither law, nor public opinion, nor my own conscience suggested a doubt of its correctness, I engaged myself to secrecy, and I cannot, without a sense of treachery and degradation which would embitter all my future life, prove false to my promise. Better, by far, endure the penalties of alleged contumacy, be they what they may.

88

DALLAS.

I have thought it due to the committee and to myself, to preface, by these explanatory remarks, my refusal to be sworn.

G. M. DALLAS.

AND HE REFUSED TO BE SWORN.

What a sublime spectacle do not this language and this attitude of our departed brother exhibit to us!

In adverting to these proceedings, P. Grand Master Brother Chandler writes:

"There are few who were present in the Hall of the House of Representatives that will ever forget the impression made by the manly appearance and important protest of Mr. Dallas. Of course he would take no oath which would make it incumbent on him to answer every question which ingenuity had been long contriving, and so he and the other recusants were ordered into a quasi custody, while the miserable committee made a report of the contempt with which their authority had been treated. And so day by day the whole number of masonic prisoners, from all parts of the State, were paraded before the House and made to hear the silly diatribes of a parcel of weak-headed or bad-hearted men, and to be denounced as incipient traitors. It became necessary from time to time to make some response to the questions propounded and charges made against the prisoners. On such occasions Mr. Dallas, by general consent, was the orator of the recusants, and his withering sarcasm told strongly on all the auditors. It was then remarked, that while Mr. Dallas defended his right as a citizen, he never lost sight of the fact that he was standing in the Hall dedicated to the enactment of the laws of the Commonwealth, and in the presence of those who had been constitutionally chosen to make those laws. He paid the deference, all the deference possible, to the nominal representatives of the people, but he let them understand that neither he nor his companions considered them anything more than .the accidental result of a morbid feeling, unworthy of freemen, and that the bad sentiment had in them fit representatives. There were those present who for a moment thought the forbearance of Mr. Dallas too great a leniency, but events showed that his judgment was good, and that though persecuted and outraged in their civil rights, the Masons knew how to defer to existing authorities.

DALLAS. 89

Perhaps it was in part to this most patriotic discrimination of Mr. Dallas that was due the triumph of the recusant Masons over the miserable faction which for a single election had obtained political power, and for a single year disgraced the State. The whole deportment of Mr. Dallas while obeying the call of the Legislature was dignified and loyal, securing to him the continued respectful consideration of all who witnessed his gallant defense of individual rights, and his truly dignified forbearance when protesting against the wrong that did more discredit to the fair fame of the Commonwealth than to those who were the immediate objects of the silly persecution. It was painful for a citizen to feel himself injured by such monstrous proceedings, but it was scarcely less painful to contemplate the mortifying fact, that even the great wrong had with it none of the amelioratory circumstances with which good manners and social propriety sometimes invest a public outrage."

A late writer, in alluding to the action of Brother Dallas before the committee, says:

"When he was asked to take the oath by which he was required virtually to acknowledge the right of instituting an inquisition so unheard of, into the private and harmless conduct of himself and his associates, he refused in a short, but most impressive address, and displayed in terms that led to the abortive termination of the disreputable affair—its injustice, its illegality and folly. His manly and decided course upon this occasion gained for him the grateful acknowledgments of many, who, though opposed to him in the ordinary contests of party, yet appreciated, as he did, the sanctity of social intercourse and domestic privacy."

Other and able protests were presented by eminent Masons from this city, who were compelled to attend before this committee, among them those of P. Grand Masters Josiah Randall, Tristram B. Freeman, Samuel H. Perkins, and Joseph R. Chandler; R. W. Grand Secretary Samuel M. Stewart, and the Grand Tyler Charles Schnider.

There were other brethren, some now present, who, although summoned, were not examined. They were equally as determined in their open adhesion to, and in

8*

90 *DALLAS.*

their earnest defense of the rights of the craft "in these times that tried Masons' souls," and which mark an important epoch in the history of Masonry, the State and the Nation. P. Grand Masters Brothers Kittera and Badger, the one long since dead, and the other still with us, but advanced in years and prostrated and languishing under life's slow decay, whose dying pillow is made easy by fraternal kindness, were also summoned and went to Harrisburg, as also P. Masters Charles Stout, Robinson R. Moore, and Allen Ward, now dead. The Rev. Brother William T. Sproul was also before that committee, and startled its members in his stirring protest by the remarkable expression : " Gentlemen, if you are willing to convert yourselves into a modern Juggernaut—*Roll on!*"

The refusing brethren, as stated by Past Grand Master Brother Chandler, were taken into custody and brought before the bar of the House of Representatives. Various motions were made and long debates ensued. Finally, after being in the charge of the Sergeant-at-Arms for some two days, they were released and permitted to return to their homes in various parts of the State, and this vexatious, unjust, and tyrannical proceeding came to an end.

Some time thereafter, most if not all of those who had been so foully wronged by the proceedings of the Legislature, with a view to protect their own characters and to place upon record their solemn denial of the evils attached to the order, and vindicating it from the vile and slanderous aspersions with which it had been so unjustly and cruelly assailed, prepared and published their several affidavits, as follows:

"TO THE PUBLIC.

" The subjoined statement is believed by the signers thereof to be due to themselves and to the society of which they are members; and its publicity seems to be further called for by the asser-

DALLAS. 91

tion of some members of the House of Representatives, that the asseverations in favor of Freemasonry, made by many of the witnesses recently before that body, are not, and would not be sworn to.

"The subscribers, citizens of the Commonwealth of Pennsylvania, were recently summoned before a committee appointed by the House of Representatives, and required to testify, as witnesses on oath, in relation to what are called the evils of Freemasonry. They believed it to be a duty to the cause of civil liberty, to the Constitution, to the community, to their families, and to themselves, to resist a compulsory examination for that purpose; and they obeyed the dictates of their consciences, by respectfully but firmly pursuing that course. Many of them have long ceased to participate in the meetings or deliberations of masonic societies, and retain in recollection very little more than their general objects, principles, and tendencies: but all of them are able to give to their fellow-citizens, under the most solemn of sanctions, and with the pledge of their characters as Christians and men, certain assurances which may be calculated to remove erroneous impressions and to dispel ungenerous suspicion.

"Appealing, therefore, to the Searcher of all hearts for the truth of what they say, they declare—

"*First.* That they do *not* know, and do *not* believe that Freemasonry enjoins upon, or sanctions in its members, any conduct incompatible with the strictest and purest citizenship, with the most absolute obedience to the laws of their country as paramount to all voluntary rules and regulations, and with the fairest administration of justice.

"*Second.* That they do not know, and do not believe that Freemasonry is, or can be made an engine of political party, or of religious sectarianism; having always observed and understood that its societies were indiscriminately comprised of men hostile in political sentiment and action, and of every religious persuasion.

"*Third.* That they do not know, and do not believe that what are termed '*the secrets*' of Freemasonry can impair the personal independence, or injuriously affect the morals of its members.

"*Fourth.* And that, while humbly sensible that wherever human beings associate or exist, there must be error, misjudgment, and

92   *DALLAS.*

folly in individuals, they do not know, and do not believe that Freemasonry, as a society, has for its foundation or cement, any principle or motive at variance with the cardinal ones of Charity, Friendship, Virtue, Knowledge, and Industry.

"(Signed)   GEORGE WOLF, Harrisburg.
JOHN MACLAUGHLIN, Elizabeth, Lancaster County, Pa.
N. W. SAMPLE, Lancaster County.
JOHN MATHIOT, Lancaster City.
HENRY KIFFER, Lancaster City.
SAMUEL C. BONHAM, York, Pa.
THOMAS McGRATH, York, Pa.
ALLEN WARD, Philadelphia.
JOHN STEELE, Lancaster County.
ROBERT CHRISTY, Pittsburg.
GEO. K. HARPER, Chambersburg, Pa.
FR. R. SHUNK, Harrisburg.
E. PENTLAND, Pittsburg.
ROBERT RICHARDSON, Mount Joy, Lancaster County.
JACOB EMMETT, York, Pa.
SAMUEL RINGWALT, Lancaster County.

"*Dauphin County,* ss.
"Sworn and subscribed to before me, this
23d day of January, A.D. 1836.
"(Signed) W. KLINE, J. P.   [L. S.]

"T. B. FREEMAN.   WILLIAM STEPHENS.
SAMUEL H. PERKINS.   CHARLES STOUT.
JOSEPH R. CHANDLER.   JOSIAH RANDALL.
SAMUEL M. STEWART.   WILLIAM T. SPROUL.
CHARLES SCHNIDER.   GEORGE M. DALLAS.

"*City of Philadelphia,* ss.
"Sworn and subscribed to before me, this
26th day of January, A.D. 1836.
"(Signed) JOHN BINNS, J. P.   [L. S.]

DALLAS. 93

"The undersigned, who were summoned to, and did, appear before the said committee, but were discharged without being required to give evidence, and would, if they had been required, have declined taking the oath, do severally swear or affirm to the truth of the foregoing statement.

"(Signed)   JAMES PAGE.
SAMUEL BADGER.
ROBINSON R. MOORE.

"Sworn and affirmed to before me, this
26th day of January, A.D. 1836.
"(Signed)   JOHN BINNS, J. P.   [L. S.]

"I was summoned, and did not appear, in consequence of a very severe indisposition; but if present, and required, I should have declined taking the oath; but I do now swear to the truth of the foregoing statement.

"JOHN M. READ.

"Sworn and subscribed to before me, this
27th day of January, A.D. 1836.
"(Signed)   JOHN BINNS, J. P.   [L. S.]"

G. M. Page continues:

"From the commencement of this extraordinary persecution of Freemasonry, and for a time afterward, so great was the depression, and so wide the dismay in our ranks, that it was frequently the case that a few prominent brethren who took an open and active part in sustaining and upholding the order were obliged to seek out and obtain the services of others in assisting them in doing the work of many of the subordinate Lodges, to prevent them from perishing."

On the appointment of Brother Dallas as Minister to the Court of St. Petersburg, the Grand Lodge, at a session on 3d April, 1837, passed a resolution declaring

"That it entertained a due sense of the services of Brother Dallas to that body, and to Masonry in general, as well for his

94 DALLAS.

manly firmness in sustaining the rights of the craft, as for his urbanity as a brother, and dignified deportment as Grand Master, and respectfully and affectionately tendered him their congratulations upon his honorable appointment, and their hearty wishes for his health and happiness and that of his family."

He refers to this event in his Diary, under date of 11th of April, "as a most flattering communication from the Grand Lodge."

In the same Diary, under date of 26th of April, he says :

"Last evening, after suffering famously all day, I had the hardihood to retract an apology to my masonic friends, and to accompany Major Benjamin Russel (the old Editor), Mr. Lewis, and Mr. Sibley; as a committee, to East Boston, and a supper at Maverick-House. This entertainment, like the Bar dinner, was exceedingly well done and most flattering. Dr. Flint presided, and Mr. Power (poet and musician), was one of the vice-presidents. The basis of the compliment to me was explained by Dr. Flint, in preparing his toast, to be the decisive course I had taken at Harrisburg in January, 1836, when before the Committee of Investigation; and, to be sure, they seem to have viewed that incident of my public life in the most flattering and enthusiastic manner. I endeavored to answer as well as I could, gave them a rapid sketch of the proceeding, and, although deprived almost entirely by illness of voice or energy, their prolonged and often interrupting plaudits, convinced me that the subject was one on which I could not fail to succeed. Old Russel, who sat by me, was particularly marked in his expressions of approbation, and assured me when he left me at the door of the Tremont at eleven at night, that he had never been more gratified by a public entertainment."

On 1st May, 1847, the corner-stone of the Smithsonian Institute, Washington, D. C., was laid with masonic ceremonies. Br. B. B. French, G. M. of G. L. of D. C., supported by G. M. Charles Sulivan, of Maryland, G. M. James Page, of Penna., had charge of the masonic ceremonies. After the completion of the ceremonies, Bro. Dallas, Vice-President of the United States, made an elo-

DALLAS.   95

quent address, and read the following extracts from the Bequest.

"James Smithson, a Londoner born, and claiming to be the son of a distinguished nobleman, gave his life exclusively to intellectual pursuits, and especially to researches in physical and experimental science. Supplied with larger means than his wants required, and steadily practicing a strict scheme of personal economy, he amassed a considerable fortune. He died in Genoa, 1829, and by his will bequeathed his accumulated property to this Union, a country that, notwithstanding his change of abode, he had never visited, whose citizens he had never associated with, but in whose inevitable future he saw the most solid ground on which to cast the anchor of his fame. His legacy, for some time the subject of litigation in the British Court of Chancery, was finally secured, brought over, and received in the Treasury of the United States, on the 1st of September, 1838. Its exact amount when deposited was $515,169.

"This legacy was accompanied by a declaration of its design, and the execution of that design has been assumed as well by an acceptance of the money as by several open and formal avowals by our Government. It was to found an Institution at Washington for the increase and diffusion of knowledge among men— to found, not an academy, not a college, not an university, but something less technical and precise, something whose import and circuit should be bolder and more comprehensive—an Institution not merely for disseminating, spreading, and teaching knowledge, but also and foremost for creating, originating, increasing it. Where? In the city whose name recalls the wisest, purest, and noblest spirit of the freest, newest, and broadest land. And among whom? Not a chosen or designated class—not the followers of a particular sage or sect—not the favorites of fortune nor the lifted of rank—but among men! Men of every condition, of every school, of every faith, of every nativity—MEN! It was with a purpose thus elevated and expansive, thus as well distinct as undiscriminating, that James Smithson committed his wealth to the guardianship of the American Republic."

The Grand Lodge of Pennsylvania, in participating in these ceremonies, was represented by its Grand Master and

96 DAUGHTERS—DAVIE.

Grand officers. Bro. Dallas received and welcomed his brethren in the most cordial and fraternal way, and extended to them those attentions which constituted one of the charms of his life. The name of Bro. Dallas has passed down to history, honored and esteemed for a correct and ennobling life, as a Citizen, Statesman, Christian, and Mason.

Daughters of Zelophehad.—This system of Adoptive Masonry was first practiced in France. It is a system taken from the Scriptures. In the 27th chapter of Numbers, the "daughters of Zelophehad came to Moses." This Zelophehad was of the tribe of Manasseh, and a person of eminence. The occasion selected for the appeal made by these fine women was when Moses, accompanied by Eleazar, the high priest, and the princes, and all the congregations, was standing before the door of the Tabernacle. This was just prior to the consecretion of Joshua as the successor of Moses.

David.—In order to preserve the ark of God and render him just and befitting homage, conceived the idea of building him a Temple. Moses had foretold the erection of a Temple to Jehovah's honor, and the place it was to be built upon remained a secret among the Jebunites. God, however, seeing David's determination, directed Nathan, the prophet, to communicate to him, that he should build an house, that when his days were fulfilled, he should sleep with his fathers, and from his seed he would establish his kingdom.

Davie, Wm. Richardson.—Was born in Egremont, England, June 20th, 1756. In 1760 he came to America, and located in North Carolina. He enlisted with the Federal army at the opening of the struggle. He was commissioned general under General Green. In 1798 Washington appointed him a brigadier in the regular army. In the same year he was elected Governor of South Carolina. President Adams appointed him Minister Extraordinary to France. He was a Mason, but the date and place when made is lost, but it is held that it was in one of the Military Lodges. A Lodge had been opened at Halifax, in 1767, and re-opened after the war in 1787. During this year a Grand Lodge was formed, and Bro. Davie was its 3d Grand Master. He laid the corner-stone of the "University of S. C." as Grand Master, in April 14th, 1798. He died at Tivoli, S. C., December, 1824, aged 64 years.

Daviess, Jo. H.—Grand Master of Kentucky. Died upon the battle-field of Tippecanoe. He was elected Grand Master in 1811. On August 25th, 1812, the Grand Lodge was convened to perform appropriate honor of the deceased G. M. Jos. Hamilton Daviess, killed Nov. 7th, 1811, at Tippecanoe. Bro. Henry Clay was the designated orator, but not being able to attend, Dr. C. W. Cloud took his place. In August 20th, 1814, the Grand Lodge ordered a vote of thanks to Bro. W. A. Lee, for a portrait of the deceased Grand Master Daviess. In October 11th, 1858, Hon. Levi L. Todd, of Indiana, P. G. M. Wm. Sheets, and others, presented the Sword of G. M. Daviess to the G. L. of Ky. Bro. Daviess was a hero and patriot, and his character was written upon the blade of his sword—"Liberty and Independence."

Deacon.—An officer of the Lodge who conveys messages, assists in ceremonies, and obeys commands.

Deacons.—Each Lodge has two Deacons.

Decalogue.—The Greek name given to the law of the two tables of stone given by God to Moses on Mount Sinai. They are said to have been written by the finger of God. They are in symbolized use in the R. A. Chapter.

Declaration.—A candidate when he applies to obtain the honors of Masonry, petitions and declares therein that he is a freeman, of mature age, that he is unbiased by the improper solicitations of friends, and uninfluenced by mer-

98 — DECLARING — DELAWARE.

cenary motives, that he freely and voluntarily offers himself a candidate for Masonry, that he is prompted so to do by a favorable opinion conceived of the institution, and a desire of knowledge, and that he will conform to the ancient usages and customs of the order.

Declaring Off.—A term when Lodges have ceased to meet regularly. Again, if a brother ceases to visit his Lodge and pay his dues.

Deconus.—In the Baron Hunde system of Templars, an honorary officer who presides in the absence of the Grand Master and the Prior.

Dedication.—Masonic Lodges were in the first dedicated to King Solomon, and continued so to be until the Jews were carried into captivity. The dedications were made from that period to Zerubbabel, until the coming of Christ. After the destruction of the Temple by Titus, they were dedicated to St. John the Baptist. Masonry having received a severe shock at this time, the craft held a meeting in the City of Benzoimie, and solicited the Bishop of Ephesus, St. John the Evangelist, to accept the Grand Mastery, which he did. Since his death, Lodges have been dedicated to St. John the Baptist and to St. John the Evangelist.

Degrees.—Steps, Distinction in Honors. Masonry consists in separate degrees. A science cannot be imparted in a single moment, but there are variations and rules that must be acquired and understood to ascertain their value. So with Freemasonry. The candidate must be tried step by step, to ascertain if he is worthy of other honors. If he is found proficient in his duties, he is permitted to advance one step after another, in accordance with masonic regulations.

Delaware.—Freemasonry was introduced into this State about 1796, through the Military Lodges. On May 17th, 1814, the Grand Lodge of Pennsylvania granted a warrant for a Lodge to be held at Wilmington. On June 1st, 1806, the Grand Lodge was organized. On Jan. 19th, 1818, the Grand Chapter was organized. No Commandery, Council G. and R. Masters, or A. and A. Rite are practiced in this State now.

Delta (*Δ*).—A letter of the Greek alphabet. It is used in the Knights Templar. It is a symbol of the unspeakable name.

Demit.—To withdraw from a Lodge by its permission.

Demiurgis.—Classical authors give it as an artificer employed in ordinary handicraft. In the language of the Platonists it denotes an exalted and mysterious agent, by whose means God is supposed to have created the universe. Hence the Demiurgis, or Logos, as the same imaginary is termed in the *Sinetus* of Plato, is identified by the Platonizing Christians with the second person of the Trinity.

Denmark.—In 1743, the Grand Lodge of Berlin granted warrant for a Lodge to be opened at Copenhagen. In 1745 and 1749, the Grand Lodge of England granted a similar favor. In 1792, the office of Grand Master was assumed by Charles of Hesse. Freemasonry has become a recognized institution of the government.

Deputy Grand Master.—Next in rank to the Grand Master, and elected annually.

Deus Menengue Lus.—The motto 33d degree A. and A. Rite. It means " God and my right."

Dieu Le Veut (*God will it*).—The battle cry of the Crusaders.

Dionysian Architects.—The followers of Dionysius or Bacchus. The order of Sidinian Builders was opened by this order. It existed before King David's time. The Roman Architects also sprung from this order. Some contend that Freemasonry sprang from this order.

Director of Ceremonies.—An officer whose duty it is to usher and assist in masonic ceremonies.

100 DISCIPLINE—DISCOVERY.

Discipline of the Secret.—A name given by theological writers to a system supposed to have been in force in the primitive church, by which its mysterious doctrines were concealed from the mass of believers, and developed only to a select class. It was represented in four degrees: Faithful, Enlightened, Initiated, and Perfect.

Disclosing.—To impart the secrets of Masonry would be dishonorable in the extreme, and hence the means of securing the good of Masonry are good government and a silent tongue. Secrecy is one of the virtues of a good Mason. The profligate and unprincipled Mason never forgets this virtue; although tortured, abandoned, and discarded by his associates, he will not disclose or expose the secrets imparted to him.

Discovery.—The sojourners discovered the secret vault which Solomon had constructed for securing the valuables of Masonry, while engaged in clearing away the rubbish in the building of the second Temple. This vault was supported by seven pair of pillars, and had not been destroyed when the Temple was demolished. The rubbish having covered up the keystone of this vault under the Sanctum Sanctorum, it was only ascertained, after careful inspection, the valuables that it contained and preserved. The valuables were then removed and placed in a secure place.

According to the *Jewish Chronicle*, the foundation of the inner wall of Jerusalem (referred to in Lam. ii. 8, under the name of rampart; and also in Isaiah, xxii. 11, where the two walls are spoken of) has lately been discovered. As far as it is laid bare, it consists of very large stones, and the solid masonry is just the same as that of the western wall of the Temple. It is about four yards distant from the present wall. The spot was visited by many Europeans, among whom are mentioned the Austrian and French consuls, as also by Dr. Rosen, the Prussian consul, distinguished for his topographical knowledge of the Holy

DISPENSATION—DOW.

City, and they all agreed in pronounciug this remnant of hoary antiquity the foundation of the "rampart." It was discovered while digging to lay the foundation of a new building, the "Abode of Peace," erecting for the Jewish poor at the expense of a deceased benefactor. On the same plot of ground was also discovered a very large and equally ancient cistern, thirty-six yards long by nine and a half wide, and fourteen deep.

Dispensation.—A warrant to open a Lodge, make Masons at irregular times, and confer honors, is called a Dispensation. The granting of these Dispensations is vested in the Grand Master and his Deputies.

Distress.—The sign of distress was derived from the expulsion of Adam and Eve from the Garden of Eden. The divine mysteries that he had been intrusted with, he handed down to his son Seth, and he to Enoch, and from Enoch to Methuselah, Lamech, Noah, Geon, Abraham, Isaac, Jacob, Levi, Kelbath, Annam, Moses, Joshua, the Elders, the Prophets, and so on until they were intrusted to Solomon.

Dominica.—Freemasonry was introduced here in 1844. On the 11th December, 1858, the Grand Lodge was organized.

Dove.—Emblem of Innocence. It is among the symbols of Masonry. With the olive branch in its mouth, it is acknowledged as the harbinger of peace and safety.

Dow, Lorenzo.—This eccentric individual was a Mason, and initiated Christmas-day, 1824, in No. 6, St. Alban's Lodge, Bristol, R. I., and the following day, Sunday, was passed and raised. On a preaching tour, and being able to remain no longer, when it was proposed, he replied that there was nothing incompatible with the Lord's day in the institution. After preaching in the afternoon, he went to the Lodge and left it a Master Mason. The record of the Lodge is "Lodge closed with exhortation and prayer by

102 DRESS—DUPLICATION.

Brother Lorenzo Dow." Upon being invited by the M.·., he knelt in the center of the Lodge, and thus exhorted them to an exemplary life. It was an impressive scene, and deeply affected those present.

Dress.—The dress of a Master Mason has been the subject of change. In 1717, it was a small cap and yellow jacket, and blue garments. In 1813, it was arranged that the dress should be, that of Grand Officers, *purple;* Grand Stewards, *crimson;* and the Master, *blue,* being the original colors adopted by the primitive Masons.

Druids.—The priests of the Celtic inhabitants of ancient Gaul and Britain. It is derived from the Greek δρυς, *oak.* They worshiped the gods Jupiter, Apollo, Mars, etc., whom they believed to be the same with personages of the Grecian mythology. They sacrificed human beings, and worshiped in groves. The rock altars that are scattered over France and England are attributed to the Druids. Claudius and other Roman generals endeavored to extirpate them; but it was reserved for Christianity to work the reform.

Due and Ancient Form.—A term used by Masters in their masonic ceremonies.

Due Form.—An act performed by the Grand Master is in "ample form;" by his Deputies, in "due form."

Due Form.—The performance of any ceremonies by the D. G. M. is done in *due form.*

Due Guard.—So to guard our actions and words, that no reflection may come upon the order.

Duplication.—A celebrated problem of ancient geometry. While a plague devastated Athens, deputation was sent to consult the oracles of Apollo, at Delphi, who sent an answer that the plague would cease when they had doubled the altar of God. The altar was cubical, consequently the problem was to find the sides of another cube of twice the solid contents. This was reduced to another equation by the insertion of two mean proportionals between two given straight lines, a problem which the ancient philosophers discovered by methods of constructing higher curves. The solution of the duplication constitutes the point of the Temple.

E.

Eagle.—Is called the king of birds, on account of its strength, elevation, and rapidity of flight. Daniel referred to it, and St. John, in Revelations, likens the divinity of Christ, as an eagle that soars to heaven. It was a symbol of the cherubim.

Ear of Corn.—The ear of corn is a symbol of plenty, and had its origin from the fact that when the Israelites passed over Jordan into Canaan, they found the country abounding in ripe corn, which they hailed with universal joy, as their journeyings through the wilderness gave them but manna as food.

East.—The position of the Master of a Lodge; whereas the sun rises in the east, to open, rule, and govern the day, so presides the Master in the east, to open the Lodge and govern it.

Eastern Star.—This system of Adoptive Masonry was introduced into the United States in 1778. Master Masons, their wives and sisters, are admitted into the Lodge as members. It has five degrees: 1. Jephtha's Daughter. 2. Ruth, or the Mason's Widow. 3. Esther, or the Mason's Wife. 4. Martha, or the Mason's Sister. 5. Electa

Eavesdropper.—A watcher under the eavedrop of a building to hear private conversation of others. As a punishment for such evil disposed ones, the Masonic Lectures of 1777 inflicted that they be placed under the cavedrop of a house, and there remain until the water run in at the shoulders and out at the boots.

104   EBAL — EDWARD.

Ebal.—Moses enjoined upon Joshua, that after passing Jordan they should proceed to Scheckun and then separate into two parties, the one to proceed to Gerizim and the other to Ebal. They were divided into six tribes each. When arriving at Gerizim, the one party was to pronounce blessings on those who observed the law, and the other, on reaching Ebal, were to pronounce curses on those who violated the law. They erected an altar upon Mt. Ebal and lettered the law upon it.

Eclectic Masonry.—Instituted by Baron Knizze, in 1782, and worked Masonry in three degrees, and held the higher for recreation.

Eclectic Rite of Masonry.—In 1783, the Grand Lodges of Frankfort and Welzlor organized the Eclectic Rite of Masonry at Frankfort. It was made of all the Rites and Systems represented at the Wilhelmsbald Congress in 1782. They renounced all speculation in Magic, Cabalistic, Templarism, etc., and declared that the order of Masonry should and would be governed in accordance with the Grand Lodge regulations of England, adopted in 1723.

Ecossars.—A degree of the French Rite, and is almost the same in its character as the degree of Select Master in Cryptic Masonry.

Ecuador.—The history of Freemasonry in Ecuador is exceedingly lame. In 1857, a Lodge existed at Guayaquill under the authority of the Grand Lodge of Peru. Masonry meets with the opposition of religious fanatics here, and consequently has but little show. Those Lodges that now exist are conducted secretly.

Edict of Cyrus, King of Persia.—It gave permission to the captives, to Jews, to repair to Jerusalem to rebuild the Temple, under the leadership of Zerubbabel, accompanied by Joshua and Haggai.

Edward I.—Brother of King Athelstane, and succeeded

him in 941, was an able and spirited prince. He obtained a charter from his brother Athelstane, and established a Lodge at York, in 930. By virtue of this charter, all Masons of the Kingdom were assembled at York, where they formed the General Grand Lodge, of which Prince Edwin became the Grand Master. Edwin met with an untimely end, being stabbed by Lealf, an outlaw, while presiding at a banquet. The Charter of York was lost during the Contest of the Roses, but its contents were preserved in the Constitution of Edward III.

Edward Pierpont.—First Grand Master of Connecticut, was born in Northampton, Mass., in 1750. He became a Mason in Haven Lodge, New Haven, Dec. 28th, 1735. He was elected Grand Master 8th July, 1789. He died 14th April, 1826, aged 76.

Elected Cohens.—Introduced into France in 1757, and had nine degrees: The Blue Lodge degrees, Grand Elect, Apprentices Cohen, F. C. Cohen, M. Cohen, Grand Architect, and Knight Commander.

Elected Knights of Nine.—This degree is a rehearsal of the mode in which a member of Solomon's Overseers obtained a knowledge of a certain degree, and for the transgression was punished. The chief officer is King Solomon. The Lodge is Solomon's Secret Chamber, and the Assembly is styled a Chapter.

Election.—An election of officers takes place annually. Every Master, *who having served a term as Warden* of a Lodge, may be elected as Worshipful Master, *and not otherwise.* All members are eligible to vote who have paid their dues to the day of election.

Elect of Perignon.—A degree of the French Rite, and relates to certain criminals who were punished for their disobedience, etc.

Elect of Truth.—A Rite adopted at Remes, France. It had 14 degrees, to wit: The Blue Lodge degrees, Perfect

106   *ELEPHRATA — ENDLESS.*

Master, Elect of Nine, Elect of Fifteen, Master Elect, Minor Architect, 2d Architect, Grand Architect, Knight of Earl, Rose Croix, Knights Adepts, Elect of Truth.

Elephrata.—The seat of Indian mysteries, situated on the west coast of Hindostan. A great cave exists on the island, which contains many hieroglyphics.

Eleusian Mysteries.—The secret religious rites performed in honor of Ceres and Proserpine, at the Attic town of Eleusis. To these mysteries all the Greeks of both sexes, if unpolluted by crime, were admitted; and as the persons thus initiated were considered to be peculiarly under the protection of the gods, and to enjoy their favor, it was a privilege much sought after.

Eleusis.—The 75th deg. of Rite of Memphis is called Knights of the Golden Branch of Eleusis.

Emanuel or Immanuel.—A name given to our Saviour, signifying that he is *God with us*—in our nature and our side. Referred to in the Knights Templar system.

Emergency Lodge.—Is called at any time by the Master, or in absence of the Master by the Senior Warden. The reasons for calling such Lodge must be explained in the summons.

Emperors of the East and West.—Instituted in France, in 1758. It consisted of 25 degrees, and the first 19 are those of the Scotch Rite; the 20th, Grand Patriarch Noachite; Key of Masonry; Prince of Lebanon; Knight of Sun; Kadosch; and Royal Secret.

Encampment.—An assembly of Knights Templar.

Encampment, Grand, of the United States.—Was organized June 22d, 1816. The officers are Grand Master, D. G. M., G. G., G. C. G., G. P., G. W., G. J. W., G. T., G. R., G. St. Br., G. Sad. Br., G. W., P. G. M.'s., D. G. M., G. Gen., G. C. G., of all Commanderies.

Endless Serpent.—A symbol of Divine wisdom, regeneration, and eternity, having creative power, immortality, and eternal existence.

ENGLAND. 107

England.—The introduction of Masonry into England occurred during the 3d century. In A.D. 300, an organization, protected by Emperor Caraucius, who granted them a warrant, was greatly prospered. A Roman general, Albanus, was Grand Master. Freemasonry continued in a feeble state until 926, when Athelstane became King of England. He made his brother Edwin overseer of the craft and granted him a warrant. In accordance with this warrant, Edwin convened all Masons at York, and formed a General Lodge, of which he assumed the Grand Mastership. This Lodge of York exercised its authority over England until 1567, when those Masons in the southern part of England met and appointed another Grand Master. The General Assembly still holds its sessions at York, where all the valuable masonic papers and documents are kept. Masonry having fallen into disrepute in the 17th century, it was resolved that the privileges should no longer be restricted to operative masons, but extend to men of all professions, thus changing the system from the operative to speculative. In changing the system it became necessary to make new rules and regulations, but it was not effected until 24th June, 1717, when the Grand Lodge was formed. Friendly relations existed between these two Grand bodies until 1734, when the London Lodge granted charters to a number of dissatisfied members of the York Lodge. In 1738, a number of dissatisfied members of the York and London Lodges withdrew and established themselves as *Ancient Masons.* They alleged that the new Lodges had departed from the old system, and worked and adopted new plans, and hence they were *Modern Masons.* In 1739, they established a Grand Lodge in London, as the "Grand Lodge of Ancient York Masons." These two bodies continued to exist and war with each other until 1813, when the Grand Master of the Moderns, Duke of Sussex, and the Grand Master of the Ancients,

108   *ENOCH—ESCALLOP.*

Duke of Kent, had them united as the "United Grand Lodge of Ancient Freemasons of England."

Enoch.—Fearing that the secrets of Masonry would be lost by the deluge, had them engraved on porphyr stone and placed in the earth, and marked the place with two pillars, which inscriptions designated the spot where treasures were hidden and dedicated to the ever-living God.

Enos, Joseph.—Grand Master of Masons of New York, in 1822–23–24. Died October 31st, 1866, aged 84. He presided over one of the divisions of the body arising from the troubles of 1823. He was an earnest and zealous Mason, and filled a prominent space in the masonic history of New York.

Ensigns (*Flag or Banner*).—The ensign of Judah was a lion; Issacher, an ass; Zebulun, a ship; Reuben, a river, or figure of a man; Simeon, a sword; Gad, a lion; Ephraim, a unicorn; Manasseh, an ox; Benjamin, a wolf; Dan, a serpent; Asher, an ear of corn; and Naphthali, a stag.

Entered Apprentice.—The 1st degree in Masonry. In ancient times few Freemasons enjoyed the privilege of more than this degree. In fact, the Grand Lodge of England did not allow any to be made Fellow Crafts or Masters outside of London, without dispensation first being granted.

Entering.—A term used when a profane is permitted to see the mysteries of Masonry, and contemplate the works of the G. A. O. T. U.

Ephod.—A species of ornament worn by the High Priest. It was richly composed of gold, blue, purple, crimson, and twisted cotton, and upon the part which came over his shoulders, were two large precious stones, upon which were engraved the names of the twelve tribes of Israel; six names on each stone. The ephods worn by the ordinary priests were of fine linen.

Epopt.—A functionary of the Eleusian mysteries.

Escallop.—The escallop, or scallop shell, first brought

ESOTERIC — ESSENES. 109

back from the East by those who, as true pilgrims, had visited the Holy Land, afterward became the badge both of pilgrims and Crusaders. It was the especial cognizance of the Knights of Santiago, and is said to have decorated the housings of the horse on which S. James was mounted at the battle of Clavigo, when, as on many other occasions, as Don Quixote assured Sancho, "he was personally seen cutting and slaying, overthrowing, trampling, and destroying the Moorish squadrons; of which," continues the Knight-errant, "I could give thee many examples derived from authentic Spanish histories."

The order of S. James, in Holland, bore a badge and collar of escallop shells, and they are introduced also into the Collar of S. Michael, an order of knighthood established by Louis XI. Buckenham Priory, Norfolk, founded by William de Albini and his wife, Queen Adeliza, the widow of Henry I., had for Arms "*Ar.* three escallops *sa.*;" while on the ancient seal, S. James himself is represented wearing in his pilgrim's hat an escallop shell. This shell belongs also to the Arms of the Abbey of Reading, dedicated to S. James. The famous Jacques Cœur bore two escallops, in allusion to his patron saint, with three hearts for his own name.

Esoteric.—A set of mysterious doctrines which the ancient philosophers communicated only to the more enlightened of their disciples, and another more popular doctrine that they promulgated to the people.

Esquire.—A title used in the English system of Templars. It was much used in the days of chivalry

Essenes.—A sect of Jews in the time of our Saviour. They were few in number and lived chiefly in solitude, taking no part in public matters, but giving themselves up to contemplation. They believed in the immortality of the soul, and revered the Scriptures highly. Its members were admitted by oath at mature age. After a three years'

10

110 ESSENTIAL — EZRA.

probation of self-denial, and if faithful, they were clothed with an apron and small axe; this being the sign of their acceptance to the full privileges of the order.

Essential Secrets of Masonry.—Are such as to prevent imposition and obtain recognition. They are grips, words, signs, and tokens, whereby one may know another as well in the dark as in daylight.

Established Religion.—Freemasons are enjoined to comply with the religion recognized or established by a kingdom or power. This is not to be understood, however, as applying to their own private opinion and belief.

Exalted.—A line used in the Royal Arch. The candidate is exalted to a position of sublimity and perfection of Masonry, as practiced in ancient days.

Exclusion.—A member of a Lodge cannot be excluded without giving him proper notice of the charges against him, and the time and place of the investigation. A record of such exclusion must be reported to the Grand Lodge.

Exemption.—The term Free and Accepted Mason was derived from the fact that those Masons who were employed in the work of the Temple building were relieved from taxes and duties. The privilege of bearing arms was also accorded to them. From the period of the building of the second Temple the term Free and Accepted was applied to Masons.

Expenses.—The expenses of building the Temple were enormous. It was reckoned at £750,000 of our money. Whether these talents were held at the value of a Mosaic talent or not, is a question. However, the display of precious metals was prodigious.

Expert.—An officer to examine visitors in French Lodges.

Ezra.—The Jewish High Priest; was a zealous servant of God. He is supposed to have returned to Jerusalem with Zerubbabel from Babylonish captivity.

F.

Fall of Water.—The waters of Jordan were divided, so that the Israelites might pass over, and the water then fell and returned to its natural course. From this miracle, an emblem of the Fellow Craft degree is derived.

Family Lodges.—Lodges of this description are in use in Germany.

Feasts.—Have been celebrated in all ages of the world. At stated times and appropriate seasons, Masons have their feasts. In the United States, feasts are held on St. John the Baptist's day and St. John the Evangelist's day, respectively, June 24th, and December 27th.

Fees of Honor.—Every brother on his first appointment to either of the following offices shall pay to the Benevolence Fund, *i.e.:* Prov. Grand Master, 10 guineas; Deputy G. M., 10 guineas; Grand Warden, 10 guineas; Grand Treasurer, 10 guineas; Grand Registrar, 10 guineas; President of Board of General Purposes, 10 guineas; Grand Secretary, 10 guineas; Grand Deacon, 5 guineas; Grand Director of Ceremonies, 5 guineas; Grand Supt. of Works, 5 guineas; and Grand Sword Bearer, 5 guineas.

Felicite.—Organized in Paris in 1742, by naval officers. The initiation was the representation of a voyage in quest of the Island of Happiness. There were four degrees: Cabin Boy, Patron, Commander, Vice-Admiral. Its motto, *Peace be with thee* (*Schalona lecka*). Its emblem, the anchor.

Fellow Craft.—This is the second degree in Masonry. It is scientific.

Females.—It is often urged, why are ladies excluded from Freemasonry? Simply, that the labor is such that it cannot be performed by them. The wife and daughter of

112   *FENILLANTS—FIRE.*

a Master Mason receive indirectly all the benefits that can accrue from the order to her husband. The social reform and influence effected upon society she may assist in. The labors of love and charity are peculiar virtues with Masons, and in these labors the wife, daughter, and sister may assist and receive therefrom much pleasure and enjoyment.

Fenillants.—An order holding the St. Bernard views, and a system of Adoptive Masonry.

Fersler's System.—This system embraced nine degrees: G. A. P., F. C., Master, Holy of Holies, Justification, Celebration, True Light, Fatherland, Perfection.

Festivals.—The 24th of June, St. John the Baptist's anniversary, 27th of December, St. John the Evangelist's anniversary, are observed in the United States. The 23d of April, St. George's anniversary, observed in England. 30th of November, St. Andrew's anniversary, observed in Scotland.

Fidelite.—Organized in 1740, at Paris, and termed Knights and Ladies of Fidelity.

Field Lodges.—No Military Lodge shall initiate into Masonry any inhabitant or sojourner, at any place its members may be stationed, nor those in the military below the rank of corporal, without dispensation. If the military body is disbanded, the warrant must be returned to the Grand Lodge. The custom of warranting these Lodges has become common in all nations. In the recent rebellion, Lodges were formed in both the Union and Rebel armies.

Fiery Cloud.—The pillar of fire guided the Israelites through the wilderness during the night-time, while the guide during the daytime was a pillar of cloud. It was the divine presence of Jehovah, overshadowing his chosen with his protection.

Fire.—The Great I am that I am appeared to Moses in a burning bush, and to Abel and Noah His presence was manifest in a flame of fire.

FITZ. 113

Fitz, John.—One of the most interesting masonic sketches, that awaken emotions of sympathy, is that of John Fitz, of London, in 1425. In 1425, he made application for the honors of Freemasonry in St. John's Lodge, London, which was held at a private house. At this period, Freemasonry was interdicted. Robert Sprang was an applicant at the same time, and was rejected, which so enraged him that he gave information to Beaufort, then Bishop of Winchester, who took measures to arrest the party. Information, however, being received, the Lodge adjourned, and the bishop's efforts were thus frustrated. Sprang then directed their attention to the whereabouts of John Fitz, who was apprehended and cast into prison. Upon Fitz's examination, he refused to give any information of the order, and declared that he would rather lose his hands and tongue than divulge the secrets of Freemasonry. Beaufort, fully aroused by this refusal, declared he should be treated in accordance with his declaration. Fitz was then cast into prison, and the story became patent that he had escaped during the night. In course of time, the case of Fitz was forgotten, and his incarceration was seldom mentioned. However, the most interesting sequel to this affair occurred in 1449, or about that period. The interdiction of Freemasonry having been removed, St. John's Lodge met at the Appletree Tavern. It was during one of its sessions that an application was made for visitation by an individual who had lost his tongue and hands. Much difficulty was encountered in the examination, which finally resulted in his being declared worthy of admission. He gave his name as John Fitz, or at least satisfied the brethren that he was the individual that had been arrested by Beaufort. Did he suffer by Beaufort's order? It is for the reader to surmise, as it never became known who his cruel and savage tormentors

10*

114 FIVE—FLORIDA.

were. Fitz lived and enjoyed the unbounded sympathy of the brethren for many years.

Five Points of Fellowship.—To aid and assist our distressed brethren; to remember our Creator; the poor and needy; to keep secure our brethren's secrets when imparted to us; to defend the character of a brother when his cause is just; and to admonish our brethren from evil. The whole may be summed up in duty to God and man.

Fleeces, the Order of the Three Golden.—August 15th, 1809, in the camp of Schönbrunn, Napoleon added a third order to those of the Legion of Honor and Iron Crown. It was intended to consist of one hundred grand officers, four commanders, and one thousand members, chiefly military men. The Emperor was to be Grand Master, and the King of Rome the only hereditary member. Princes of blood had first to serve two years in the army before being admitted.

Floats.—The Bible narrates that the stone used in building the Temple was brought from the quarries on floats to Joppa, and thence were taken to Jerusalem on wagons prepared for this express purpose.

Floor Cloths.—An old custom prevailed up to 1760 of drawing necessary figures with chalk upon the floor. The custom has given way to ornamented cloths for this purpose.

Florida.—Freemasonry was introduced into the State about 1805-6. A Lodge was opened at this time at St. Augustine, under a charter from the Grand Lodge of Georgia. This Lodge worked until it was suppressed by the Spanish Government in 1811. In 1820, the faithful few were granted a warrant by the Grand Lodge of South Carolina, to open a Lodge in St. Augustine, but did not long survive. In 1822, De Witt Clinton, General Grand High Priest of the United States, granted a warrant for a Mark Master's Lodge at St. Augustine, which ceased to

FORTY-SEVENTH—FRANCE. 115

work in a short time. In 1824, the Grand Lodge of South Carolina chartered a Spanish Lodge at St. Augustine, and it ceased to work in a few months. In 1826, the Grand Lodge of Alabama granted a charter for a Lodge at Tallahasse, known as Jackson Lodge. The Grand Lodge of Tennessee, about this time, organized Washington Lodge at Quincy. On the 5th July, 1830, the Grand Lodge was organized at Tallahassee. On the 11th Jan. 1847, the Grand Chapter was organized, and in Jan. 1852, a Council of Royal and Select Masters was duly formed.

Forty-seventh Problem of Euclid.—Four times ten and seven. This figure depends on the connection of its lines, which make up the whole. Thus it is with Masonry, which is made up perfectly by the union of its members.

Foundation Days.—The days for laying the foundation of masonic Lodges are from April 15th to May 15th.

Four.—The mystic number of Four with the Jews.

France.—At what period Freemasonry was introduced into France, is not known. The first Lodge was at Dunkirk; it was opened 13th Oct. 1721. Another was opened at Mons about this time. In 1726, a Lodge was formed in Paris by Lord Derwenwater. In 1729, two other Lodges were organized in Paris. In 1732, another was organized. In 1735, Lord Derwenwater was appointed Provincial Grand Master by the Grand Lodges of England, which he transferred to Lord Harnonester. In 1736, Lord Harnonester was appointed Grand Master by the four Lodges of Paris, which had formed a Prov. Grand Lodge. In 1738, Duke D'Autine succeeded him, and held the position to 1743, when the body assumed the name of "English Grand Lodge of France." Louis XV., at this period, interdicted the assemblage of Masons. The Grand Lodge then formed the Grand Orient of France, and severed its connection with England. It was a custom at this date to sell warrants to Masters for life, and they continued to

116 FRANCE.

sell to others, thus producing great confusion and disturbance. At this time, the Grand Master appointed Bouse as a proxy, but afterward appointed in his stead Lacome, a brainless dancing-master. The members refused to recognize him, and Chaillon de Joinville took his place. At this period a strife began to show itself between the rival parties, and was followed by a bitter contest. In 1770, a reconciliation took place, which only lasted a sufficient time to gather strength for a fresh outburst. The government again interdicted them. In 1772, the Grand Lodge assumed the name of Grand Orient. In 1799, the rival factions were again reconciled. In 1802, the Scotch Rite refused to recognize the authority of the Grand Orient; and in 1803, they established the "Scottish G. L. of A. and A. Rite." In 1804, they both reunited. This, however, only lasted one year. In 1802, the Sovereign Grand Inspectors were organized by Count de Grasse-Tilly, and termed the 33d deg. In 1814, the Scotch Rite had ceased to work, and the Grand Orient exercised jurisdiction over all the degrees. On 9th April, 1815, the Rite of Misraim was introduced by Bedarridel, but was not recognized by the Grand Orient, and in 1862 it was swallowed up in the Scotch Rite. In 1852, Lucien Murat was elected Grand Master, and 1861, an effort was made to displace the imbecile by electing Napoleon. Discord reigned without any restrictions in the order until 11th Jan. 1862, when Napoleon appointed Marshal Magnon Grand Master for three years. Magnon was not a Mason at this time, but was immediately invested with 33d degree. Magnon succeeded in placing all things in a healthy condition, and at the expiration of his appointing, he was unanimously elected Grand Master. He remained in office until his death, 29th May, 1865. The Grand Orient then elected Gen. Mellinet. In this year the order was remodeled, and is now in flourishing condition, freed from the dross of fanaticism that had sought to engulf it in ruin.

Franklin, Benjamin.—Born in Boston, 17th Jan. 1706. No date is known when he became a Mason. In 1732, he was S. W. of the Tun Lodge, Phila. On the 24th June, 1734, Henry Price, G. M. of Mass., appointed him Master of a Lodge in Phila. About this time, the G. L. of England appointed him Pro. G. Master. In 1749, he was still continued as Grand Master of Pa. by Thomas Oxnord, G. Master of N. A. He died 17th April, 1790, aged 85.

Franklin, Wm.—Son of Benj., born in Philadelphia, March 2d, 1731. He was made a Mason in the old Lodge at Philadelphia. He was the first Royal Governor of New Jersey. He was the first Secretary of Grand Lodge of Va. Died Nov. 17th, 1813, aged 82.

Frederick II. of Prussia.—The greatest monarch of the 18th century, born 21st Jan. 1712. He was one of the originators of the order of African Architects, which was established in Germany in 1767.

Free-born.—One of the qualifications of the candidate is that he must be *free-born.* This has simply been an usage of the order which was in the old York Constitution in 926. The G. L. of England holds "that it is inconsistent with the principles of Freemasonry to make, pass, or raise Masons in any prison or place of confinement." The old English lectures also speak of that grand festival which Abraham made at the weaning of his son Isaac, when Sarah, seeing Ishmael, the son of Hagar, the bondwoman, teasing her son, she feared that if reared together, he might imbibe of the slavish principles, and hence asked Abraham to put away the bondwoman's son. The social equality of the Lodge would not be *free* if the freeman and the imprisoned man sat together. In 1782, a Lodge was held in the Kings' Bench prison to make certain Masons, and hence the universal condemnation of this action.

118   *FREEDOM—FREEMASON.*

Freedom, Order of.—This order of American Knighthood was contemplated in 1783. The order, however, was never constituted, but we herewith give an account published in Philadelphia, 25th March, 1783, as the names of prominent personages appeared in the formation: On the 4th of July next, a new order of Knighthood, called the Order of Freedom, will be established.

Patron of the order, St. Louis, Chief of the order, President of the order for the time being; Grand Master, General Washington; Chancellor, Dr. Franklin; Genealogist, Mr. Payne; Usher, Mr. Thompson; Prelate, Dr. Witherspoon; Secretary, Mr. Diggs; Herald, Mr. Hutchinson: 24 Knight's companions, consisting of the Governor of each State for the time being, which they reckon 19, Generals Lincoln, Greene, Wayne, and Col. Lee. The robe is to be scarlet and blue, with ermine; the ribbon, a broad satin with 13 stripes of red and white, to which will be suspended a medal, in front, representing Virtue, the genius of the U. S., dressed like an Amazon, resting on a spear with one hand, holding a sword in the other and treading upon it. Tyranny, represented by a man prostrate, a crown fallen from his head, a broken chain in his left hand, and a scourge in his right; in the exerque, *Sic semper tyrannis.* On the reverse, Liberty, with her wand and Pileus; Ceres, with a cornucopia in one hand, and an ear of wheat in the other, on one side, and Eternity, with the globe of Phœnix on the other. In the exerque, *Deus nobis hoc otia fecit.* The loof of the medal is formed by a rattlesnake with the tail in the mouth, an emblem of eternity. A staff of liberty, with a cap on the top, fixed to the body of the snake. The motto, *In recto decus.*

Freemason.—A definition and explanation so various, that it may be found in all languages differing. The term originally was only Mason, but it appears that the privi-

FREEMASONRY—GAVEL. 119

lege granted, and the relief given them from fines and duties, led to the adoption of the term.

Freemasonry.—The *alpha* and *omega* of philanthropy, charity, reason, truth, temperance, justice, science, art, morality, brotherly love, and Christian intention and disposition toward all men.

French Rite.—In 1786, the Grand Orient of France organized this system to preserve the higher degrees in simplicity of form, style, and access. The degrees are seven: the Blue Lodge, Rose Croix, Scotch Order, Knights of the East, and *Ne Plus Ultra.*

Freres Pontines.—This order of speculative Masons organized in the 12th century at Avignon. It has ceased to exist.

Funerals.—Masonic funerals are only conducted at the express wish of the deceased brother.

G.

This letter refers to Geometry; and also may stand for the name of God.

G. A. O. T. U.—Grand Architect of the Universe. An effort was recently made in some of the French Lodges to strike out the use of these abbreviations, but upon vote it was decided to continue them. They are used upon official documents.

Garter, Order of.—The commonly received account of this order is, that Richard I. tied thongs of leather as a mark of distinction round the legs of several of his officers at the siege of Arc. The order was restored about 1344 by Edward III. The statutes of the Garter were received by Kings Henry V., Henry VIII., and George III. It is also called the Order of St. George.

Gavel.—The gavel is an instrument made use of by

120 GEDELIAH — GENERAL.

operative masons to fit the rough stone for the builder's use. Speculative Masons use it to divert the character from the superfluities of life, and fitting their bodies as living stones for that spiritual house not made by hands, eternal in the heavens. It is an emblem of the E. A. P.

Gedeliah.—A Jewish Prince who went over to the Chaldeans before the destruction of Jerusalem. Nebuchadnezzar made him governor of the poor people left in Judea.

General Grand Chapter of the U. S.—The first R. A. Chapter in America, of which any definite account is extant, is that held in Philadelphia prior to 1758. This Chapter worked under No. 3 warrant of Master Masons, and had communion with Military Lodge, No. 351, under jurisdiction of G. L. of all England. In November, 1795, Molan made an irregular attempt to introduce innovations with the Chapter degree, and form an independent Grand Royal Arch Chapter, under the warrants of Nos. 19, 52, and 67 of Philadelphia. The Grand Lodge, upon complaint, suspended these Lodges. On November 23d, 1795, Lodge No. 3 held a session to devise a plan for forming a Grand Chapter, and accordingly organized. This was the first Grand Chapter of the U. S. On October 24th, 1797, the Chapters of Massachusetts, New Hampshire, Rhode Island, Connecticut, Vermont, and New York met in convention at Boston, to deliberate on the question of forming a General Grand Chapter. This convention issued an address, and agreed to meet in Boston, January 24th, 1798, which they did, and organized a Grand Chapter for the States of New York, New Hampshire, Massachusetts, Rhode Island, Connecticut, and Vermont, and styled the Grand Royal Arch Chapter of the Northern States of America. The Grand Lodge of Pennsylvania did not unite with this body on account of considering the Arch as under the jurisdiction of the Grand Lodge. In 1806, the title of the Grand Royal Arch Chapter of the Northern

GENERALISSIMO — GIBEON. 121

States of America was changed to "The Gen. G. Chapter of R. A. M. of the U. S." Under this title all the Grand Chapters of the various States united and acknowledged its jurisdiction.

Generalissimo.—The second officer in the Knights Templar.

Geometry.—The science which treats of the properties of figured space. Freemasonry is sometimes named Geometry.

Georgia.—Freemasonry was introduced into this State about 1730–1734. In 1735, the Grand Lodge of England granted a Charter for a Lodge at Savannah. In December 16th, 1786, the Grand Lodge was organized.

Germany.—Freemasonry was introduced into Germany about the 10th century. The operative masons were organized as Apprentices, Fellow Crafts, and Masters. In 1733 the Grand Lodge of England granted a warrant for a Lodge to be held at Hamburg. On August 11th, 1738, Frederick II. was initiated at Brunswick. In 1741, a Provincial Grand Lodge was organized for Hamburg. In 1743, another Lodge was opened in Hamburg. In 1744, a Lodge was opened in Hanover. In 1738, a Lodge was opened in Dresden. In 1741, one at Leipsic. In 1742, one at Frankfort-on-the-Main. In 1751, the "Strict Observance" was organized. In 1756, a Provincial Grand Lodge was opened at Frankfort-on-the-Main. In 1776, the Illuminati was organized. In 1780, the Swedish Rite was organized. In 1783, Eclectic Rite was organized to swallow up the various rites that was practiced. In 1789, the Grand Lodge of England established the Provincial Grand Lodge.

Ghiblim.—A tribe allied against Jehosaphat, King or Judah. The land was south of Canaan. From this place Solomon had his Tyrian stone-squarers, or Ghiblims or Ghiblimites.

Gibeon.—Mentioned only in the Old Testament. It was a great city in Judea. It was upon this place that the sun

11

122 GIBLIMITES—GNOSTICISM.

stood still while Joshua gained a signal victory over the Canaanites. It was here that the young Solomon offered a thousand burnt offerings, and was rewarded by the vision which left him the wisest of men. It had a peculiar place of worship. It is in symbolical use in France as the name of Master, and the Swedish Rite uses it in the same light.

Giblimites.—Were the inhabitants of Gabal in Phœnicia, near Mt. Lebanon, under the dominion of King Hiram. The Phœnician *gibal*, which makes *giblim* in the plural, signifies a mason, or stone-cutter, or stone-squarer. The Gibalons were Master Masons who put the finishing stroke to King Solomon's Temple.

Gilead.—A group of mountains connected with Lebanon by means of Mt. Herman. It is the name of the keeper of the Holy Sepulcher of James VI. in the Scottish degree.

Gist, Mordecai.—This distinguished general of the Union army of the United States is supposed to have become a Mason in Maryland prior to the Revolution, in the Baltimore Lodge, under warrant from Grand Lodge of Penna. At an army festival in 1779, a petition was circulated for the purpose of uniting all the Lodges under one grand head, and a committee appointed to consider the matter. When, in June 7th, 1780, this committee met, Gist was chosen the President. On April 4th, 1780, the Grand Lodge of Penna. granted a warrant for an Army Lodge, No. 27, of which Gist was appointed Master. At this time the general was in South Carolina. At the conclusion of the war, the Grand Lodge of Penna. revoked the charter of the Lodge, and granted in place a Local Charter in 1786 for a Lodge at Charleston, No. 27, and made Gist the Master. When the Grand Lodge of South Carolina was formed, General Gist was elected the Dep. Grand Master. In 1790, he became Grand Master, and filled the position two terms. He died September, 1792, aged 50 years.

Gnosticism (Gr. *Knowledge*).—A philosophical sect or

GOD.

123

system of religion, which prevailed in the East during the first four centuries of our era, and exercised much influence on the Christian theology, giving birth to many hideous heresies, and insinuating itself in a moderate form in the writings of the orthodox fathers. Its origin is involved in mystery, its principles seem to point to the Oriental philosophy as its genuine parent, but the fathers refer it to a Greek origin, and appeal to the cosmogonies of Hesiod and others, as the real exemplars from which it is imitated. Another solution places Alexandria as the place from whence it originated. It was, however, certainly a resort of Gnostic opinions, in and out of the church. The principle of this philosophy was an attempt to reconcile the difficulties attending upon the existence of evil in the world. Evil, being the contrary of good, must be contrary to, and therefore the opponent of, God; if the opponent of God, then independent of him, and coeternal. The human soul, which tends to a higher development, was held to be the gift of the Supreme Deity imparted to man to combat against the material principle, with the end of subduing it. From the Supreme God on one hand, and material on the other, the philosophers produced fanciful genealogies of superior intelligence, under the name of Æons, a Greek word, meaning *periods*, representing these deities or divinities by a name expressive of the time and order of their generation. The Demiurgus, who formed the world out of matter, was an Æon, derived from the Evil principle. Also God, of the Old Testament, considered by the Gnostics an object of aversion to the one Supreme God, to counteract whose machinations the Æon, Christ, was sent into the world. The Gnostics ceased in the fifth century. Traces are, however, found in the degrees of Adepts of the Sun, in Masonry, and several of the old Rites.

God.—The two principal names of the Hebrew are *Jehovah* and *Elohim*,—Elohim, the Creator, and Jehovah,

124 *GOLDEN—GOLGOTHA.*

the Redeemer. He is the first and the last and changes not; the earth and heavens shall perish, but he shall endure forever. The human race believes in a God, and by necessity there must exist a God. The reasoning faculty of man, the beauty and glory was opened unto him, yet when he had contemplated this he conceived a greater and more glorious world, the master-place of a God. It is in this sense of superiority and divinity that Freemasons look for God, as the perfect Being from whom all good emanates, and through whom all things have their being and existence. The fact then is clear to all intelligent minds why the *atheist* cannot be admitted into Masonry.

Golden Candlestick.—It was made of pure gold, and for the use of the Temple. It had seven branches, and was placed in the Holy Place to illuminate the Altar of Incense and Shew-Bread.

Golden Fleece.—An order of European knighthood, and founded in 1430, by the Duke of Burgundy, Philip II. It is supposed that Jason, on his expedition to Colchis, entertained a commercial expedition. The masonic apron is said to be more ancient than any other badge. The Argonautic campaign by Jason is supposed to be only an account of the Deluge figuratively described. Be that as it may, there can be no doubt that the masonic apron was in use long before the abortioned attempts to counterfeit Masonry.

Golgotha.—Signifies the place of *Skull*, so called either from its resemblance to the skull of a man's head, or because it was the place where malefactors were beheaded; a small hill to the west of Jerusalem. It is said Adam was buried here: but it is certain Jesus was crucified here, and buried in an adjacent garden. Over Jesus' sepulcher, Helena, mother of Constantine, built a grand church, in A.D. 330. The word is used in the Knights Templar and Scottish system.

GOTHIC—GRAND. 125

Gothic Constitution.—A revision of Freemasonry from 926 to 1717.

Grand Architect of the Universe.—Freemasons recognize, adore, and obey, the All-wise God, as the Grand Architect of the Universe. Being the Creator of all things, He is the Architect of all things, and as such we bow in humble submission to His will.

Grand Bodies of Masons.—Up to the year 1717, all Lodges of Masons were entirely independent of each other. They met to practice Masonry and confer its honors upon the worthy one, by and with the consent of the English Government. At the General Assembly, at York, in 1787, a new regulation was adopted, that all Lodges should act by virtue of a warrant from the Grand Lodge, and that no Lodge would be considered hereafter legally and justly constituted, unless warranted by the Grand Lodge.

Grand East of Masonry.—The place permanently selected for the assemblage of the Grand Body is termed the Grand East. In the United States we term the Grand East, the Grand Lodge that meets annually in the several States. So, too, in Europe, the Grand East of England meets in London, the Grand East of Ireland at Dublin, the Grand Orient of France at Paris, etc.

Grand Inquisor Commander of Masons.—31st degree of Ancient and Accepted Rite. It is an administrative degree.

Grand Lodge.—The body that has exclusive jurisdiction in a State or kingdom over the Subordinate Lodges, and all Masons within its bounds. It empowers subordinate bodies to practice all the rights of Masonry. Originally the order was not governed by Grand Lodges, but the right existed inherently to act as individuals. However, the ancient brethren met annually, to consult upon Masonry and select a Grand Master. But as the order increased in power and numbers, it became necessary to establish

11*

126 GRAND.

Grand Lodges, for the interest of the order. The first charter granted was to St Alban's, for a General Assembly, and subsequently Prince Edwin obtained a charter to assemble all Masons at York. It was thus the order obtained and has ever since recognized the necessity of a Grand Lodge.

Grand Lodges and their Jurisdiction.—A Grand Lodge has jurisdiction over the territory of the State in which it is organized, and no other Grand Body can exercise any authority or charter Lodges therein. It is governed by the ancient usages and landmarks of the order, and acknowledges no superior authority than these.

Grand Master.—The superior officer of the Grand Lodge. The following is a list of Past Grand Masters of the Grand Lodge of Pennsylvania, from the year 1779 to the present time, in the order of their election:

William Ball, Esq.	Tristram B. Freeman.
William Adcock.	John M. Read.
Jonathan Bayard Smith.	Samuel H. Perkins.
Wm. Moore Smith.	Joseph R. Chandler.
Israel Israel.	Cornelius Stevenson.
James Milnor.	William Barger.
Richard Tybout.	James Page.
Samuel F. Bradford.	Peter Fritz.
Walter Kerr.	William Whitney.
Bayse Newcomb.	A. Bournonville, M.D.
Josiah Randall.	James Hutchinson.
J. B. Gibson.	Peter Williamson.
James Harper.	John K. Mitchell, M.D.
Thomas Kittera.	Henry M Phillips.
Samuel Badger.	John Thomson.
Michael Nisbet.	David C. Skerrett, M.D.
John Steele.	Lucius H. Scott.
Geo. M. Dallas.	John L. Goddard.

Richard Vaux.

GRAND. 127

Grand Master Architect.—In the Ancient and Accepted Rite, the 12th degree, which is entirely scientific. The Assembly is termed Chapter. The officers are Thrice Illustrious, and two Wardens.

Grand Master of Symbolic Degrees.—In the Ancient and Accepted Rite, the 20th degree. It is philosophic in its exemplifications of Masonry. The chief officer is called Venerable Grand Master. It requires nine members to open a Lodge.

Grand Masters.—The following list of Superintendents, Patrons, and Grand Masters, presided over the Masons in England to 1790.

Carausis, a Roman general, first patronized the order.
St. Albanus also protected it.
640. Rennet, Abbot of Winal, became Superintendent.
924. Prince Edwin, Grand Master.
1041. Leofrick, Earl of Coventry, Superintendent.
1066. Gundolp, Bishop of Rochester, and Roger de Montmorency, Patrons.
1087. Gilbert de Clare, Marquis of Pembroke, Presided.
1199. Peter de Colechurch, Grand Master.
1204. Peter de Rupibus, "
1272. Walter Gifford, Archbishop of York, G. M.
1307. Walter Stapleton, Bishop of Exeter, "
William Wykeham (in reign Richard II.), G. M.
Thomas Fitz Allen (" Henry IV.), "
1424. Henry Chichely, Archbishop of Canterbury, G. M.
1442. Wm. Wanefleet, Bishop of Winchester, "
1471. Robt. Beauchamp, " Sarum, "
1502. Henry VII., "
Cardinal Wolsey (reign Henry VIII.), "
1534. Thomas Cromwell, Earl of Essex.
1540. John Lanchet, Lord Audley.
1547. Duke of Somerset.
1552. John Poynet, Duke of Somerset.

128   *GRAND.*

1553. Thomas Sackville.
1567. Francis Russell, Earl of Bedford.
1569. Thomas Gresham.
1588. Charles Howard, Earl of Effingham.
1603. Geo. Hastings, Earl of Huntingdon.
1604. Inigo Jones.
1619. Earl of Pembroke.
1630. Henry Danvers, Earl of Danby.
1633. Thomas Howard,   "   Aurundale
1635. Francis Russell,   "   Bedford.
1663. Henry Jennyn,   "   St. Albans.
1666. Earl Rivers.
1674. Geo. Villars, Duke of Buckingham.
1679. Henry Bennet, Earl of Arlington.
1685. Sir Christopher Wren.
1697. Charles, Duke of Richmond.
1698. Sir Christopher Wren.
1705. John Lampert, Baronet.
        Anthony Sayer (accession Geo. III.)
1719. Dr. Dersaguliers.
1723. Duke of Buccleugh.
1730. Thomas Howard, Duke of Norfolk.
1731. Lord Lovel.
1732. Anthony Brown.
1733. James Lyon, Earl of Strathmore.
1734. John Lindsey, Earl of Crawford.
1735. Thomas Thynne, Viscount Weymouth.
1736. John Campbell, Earl of London.
1738. H. Brydges, Marquis of Carnarvon.
1739. Robt., Lord Reymond.
1740. John Keith, Earl of Kingston.
1741. James Douglas, Earl of Morton.
1742. John Ward, Viscount Dudley and Ward.
1745. James Cranston, Lord Cranston.
1746. William, Lord Byron.

GRAND. **129**

1750. Lord Byron.

1754. James, Marquis of Carnarvon.

1757. Gholto, Lord Aberon.

1758. John Paby, Lord Caryfort.

1760. Earl of Drogheda.

1762. Washington Shirley, Earl of Ferres.

1764. Cadwallader, Lord Blany.

1767 to 1771. Henry, Duke of Beaufort.

1772. Robert Edward, Lord Petre.

1777 to 1781. George, Duke of Manchester.

1782 to 1789. Frederick, Duke of Cumberland.

1790 to 1813. Augustus Frederick, Duke of Sussex.

Grand Masters of Knights Templar, with their date of election:

1. Hugh de Paynes, 1118.

2. Robert of Burgundy, 1139.

3. Everard de Barri, 1147.

4. Barnard Trenellope, 1151.

5. Bertrand de Blouchefort, 1154.

6. Andrew de Montbar, 1165.

7. Philip of Naples, 1169.

8. Odo St. Amand, 1171.

9. Arnold de Troye, 1180.

10. John Terricus, 1185.

11. Gerard Ridefort, 1187.

12. Robert Sablaens, 1191.

13. Gilbert Gralins, 1196.

14. Philip de Plessis, 1201.

15. William de Carnita, 1217.

16. Peter de Montague, 1218.

17. Armand de Petragrosa, 1229.

18. Herman de Petragrosins, 1237.

19. William de Rupefort, 1244.

20. William de Sonnoe, 1247.

21. Reynald Vichierius, 1250.

130

GRAND.

22. Thomas Berand, 1257.
23. William de Beaujean, 1274.
24. Theobald Gondinius, 1291.
25. James de Molay, 1298.
26. John Mark Laurienius, 1314.
27. Thomas Theobald Alexandrinus, 1324.
28. Arnold de Brayne, 1340.
29. John de Claremont, 1349.
30. Bertrand du Gueschi, 1357.
31. John Arminiacus, 1381.
32. Bernard Arminiacus, 1392.
33. John Arminiacus, 1419.
34. John de Croz, 1451.
35. Bernard Imboult, 1472.
36. Robert Senancourt, 1478.
37. Goleatius de Solazar, 1497.
38. Philip Chabot, 1516.
39. Gaspard de Jalliaco Taranensis, 1544.
40. Henry de Montmorency, 1574.
41. Charles de Valois, 1615.
42. James Ruxellius de Grouceir, 1651.
43. James Henry de Durefort, 1681.
44. Philip, Duke of Orleans, 1705.
45. Louis de Bourbon, 1724.
46. Louis Henry Bourbon, 1737.
47. Louis Francis Bourbon, 1741.
48. Louis Henry Trimaleon, 1776.
49. Claud M. R. de Chevillon, 1792.
50. Bernard R. Fabre Palaprat, 1804.
51. Sir Sidney Smith, 1838.

Grand Officers' Club.—A club to which all Grand Officers are admitted.

Grand Prelate.—An officer of the Royal Arch Chapter.

Grand Principal Sojourner.—In the American Accepted Rite, the 19th degree. It is a history of the Apocalypse, so far as refers to the New Jerusalem, according to St John's revelation. The principal officer is called Thrice Illustrious Grand Pontiff.

Grand Priory.—The Grand Body of Templars of Scotland assumes this name.

Grand Scottish Knight of St. Andrew.—In the Ancient and Accepted Rites, the 29th degree, which is dedicated and consecrated to the freedom of man in the moral attributes. It is founded upon equality, and the humble member is equal to the greatest potentate. The meeting is termed a Chapter. It has two rooms; the first is the Court of Saladin, Sultan of Egypt. Its principal officer is styled Venerable Grand Master.

Grand Stewards' Lodge.—This Lodge has no power to make Masons. It is, however, represented in the Grand Lodge by its officers.

Grand Wardens.—Officers of the Grand Lodge. While serving in this capacity, they cannot act as Warden of any other Lodge.

Grecian Masonry.—In the Rite of Memphis, the 13th and 14th degrees.

Grip and Sign.—These are among the masonic modes of recognition, by which one Mason may be known to another, upon trial.

Grovesnor, Daniel.—Was born in Vermont, and removed to Troy, Ohio, over forty years ago, where he resided until his death. He was a true Mason, and during the anti-masonic excitement stood firm and unflinching at his post, and, with Bros. Asa Coleman and John Brown, kept Warren Lodge above the wave of opposition, of which he was then Master. Before he was Master of the Lodge, a Bro. Spinner held that post. Both were members of the Baptist Church, but Rev. Eaton, the pastor, refused to receive their certificates unless they would renounce Masonry. Spinner acquiesced to this demand, but

132   *HAGAR — HAMMATT.*

Grovesnor refused to do so, preferring to connect with a church less bigoted. He kept his post unflinchingly until Freemasonry had triumphed over fanaticism.

H.

Hagar.—Was an Egyptian bondwoman, that Sarah gave to Abraham. He was much attached to her son, and earnestly prayed Jehovah that he might be the child of promise. But this was denied, as a free spirit could not spring from a bondwoman.

Haggai.—The first of the three Jewish prophets that flourished after the captivity. He, with Zechariah, exhorted them to complete the Temple. He assured them that Messiah would appear in the flesh, teach in their courts, and render the second Temple more glorious than the first.

Hallelujah, or Alleluiah.—A word that stands at the beginning of many Psalms. It was used as a formula of praise on solemn occasions. This is intimated by the Apocryphal Book of Tobet, when speaking of the rebuilding of Jerusalem, "And all her streets shall sing Alleluia." In the degrees of Sublime Scotch, Heavenly Jerusalem, and Apprentice degree, in the Rite of Misraim, it is the expression of applause.

Ham.—Youngest son of Noah, who mocked at his father's shame, and was cursed on that account. His posterity peopled Africa and Asia. Reference is made to this in the Templar system.

Hammatt, John B.—One of the oldest Masons of Massachusetts. He was Past Grand High Priest of the Grand Chapter of Massachusetts. He organized Trinity Chapter, at Hopkinton, the second in the State. He was about 90 years of age at his death.

Hammer or Gavel.—With this instrument the Lodge is governed. Its sound commands respect and obedience, and is the Master's authority.

Hand Clapping.—Applause, Consent. Used in Freemasonry.

Haran.—The sacred word and name of the Chief Officer of the 71st degree in the Rite Misraim.

Harmony, Order.—Founded by Grossinger, in 1778. The Grand Mistress was the Duchess of Newcastle. The object was friendship and love.

Harodim.—The overseers placed by King Solomon; the bearers of burden and hewers in the mountain are called princes or Harodim.

Harodina.—A sect of Jews in the time of Christ. Some held them to be political, and others a social organization. The lectures include many of the masonic features. Each class has a particular lecture. The Chief Harod annually assigns to each class a number of leaders, termed Sectionists, and they distribute the portions of their Sections among the clause-holders, who are the private companions.

Harpocrates.—An Egyptian God. He was worshiped under the title of Sigolion. He is represented as a young man with a cornucopia and quiver, in connection with the owl and poppy.

Hays, Daniel R.—Grand Lecturer of G. L. of Indiana, died at Allicia, Dec. 26th, 1866, in the fifty-first year of his age. He entered the Grand Lodge in 1850, as representative of No. 18. He was made a Mason March 22d, 1845, and received the third degree August following. He was for several years High Priest of Chapter No. 23, and Grand High Priest of Grand Chapter of the State. He was T. I. G. M. of Council No. 12, and received the orders of Christian Knighthood in Lafayette Commandery, No. 3. He was also a member of the Ind. Order of Odd Fellows,

134 HEALED — HERMANDAD.

and Good Templars. In 1860 he was appointed Grand Lecturer by the Grand Lodge, which duty he discharged to the lasting honor of the fraternity. He died universally lamented by the order and the Christian church.

Healed.—A masonic term, used when a Mason is irregularly made, and afterwards taken into a regular Lodge. The question is now exciting considerable interest in masonic circles, how those Masons who have been made in the Military Lodges, North and South, during the recent civil strife, shall be healed. In many instances the parties know nothing by which to make themselves known, and hence the necessity to *heal* them and take them into fellowship.

Helm, Hon. John L.—Deceased Governor of Kentucky, was born in Hardin County, July 4th, 1802, and died at Elizabeth, Sept. 8th, 1867. His parents were natives of Virginia. He read law under General Duff Greene and Ben Hardin, and was admitted to the bar at the age of 21. He was first elected to the Legislature from Hardin, by the "Old Court" party, and subsequently was elected Senator. He was the author of the "Sinking Fund System," and presided frequently as Speaker of the House of Representatives. In 1848, he was elected Lieutenant-Governor on the same Whig ticket with Brother John J. Crittenden, and upon Mr Crittenden becoming a member of President Fillmore's Cabinet, he became Governor of the State. In 1865, he was elected to the State Senate, and at the last election, Governor of Kentucky.

Hendrix, Wm.—Past G. M. of G. L. of Alabama, died Aug. 27th, 1866, at Montgomery. In 1844 he served as J. W. of the Grand Lodge; in 1846–47, as Dep. G. M.; and in 1851, as Grand Master. His virtues were those of a just and upright Mason, a Christian, and a citizen.

Hermandad Brethren.—In 1295, a Spanish order was organized in Castile and Leon under this appellation. It had for its object a joint administration of the laws of society, to prevent and punish crimes. It had immense influence and power, and exerted it for good.

Hermaphrodite.—From the Greek mythological fables of union and confluence of the bodies of the Nymph Salmacis and Hermaphroditus, son of Mercury and Venus.

Hermetic Masonry.—Hermes Trismegistus, a person of questionable reality, was looked upon as the founder of the ancient art. This philosophy found its place in Freemasonry in 1800.

Heroden (*Halig Houri*).—The name given a mountain near Kilwinning, in the degree of Grand Architect. Sir Robert Bruce united the orders of St. Andrew of the Thistle and Knights Templar, and gave it the name of Heroden.

Heroden, Order of.—This order is said to have been instituted after the battle of Bannockburn, by Sir Robert Bruce, on St. John's day, 1314. The King of Scotland was the Grand Master. The Grand Lodge is said to have been first established upon the summit of Mount Moriah, in Judea, and afterwards at I-colm-kill, and finally at Castle Kilwinning, where changes were made in the ritual.

Heroines of Jericho.—A degree of Adoptive Masonry, conferred upon wives and widows of Royal Arch Masons. The Easter Star has superseded this rite in the United States.

Hieronymites.—This order was founded by St. Jerome. It originated in Spain, and admitted both sexes. It had masonic form, but no connection with Freemasonry. The order also received the title of Zeromists.

Hierophants, or Hierophant.—The title of the priest who initiated candidates into the Eleusian mysteries. He resided at Athens, and filled the position during his life.

High Priest.—A man who officiates with Jehovah on behalf of others, for the occasion. The chief of the priestly order among the Jews. In the Jewish system, Adam is said to have been the first priest. The High Priest entered

136 HIGH — HIRAM.

the Holy of Holies of the Temple once a year, to intercede with Jehovah on behalf of the sins of the people. The first officer of Royal Arch Masons is termed the High Priest.

High Priesthood.—This order is conferred on Past High Priests of Chapters.

High Twelve.—A tradition exists among Masons, that Hiram Abiff was the superintendent among the workmen at the Temple, and it was his custom at the opening of each day, as the sun rose in the east, to retire into the Temple, and offer prayer and thanksgiving, and invoke God's blessing upon his labors; and in the evening to render thanks for His care and protection. Yet not satisfied with his devotions at morn and eve, he repaired to the Temple at *High Twelve*, when the craft were at refreshment, to inspect the work and lay out new designs upon the trestleboard. He performed these devotions the first six years in the Lodge, and the last year in the Most Holy Place. When the day was announced for celebrating the completion of the Temple, he performed his accustomed duty at the hour of *High Twelve*, and never returned from his devotions. His death occasioned much sorrow, and his loss was deeply felt.

Hiram.—In England the gavel is termed Hiram. It is to commemorate the virtues of that eminent craftsman who assisted in building the Temple.

Hiram Abiff.—Was of the tribe of Naphthali. His father was called a Tyrian, and a worker in brass. He is represented as the father of Kings Hiram and Solomon, either because he was the director in their *curious* and *mystical* work, or perhaps *Abi*, which signifies father, was his surname. He was a most skillful designer, and executed the most curious workmanship of brass, copper, etc. He made the brazen pillars, lavers, sea, etc., of the Temple. See I. Kings, vii., and I. Chronicles, ii.

HIRAM — HOLY. 137

Hiram, King of Tyre.—Was the son of Abibal. When David came upon the throne, Hiram sent messengers to congratulate him, and sent him cedar-trees and artificers to build him a palace. He, or his son, of the same name, congratulated Solomon on his accession to the throne. He furnished him with timber, artificers for building the Temple, and lent him 120 talents of gold. To direct the proceedings of the Temple, he gave him the chief architect in the person of Hiram Abiff.

Hirimites.—The adherents of King Hiram.

Holiness to the Lord.—The motto worn by the High Priest of a Royal Arch Chapter.

Holland.— The introduction of Masonry in Holland occurred in 1731, at Hague, under the authority of the Grand Lodge of England. In 1734, a Lodge was regularly formed at Hague. In 1756, the Grand Lodge was organized.

Holland, John Henry.—Died in the city of New Orleans, March 29th, 1864, aged 78. He was a native of Connecticut, but for many years made New Orleans his home, where he presided with honor and dignity over Indivisible Friends' Commandery, and at the time of his death its Eminent Grand Commander. The last Templar duty he performed was to constitute the Grand Commander of Louisiana, in February, 1864.

Holy Fire.—At the time when the authority was given to finish the second Temple, Nehemiah was appointed to the government of Judea. The Holy Fire, which was hidden in a pit when the captivity of the Jews took place, was yet to be found. The priests on searching could find nothing but muddy water, which they took and sprinkled the wood on the altar with, and when the sun shone upon it, the wood commenced to burn. This miracle, on reaching the King of Persia, caused him to encompass the spot where the miracle occurred with a wall.

12*

138   *HOLY—HUBBARD.*

Holy Ghost.—This order was organized by a son of Count Montpellier, about 1200. It admitted both sexes, and was a charitable institution. A hospital was built by Innocent III. for this order. Henry III. of France organized a military order under this title in 1514.

Holy Lodge.—This Lodge was opened on the spot where Moses was directed by Jehovah to put off his shoes, as the ground upon which he trod was holy. It was in the Wilderness of Sinai, at the foot of Mt. Horeb. It was instituted two years after the Israelites had passed from Egyptian bondage. The decalogue, and the designs of the Tabernacle and Ark, were delivered to Moses by Jehovah at this place. This Lodge was governed by Moses, Ahaliad, and Bezoleel.

Holy of Holies.—The Holy of Holies was the innermost part of the Temple. It was the resting-place of the Ark and the Covenant. The place was 30 feet square, and 30 feet in height. The Ark was placed in the center, upon a stone. On each side stood two cherubim, whose wings touched the walls and met over the center of the Ark.

Horeb.—The mountain where the miracles of the burning bush, the water gushing from rock by a stroke from Moses' rod, the raising up by Aaron and Hur of Moses' hands, which caused the destruction of the Amalekites, delivery of law upon tables of stone, the destruction of the tables of stone that contained the law when Moses beheld the idolatrous worship of the golden calf, and the vision of Elijah, were performed and transacted under the eye of Moses.

Hubbard, Wm. Blackstone.—Born in Lonville, New York, August 25th, 1795, and died in Columbus, Ohio, January 5th, 1866. In 1816, he emigrated to St. Clairsville, Ohio, and prepared himself for the practice of law. He was District Attorney for several years in that county, and in 1829, was elected to the Legislature. In 1839, he removed to Columbus, and engaged in banking. He was made a Mason in the Lodge of St. Clairsville. In 1843 and 1844, he was elected Junior Grand Warden of the Grand Lodge. In 1850, he was elected Grand Master of the G. L. of Ohio, and continued as such until 1853. His administrative abilities were of the highest order, and won for him the honors of the craft.

Huntoon, Rev. Benj.—A native of Salisbury, and graduate of Dartmouth College, in 1817. He was a distinguished Mason, and held the office of M. G. Grand High Priest of the Grand Chapter of Mass. in 1849–50 and 51. He died in 1864.

I.

I Am That I Am.—This was the message that God bade Moses carry to the Hebrews, when he appeared to him in the burning bush, that the *I am* fulfills every promise, had heard the cry of his people, and intended delivering them from bondage.

Illinois.—The exact date of the introduction of Freemasonry into the State is not known. In 1805, a Lodge was held at Kaskaskia. The Grand Lodge was formed about 1840, April 6th, at Jackson. On April 9th, 1850, the Grand Chapter was organized. In 1853, the Grand Council was organized. On October, 1857, the Grand Commandery was organized.

Illuminati of· Avignon, or Swedenborg Rite. — This system was organized in 1760, by a monk named Pernetti, and a Pole named Gabrianca. In 1773, it was resuscitated by Marquis de Thorn, at Avignon, and from that period known as the Swedenborg Rite. It included the three Blue Lodge Degrees, Theosophite, Illuminated Theosophite, Blue or Red Brother, in six degrees. The first organization was partially political, and intended to bring

140 ILLUMINATI—IMPOSTS.

into disrepute the masonic system. It was afterward purged from its political ideas entirely, and reduced to a strict moral system.

Illuminati of the Enlightened.—A secret society formed in 1776, chiefly under direction of Adam Wishaupt, of Ingolstadt, Bavaria. Its professed object was the attainment of a higher degree of virtue and morality than that reached in the ordinary course of society. It numbered as high as 2000 members. In 1784, the Bavarian government suppressed it.

Immanuel or Emanuel (*God with us*).—The term is used in the Knights Templar.

Immovable Jewels.—Are the square, level, and plumb. Their positions are fixed in the Lodge, and hence they are called immovable jewels.

Impeachment.—A Master of a Lodge can only be impeached by a Grand Lodge. The members of his Lodge are bound to obey his commands. If he oversteps his authority, charges may be preferred against him to the Grand Lodge. In a masonic dictionary, edited by the learned Robert McCoy, Inspector-General of the 33d degree, he mentions a case that occurred in New York in 1842. The Master being absent, the Wardens opened the Lodge, preferred charges against him, appointed a committee to try the case, and refused to return the Master the warrant and gavel. Complaint was made by the Master to the Grand Officer, who directed that the warrant and gavel be forthwith returned to the Master, and that the members hold themselves in readiness to maintain their charges before the Grand Steward's Lodge. This order was promptly complied with.

Imposts.—King Solomon relieved the members of Tyrian artist's society from imposts, that they might be distinguished from the Jews who performed more humble labor. They received as an honorary title the name *Free*. The members of this society were mostly foreigners.

INCOMMUNICABLE—INNER. 141

Incommunicable.—It is held that Moses requested of the Almighty, at the burning bush, the correct pronunciation of God, which was lost through the sinfulness of mankind. The word *ghalam*, it is asserted, being written without a *van*, should be rendered to hide, and not as formerly, forever. The Jews call it Shemhampharoh, the unutterable name; and hence they use Elohim, Adonai, or Hashem to express the name.

Indiana.—The exact date when Freemasonry was introduced into this State is not known. The first Lodges worked under warrants from the Grand Lodges of Kentucky and Ohio. On December 2d, 1718, Vincennes, Lawrenceburg, Veray, Rising Sun, Madison, Charleston, Brookville, Salem, and Corydon Lodges met at Corydon, and organized the Grand Lodge. The first communication was held at Madison, Jan. 12th, 1818, and the constitution adopted Jan. 14th. During the anti-masonic crusade in 1828–30, the order fell into the background, and in 1834 the Grand Lodge opened with the representatives of but four Lodges. From thirty Lodges it dwindled down to but nine. But from this period, under the zeal of Mason, Sheets, Smith, Morris, Carter, and others, the order prospered, and now there are over 350 Lodges under its jurisdiction. In Nov. 1846, the Grand Chapter was organized. In 1856, the Grand Council of Royal and Select Masters was organized. In 1854, the Grand Commandery was organized.

Induction.—Used when the Master is conducted to the Oriental Chair of King Solomon. The term is found in the system of the Illustrious Order of the Cross.

In hoc signo vinces (*In this sign thou shalt conquer*).— The motto of the Knights Templar.

Initiated.—Received into a society by proper ceremonies.

Inner-Guard.—An officer placed at the inner door of the

142   *I. N. R. I.— INTERDICTED.*

Lodge, to prevent improper intrusion, receive the brethren, candidates, etc.   ❧

I. N. R. I.—Tit. ab.: Jesus of Nazareth, King of the Jews. This was the inscription placed upon the cross on which the Saviour of mankind was crucified. The term is in use in Templar system.

Insect Shermah.—There is a legend among the Jews that the stones of the Temple were made into proper form by a worm called Samir, and that the stones reached the Temple of their own agreement, and angels directed the placing together. The word signifies a hard stone. According to masonic accounts, the worm is called the *insect shermah.* However, it may be stated that this legend among the Jews is accepted by but few.

Insignia.—Badges of distinction among officers. The square, triangle, circle, compasses, level, plumb, designate the position of the wearer.

Instruction Lodges.—The proficiency of the brethren in the ceremonies of the order may be vastly improved by attending these Lodges. It is only by great care and attention that the discipline required in the ceremonies can be properly discharged. The benefit arising from such instruction is obvious to all Masons. In England, great attention is given to Chapters of Instruction.

Instruments.—The instruments of the Lodge are the Setting-maul, Square, Rule, Level, and Plumb.

Intendant.—The term originated from the Intendant who was placed at the Temple.

Interdicted Masonry.—As the principles of Freemasonry have ever been antagonistic to Romanism, and has always been found upon the side and connected with Christianity, in principle, doctrine, and practice, it will be no matter of astonishment to the reader to learn that numerous edicts and interdictions have been thundered against it at various times, and its members subjected to

INTERESTING.

all kinds of corporal punishment and death, by the powers of the Catholic Church. Annexed is a list where Freemasonry has been interdicted and prohibited, with the date, during the 17th century:

Russia, 1731–'94–'97.	Vienna, 1743.
Holland, 1735–'37.	Canton of Berne, 1743–'70–'82.
Paris, 1737–'38–'44.	Austrian States, 1742–'64.
Sweden, 1738.	Turkey, 1748.
Hamburg, 1738.	Spain, 1751.
Geneva, 1738.	Naples, 1752–'75.
Roman States, 1739–'51.	Dantzic, 1763.
Portugal, 1739–'42–'76–'92.	Aix-la-Chapelle, 1779.
Florence, 1739.	Morocco, 1784.
Marseilles, 1742.	Basle, 1785.

Interesting Forms of Prayer (*Knights of Malta*).—In "Parkes's Library of the English Fathers" are two forms —one of prayer and one of thanksgiving—for the delivery of the Island of Malta from the Turk. They are found in full on pp. 519 to 535, in the volume of Liturgical Services of Queen Elizabeth, title as follows:

1565. A FORME to be evsed in Common praier every Wednesdaie and Fridaie, within the citie and Dioces of Sarum; to excite al godly people to praie vnto God for the delivery of those Christians that are now inuaded by the Turke. London: Jhon Waley, n. d. Quarto.

1565. A SHORT FORME OF THANKESGEUVING TO GOD for the delyuerie of the Isle of *Malta* from the invasion and long siege thereof by the great armie of the Turkes, both by sea and lande, and for sundry other victories lately obtained by the Christians against the saide Turkes, to be vsed in the Common praire within the province of Canturburie, on Sundayes, Wednesdaies and Fridaies, for the space of six weekes next ensuinge the receipt hereof.

Set forthe by the Most Reverend Father in God, Matthew, by Goddes Prouidence, Archebyshop of Canterburie,

144   *IOWA — IRISH.*

Primate of all Englande, and Metropolitane. London: Wyllyam Seres, 1565.

There is still one other form of 1566, of same tenor.

1566. A FOURME to be used in Common Prayer every Sunday, Wednesday and Fryday throughout the whole Realme: to excite and stirre all godly people to pray vnto God for the preseruation of those Christians and their Countreys that are nowe inuaded by the Turke in Hungary or elsewhere.

Set foorth by the Most Reuerende father in God, Mathewe, Archbyshop of Canterbury, by the aucthoritie of the Queen's Maiestie. Jugge and Cawwood.

Iowa.—The Grand Lodge of Missouri granted authority for a Lodge at Desmoines, on 20th November, 1840. On February, 1841, a Lodge opened at Bloomington, and in October, 1842, a Lodge was opened at Dubuque. In January, 1844, the Grand Lodge was formed at Iowa City. On the 8th June, 1854, the Grand Chapter was opened. On the 6th January, 1864, the Grand Commandery was organized. The Grand Council was organized in 1857.

Ireland.— Of the early Masonry of Ireland little is known. In 1729, the Grand Lodge was formed. In 1809, the 33d degree, Ancient and Accepted Rite, was organized, under the authority of the Supreme Council of South Carolina, N. A. In 1820, the Rite of Misraim was organized. The Grand Chapter, Grand Commandery, and Supreme Grand Council are embraced within the Grand Lodge.

Irish Chapters.—Organized in Paris in 1730, and proposed to introduce a form of the Scottish Rite, but signally failed.

Irish Masonry.—A political system introduced in 1735, and consisted of three degrees: Irish Master, Perfect Irish Master, and Puissant Irish Master. It had especi-

*ally as its object the restoration of the Pretender to the crown of England.

Ish Chalzeb.—The hewers of stone in the Syrian quarries were called *ish chalzeb*.

Ishmael.—The son of Hagar, who was driven to the wilderness by Sarah, wife of Abraham.

Ish Sabal.—The remnants of the Old Canaanites, in all 70,000, employed as men of burden in the work of building the Temple.

Italy.—In 1733, Lord Charles Sackville introduced Masonry at Florence, by authority of the Grand Lodge of England. The order rapidly increased, and exerted a great influence. In 1738, Pope Clements XII. interdicted the order, and introduced a system of persecutions against it. In 1776, the interdiction was removed by the efforts of Queen Caroline. In 1805, Ancient and Accepted Rite was organized at Milan. In 1809, the Grand Lodge was organized. During the interval, between 1814 and 1860, the order almost ceased to live, the persecutions having been renewed. In 1861, Bro. Joseph Garibaldi organized a Grand Lodge at Palermo. At present the order is flourishing.

J.

Jachin.—One of the pillars at the entrance of King Solomon's temple. In the dome of Wortsberg, in the entrance to the chamber of the dead, on the chapter of the column is written *Jachin*, and on the shaft the word *Boaz*.

Jackson, Andrew.—Seventh President of U. S., born in South Carolina, March 15th, 1767, died at Nashville, Tenn., June 8th, 1845. The life of this illustrious patriot and statesman is too voluminous for our pages, and as it is within the reach of all persons, we give only such history

146 JACKSON—JACOBINS.

of his masonic life that we find. In 1822 and 1823, he was Grand Master of Masons in Tennessee.

Jackson, James, Maj.-Gen.—Born in Devonshire, England, 21st Sept. 1757, died at Washington, D. C., 15th March, 1806. He came to America in 1772, and read law at Savannah, Ga. In July, 1782, Gen. Wayne selected him to receive the keys of Savannah from the British upon their evacuation. In 1778, he was appointed a brig.-general of Georgia militia, and was wounded in the engagement of Ogeechee. He was at the siege of Savannah in Oct. 1779, and at the battle of Blackwater in 1780. Gen. Andrew Pickens made him his brigade-major in 1781. He participated in the siege of Augusta in June, 1781. He filled an important post in the Southern revolutionary struggle. In 1778, he was elected Governor of Georgia, but declined to serve. He was one of the first representatives of Georgia in Congress after the organization of the Federal Government, and from 1792 to 1795, a member of U. S. Senate. About this time he was made a major-general. He assisted in framing the Constitution of Georgia, and from 1798 to 1801, was their Governor, when he was again chosen U. S. Senator. In 1785, in King Solomon's Lodge, at Savannah, which had commenced its work under an old oak-tree in 1733, and belonged to the *Modern*, we find his first Masonic Records. In July, 1785, he proposed that they form themselves into the *Ancients*, which was done. In 1786, when the Independent Grand Lodge was formed, he was elected Dep. G. Master, and the following year elected Grand Master, which he held until 1789.

Jacobins.—A religious order of St. Dominic, so called in France from the situation of their principal convent at Paris. Second Jacobins in French history, a political party that took a prominent part in the French Revolution. Both were fashioned after the masonic system, but had no connection with it.

Jacobites.—A religious order of Christians of Syria, organized in the 6th century by Jacob Baredzi. Second, a party in England, that adhered to the dethroned monarch James II. and his descendants. They have no relation to Freemasonry.

Jacob's Ladder.—Jacob was the younger son of Isaac. He bought the birthright of his brother for a mess of pottage. Esau, on receiving a knowledge of this, resolved to slay his brother. His mother informed Jacob of this, and desired him to retire to Mesopotamia, to her brother Laban. Isaac obtained a knowledge of the affair, and directed Jacob to go to Padanaram and marry one of his uncle's daughters. He departed, and in the second day of his journey lighted on a place called Luz, on account of the multitude of almonds and hazels that grew there. Here, at night, he lay himself down to rest, under the open sky, with a stone for a pillow. In a dream he saw a *ladder*, whose foot stood on the earth, and its top reached into heaven, and the angels of God ascended and descended upon it. Above the top of it stood the Lord God Almighty, and assured him that he was the God of his fathers, Abraham and Isaac, that he would give him and his seed the land of Canaan for their inheritance, and render them as numerous as the sand upon the sea-shore. Waking from his sleep, Jacob erected a monument, and called the place Bethel. The use of Jacob's ladder is known to every Mason. The rounds in it are represented as Faith, Hope, and Charity.

Jael.—The wife of Heber, the Kenite. When Sisera had been defeated, he alighted from his chariot, hoping to escape the Israelites. He asked hospitality of Heber's household, Heber being absent, which was granted. He then betook himself to repose, and while in deep sleep Jael drove one of the tent nails through the temples of Sisera. The nail of Jael is referred to in a high masonic degree.

148 JAH—JERICHO.

Jah and *ehyeh, asher, elijeh.*—I am that I am; are the incommunicable names of God. It was not used in primitive times. The modern Jews' Jehovah, Jero, Jao, Jahah, Jaon, Jaod, and even Judah, seem to be all pronunciations of Jehovah.

Jansenists.—A sect who followed the opinion of Jansen, Bishop of Ypres, in the seventeenth century. They were celebrated for the contest they maintained against the Jesuits, whom they overcame. This was a secret religious order of Catholics.

Japheth.—The elder son of Noah. To reward the covering of his father's nakedness as he lay drunk, his father blessed him, saying, God would enlarge and persuade him, and make him to dwell in the tents of Shem, and render the offspring of Canaan his servants.

Jedediah.—Anderson states that a Jewish tradition holds that King Hiram has been the Grand Master of all nations. That on completion of the Temple, finding that the Great Architect had inspired Solomon above all men in the world, he yielded the pre-eminence to Solomon. Jedediah—which is rendered the beloved of God.

Jehoshaphat.—The name is taken from Jehovah, and Shaphat, meaning Christ, and to judge. When the elements of scattered Masonry were gathered together, it was held that the Lodge was in the vale of Jehoshaphat. All nations are to be gathered together into the valley of Jehoshaphat, according to the prediction of Joel, in the great day of judgment.

Jehovah.—The Scripture name of Supreme Architect of the Universe. The Jews avoid the pronunciation of the name, and use Adonai in place. The Jewish idea is, that in the world to come the name of God will be both read and written, with divine permission. The Hebrew name is יהודה.

Jericho.—The masonic legend regarding Jephtha may

be summed up as follows : The Ephraimites had conspired to overthrow Jephtha, and even encamped around a certain pillar. The Ephraimites being defeated, they retreated. Jephtha, in order to intercept them, placed guards on the banks of Jordan, and gave them a countersign. And when an Ephraimite attempted to pass the guard, said: Art thou an Ephraimite? and if he said nay, he commanded him to say Shibboleth; and he said Sibboleth, as he could not pronounce it right. Then they took and slew him; and history records, in Judges, that forty-two thousand perished that day from the sword of the Gileadites.

Jerusalem (*Habitation of Peace*).—It is held that it was formerly Eden, of which Melchisedek was king. Jerusalem is first mentioned when Adoni-zedek, the king, entered into an alliance against Joshua. After Joshua's death, the Judahites took it and set it on fire. After that the Judahites, Benjaminites, and Jebusites dwelt in it. At a later period David conquered the mountain of Zion from the Jebusites, and fixed his abode here, and called it City of David. He replaced the covenant, and built an altar on the threshing-floor of Araunah, where the angel stood who threatened Jerusalem with pestilence. David was not able to build a temple to the Lord on account of the wars, but the Lord, through Nathan the prophet, promised to appoint a place for his people. The promise made David was fulfilled by Solomon building the Temple on Mt. Moriah.

Jesuits (*Society of Jesus*).—It was founded by Ignatius Loyola, a Spaniard, in 1534, when he and Francis Xavier, and four other students, found themselves laboring together for the conversion of unbelievers. The first principle was implicit obedience to the Holy See. Pope Pius III. confirmed the order in 1540. They appear to have taken their system of mysteries from the Egyptians. The Popes granted the Jesuits greater indulgence than any

150
JESUITS—JEWELS.

other of their subjects. It soon became powerful in intrigue with all crowned heads and governments; but having lost its original ideal, it soon became a viper nest of assassins and treason hatchers.

Jesuits of St. Jerome.—A religious order, organized in 1363, by Giovanni Calombina, of Vienna, of extremely ascetic habits in its origin. It had no connection with Freemasonry, yet it assumed some of its forms.

Jewels.—We herewith annex a list of the jewels worn by the officers of the respective orders of Freemasonry.

Masters' Lodge.

W. Master—Square.

P. Master—Compass opened on a quarter circle.

S. Warden—A Level.

J. Warden—A Plumb.

Secretary—Cross Pens.

Treasurer—Cross Keys.

S. Deacon—Square and Compass, with Sun.

J. Deacon—Square and Compass, with quarter Moon.

Stewards—A Cornucopia.

Master of Ceremonies—Cross Swords.

Tyler—A Sword.

Grand Lodge.

Grand Master—A Compass, at a quarter circle, with medallion of Sun.

P. G. Master—Same, with Triangle.

D. G. Master—A Square.

S. G. Warden—A Level.

J. G. Warden—A Plumb.

G. Secretary—Cross Pens.

G. Treasurer—Cross Keys.

G. Chaplain—Holy Bible.

G. Marshal—Scroll, with Crossed Swords.

G. Standard Bearer—A medallion Banner.

JEWELS. 151

G. Sword Bearer—A Sword.
G. Steward—A Cornucopia.
G. Deacon—A Dove, with an Olive Branch.
G. Pursuivant—Sword and Trumpet, crossed.
G. Tyler—Crossed Swords.

Royal Arch Chapter.

M. E. High Priest—A Miter.
King—A Level, with a Crown.
Scribe—A Plumb, with a Turban.
Captain of Host—Triangular Plate, with figure of a Soldier.
Principal Sojourner—Triangular Plate, with figure of a Pilgrim.
Royal Arch Captain—A Saber.
Master of Veils—A curved Sword.
Treasurer—Cross Keys.
Secretary—Cross Pens.
Chaplain—Holy Bible.
Steward—A Cornucopia.
Sentinel—Cross Swords.

Knights Templar.

Grand Commander—A Cross.
Generalissimo—A Square, with Paschal Lamb.
Captain-General—A Level, surmounted by a Cock.
Prelate—Triple Triangle.
S. Warden—Hollow Square and Sword.
J. Warden—Eagle and flaming Sword.
Treasurer—Cross Keys.
Recorder—Cross Pens.
Standard Bearer—Plumb and Banner.
Sword Bearer—Triangle and Cross Swords.
Warden—Square Plate, with Trumpet and Cross Swords.
Three Guards—Square Plate, with Battle-axe.

152

JEWELS—JEWS.

Royal and Select Masters.

G. Master—Trowel and Square.
Hiram of Tyre—Trowel and Level.
Commander of Works—Trowel and Plumb.
Treasurer—Trowel and Cross Keys.
Recorder—Trowel and Cross Pens.
Captain of Guard—Trowel and Battle-axe.

Jewels, Lodge.—The masonic jewels of the Lodge are the Square, Level, and Plumb.

Jewish Shekel.—This was of great antiquity among the Jews, and worth about an American half dollar. It is more than probable that a coin of fixed value was circulated in Solomon's time, but the earliest specimens that can be found are of the coinage of Simon Macaebeus, 144 B.C. On the obverse is a sacred pot of manna, and "Shekel Israel," in Samaritan characters; on the reverse, the rod of Aaron, having three buds, and the inscription, "Jerushalen Kadoshah," or Jerusalem the Holy. Every Israelite above twenty years of age was compelled to pay an annual polltax of half a shekel, as a contribution to the sanctuary, and hence called "the offering of the Lord." The consecration of the shekel to this holy purpose is undoubtedly the reason it has been held as the value of the Mark.

Jews.—The name was formed from that of the Patriarchs of Judah. During the captivity, the term was applied to all the Hebrew people. It appears that the only masonic tradition left by the Jews is that of the first degree. The second degree originated in some other locality, as the Hebrew laws were a stumbling-block to the higher studies. The priests held that the sciences were not necessary, and hence arises the want of information regarding a true idea of the Jewish Masonry.

Many Lodges do not admit Jews as Masons, alleging that they cannot accept the Gospel of John as their faith.

JOABERT—JOHNSON. 153

The Jews assert that they can be made Master Masons, as they venerate the memory of the Saints John. This is a question for each individual brother to decide. The duty of a Mason is plain, and he cannot err. Certain qualifications are required of a candidate, which he answers in the petition for membership, and a decision is made upon the report of the committee by a vote of the Lodge.

Joabert.—Companion of Solomon.

Joachin, St.—An order organized in Bernberg, in 1800, into which both sexes were admitted. They avoided dancing, and believed in the Trinity; practiced virtue, morality, and perfect friendship.

Johannite.—The term is applied to Freemasonry. Formerly Lodges were dedicated to King Solomon, but now they are dedicated to the Saints John the Baptist and the Evangelist.

John Brothers.—It appears, up to 1440, that Freemasonry flourished under the name of John Brothers. After that period the John Brothers merged into Free and Accepted Masons. There are many localities where organizations holding masonic rites and ceremonies assumed other names, but at this date Freemasonry knows but one organization, and is regular throughout the world.

Johnson, Sir John.—Son of William; born at Johnsontown in 1742. He was initiated into Masonry at London, in 1767, and soon after was commissioned Prov. Grand Master of New York by the Grand Lodge of England. He was installed in 1771. Dr. Peter Middleton was his Deputy. After the Revolution he went to Canada, where the English Government appointed him Governor-General. He died at Montreal in 1830, aged eighty-eight years.

Johnson, Sir Wm.—Was a native of Ireland. He came to America in 1735, and settled at Caughnawaugua, on the Mohawk. The Lodge at that place was chartered 23d August, 1766, and Johnson was made first Master. He

154 *JOHN—JUDAS.*

obtained the jewels in England, and presented them to the Lodge. On the 6th December, 1770, he was elected Master of "Ineffable Lodge," Albany, when he resigned the former Mastership. He died July 11th, 1774, aged sixty.

John the Baptist.—The celebrated forerunner of Christ, the son of Zechariah. He it was who baptized Christ in the River Jordan, and it was this man who, to gratify the malice of Herodias, suffered death by beheading.

Joppa.—A seaport on the coast of Palestine. From the first Crusade to the present day it has been the landing-place of pilgrims on their journey to Jerusalem. An old tradition among Masons is, that its banks were so steep that it became necessary to assist any one in getting up it. Reference is made to this city in the Mark Degree.

Joseph.—The son of Jacob. The history of this distinguished person is known to all Bible readers.

Joshua.—A descendant of Ephraim. His name was *Hoshea*, but to mark that it would render Israel safe and happy, he was called Jehoshua or Joshua. He was the companion of Moses, and governed Israel, after the death of Moses, twenty-five years.

Joshua.—The High Priest, a descendant from Seraiah, who held the dignity of High Priest when the Temple was destroyed. At the building of the second Temple, he was one of Zerubbabel's assistants.

Jubal.—One of Cain's descendants. Son of Lamech and Adar.

Judah.—Fourth son of Jacob. He recommended his brothers to sell Benjamin to the Arabian merchants, instead of killing him. Jacob gave him his last benediction, and predicted that the Messiah should be born of his line.

Judah and Benjamin.—They are the only two tribes that returned from the Babylonish captivity. What became of the other tribes is not known.

Judas Iscariot.—Why he was called Iscariot—whether

because he was *Ish-Karioth*, or inhabitant of Kerioth; or *Ish-scariota*, the man who had the bag; or *Ish-coral*, the man that cuts off; or *Ish-shokrat*, the man of reward of bribes—is mere conjecture. He was one of Christ's disciples, and a covetous man, and sold his Master for twenty pieces of silver. When Christ was condemned, he told his crime and returned the money. He attempted suicide, but the rope breaking, his body fell, burst asunder, and his bowels gushed out. Mention is made of this man in the lectures of the Templar system. Among Masons there have never yet been any Judas Iscariots who would sell the mysteries of the order for a bribe. During the antimasonic excitement heavy bribes were offered for a Judas, but none could be found so base as to betray the order.

Junior Warden.—The third officer in rank in a masonic Lodge.

K.

Kansas.—In 1854, the Grand Lodge of Missouri granted authority for opening of Lodges. In 1855, November 14th, the Grand Lodge was organized.

Kentucky.—About 1790, Freemasonry began to exert its influence in Kentucky. The Grand Lodge of Virginia granted warrants for several Lodges. On the 8th September, 1800, the Grand Lodge was organized at Lexington. On the 4th December, the Grand Chapter was organized at Frankfort. On the 5th October, 1827, the Grand Commandery was organized. On the 10th December, 1827, the Grand Council of Royal and Select Masters was erected. On the 21st August, 1852, M. P. G. C. of 32d degree was organized by Brother Mackey, of Charleston, S. C , at Louisville. Henry W. Grey was the first G. C. in C., who was succeeded by Robt. Morris, in 1858, and he by Fred. Weber, in 1859, and John H. Howe, in 1866.

156

KEYSTONE — KING.

Keystone. — The keystone is a symbol in the Royal Arch Degree. It is sometimes called the copestone. The knowledge of the arch and keystone is very ancient, as many of the ancient works of the Egyptians are found to be formed upon this principle of science.

Kilwinning. — At this place Sir Robert Bruce, of Scotland, organized the order of St. Andrew, about the 1st July, 1314, to which he added the order of Herodem. Bruce retained the right of Grand Master, and then it passed to his successor. It is supposed that Freemasonry made its start in Scotland at this place. The Ancient Mother Kilwinning Lodge is still working.

King. — The chief officer in a chapter of Holy Royal Arch Masons. He is looked upon as being the Governor of Judea at the erection of the second Temple, known as Zerubbabel.

King Henry's Questions. — *Certayne Questyons, with Answeres to the same concerning the Mysteries of Maconrye. Writtene by the hande of Kynge Henrye, the sixthe of the name, and faithfullye copyed by me, Johan Leylande, Antiquarius, by the commande of his Highnesse; they be as followethe:*

Q. What mote ytt be?

A. Ytt beeth the skylle of nature, the understandynge of the myghte that ys hereynne, and ytts sondrye wreckynges; sonderlyche, the skylle of reckenyngs, of waightes and metynges, and the treu manere of façonnynge al thynges for mannes use; headlye, dwellinges, and buyldynges of alle kindes, and all odher thynges that make gudde to manne.

Q. Where dyd ytt begynne?

A. Ytt dyd begynne with the ffyrste menne in the este, whych were before the ffyrste manne of the weste, and comynge westlye, ytt hathe broughte herwyth alle comforts to the wylde and comfortlesse.

KING. 157

Q. Who dyd brynge ytt westlye?

A. The Venetians, who beynge grate merchaundes, comed ffyrst ffrome the este ynn Venetia, for the commodytye of marchaundysynge beith este and weste bey the redde and myddlelonde sees.

Q. How comede ytt yn Engelonde?

A. Peter Gower, a Grecian, journeyedde ffor kunnynge yn Egypte, and yn Syria, and yn everyche londe whereas the Venetians hadde plauntedde maçonrye, and wynnynge entraunce yn al lodges of maçonnes, he lerned muche, and retournedde, and woned yn Grecia Magno, wacksynge, and becommynge a myghtye wyseacre, and gratelyche renowned, and her he framed a grate lodge at Groton, and maked manye maçonnes, some whereoffe dyde journeye yn Fraunce, and maked manye maçonnes, wherefromme, yn processe of tyme, the arte passed yn Engelynde.

Q. Dothe maçonnes descouer here artes unto odhers?

A. Peter Gower, whenne he journeyede to lerne, was ffyrste made, and anonne techedde; evenne soe shulde all odhers beyn recht. Natheless maçonnes haueth alweys yn everyche tyme, from tyme to tyme, communycatedde to mannkynde soche of her secrettes as generallyche myghte be usefulle; they haueth keped backe soche allein as shuld be harmfulle yff they comed yn euylle haundes, oder soche as ne myghte be holpynge wythouten the techynges to be joynedde herwythe yn the lodge, oder soche as do bynde the freres more stronglyche togeder, bey the proffytte and commodytye commynge to the confrerie herfromme.

Q. Whatte artes haueth the maçonnes techedde mankynde?

A. The artes, agricultura, architectura, astronomia, geometria, numeres, musica, poesie, kymistrye, governmente, and relygyonne.

14

158   *KING.*

Q. Howe commethe maçonnes more teachers than odher menne?

A. The hemselfe haueth allein yn arte of ffyndynge neue artes, whoche arte the ffyrste maçonnes receaued from Godde; by the whyche they fyndethe what artes hem plesethe, and the treu way of techynge the same. Whatt odher menne dothe ffynde out ys onelyche bey chaunce, and herfore but lytel I tro.

Q. What dothe the maçonnes concele and hyde?

A. Thay concelethe the art of ffyndynge neue artes, and that ys for here own proffytte, and preise. They concelethe the arte of kepyng secrettes, that soe the worlde mayeth nothinge concele from them. They concelethe the arte of wunderwerckynge, and of foresayinge thynges to comme, that so the same artes may not be usedde of the wyckedde to an euyell ende. They also concelethe the arte of chaunges, the wey of wynnynge the facultye of Abrac, the skylle of becommynge gude and parfyghte wythouthen the holpynges of fere and hope; and the uni-verselle longage of maçonnes.

Q. Wylle he teche me the same artes?

A. Ye shall be techedde yff ye be werthye and able to lerne.

Q. Dothe all maçonnes kunne more then odher men?

A. Not so. Thay onlyche haueth recht and occasyonne more than odher menne to kunne, butt manye dothe fale yn capacity, and manye more dothe want industrye, that ys pernecessarye for the gaynynge all kunnynge.

Q. Are maçonnes gudder men than odhers?

A. Some maçonnes are not so virtuous as some odher menne; but, yn the moste parte, they be more gude then they would be yf thay war not maçonnes.

Q. Dothe maçonnes love eidher odher myghtylye as beeth sayde?

A. Yea verylyche, and yt may not odherwise be; for

KING — KNIGHT. **159**

gude men and treu, kennynge eidher odher to be soche, dothe always love the more as they may be more gude. [Here endethe the questyonnes and awnsweres.]

A GLOSSARY OF ANTIQUATED WORDS IN THE FOREGOING MANUSCRIPT.

Allein, only.
Alweys, always.
Beithe, both.
Foresayinge, prophesying.
Freres, brethren.
Headlye, chiefly.
Hem plesethe, they please.
Hemselfe, themselves.
Her, there, their.
Hereynne, therein.
Herewythe, with it.
Holpynge, beneficial.
Kunne, know.
Kunnynge, knowledge.
Make gudde, are beneficial.
Metynges, measures.
Mote, may.
Myddlelonde, Mediterranean.
Myghte, power.
Occasyonne, opportunity.
Commodytye, conveniency.

Confrerie, fraternity.
Façonnynge, forming.
Odher, other.
Onelyche, only.
Pernecessarye, absolutely neces-sary.
Preise, honor.
Recht, right.
Reckenyngs, numbers.
Sonderlyche, particularly.
Skylle, knowledge.
Wacksynge, growing.
Werck, operation.
Wey, way.
Whereas, where.
Woned, dwelt.
Wunderwerkynge, working mir-acles.
Wylde, savage.
Wynnynge, gaining.
Ynn, into.

(*Freem. Mag. and Mas. Mirror.*)

King Henry VI.—This King of England was made a Mason about the year 1442. A Lodge was held in Canterbury and London in his youthful days.

King of Sanctuary.—A side degree, conferred upon Acting Past Masters of a Lodge.

Knight of Red Cross.—This order was founded when incidents that occurred in the reign of the King of Persia, Darius, and illustrates the interruptions the Jews occasioned in building the second Temple, and a history of Zerub-

160   *KNIGHT—KNIGHTS.*

babel at the Court of Persia. It is a portion of the K. T. system.

Knight of the Lilies.—Sometimes called Knight of the Lily of the Valley. It is in use in the Templar system of France.

Knight of True Light.—Organized by Baron Haus Heuiride, in 1780, in Austria, and had five degrees: Knight Novice of 3d year, K. M. of 5th year, Levite, Priest.

Knights and Ladies of Hope.—A French Adoptive degree, about the first in the line of Androgynal Masonry.

Knights of Constantine.—A side degree, conferred upon Master Masons. Constantine Perphyrogeintus is the author of this degree.

Knights of East and West.—This order originated in 1118, when the vows of secrecy and friendship were taken between eleven Knights and Birinus. The first of office is called Venerable, and represents John the Baptist. In the Ancient and Accepted Rite it is the 17th degree.

Knights of John the Baptist.—This order arose in Ireland, in latter part of 18th century, and is connected somewhat with the Templar system.

Knights of Kadosh.—30th deg. A. and A. R. Seven orders by this name exist: The Hebrews, First Christians, Crusades, Templars, Cromwell, Jesuits, and Grand Kadosh.

Knights of Malta.—This order, first known as the Hospitallers of St. John of Jerusalem, and afterward as the Knights of Rhodes, and lastly as the Knights of Malta, was organized about the commencement of the Crusades, and was a religious order, with military form and protection. A number of merchants from Amalfi, Naples, seeing the exposure and misery occasioned to the pilgrims on their journey to the Holy Land, obtained the consent of the Caliph of Egypt to erect a monastery near the Holy Sepulcher at Jerusalem, in 1048, which was dedicated to St. John

KNIGHTS. 161

the Baptist, who was their patron. They took the black habits of the Hermits of St. Augustine, and wore a cross of eight points on the left breast. The Knights were finally driven from Palestine, after a protracted struggle, and planted themselves near Cyprus, which they were compelled to surrender to superior strength soon afterward. From this point they reached the Island of Rhodes, and here established themselves for about 200 years, but were finally routed by the Turks. Castro, Messina, and other points became the headquarters, and respectively abandoned, as circumstances required, until finally, in 1530, they established themselves on the Island of Malta. In 1565, Solyman II. besieged the island and wrested it from their protection. It was during this campaign that the fortress of St. Elena was taken by the Turks; but reinforcements arriving from the Viceroy of Sicily, the Turks were defeated, and the siege raised in 15—. Napoleon I. captured the island in 1798. Paul I. of all the Russias was chosen Grand Master in this year, and he took the order under his protection. In 1800, the English reduced the island, and the headquarters of the Knights was transferred to Calowa, Sicily. In 1826, it was transferred to Ferrara by order of the Pope. In 18—, the last public procession took place at Sonneburg. The King of Belgium, Leopold, and others, were made Knights at this time. The history of the order is a living page of heroic martyrdom and self-denial in spreading the true religion among the infidels. The degree is conferred in the Knights Templar system.

Knights of St. Paul.—It was organized in 1367, in commemoration of a body of knights, at the River Affanta, who were attacked by Amureth I. and a host of Saracens. The enemy lying in ambush, waited until the knights had reached the center of the bridge, when they attacked them at both ends of the bridge. The knights, however, after

14*

162   *KNIGHTS.*

a desperate struggle, were victorious. It is known also as Knights of Mediterranean Pass.

Knights of the American Eagle.—In Texas, a military degree.

Knights of the Brazen Serpent.—This degree of the Ancient and Accepted Rite arises from the history of the serpents sent among the Israelites to punish their transgressions. Moses put a brazen serpent upon a pole, and those who had been bitten by the serpents, when they looked upon it were healed. The jewel is a cross with a serpent upon it.

Knights of the Christian Mark.—Its motto is, Christ reigns, conquers, and triumphs, King of kings, and Lord of lords. Pope Alexander instituted this order at Rome, for the protection of the Holy See.

Knights of the Dane.—A system of Adoptive Masonry, originating at Versailles in 1784, which admitted both sexes.

Knights of the Dragon.—A degree which was practiced by the Templars of Strasbourg and Lyons, in 1766.

Knights of the East.—In the Ancient and Accepted Rite system it is the 15th degree. The allegory is, that those Masons who were ready with trowel and sword to build or defend the Temple and City of Jerusalem, founded it when assistance was rendered by Darius against those who sought to prevent their accomplishing the rebuilding of the Temple. King Cyrus, upon releasing the captives, sent them under command of Zerubbabel to Jerusalem. To prevent surprise, he elected 7000 Masons, when he arrived, as a guide. At the Euphrates they were assailed by a force who sought to destroy them, but were defeated by the captives at the passage of a bridge. The Samaritans sought to impede the work of the Temple, and hence the workmen were provided with arms, so as to defend themselves against surprise. As a recompense for their

KNIGHTS. 163

fidelity, King Cyrus conferred the degree of Knights of the East upon them.

Knights of the Holy Sepulcher.—This order was instituted by St. Helena, daughter of Colyus, King of Britain, in 302. She searched for the Sepulcher and the Cross of Christ, and when she had found them, organized this order. It was purely charitable in its design, and Pope Marcellinus gave it his sanction in 304.

Knights of Three Kings.—A side degree in Masonry. King Solomon is the presiding officer. It is conferred in the presence of at least five Knights. It shows the peace and harmony that exist among Masons.

Knights Templar.—The Hospitallers of St. John of Jerusalem, after certain events took upon themselves the title of Malta. It was organized 1099. Nine gentlemen formed the society, to protect Christian pilgrims who traveled to the Holy Sepulcher. These men received the sanction and encouragement of the Abbot of Jerusalem, who assigned them a place of retreat in a Christian church, called the Church of the Holy Temple, from whence they received the title *Templars*. The religious fervor at this time was great. No less than 7000 pilgrims visited the Holy Sepulcher in 1064. The Turks, in 1065, obtained possession of Jerusalem, and organized a system of barbarity against the Christians. These outrages aroused the Christians of Europe, and the Crusades followed. In 1099, Jerusalem was wrested from the hands of the Turks by the Crusaders, and at this time the order was formed. Baldwin II., King of Jerusalem, gave them a habitation on Mt. Moriah, in 1118, and they were then termed Knights of the Temple of King Solomon, and Hugh de Perganes was chosen superior. In 1128, the Pope ordered to arrange a form of government for them. The order from this time to the martyrdom of Jacques de Molay passed through many shifting scenes, and from the latter period to the present day the order has

164 KREIDER—LAFAYETTE.

gradually gained strength in all quarters. In the United States, the order is flourishing. St. John the Almoner is the patron to whom Commanderies are dedicated. The motto is, *In hoc signo vinces.*

Kreider, Dr. M. Z.—A zealous Mason, who died in 1853, at Lancaster. He was Grand Master of Masons in Ohio, in 1848 and 1849. He was also Most Em. G. Commander of Knights Templar of Ohio, for two years. He devoted special attention to the mysteries of the Royal Arch degrees and the order of Christian Knighthood.

L.

Labarum.—The standard of Constantine the Great was called Labarum. Constantine being on the march to meet the enemy, a pillar appeared in the heavens, like unto a bow, with the inscription upon it, *" In this we conquer."* Εν. ΤΟΥΤΩΜΙΚΑ.

Labor Vivis Convenit (*Labor is useful to Men*).—In the Scottish Lodge of Nine Sisters, it is used as the device, and likewise in the Baron Hunde Templar system.

Lafayette, Marquis de.—Born at Chavagnac, Auvergne, 6th September, 1757. At the age of seventeen he was an officer in the Royal Guards. We pass over his life until 1777, when he left France secretly for America. His connection with the revolutionary struggle, and his intimacy with Washington, are known to all Americans. He was made a Mason in one of the Military Lodges, either at Morristown or Albany. He visited Lodge No. 9, Yorktown, with Washington, after the siege of that place. In 1784, on a visit to America, he presented Washington with a beautiful masonic apron, wrought by Madame Lafayette, which is now in possession of the Grand Lodge of Pennsylvania. October 21st, 1824, he visited the Grand

Lodge of Louisiana. On May 4th, 1825, he visited the Grand Lodge of Tennessee. On the 8th October, 1825, he visited the Grand Lodge of New York. On the 10th October, 1830, he visited the Grand Lodge of Tennessee. All these Lodges conferred the honor of an honorary member upon him. In October, 1830, as a token of the high esteem the fraternity held of his masonic virtues, the Grand Orient of France tendered him a public dinner. He was a great and good man, and the fraternity will ever acknowledge the memory of such patriots, soldiers, and Christians. Since writing the above, a brother has sent us the item where Lafayette was made a Mason. In a room over the bar-room of the old Freemen's Tavern, on the north side of the green in Morristown, N. J., 1777. General Washington's winter quarters were at Morristown during the winter of this year. General Washington presided in person. General Lafayette was but twenty years of age, just Washington's when he was made a Mason, 1752, twenty-five years before.

Lambskin.—It has in all ages been deemed an emblem of innocence; he therefore who wears a lambskin, as a badge of Masonry, is thereby reminded continually of that purity of life and conduct which is essential to gaining admission into the Celestial Lodge above.

Lamech.—Masonic tradition states that in the seventh age from Adam, there was born unto Methuselah a man named Lamech, who had taken unto himself two wives. The first wife, Adah, bore him two sons, whom he named, one Jabal and the other Jubal. Jabal is said to have been the originator of geometry, and Jubal the inventor of music. Zilla, the second wife, bore Tubal Cain, the workman in brass and iron. She also bore a daughter, who was the founder of the weavers' craft, whom she named Naomi.

Lamson, William.—Excellent King of Cheshire Chapter, No. 4, New Hampshire, died in Keene, November 1st,

166

LANDMARKS.

1864. He was much esteemed as a citizen and Mason. At the time of his death he was a member of the Grand Chapter.

Landmarks. — A mark fixed to designate an object. Masonic landmarks may be summed up as follows:

1. Belief in a Supreme Being.
2. The Bible, the rule and guide of all Masons.
3. Voluntary assumption of masonic authority is binding always.
4. The rites and law of the Ancient York Rite are immutable.
5. Contentions are contrary to the genius of Masonry.
6. Charity, a peculiar virtue.
7. The right of visit, absolute.
8. A candidate must be of proper age, hale and sound, and no woman or eunuch.
9. None can make Masons but legally warranted Lodges.
10. The ballot-box, an inviolable secret.
11. A petition after reference cannot be withdrawn, but must be reported and balloted upon.
12. A ballot for each degree, when demanded, an undeniable right.
13. Initiation makes a Mason, and a M. M. a member.
14. Every Mason must contribute.
15. A Lodge U. D. cannot be represented in the G. L., and its officers do not destroy their membership in other Lodges.
16. The Master and Warden must be chosen annually, and if installed cannot resign.
17. No one can be elected Master of a Lodge unless he shall have served as a Warden.
18. No appeal from the Lodge can be taken from decision of W. M.
19. Masons must be tried by *their peers.*

20. Intercourse with clandestine Lodges, a masonic offense.

21. Restoration to privileges of Masonry does not restore to membership.

22. Unaffiliating Masons are subject to masonic discipline.

23. A Lodge failing to meet for one year, gives cause to forfeit its charter.

24. Every warranted Lodge must meet in the G. L.

25. A G. L. has supreme control, within its limits, over all matters of Ancient Craft Masonry.

26. No appeal lies from the decision of the G. M. in chair.

27. The office of G. M. is elective, and filled annually.

28. A G. L. must meet at least once a year.

The above is the substance of the landmarks. Many writers differ as to the number of these marks. The Ahiman Rezon lays down the law upon these questions.

Lawrence, Henry C.—Past Grand Senior Warden of the Grand Encampment of Knights Templar of the United States, died on the 9th December, 1862, from injuries received upon the 9th of that month, in attempting to leap from a railroad car while still in motion. He was in the prime of his manhood, and in the midst of his usefulness. He was the Grand Commander of the Grand Encampment of Indiana in 1854, and again in 1857, and was Grand Senior Warden of the Grand Encampment of the United States in 1856 and 1859. He was universally respected in all the relations of life.

Laws of Masonry.—The Grand Lodge is the creative power of the laws that govern Masonry. All alterations and abrogations are determined by it, so long as it does not conflict with the old established landmarks of the order. Its rules of action are based upon long established customs and usages, and these constitute the landmarks, which are

168   *LAY—LEVY.*

unrepealable. And it is fortunate for the stability of the institution that they should not change, as they stand in the way of many innovations that would creep into the order.

Lay Brothers.—A sect in the 11th century, skilled in the arts and sciences. They were dressed somewhat differently from the other monks. The Carthusian and Cistercian orders made the first distinction.

Lazarists.—In 1632, St. Vincent de Paul founded an order under this caption at Paris. They occupied the Priory of St. Lazarist.

Lebanon.—A chain of mountains on the northern borders of Palestine. Its forests abounded with cedar-trees. It was in possession of the Phœnicians at the time the Temple was being erected, and they being skilled in felling timber, the importance of this acquisition of an alliance between Solomon and Hiram is apparent. The timbers were taken in floats to Joppa, and from there to Jerusalem.

Left Hand.—The left hand is noticed as being nearest the heart in masonic ceremonies.

Leprosy.—A disease that manifests itself upon the body with a kind of white scale. To soften the hardness of Pharaoh's heart, and show how easily his power would be weakened, Moses was commanded to put his hand into his breast, and it immediately became leprous, or white as snow; again returning it into his bosom, it became sound.

Level.—The level is one of the immovable jewels, and used by operative masons to prove horizontals, etc.

Levy.—A levy of 30,000 men of Jerusalem was employed in divisions of 10,000, and changed monthly, for felling the timbers in Lebanon: 80,000 were employed in the quarries of Judea, who were assisted by 70,000, who were styled burden-bearers, the ancient Hebrews.

LEWIS. 169

Lewis.—A name given to the son of a Mason. He had the privilege of being entered in his eighteenth year.

Lewis, Winslow, M.D.—Born in Boston, July 8th, 1799. He was a graduate of Harvard University, in 1819, and took his degree of M.D., 1822. Dr. Lewis's career as a physician and scientific writer has been eminently successful. He was a representative from Boston to the General Court in 1835, '53; one of the Common Council of the city in 1839; on the School Committee, 1839, '40, '41, '44, '45, '57, and '58; visitor of the U. S. Marine Hospital, 1856 to 1862; one of the overseers of Harvard University from 1856 to 1862, and lately re-elected for six years more; consulting physician of the city, 1861; counselor of the Massachusetts Medical Society; a member of the American Medical Society of Paris. For three years he was Grand Master of Masons in Massachusetts, viz., in 1855, '56, and '60, and has been at the head of several orders in Masonry, a recapitulation of which would sound strange and forthputting to the uninitiated, and give no information to those who are. He has for many years been a fervent and active friend to that noble institution. The reason of his becoming a Mason was singular. In the days when the fraternity were abused without mercy and persecuted to the utmost, he saw an advertisement in a paper of one of the furious Anti-Masons, Avery Allyn—a name now almost forgotten—that on a certain day, in 1829, he would deliver a lecture, showing up the weakness and hypocrisy of Freemasonry, and its dangerous tendency. The doctor was led by curiosity to go and hear him; and the very sophisms this arch-enemy of the brotherhood used, and the abuse he heaped upon many of them, who were men without fear and without reproach, made him a convert on the other side, and he became a Mason in Columbia Lodge, then under the government of Joshua B Flint, M.D., since G. M. of the Grand Lodge of Massachusetts. In 1861, he

15

LIBATION — LIBERTINE.

was elected President of the New England Historic-Genealogical Society. To this society and Harvard University he made several large donations of valuable books.

Brother Winslow Lewis was initiated in Columbia Lodge, November 3d, 1830; passed January 6th, 1831, and raised February 3d, 1831. He is a member of St. John's Lodge, St. Paul's Chapter, Council of Royal and Select Masters, Boston Encampment, Grand Chapter, Grand Encampment, affiliated member of the "Loge Clement-Amitie," at Paris, and honorary member of Pythagoras Lodge, No. 86, at New York. He has been Senior Warden of St. John's Lodge, High Priest of St. Paul's Chapter, Commander of the Boston Encampment, Grand King of the Grand Chapter, Grand Master of the Grand Encampment of Massachusetts and Rhode Island, Grand Generalissimo of the Grand Encampment of the United States, Grand Master of the Grand Lodge of Massachusetts, a Trustee of the Grand Charity Fund, and a Trustee of the Masonic Temple. This enumeration does not evidence the extent of his official services, as he has also held many subordinate stations.

Libation (*to pour out*).—The Hebrews and Greeks practiced libations. It was a solemn act. In the K. T. system libations are used.

Libertas.—In mythology of the Greeks and Romans was a goddess worshiped with peculiar veneration. By the former she was invoked by the synonymous title Eleutheria. At Rome, her most famous temple, Gracchus, was situated on the Aventine Mount. She was represented under the figure of a woman holding in one hand a cap, the symbol of Liberty, and in the other a dagger. Libertas is used in the higher masonic degrees.

Libertine.—Dissolute, under no restraint to law or religion, a debauch in lust and lewdness. The ancient laws forbid the making of such persons Masons.

Light.—The term is used figuratively; as those without the pales of Freemasonry are considered in darkness as to its mysteries and ceremonies, and hence the candidate is brought from darkness or ignorance to true masonic light, or a practical knowledge of its usefulness and design.

Linear-Triad.—A geometrical term, used at one time on the floor-cloths of the Royal Arch, and had reference to sojourners; and the three stones, on which prayer was rendered on discovery of the Great Word that was lost.

Lobdell, Charles.—Born 24th June, 1834, in the City of New York. He sent in his petition for membership to St. John's Lodge, No. 3, Bridgeport, Connecticut, 21st June, 1865. He was initiated 12th July, 1865, passed 2d August, 1865, and raised 28th September, 1865. He was passed in Jerusalem Chapter, No. 13, same place, 10th November, 1865, acknowledged 24th November, 1865, and exalted December 1st, 1865. He received the degrees of Cryptic Masonry in Jerusalem Council, No. 16, 7th January, 1867. Brother Lobdell was the masonic editor of the *La Crosse Democrat*, and filled the station with marked ability. His course of usefulness terminated with the frightful railroad accident at Angola, New York, December 18th, 1867. The memorial services were held at La Crosse, by Lodge No. 45, in honor of his being the first masonic editor in Wisconsin.

Lodge.—The refuge of Masons. The place to practice the ceremonies of Masonry, hear the Bible teachings, squaring their actions, and compassing them within the bounds of prudence. Three members form a Lodge; seven members perfect it. It is formed by three, improved by five, and perfected by seven.

Lodge Furniture.—Holy Bible, square, and compass.

Lodge of Good Council.—A Lodge which worked in the Latin language, and organized in Warasdin, Hungary, 1791.

172 LODGES—LUTHER.

Lodges of Lebanon.—These Lodges were skillfully arranged, and order was perfect. The Apprentices went in squads of seven, and the Fellow Crafts in squads of five.

Lodges of Tyre.—Two Lodges of Super Excellent Masters, six Lodges of Excellent Masters, eight Lodges of Grand Architects, and sixteen Lodges of Architects composed the Lodges in the quarries of Tyre. Three classes of Masters existed in thirty-six Lodges; these were called Menatzchim; together with seven hundred Lodges of Ghiblimites, who were superintended by Hiram Abiff, the Grand Master.

Lord's Prayer.—Our Father who art in heaven, Hallowed be Thy name. Thy kingdom come. Thy will be done, on earth as it is in heaven. Give us this day our daily bread. And forgive us our trespasses as we forgive those who trespass against us. And lead us not into temptation, but deliver us from evil. For Thine is the kingdom, and the power, and the glory, forever. Amen. Used in the Christian Orders of Knighthood.

Louisiana.—In 1790, the Grand Lodge of South Carolina granted a warrant for a Lodge. In 1794, a warrant was issued from the Grand Orient of France. In 1800, the Grand Lodge of Pennsylvania granted a warrant. On the 11th of July, 1812, the Grand Lodge was organized. On March 5th, 1813, the Grand Chapter. On the 16th of February, 1856, the Grand Council of R. and S. Masters; and on the 4th of February, 1864, the Grand Commandery of Knights Templar was organized.

Lowton.—In the French Rite, the son of a Mason is called "Lowton," and among the English he is called "Lewis," and is entitled to the privilege of being initiated three years before his majority.

Luther, Martin.—The great Reformer was a Freemason. We give Luther's own statement regarding it, as given to his son, Martin Gotlieb, Christmas Eve, in 1536,

LUTHER

173

at his home in Wittenberg, who requested him to sing "that strange song" which he had learned when he got his *medal.* It was the "Mark Master's song." (From the *Nat. Freemason.*)

"During the night of Christmas, 1520, when I had just fifteen days before publicly burned the Pope's Bull, I sat in my study weary and heavy laden. For the bold act, while it drew my stanch friends closer around me, alienated also at the same time the more timid multitude, and I was left to a certain degree alone. Melancholy and a certain sad feeling crept over me, as the twilight passed away and darkness threw a still greater gloom over the study. But at last I aroused myself, and said, 'A helper will be raised up for me—I will have faith in this my darkest hour.' Hardly had I come to this conclusion when there came a rap at the door, and three men entered, and congratulated me upon the bold steps I had taken that day. The eldest inquired of me whether I had considered the danger and risk I ran in thus bidding defiance to the whole papal power. I replied that I did not stop to consider the probable peril in my way as long as I knew myself in the path of duty.

"'Well said, Brother Martin,' replied Hans Stauffenacher, who had until then stood behind his companions; 'well said! the Guild has long thought that in thee we have found a kindred spirit, and is now ready therefore to throw its protection around thee. What sayest, art willing to become one of us ?'

"I answered, 'But I am not skilled in the using of the implements of thy calling; how can I then become one of you ?'

"A quiet smile played around Hans's mouth, as he said, 'Ah! there are other implements we use than thou wot'st of, implements which thou wilt find that thou canst handle with a master's hand. In the mean time, for thy satisfaction, thou mayest know that many honorable knights and princes have been made free of the Guild, and they knew far less of its implements than thou. We have departed from our ordinary usage in making thee this offer, but the Guild thought that thou wert not only a kindred spirit, but a master, in carrying out the great principles of true and untrammeled religion. It is therefore ready to extend to thee its privileges and help.'

15*

174 LUTHER.

"After a few seconds of hesitation I answered, 'Hans, I have known thee for many years, and am fully convinced that thou wouldst not lead me into any place where, in consistence with my calling, I ought not to go. But thy coming to-night seems to have been a special providence, for only a few minutes ago did I feel cast down in my soul, when the thought that God would raise me up help strengthened me. I am ready, therefore; lead on, I'll follow.'

"My three companions then conducted me to the Guildhall, where I was, with many and ancient ceremonies, introduced among the brethren of the Mystic Tie. Judge my delight and surprise when the first thing I beheld in the room was a beautiful copy of the Holy Bible, the book which I ever acknowledged the rule for our faith. I was then told that that volume lies ever open in the hall, to be consulted by the brethren.

"Rapidly was I advanced that night from step to step, until I reached the grade which entitled me to wear this medal, and know the meaning of its mystic inscription. That night I learned, too, the beautiful song which you seem to like so much.

"Months passed by, and the multiplicity of my labors did not permit me to meet my new brethren more than once, but they did not forget *me*.

"On the 2d of April I was waited upon by three of the Guild, who presented me, in its name, with this medal, which I was now entitled to wear. They at the same time earnestly entreated me always to wear it when abroad, and particularly when surrounded by enemies.

"A few days after this interview I left for Worms, to defend myself before the Diet. I need not now repeat to you what took place there. You and your mother have made me relate it so often that you ought to know it by heart. Enough, the trial over, I set out on my way home. Twice before I reached Moera, the residence of my grandmother, was I accosted by riders in rather a suspicious way, but each time, when they caught sight of the medal, they stopped short, asked permission to examine it, cast meaning glances at one another, then shook hands with me and left.

"When we came near the castle of Altenstein I perceived one of the riders who had been left with me become sad and cast

LUTHER.

175

down; at the same time he always kept close to my side. I entered into conversation with him, and endeavored to ascertain the cause of his grief. At first he remained silent, until it appeared that the words forced themselves to his lips, when he said: 'Thy danger, Brother Martin, makes me sad. I felt a great struggle between my duty to keep concealed the order of the Holy Vehme, and the duty which I owe to thee as a brother of high degree in the Ancient Guild. I have, however, given notice to the Guild, of which the noble Elector, Frederick the Wise, is an illustrious member.'

"When I had heard the cause of his uneasiness, I replied: 'Be not troubled on my account; the Lord will raise up help for me.' Hardly had the words escaped my lips, before a troop of savage-looking riders, perfectly disguised, rushed down upon us, tore me from my horse, and, tying my hands, one of them took me up behind him, while the rest surrounded him, and then they all galloped off in a westerly direction. Rapidly they now continued to ride through the woods, nor did they slacken their pace until the Wartburg was in sight.

"When they drew up before the bridge of that strong castle, they lifted me gently from my horse, and led me into the hall of the castle. When arrived there, and I looked around me, I found assembled many of the noblest knights of the empire, and among them the venerable elders of the Guild: and each of them, as well as those who were my late captors, wore upon their breast a medal similar to the one you now see.

"I was then told that my enemies had succeeded in arousing the Vehme against me; that that day the fearful summons was to be delivered; but the man who had charge of it, seeing the medal upon my breast, and having himself received one like it, informed the Elector of the pending summons, and the place where it was to be delivered. The trusty brethren of the *Mark*, when informed thereof, immediately assembled to rescue a brother from the clutches of the dark tribunal. You have seen how they executed their task.

"'But now, my brother, you must change your garb, and assume that of an esquire, until this storm shall have blown over.'

"My theological and literary labors, in which I engaged during

176 MACBENEC—MAGNON.

my stay at the Burg, were much facilitated by the lore which I found among the brethren of the Guild; and the connections I formed during that time have continued to be among the dearest and most profitable I have made in life. I shall ever bless the day when I became free of the Guild."

" And I, too, will join the Guild when I shall be big enough," exclaimed little Martin Gotlieb.

In 1759 was buried in Dresden, Martin Gotlieb Luther, a lawyer, and worthy member and P. M. of the Guild, and the silver *Mark* was placed in his coffin, in accordance with his last request.

M.

Macbenec. Heb.—*He lives in the Son.*

Made.—A term used in masonic ceremonies. It is a solemn ceremony, and should be seriously contemplated.

Magians.—A caste of hereditary priests among the Persians and Medes. The name comes from *mog* or *mag*, meaning priest in the Phlevi language. Zoroaster was the great reformer of this order. Its two principles, good and evil (Oromastes and Arimones), divided the dominion of the world into alternate periods, during its predestined existence of 12,000 years. The book Zendustra contains the doctrines. The fire worshipers of Persia still hold them in great reverence. There were three degrees: Harbeds, Mobeds, Dester Mobeds. The order was organized in Florence in 1700.

Magnon, Bernard Pierre.—Marshal of France and Grand Master of the Grand Orient, died May 29th, 1865. He was made Grand Master Jan. 11th, 1862, by decree of the Emperor Napoleon, in which he prohibited the Grand Orient from electing its principal officer. In 1864, when the Emperor, at the instance of Marshal Magnon, by another decree restored to them the right of election, so

MAHER — MARIA. 177

much had the Marshal endeared himself to the craft by the able manner in which he had discharged the functions of the office, that he was unanimously elected Grand Master, and continued in discharge of the duties of G. M. until his death.

Maher-Shalal-hash-Baz (*He hasteth to spoil*).—A son of Isaiah. It is used in the Knights Templar.

Mallet.—An implement used by operative masons. Freemasons use it in the moral sense, to divert the character from the vices and superfluities of life.

Manna.—The name given to the miraculous food upon which the Israelites were fed for forty years. It is a symbol of the degree of Holy Royal Arch Masonry. The manna that fed the children of Israel fell every morning. They called the food *manna*, for the particle *man* in our language is the asking of a question, what is this? (*man-hu*). Moses answered, "that it was the bread that the Lord had given them to eat." A miraculous event was that "he who gathered much had nothing over, and he who gathered little had no lack."

Manual Workers.—Those Masons who perform their work by the aid of the Manual.

Manuscripts.—All the ancient masonic manuscripts were called out in 1717, by G. M. Payne; and in 1721, Dr. Anderson prepared from them the Book of Constitutions. A valuable collection by Nicholas Stone was burned through the mistaken zeal of some brethren, who imagined that the printing of anything that related to Masonry might prove an injury to the order. (See Ant. Mas.)

Maranatha.—A form of anathematizing among the Jews. It signifies that the Lord will come to take vengeance.

Maria Theresa.—In 1764, Maria Theresa, then Empress of Austria, seeing the usefulness of Freemasonry, applied to the Grand Master for the honors of Masonry. The Grand Master declined to initiate her, or inform her

MARK—MARTINISTS.

of the secrets of the order. This so enraged Maria that she interdicted the order in Austria.

Mark.—The Tyrian Signet which King Hiram sent to King Solomon. It is the medal of a Mark Master, and in the form of a keystone.

Mark Masons.—By this degree each Mason was known and distinguished by the Senior Warden at the erection of the Temple, and the disorder and confusion that might have attended the work was prevented. If defects were found, the overseers, by this degree, found where the fault originated.

Mark of Cain.—Some mystery attends the punishment of Cain. " Cain went from the presence of the Lord," probably means that he was exiled to some place where the Almighty still manifested himself to his fallen creatures. God, however, gave him the assurance that he was to be protected against the wrath of his fellow-man. This assurance was not, as falsely translated, a mark set upon him; but by appointing a sign or token, which he might understand as a sign or token, that he should not perish by the hands of another. Some authors hold that the mark set upon him was the circle of the sun rising on him, or Abel's dog that was always with him, or that it was a long horn growing out of his forehead.

Mark of the Craft.—It was the custom of the ancient workmen to make their mark upon their work, and for this reason each had a separate design, to designate who had performed it. At Strasbourg, the mark of the mason is found upon the stone and brick. Many of these marks were put upon them in the quarries by the hewers, as they prepared them for the builder's use.

Martinists.—This order was organized by Marquis de Martin, about 1780, and devoted to philosophy, good works, religion, art and science, and regeneration of mankind. It had ten degrees : the E. A. P., F. C., M.,

MASONIC. 179

Ancient M., G. Architect, and Master of the Secret; this formed the first temple. The Prince of Jerusalem, Knights of Palestine, and Knights of Kadosh, the second temple.

Masonic Anniversaries.—St. John the Baptist's, the 24th day of June; St. John the Evangelist's, the 27th day of December; St. Andrew's day, 30th November; St. George's day, 23d April.

Masonic Dates.—

Ancient Craft,	add 4000 to the Christian era.		
Scotch Rite,	" 3760	"	"
Royal Arch,	" 530	"	"
Royal and Select Master,	" 1000	"	"
Knights Templar,	sub't 1118 from	"	"

Ancient Craft Masonry dates from the creation of the world.

Scotch Rite dates from the creation, but uses the chronology of the Jews.

Royal Arch Masons date from the commencement of the second Temple, 530 before Christ.

Royal and Select Masters date from the completion of Solomon's Temple.

Knights Templar date from organization of the order, 1118.

Masonic Emblems.—

The Templar's Cross is prefixed to the signatures of the officers of G. C.

The Passion Cross is prefixed to Knight Templar's signature.

The Patriarchal Cross is affixed to the signature of G. E. C. of U. S.

The Cross of Salem is prefixed to the signature of G. M. of K. T.

The Delta is used in the H. R. A. C.

The ☐ is used as an abbreviation for the word Lodge.

180

MASONIC.

The ⊟ is used in the plural for Lodges.

The Tau Cross is a distinction between the Apron and Jewel of the R. A. M.

The Water Triangle represents the Kind God of the Egyptians.

The Fire Triangle, as the Egyptians' Angry God.

The Six-pointed Star, as the Sacred number.

The Seven-pointed Star, used as a Perfect Godhead.

The Seven-pointed Star, with a circle around it and a dot in the center, used as the Sacred number.

The letter G. symbolizes Geometry.

The Lambskin, used by the E. A. as an emblem of purity.

The 24-inch Rule is the working tool of the E. A.

The Common Gavel, as a mark of authority.

The Charter, as the authority for opening and holding a Lodge.

The Shoe, as a Contract. An Israelitish custom.

Jacob's Ladder, symbolizing Faith, Hope, Charity.

The Bible, as the gift of God.

The Compasses, to limit the desires.

The Square, to perfect the actions.

The Masonic Pavement represents the ground-floor of the Temple.

The Level is an Immovable Jewel.

The Plumb   "   "   "

The Rough Ashler represents the crude material.

The Perfect Ashler, finished work.

The Trestle Board, the place for laying out the work.

The Bible upon Staves, with circle within, a point within a circle.

The Globe upon a Column, Architecture.

The Trowel, cementing Brotherly Love.

The All-seeing Eye, the God who protects and seeth all.

The Sun, the post of the W. M.

MASONIC—MASSACHUSETTS. 181

The Moon, one of the lesser lights.
The Seven Stars are the Sacred numbers.
The Sword, Justice.
The Ark, Place of Refuge.
The Anchor, Place of Safety.
The 47th Problem of Euclid, Science.
The Hour-Glass, Human Life.
The Scythe, Time.
The Three Steps, Youth, Manhood, Age.
The Coffin, Mortality.
The Chisel, Discipline.
The Penny, Wages.
The Chair, the Oriental Seat.
The Altar, Offering.
The Burning Bush, Holiness.
The Ark and Cherubim, Divine Presence.
The Rod of Aaron, Superiority.
The Ear of Corn, Plenty.
The Bee-Hive, Industry.
The Pot of Incense, Sacrifice.
The Mallet, Correction.
The Skull and Bones, Reflection.
The Mark, a Signet.
The Blazing Star, emblem of Deity.

Masonic Monitor.—A book with the regulations, charges, emblems of the order, etc.

Masonic Year.—The masonic year commences on June 24th. It dates from the creation of the world, thus showing 4000 years more than the calendar A. D.

Mason-Marks.—The degree of Mark Mason was only conferred upon those who had proved their skill in the use of the plumb, level, and square.

Mason's Wind.—A breeze that cooled and refreshed the laborers who worked upon the Temple.

Massachusetts.—Freemasonry was introduced here on

182 MASTER — M'FEE.

30th July, 1733, by the Grand Lodge of England appointing Henry Price Provincial Grand Master of New England. He organized the first Lodge at Boston, at that date, under the name of St. John's Lodge. On the 30th Nov. 1752, the Grand Lodge of Scotland granted a warrant under the title of "St. Andrews," to be held in Boston. This Lodge, in connection with the Military Lodges of the British army, established the "Massachusetts Grand Lodge," 27th Dec. 1769. Thus were two Grand Lodges established. During the occupation of Boston by the British troops in 1775, the two Grand Lodges were suspended. On the 6th Oct. 1779, the Grand Lodge of Mass. granted a warrant for a Military Lodge to the officers of the Federal army. On the 5th of March, 1792, a reconciliation was effected between these two Grand Bodies, and on the 9th June, 1792, they met and organized the Grand Lodge of Ancient Free and Accepted Masons of Mass. Since that event, prosperity has attended the order in this State.

Master of a Lodge.—A Master of a Lodge must have been previously appointed or *served as a Warden*, before he can be elected as a Master of a legally warranted Lodge. This is an important landmark of the order.

Master Mason's Daughter.—A degree of Adoptive Masonry, conferred upon the wives, sisters, and daughters of Master Masons. The 11th and 12th chapters of St. John are read as Scripture lessons.

Master of Ceremonies.—An officer to whose charge are left the ceremonies of the order. He must see that everything is well and duly prepared.

Mature Age.—The ancient landmark in reference to this is, that no one's son be made a Mason before he becomes of mature age. Under date of Dec. 27th, 1729, the English Constitutions made the age of 25 as the proper maturity. (See "Lowton.")

McFee, Wm.—District Deputy Grand Master of Grand

Lodge of Louisiana, was born in Philadelphia, Pa., April 14th, 1817. At an early age he removed to Jefferson County, Miss. In 1844, he removed to Morehouse Parish, La., where he resided up to the time of his death. He was the first Clerk of the District Court in that parish, and continued in that office until 1854. He represented the parish in the Legislature in 1860 and 1861. He was made a Master Mason in Union Fraternal Lodge, No. 53, in 1846. In the same year he assisted in forming Mount Gerizim Lodge, No. 54, at Bastrop, and was for many years W. M. of that Lodge. He also for many years occupied the station of M. E. H. Priest of Living Stone R. A. Chapter, No. 16 (alternating with M. E. Comp. A. S. Washburn). As a Mason, he was universally beloved and respected for his uprightness, integrity, and zeal. In 1865, he was appointed D. D. Grand Master for the 7th district, which had been vacated by the death of his intimate friend and brother, A. S. Washburn. He died on Jan. 29th, 1867, in the 50th year of his age, and was interred with all the honors conferrable by the fraternity, of which he was so long a worthy and zealous member.

McGreggor, Alexander.—One of the representatives from Lexington Lodge, in convention, Sept. 8th, 1800, and one of the committee to draft an address to the Grand Lodge of Virginia, detailing the necessity for a separation. He was chairman of the first Grand Lodge Committee. On Oct. 13th, 1801, he opened the Grand Lodge. He occupied a number of important positions in the Grand Lodge, and was looked upon as a zealous, worthy Mason. He died in Sept. 1805.

McMurdy, Rev. Robert, D.D., LL.D.—Passed through his academical and collegiate course with great credit, before reaching the age of eighteen. He immediately went abroad on an educational tour, and returned to his native country at the expiration of two years, and before reaching

184   M'MURDY.

his majority. He was immediately called to the superintendence of an educational institution, and obtained great celebrity as an educator, East and West. He resigned the Presidency of the Church College of Kentucky in 1859. In the ministry of the Protestant Episcopal Church, he has occupied a highly respectable position. He was elected repeatedly to the trusteeship of the Diocesan Institute, and of the General Theological Seminary, New York City. For twelve years, and as long as he was in his own diocese, he was one of the four clerical delegates to the General Convocation, when such men as Henry Clay and Adam Beatty were elected among the lay delegates. He was secretary of the diocese for many years. He is a member of several national societies of North and South America, and received from several colleges the degree of A. M., and that of D. D., the same year, from his Alma Mater (Jefferson), and from the Church College, of New York; and that of LL. D. from the Northwestern University. He has also served as Chaplain of the House of Representatives, Washington. Twenty-seven years ago he became a Freemason, when twenty-one years of age, and he and Grand Master Hubbard were dubbed Sir Knights the same evening and in the same asylum. He has been elected, and officiated, to high positions in several Grand Lodges and Grand Chapters, and for nine years has served in the office of second importance in the Grand Encampment of the United States. Dr. McMurdy was the founder and the editor of the *National Freemason*, the great and able expounder of masonic truths and doctrines for the masonic world. Dr. McMurdy is a connection of the McMurdys and Napiers of England and Scotland, and of an old revolutionary and masonic stock, and he does no discredit to his blood. His works will live after him, educationally, clerically, and masonically. He is doing for this country and century what Dr. Oliver did for England and his generation, and may well be styled the Dr. Oliver of America. May his days be long as his usefulness has thus far been.

Mediterranean Pass.—Referred to in Templarism.

Melchisedek.—Priest of the Most High God, and King of Salem, who went forth to meet Abraham on his return from pursuit of Chederlaomer and his allies, who carried away Lot captive. It has historical connection with the order of High Priesthood, Illuminati, and Asiatic Brothers, 5th degree.

Melek-Melek (*A King*).—A term used in the French Rite.

Melita or Malta.—An island of the Mediterranean. It seems to have had its name from being *Melit,* a place of refuge to ancient Tyrians in their voyage to Carthage and Spain. About A. D. 63, Paul was shipwrecked on this island. The people imagined Paul a God, because he shook a viper from off his hand without receiving any hurt from it. It is stated that no venomous beasts live in that country, and the earth is carried away to cure the bites of serpents. In 828 A.D., the Mohammedan Saracens seized it. In 1090, Roger of Sicily wrested it from them. In 1530, Charles, Emperor of Germany, seized it and gave it to the Knights of Rhodes, whom the Turks had driven seven years prior from Rhodes.

Membership.—The membership are those Master Masons who were concerned in the organization of the Lodge, and regularly raised to the sublime degree of Master Mason therein; those who have affiliated and been elected by unanimous vote. No Mason can be a member of more than one Lodge at a time.

Memphis Rite.—Organized in Paris, in 1839, by E. N. Moulted, and I. A. Marconis. It had 96 degrees. In 1860, it was reorganized and reduced to 30 degrees, and is now called the Grand Orient of France. The degrees are:

186 MENATZATHIUM — MEXICO.

APPRENTICE.

Symbolic Masonry.

1. Apprentice.
2. Fellow Craft.
3. Master.

Scotch.

4. Past Master.
5. Elect of Nine.
6. Knight of Sacred Vault.

Philosophic.

7. Knight of Sword.
8. Knight of the East.
9. Knight of Rose Croix.

Hermetic.

10. Knight of Kadosh.

FELLOW CRAFT.

11. Knight of Philothean.
12. Hermetic Philosopher.

Grecian.

13. Philosopher of Somothrace.
14. Child of Lyre.
15. Orphic Doctor.

Egyptian.

16. Lodge of Pyramids.
17. Knight of Phœnix.
18. Gage of the Labyrinths.

Scandinavian.

19. Knight of the Rainbow.
20. Skald.

MASTER.

21. Scandinavian Knight.

Chaldean.

22. Priest of Mathias.
23. Guard of the Three Fires.
24. Elect of Truth.

Indian.

25. Master of Staka.
26. Grand Kawi.
27. Doctor of Veda.

Synthetical.

28. Knight of Theosophist.
29. Magiian of the East.
30. Master of Grand Works.

Menatzathium.—Overseers of the people when engaged upon the work of the Temple.

Mesmerian Rite.—Instituted by Mesmer in 1784.

Metal Tools.—The materials for the Temple were prepared in the forests of Lebanon and the plains of Zeredatha. They were finished and numbered, so that in putting the building together the sound of the axe, hammer, or tools of iron did not mar the peace of the place.

Mexico.—Nothing is definite of the introduction of Freemasonry into Mexico. The opposition of the priesthood has kept it in the background. Where superstition and darkness reign, Freemasonry is discarded. A Grand Lodge was organized in the City of Mexico, in 1826.

MICHIGAN—MINNESOTA. 187

Michigan.—The Grand Lodge of Michigan was reorganized June 24th, 1826, at Detroit. In 1827, it was incorporated. In 1829, by a resolution, masonic labor was suspended. In 1840 and 1841, the Grand Lodge was reorganized. In 1858, the Grand Council of Royal and Select Masters was organized. On June 15th, 1857, the Grand Commandery was established.

Middle Chamber.—The Holy of Holies was termed the Middle Chamber, and was on an elevated position.

Millnor, James.—Was born in Philadelphia, June 20th, 1773. In 1794, he located at Norristown, as an attorney. He was made a Mason in No. 31, Norristown, August, 1795, and served as Master of this Lodge. In September 6th, 1796, he connected with No. 3 of Philadelphia. While a member of No. 31, he helped revise the Regulations of the Grand Lodge. He was elected Senior Grand Warden in 1798-9—1800. He was Dep. G. Master in 1801-1803. In 1805, he was elected Grand Master, and filled the office until 1813. The Grand Chapter then being subservient to the Grand Lodge, he acted in the capacity of High Priest of the G. L. of Pa. The old Masonic Hall was built and dedicated June 24th, 1811, while he acted as Grand Master. Between 1814 and 1816, he was ordained deacon, presbyter, and finally, rector of St. George's Episcopal Church, N. Y. After his resignation of Grand Master, the G. L. elected him G. Chaplain of the G. L. of New York. He died in New York, on the 8th April, 1845, aged 73 years.

Minerva.—A Latin goddess, said to have sprung into full armor from the forehead of her father Jupiter. She was worshiped as the Goddess of Wisdom and Patroness of Industry and Arts. Freemasons use this statue as a symbol of wisdom.

Minnesota.—The Grand Lodge of Ohio granted the first warrant for a Lodge to be held in this State, August 4th, 1829, to be opened at St. Paul. On October 12th,

188 MISCHEHAN — MISRAIM.

1850, the Grand Lodge of Wisconsin granted a charter for a Lodge at Stillwater. In 1852, the G. L. of Illinois granted a warrant for a Lodge at St. Anthony. On February 23d, 1853, the Grand Lodge was organized at St. Paul. On December 19th, 1859, the Grand Chapter was organized. In 1866, the Grand Commandery of Knights Templar was organized.

Mischehan (*Tabernacle*).—Sacred word in French Rite.

Mischpheveth (*Most Powerful*).—Sacred word in the French Rite.

Mischtar (*Fountain*), sometimes used *Mishpat.*—Sacred word of French Rite.

Misraim, Rite of.—Organized about 1800, in France, and composed of ninety degrees, and divided into four classes: Symbolic, Philosophical, Mystical, and Cabalistic.

Symbolic. Series I.	22. Architect.
1. Apprentice.	23. Grand Architect.
2. Fellow Craft.	24. Architecture.
8. Master.	25. Apprentice Perfect Architect.
4. Secret Master.	26. Fellow Craft " "
5. Perfect "	27. Master " "
6. Master through Curiosity.	28. Perfect Architect.
7. Master in Israel.	29. Sublime Scotch Master.
8. English Master.	30. " " " of He-
9. Elect of Nine.	roden.
10. " " the Unknown.	31. Royal Arch.
11. " " Fifteen.	82. Grand Axe.
12. " " Perfect.	88. Sublime Knight of Election.
18. " " Illustrious.	
14. Scotch Trinitarian.	*Philosophical.* Series II.
15. " Companion.	34. Knight of Sublime Election.
16. " Master.	85. Prussian Knight.
17. " Panisière	86. Knight of the Temple.
18. Master of Scottish Rite.	87. " " Eagle.
19. Scotch Elect of Three.	88. " " Black Eagle.
20. " Master of Sacred	39. " " Red "
Vault of James VI.	40. " " White "
21. " Master of St. An-	41. " " East.
drew.	42. Commander of the East.

MISSISSIPPI. **189**

43. Grand Com. of the East.
44. Arch. of the Sovereign Commanders of the Temple.
45 Prince of Jerusalem.
46. Sov. Prince Rose Croix of Kilwinning and Heroden.
47. Knight of the West.
48. Sublime Philosopher.
49. Chaos the First, Discreet.
50. "   " Second, Wise.
51. Knight of the Sun.
52. Sovereign Com. of the Stars.
53. Sublime Philosopher.
54. Key of Masonry, 1st degree.
55. "   "   2d   "
56. "   "   8d   "
57. "   "   4th   "
58. Freemason Adept.
59. Sovereign Elect.
60. Sovereign of Sovereigns.
61. Master of Lodges.
62 Very High and Powerful.
63. Knight of Palestine.
64. "   " the White Eagle.
65. Grand Elect Knight Kadosh.
66. " Inspector Commander.

Mystical. Series III.

67. Benevolent Knight.
68. Knight of the Rainbow.
69. "   " Banner.
70. Very Israelitish Prince.
71. Sovereign Prince Talmudim.
72. "   " Zadkim.
73. Grand Hiram.
74. Sov. Grand Prince Hiram.

75. Sov. Prince Hassidim.
76. " Grand Prince Hassidim.
77. Grand Inspector Intendant Regulator of the order.

Cabalistic. Series IV.

78. Sov. Prince of 78th degree, Chief of 4th Series.
79. Supreme Tribunal of Sov. Princes.
80. Supreme Consist. of Sov. Princes of 80th.
81. Supreme Consist. of Sov. Princes of 81st.
82. Council of Sov. Princes of 82d.
83. Sov. Gr. Trib. of Ill. Gov. Prince of 83d.
84. Council of Sov. Princes of the 84th.
85. Council of Sov. Princes of the 85th.
86. Council of Sov. Princes of the 86th.
87. Sov. Prince Constituent Gr. Master of the order for 1st Series.
88. Sov. Prince Constituent Gr. Master of the order for 2d Series.
89. Sov. Prince Constituent Gr. Master of the order for 3d Series.
90. Absolute Supreme Powerful Grand Master of the order.

Mississippi. — Freemasonry was introduced into this State by warrant from the Grand Lodge of Kentucky, in 1817. The Grand Lodge was organized July 27th, 1818, at Natchez. On May 18th, 1857, the Grand Chapter was

190

MISSOURI.

organized, at Vicksburg. On January 18th, 1856, the Grand Council of Select Masters was organized.

Missouri.—The first Masons of Missouri were merchants, who obtained their gavel at Philadelphia, Pennsylvania. They were made in the old French Lodge, No. 73, on the registry of the G. L. of Pa. In 1807–8, a warrant was granted by the G. L. of Pa. for a Lodge at St. Genevieve, Territory of Louisiana, and registered as Louisiana Lodge, No. 109; Otho Strode being its first Grand Master, Dr. Aaron Elliot and Jos. Hertick, Wardens. This was the first Lodge established in the State of Missouri. In 1811–12, Geo. H. Dodge presided over the Lodge. During the war with England, the Lodge declined, and ceased to work in 1816–17. In 1826, a petition was made for a Lodge in St. Genevieve, by the name of Tucker Lodge, which was chartered as No. 13, and continued in existence until 1831. In 1809–10, a charter was granted by the G. L. of Pa., to Brethren in St. Louis, to open St. Louis Lodge, No. 111. In 1820, the G. L. of Indiana granted a charter for a Lodge at Jackson, Cape Girardeau Co. On October 8th, 1816, the G. L. of Tennessee granted a charter to Jos. Pileper, Thomas Brady, Jeremiah Conner, and others, for a Lodge at St. Louis, Missouri Territory, as Missouri Lodge, No. 12, and signed by Robt. Searcy, G. M. On October 6th, 1819, a charter was granted for a Lodge in Herculaneum, as Jachin Lodge, No. 25, and signed by Oliver Hays, G. M. The same year and date a charter was granted to Benj. Emmons and others, for St. Charles Lodge, No. 28, at St. Charles. On the 22d February, 1821, in pursuance of an invitation sent by Missouri Lodge, No. 12, to the Lodges in the State, the following Lodges were represented in the hall of No. 12, in St. Louis, and resolved to organize a Grand Lodge for Missouri. William Bates, Nathaniel Sims, and Edward Bates were the committee to prepare a constitu-

MISSOURI.

191

tion, etc. They then adjourned to meet on 23d April following. On the 21st April, 1821, a convention was held in No. 12, and represented by Missouri Lodge, No. 12, Edward Bates; Jachin, No. 25, William Bates; J. Jones, I. Craige, T. Grinsley, W. H. Pocake, J. H. Penrose, W. G. Pelus, W. H. Hopkins, and H. Hardin. The proceedings of the meeting at St. Louis, February 22d, were adopted. On the 24th April, the following Lodges were represented: Missouri, No. 12; Jachin, No. 25; St. Charles, No. 23. The election of Grand officers resulted in choosing Thomas F. Reddick, G. Master; James Hermerly, S. G. W.; William Bates, J. G. W.; Archibald Gamble, G. Treas.; William Renshaw, G. Sec. Adjourned to May, 4th inst., when they met in a Baptist church at St. Louis, and the officers installed, and the G. Lodge consecrated by Thompson Douglass. "1822, committee appointed by Missouri R. A. Chapter and Missouri Lodge, No. 12, for procuring funds to build a hall." "1823, application for permission to initiate a man who 'had lost an arm,' another 'very much deformed,' *rejected.*" "August 31st, 1823, Grand Master N. B. Tucker lays the corner-stone of a Presbyterian church." On the 29th April, 1825, a special meeting was held. It was ascertained that Bro. General Lafayette, an officer of the Revolution, was in the city. On motion, he was elected an honorary member of the Grand Lodge. The committee waited upon General Lafayette, and he, together with his son, Bro. George Washington Lafayette, were received by the Lodge standing. Bro. Geo. W. Lafayette was then elected an honorary member. April 5th, 1830, the Grand Lodge ten years in existence, and representing four Lodges. April, 1832, resolved that one communication be held annually. October, 1833, Grand Lodge adjourned to meet in Columbia, Broome County, 2d December, 1833. October 2d, 1837, after an absence of four years, Grand Lodge returned to

192   *MITER — MOLAY.*

St. Louis. October 21, 1839, Grand Lodge laid corner-stone of Court-house, St. Louis. October 6, 1840, nine chartered and one Lodge U. D. represented. On 12th September, 1842, Grand Lodge purchased 1350 acres of land in the County of Marion, for establishing an institution and asylum for the education of indigent Masons. The purchase included the Upper Marion College. In February, 1843, Grand Lodge chartered by the State. May 9th, 1842, G. L. laid corner-stone Methodist Episcopal church. June 24th, 1845, Masonic College dedicated. March 18th, 1847, G. L. locates the Masonic College at Lexington. May 18th, 1847, G. L. lays corner-stone of Masonic College. May, 1849, G. L. meets in Booneville. June, 1852, G. L. again meets in St. Louis, permanently, and 64 Lodges represented, and 104 paid their dues.

Miter.—The covering worn by the High Priest of the Chapter; upon it is engraved "Holiness to the Lord."

Mithras.—The Grand Deity of the Persians, supposed to be the Sun or God of Fire, to which they paid adoration as the emblem of divine essence. The Romans also raised altars to the honor of this Deity, with the inscription, *"Deo Soli Mithræ,"* or *"Soli Deo unicto Mithræ."*

Mock Masons.—A term applied to a number of disappointed, worthless Masons, who were defeated in obtaining positions of honor in the order, in 1747, and made a mock procession to the grand feast.

Molay, James de.—The last Grand Master of Knights Templar. He was admitted into the order about 1265, and, on the death of William de Beaujean, was elected Grand Master. The power of the Templars created much jealousy and many enemies. In 1307, an order was issued for the general arrest of the Knights Templar throughout France. They were accused of heresies and revolting crimes. Fifty-seven were burned in 1311, and the Council of Vienna abolished the order in 1312. Molay, with his companion,

MONAD—MORGAN. 193

Guy Dauphin, of Auvergne, and Hugh de Pevalde, were detained in prison until 1313, at Paris, where their trial took place by the Commissioner of the Pope; and concurring to the accusation of being Templars, were condemned to perpetual seclusion. Molay and Guy, under hope of freedom, retracted their confession, and were burned as relapsed heretics, at Paris, 18th March, 1314.

Monad.—The real atom of nature, or the elements of things. Every monad is a living mirror, representing the universe according to its particular point of view, and subject to no regular law.

Montana.—The Grand Lodge was organized January 24th, 1866, at Virginia. This is about all the information that we have been able to get regarding this State.

Montanists.—A sect of the second century, so called after Montanus, of Phrygia. He was an original priest of Cybele, and announced himself, about the year 160, as a prophet who was to convey Christianity forward to perfection. He taught a permanent extraordinary influence of the Paraclete, manifesting itself by ecstasies and visions; assigned to doctrines and rites a subordinate significance, and demanded the most rigid ascetism as a manifestation of purity. Besides the ordinary fasts and mysteries, he prescribed annual and weekly ones. Its members were designated *psychii*, while they themselves assumed the name of *preumatii*.

Morgan, William.—Was born in Culpepper Co., Va., in 1766; adopted the trade of a stone-cutter; opened a store in Richmond in 1819; removed to Toronto, Canada West, shortly afterward, and commenced the business of brewing, and from thence to Rochester, New York, about 1825. The press of Canandaigua denounced him as a swindler and dangerous man, August 9th, 1826, which notice the two Batavia journals copied. In July, 1826, he was imprisoned for debt, and September 10th, tried for theft,

17

194 *MORIAH.*

and discharged. On the 12th September, he was released from prison by his friends upon payment of the debt. At this time it was noised about by his friends that he was engaged in publishing the secrets of Masonry (a republication of "Jachin and Boaz," which first saw light in England); and to give his intended work coloring, and excite interest and sympathy, his friends induced him to secrete himself, while they published "that he had been abducted upon his release from *durance vile*, and carried to Fort Niagara, and secured in the magazine of the fort, then unoccupied by the United States; that he was kept there for a period, and ultimately removed from thence to an unknown place." What became of him is shrouded in mystery. Governor Clinton, and a number of prominent Masons, offered handsome rewards for those engaged in the affair, and finally appointed a committee to investigate it. The rigid investigation thus instituted by the executive resulted in establishing that the so-called abductors of Morgan were his friends and chosen companions. The result of this circumstance gave prestige to the Anti-Masonic party organized in 1819. This party was vigorously pushed and stimulated by political tricksters, not out of sympathy for Morgan, nor love of morality, but for power and corruption. Old issues had become threadbare under their lashings, and new hopes sprang up in waging an anti-masonic war. Such men as the Ritners, Grangers, Sewards, Spencers, Stevenses and others, arrayed themselves on the side of the Canada brewer. A noted fact is, that all these men, except Mr. Stevens, regretted their early mistake, and he alone still adheres to his notable fame, earned in Pennsylvania, as the "Inquisitor-General" of the Anti-Masonic party.

Moriah.—One of the hills of Jerusalem on which the Temple was erected. It is supposed to be the same place where Abraham went to offer up Isaac. The Jews themselves believe that the altar of burnt-offerings stood upon the very site where the patriarch proposed to offer up his son as a sacrifice. It was also the spot where Jehovah appeared to David.

Morris, Robert.—Born August 31st, 1818. Was made a Mason at Oxford, Mississippi, in March, 1846, and Grand. Captain of the Grand Lodge of Mississippi, in 1849–50. Received the Royal Arch Degree, at Lexington, Miss., in 1848, and Council Masonry, at Natchez, Miss., 1849. Received Encampment Masonry, at Jackson, Miss., 1850; Scotch Rite, including S. P. R. S., 1855; Rite of Memphis, including 90°, 1864; and order of High Priest, in 1854. As a masonic author, Bro. Morris has earned enviable reputation. In 1849, he wrote a prize tale, entitled "Triumphs of Innocence." "Lights and Shadows of Freemasonry," in 1852; "Life in the Triangle," in 1853; "Two Saints John," in 1854; "Code of Masonic Laws," in 1855; "Masonic Reminiscences," in 1857; "History of Freemasonry in Kentucky," in 1859; "Tales of Masonic Life," in 1860; "Prudence Book of Freemasonry," in 1860; "Masonic Martyr," and "Miniature Monitor," in 1861; "Masonic Poems," in 1864; "Masonic Almanacs" for 1860–1–2–3–5; "Rosary of Eastern Star," in 1865; "Masonic Ladder," in 1866; and "Manual of Eastern Star," same year; "Guide to High Priest," in 1865; "Lodge at Mystic," in 1862; "Dictionary of Freemasonry," in 1867; "Special Helps to W. Master, Sec., and Sen. Warden," in 1866. As a publisher, Bro. Morris issued all the works of Dr. George Oliver, in American edition, together with those of De Vertal, Towne, Mackey, Creigh, Arnold, and other writers of notoriety in masonic lore. The total number of his publications and republications have reached seventy-four volumes. He was Grand Master of Kentucky in 1858–9. He received the degree "Doctor of Laws" in the Masonic University of Kentucky, in 1860. He was Grand

196

MOSAIC—MYSTIC.

Lecturer of Tennessee in 1850–1, and of Kentucky in 1853–4; and known extensively for his masonic orations and addresses, a general writer for secular papers and literary magazines. He has thus far spent a useful life to the craft, and done much to place Freemasonry before the world as a great moral, charitable, and religious institution. Few men have labored for the good of Masonry as Robert Morris, and few men have the universal esteem of the craft as he. He resides at present (1867) at Lagrange, Kentucky. At the present time Brother Morris is on a visit to the Holy Land, securing information and relics of ancient Masonry.

Mosaic Pavement.—This was before the porch of King Solomon's Temple. The figures in the pavement represented historical and other subjects.

Moses.—The lawgiver of Israel, was of the tribe of Levi, and son of Amram and Joshabad. The name means "drawn out of water." He was learned in the wisdom and mysteries of the Egyptians, which were held sacred and kept from the eyes of the people. Moses taught the Israelites the divine worship and knowledge of the true God.

Most Excellent.—The High Priest of a R. A. Chapter.

Most Worshipful.—Presiding officer of the Grand Lodge.

Mount Libanus.—A range of mountains of Lebanon. Materials for the Temple were obtained at this place. This mount is referred to in the degree of Perfect Master.

Movable Jewels.—The movable jewels of the Lodge are the compass, square, level, and plumb.

Music.—This art was invented by Jubal, one of Cain's descendants.

Mustard Seed.—Zingendorf is said to be the author of this rite, which he introduced in 1739. The parable of the mustard seed contains the history of this degree.

Mystic Mason.—This rite has three degrees, to wit:

Mystic E. A. P., Mystic F. C., Mystic M. M. It originated about 1800, and was speculative and alchemistical.

Mystic Tie.—The brethren of the Mystic Tie are found throughout the world. The term is applied to Masons in general.

N.

Naharda.—A brotherhood founded by the Jewish captives in bondage at Naharda, on the Euphrates. The mysteries were lost when the captives were released, or established by Zerubbabel in Jerusalem.

Name of God.—It is stated that the name of God was never known until communicated to Moses, and was forbidden to be used except in the Tabernacle before the Mercy-seat, by the High Priest, and that but once a year. The two principal names of the Supreme Being used in the Bible are the Hebrew names, Jehovah and Elohim.

Names of Knights of Elect of Nine.—Here are the Illustrious Knights of the 11th degree, or Sublime Knights elected, with the tribes over which they presided:

    1. Joabed, tribe of Judah.
    2. Stockin,   "   Benjamin.
    3. Terrey,   "   Simeon.
    4. Morphyr,   "   Ephraim.
    5. Alycuber,   "   Manasseh.
    6. Dorson,   "   Zebulun.
    7. Kerain,   "   Dan.
    8. Berthemar, "   Asher.
    9. Tito,   "   Naphthali.
  10. Terbal,   "   Reuben.
  11. Benechard, "   Issachar.
  12. Taber,   "   Gad.

Napoleon Masonry.—Consisted of Knight Commander, Grand Elect, Secret Judge, Perfect Initiate, and Knight

198   *NARBONNE—NEHEMIAH.*

of the Oaken Crown. Established at Paris, in 1816. These degrees were all complimentary of Napoleon.

Narbonne Rite.—In 1780, it was established at Narbonne, and consolidated with the Philoletheans, of Paris, in 1784. It had three classes: 1st. E. A. P., F. C., M. M. 2d. Perfect Master, Elect, Architect, Sublime Scotch, Knight of the Sword, Knight of the East, Prince of Jerusalem. 3d. 1st Captain Rose Croix, 2d do., 3d do. The object was devotion to the occult sciences.

Neakoras.—Warder of the Holy Place.

Nebraska.—The Grand Lodge of Illinois granted a warrant for the first Lodge in Nebraska, 3d October, 1855, to be held at Bellevue. On the 26th May, 1857, the Grand Lodge of Missouri granted a charter for a Lodge at Nebraska City. On the 3d June, 1857, the Grand Lodge of Iowa granted a charter for a Lodge at Omaha City. On the 13th September, 1857, the Grand Lodge was formed at Omaha.

Nebuchadnezzar.—A Chaldean monarch of Babylon, who led the Israelites into seventy years of captivity. In Kings, Chronicles, Daniel, Ezra, Ezekiel, and Jeremiah, reference may be found to this monarch.

Nebuzar-adan.—The name of the captain of Nebuchadnezzar's guard who completed the ruins of Jerusalem. The Hebrew *Nebu* means Lord. In Persia, it is Wise.

Negative.—The term is used masonically when a name is proposed for membership and the ballot shows that it is rejected. The constitution forbids visitors and members from discovering who the parties are that opposed the applicant, and inflicts the penalty of expulsion from the order of the informer, and forbids the admission of the visiting brother from visiting the Lodge at any time afterward.

Nehemiah (*Comforted of Jehovah*).—Three persons of this name occur in the Bible. Nehemiah the son of Azbuk, ruler in Bethzur, took a prominent part in building the

NEKAM—NEW. **199**

wall of Jerusalem, and was among those who accompanied Zerubbabel from captivity. The Jews were much distressed by Sanballat, Lobich, and Geshem. Nehemiah repaired the wall in fifty and two days.

Nekam-Nekam (Hebrew, *Vengeance*).—Allusion is made to the term in some of the high degrees.

Neophyte.—In ancient mysteries, the candidate.

New Hampshire.—The first Lodge chartered in this State was by authority of St. John's Lodge, Boston, Mass., June 24th, 1734, to be held at Portsmouth. On the 17th March, 1780, the Massachusetts Grand Lodge granted a warrant for a Lodge at Portsmouth. On the 8th November, 1781, the Grand Lodge of Massachusetts granted a warrant for a Lodge at Cornish. On the 5th March, 1784, a warrant was granted by same Grand Lodge for a Lodge at Keene. On the 8th July, 1789, the Grand Lodge was organized at Dartsmouth. In 1819, the Grand Chapter was organized. In 1824, various orders of Knighthood were organized. A State Grand Encampment of Knights Templar was formed 13th June, 1826, under a warrant of dispensation from Henry Foule, Dep. G. Master of General Grand Encampment of the United States, dated May 27th, 1826, held at Portsmouth. In 1860, there being a constitutional number of Commanderies, a State Grand Commandery was organized in June.

New Jersey.—In 1729, the Grand Lodge of England appointed Daniel Coxe Provincial Grand Master, under date of 5th June, 1730. On the 18th December, 1786, the Grand Lodge was organized at New Brunswick. On the 30th December, 1856, the Grand Chapter was organized at Burlington. On the 26th November, the Grand Council was organized. On the 14th February, 1860, the Grand Encampment of Knights Templar was established.

New Templars.—This order was composed of five degrees, to wit: Initiate; Intimi-Initiate; Adepti; Orientalis

200 NEW—NORTH.

Adepti; Magni Johannes Apostolic Adepti. This order appeared in France about 1800.

New York.—In 1737, the Grand Lodge of England granted a warrant for a Provincial Grand Lodge. On the 9th June, 1753, George Harris was appointed Prov. Grand Master. In 1760, John Johnson was appointed to fill the same position, but he having taken sides with the British, the Lodge was suspended. On the 5th September, 1781, the Grand Lodge of England appointed William Walter Prov. Grand Master. In 1783, the Grand Lodge was formed, William Walter resigning his letters patent, and the Grand Lodge electing Wm. Levek to preside. On the 14th March, 1778, the Grand Chapter was organized. In 1807, the Grand Council was organized. On the 18th June, 1814, the Grand Commandery was established.

Nile.—Masonic tradition states that Euclid taught the Egyptians to build walls to prevent the overflow of the Nile, measure their lands, that each might find their own property when the Nile overflowed them.

Nil Nisi Clavis Deest.—A motto attached to the triangle of the R. A. Masons.

Nine Masters.—After the death of Hiram Abiff, nine Masters were elected, to wit: Moabon, Jachin, Boaz, Ganigham, Azariah, Joram, Ischgi, Achal, and Abed. They were elected by the order of King Solomon.

Noachidae.—The first name of Freemasons. They were the descendants of Noah.

Noachite.—See Prussian Knight.

North Carolina.—It is conceded that St. John's Grand Lodge of Mass. granted the first warrant for a Lodge in this State, October 20th, 1767, and appointed Thomas Cooper Prov. Grand Master. However, it is stated that the Grand Lodge of Scotland granted a warrant for a Lodge in 1761. In 1787, the Grand Lodge was organized at Hillsboro.' The Grand Chapter was organized in 1822,

NUMBERS—ODD. 201

and reorganized 28th June, 1847. In 1857, it withdrew from its connection with the Gen. Grand Chapter of U. S. On the 6th June, 1860, the Grand Council was organized.

Numbers.—The numbers three, and three times three, are considered by Masons as sacred numbers. In the ancient mysteries, nine was considered the most important.

O.

Oath.—The calling of God to witness; *i. e.* take notice of what we say, invoking his vengeance or renouncing his favor, if what we say be false, or what we promise be not performed.

Obelisk (*Needle or Dart*).—A lofty quadrangular monolithic column diminishing upward, with the sides inclined so as to terminate in an apex at the top. Egypt was the land of obelisks. The two largest were at Heliopolis. They were of granite, and 180 feet in height. It was a custom to place these columns before their temples, and Solomon is said to have gotten the design of the two columns at the entrance of the porch of the Temple from the Egyptians.

Odd Fellowship.—It is supposed to have originated in England in 1788, as James Montgomery, the poet, speaks of it at that time. Odd Fellow authors state "that all beyond that time is mere conjecture of proofless tradition." They were originally a society of mechanics and laborers. The motto of the order is "Friendship, Love, and Truth." After a convention held in Manchester in 1813, where several Lodges seceded from the Union order, they were styled "Independent Order of Odd Fellows." It was introduced into the United States in 1802, at Baltimore. Thomas Wildey is styled the "Father of Odd Fellowship in the United States." The higher body is styled "Encampment." The degree of "Rebekah" was stricken out by the Grand Lodge of the United States, in session at New York, in September, 1867, but, however, left it to the voluntary acts of subordinate Lodges to retain it or discard it. The order is somewhat after the system of Masonry. It is purely charitable. A fund is held for the relief of sick brethren. It is high toned, exercises great influence for good throughout the country, and is a popular institution.

Ogden, Aaron.—Born at Elizabeth, N. J., December 3d, 1756. He took a prominent part in the revolutionary war, and a favorite of Washington. He was made a Mason in one of the Military Lodges of the army. The Grand Lodge of Pennsylvania granted a charter for a Military Lodge, No. 36, September 2d, 1782, of which Ogden was Junior Warden. He was elected Governor of New York in 1812. He died in 1839.

Ohebeloah (Heb. *whom God loves*).

Ohio.—The introduction of Freemasonry into this State was through the Grand Lodge of Massachusetts. The records of the Grand Lodge were destroyed by fire in ——, and the masonic history of this State remains shrouded in obscurity. Union Lodge, Marietta, was warranted by the Grand Lodge of Massachusetts as a Military Lodge 13th February, 1776. On 8th September, 1791, the Grand Lodge of New Jersey granted a charter for a Lodge at Cincinnati This charter was surrendered in 1805, and the Grand Lodge of Kentucky granted them a warrant. In 1805, the Grand Lodge of Massachusetts granted a charter for a Lodge at Chillicothe. On the 16th March, 1804, the Grand Lodge of Connecticut granted a warrant for a Lodge at Warren. In 1804, the Grand Lodge of Pennsylvania granted a warrant for a Lodge at Zanesville. On the 7th January, 1808, a Grand Lodge was organized at Chillicothe. In October, 1816, the Grand Chapter was

OIL — ORANGEMEN. 203

organized. In 1829, the Grand Council of Royal and Select Masters. In 1843, October 24th, the Grand Commandery was established.

Oil was more generally used among the Hebrews than in our northern climate. It was extensively used as an element of consecration. Prosperity and happiness were symbolized in oil.

Olive Branch Brotherhood.—This was organized in India by Provincial G. M. Burns, on 24th June, 1845, at Bombay.

On.—One of the oldest cities in the world, situated in Lower Egypt. On is a Coptic word, signifying light and sun. The celebrated Temple of the Sun was erected here. The Egyptians worshiped the Deity as On. They worshiped the sun as the father of creation. On was no doubt the same deity as Jehovah with the Hebrews. On was the place where Pharaoh gave to Joseph a wife, Asenatti, daughter of Potipherah, a priest of On.

Ophir.—It is supposed was situated in Arabia, Africa, and East Indies, but no positive place is fixed. It was, however, famous for its gold, where Solomon's ships visited in company with the Phœnicians. Perhaps the account that gold mines still exist in Malacca, and the name *ophirs* being given them, may fix it there. Heeren observed that all the rich countries lying south on the African, Arabian, or Indian coasts were called *Ophir*.

Ophites.—Name of an early sect of Christian heretics, who emanated from the Gnostics, so called from their worshiping the serpent that tempted Eve. They considered the serpent as the father of all sciences, which, but for the temptation of our first parents, would never have been known. The term "Brothers of the Serpent" has been applied to them.

Orangemen.—The name given to the society instituted in Ireland in 1775, to uphold the Protestant religion and

204   *ORDER.*

ascendency, and for the discouragement of Catholicism. It had office bearers, secret organization, distinctive or orange color, etc. It was suppressed by Parliament in 1836. It was masonic in its character. Thomas Wilson, a clandestine Mason, originated it. Originally it had only the degree of Orangemen, then that of Mark Mason's degree, and afterward the Heroines of Jericho.

Order, Military, of Knights of the Bath.—Was instituted in England, 1399, at the coronation of Henry IV., fell into disuse in the time of Charles II., and revived by letters patent in the reign of George I. As then constituted, it consists of the Sovereign, Grand Master, and thirty-six Companions, and has seven officers: the Dean, Registrar, Gloucester King-of-Arms, who is besides styled "principal Herald of the parts of Wales and Hanover Herald," a Herald, having the title of "Blanc Coursier," a Secretary, an Usher of the Black Rod, called also "Brunswick Herald," and Messenger. Knights of the Bath were anciently distinguished by an emcrass, or scutcheon of azure silk upon the left shoulder, charged with three crowns *proper*, with the motto, "*Trois en un.*" The collar is composed of nine imperial crowns, and eight roses, thistles, and shamrocks, issuing from a scepter, all enameled *proper*, linked together with seventeen white knots. The badge is a white Maltese cross, cantoned with four lions of England (or lions *passant gardant*). On the center is a circular compartment, charged with the rose, the thistle, and the shamrock; and, when borne by a military knight, encircled by a wreath of laurel, issuing from an escroll *az.*, inscribed *Ich dien*, in letters of gold.

At the termination of the war, 1815, it was ordained that the order should thenceforth consist of three classes, viz.: seventy-two Knights Grand Crosses (G. C. B.), one hundred and eighty Knights Commanders (K. C. B.), and an unlimited number of Companions (C. B.). Twelve of

ORDER. **205**

the seventy-two Knights of the first class are nominated for civil services. They are permitted to use supporters to their arms, which are placed within the red circle of the order, edged with gold, the old motto, " Trois en un," being replaced by the Latin legend, " Tria juncta in uno."

The Arms of Knights Commanders are similar, except that they are not permitted to use supporters, and the badge pendant from their red ribbon is smaller; that worn by Companions is smaller still.—*Ex.*

Order of Danebrog.—The most ancient of the Danish orders is that of Danebrog, instituted by William II., King of Denmark, on St. Lawrence's day, 1217. To this order belongs a legend, similar to that related of Hungus and the banner of St. Andrew. Wilderman was at war with the Livonians, and on one occasion, when engaged in a desperate battle, with but a doubtful prospect of victory, a standard, bearing a white cross, is said to have fallen miraculously from heaven, which so revived the drooping spirits of the soldiers that they gained a speedy victory. This standard was called " Danebrog," "the strength of the Danes," and gave its name to the order founded in commemoration of the miracle. The badge is a cross patonce, enameled white, charged with eleven diamonds. The collar, a chain consisting of the letters W. and C. alternately, each crowned with the regal crown of Denmark; between the letters a cross, enameled white. In the C a figure of 5. The letter W refers to the name of the founder; C, to that of Christian V., by whom the order was revived in 1671.—*Ex.*

Order of Perfect Friends.—This order sprang into existence in the 18th century, among the learned Masons of Germany.

Order of Red Men.—This society originated at Fort Mifflin, in the Delaware River, between 1812 and 1814. A portion of the soldiers organized the first council fire

18

206 ORDER.

here, fortifying it with signs, grips, and passwords. On Sept. 9th, 1824, it went under the style of *Moose Deer Bros.*, and soon after took that of "Improved Order of Red Men." Tammany is the patron saint of the order. The sacred days are February 22d and May 12th, the latter being St. Tammany's day. It is a charitable organization, with a system of benefits, fashioned after Masonry in its signs, grips, etc. The Lodge is called a "Wigwam" and the different Lodges termed "Tribes." The principal officer is called "Grand Incohenee."

Order of Regenerated Franks.—This society was organized in France, in 1815, and fashioned with masonic forms. It was a political association.

Order of St. Lazarus.—A military order of religious persons, originally an association of knights for maintaining lepers in the Holy Land. Driven from Palestine in 1253, they followed St. Louis to France. In 1490, Pope Innocent VIII. suppressed the order, and united it with that of St. John, but the edict was not universally received. In 1572, they united the order of St. Mourace in Italy. In 1608 in France, with our Lady of Mount Carmel. The knights of these orders were not permitted to marry.

Order of St. Patrick.—Was instituted by George III. in 1783. It consists of the Sovereign, the Grand Master, who is always the Lord-Lieutenant of Ireland for the time being, and a certain number of Knights, each of whom has two esquires. The collar is of pure gold, formed of harps and roses placed alternately, and connected by twelve knots. In the center is a royal crown, from which depends an appropriate badge, containing the crown, the shamrock, and a cross *saltire*, like that on the banner of St. Patrick, which was "*ar. a saltire gu,*" now transferred to the Union Jack, where it is combined with the crosses of St. Andrew and St. George.—*Ex.*

ORDER — ORIGIN. 207

Order of the Century.—A kind of Masonry which admitted both sexes, and sprung up in 1735 at Bordeaux.

Order of the Elephant.—Said to have been instituted by King Athelstane. The badge was a small elephant. The degree was only conferred upon noblemen.

Order of the Passion.—Was founded in 1380 by Richard II. of England and Charles VI. of France, for the recovery of the Holy Land from the dominion of the Saracens. The Knights wore white mantlets, on which was sewed the badge of the order—a plain red cross, fimbriated with gold, and having at its intersection an eight-foiled compartment, composed of four pointed leaves in cross and four round ones in saltire, edged *or*, and charged with an Agnus Dei *proper.—Ex.*

Order of the Star.—The Order of the Star was founded by John, King of France, in 1351, in imitation, it has been said, of the Order of the Garter, recently instituted by Edward III. The ceremony of installation was originally performed on the Feast of the Epiphany, and the name bears allusion either to the Star of the Magi or to the Blessed Virgin, who, in many ancient hymns and prayers, is addressed as "Star of the Sea," "Ave Maria Stella!" An old French writer says it was instituted by Hugh Caput "pour son heureus aunement."

Orders of Architecture.—Tuscan, Doric, Ionic, Corinthian, Composite.

Ordo ab Chaos.—"Order out of Chaos."

Oregon.—The Grand Lodge of California introduced Freemasonry into this State, by a charter for a Lodge at Oregon City, in 1849. On the 16th August, 1851, the Grand Lodge was formed.

Oriental Chair of King Solomon.—The seat of the Master of a Lodge.

Origin of the Gridiron in making Freemasons.—In years gone by, say forty or more, there lived in the City of

208 *ORIGIN.*

Gotham, a jolly good host whose physical man betokened that he was no idle workman at seasons of refreshment, and his full face denoted that good humor and a relish for jokes whetted his appetite for bibibles as well as eatables. This jolly good host was a Freemason, and his hotel was a resort for the members of the craft to while away their leisure time, where they were received with a smiling welcome, and their indulgences seasoned with a happy jest or some lively anecdote. Among the members of the Lodge to which our good host was attached, was one, a tailor by profession, who fully equaled him in pranks and jokes, and when they met some mischief was sure to be concocted, some plan devised for merriment at some one's expense. Among the inmates of the hotel was a very worthy young man, a mechanic, employed in the neighborhood, boarding there for convenience. This young man had a desire to learn the mysteries of Freemasonry, and requested the landlord to advise him the course to pursue, to which he readily agreed, as the young man was every way worthy to become a member of the fraternity. The application was made, and everything was satisfactory. Prior to his initiation, he concluded to make his debut in the Lodge in a new outfit, and he engaged a new suit from our jolly good tailor, to be finished on the night of his initiation. The tailor being cognizant of his customer's application to be made a Mason, and divining the purpose for which the suit of clothes was ordered, he, at the suggestion of the host, devised a plan for some sport on the occasion. The worthy host's wife, it was known, had some curious views concerning the mystic order, and believed it was not altogether for beneficial or charitable purposes the Masons met in their Lodges. The tailor prepared a piece of cloth, and scorched it in stripes, as if it had been burnt on a gridiron, this he neatly basted on the seat of the pantaloons. The clothes arrived in due time, and soon incased the physical man of the candidate for initiation. He presented himself before the host before going to the Lodge, who, in the presence of his better half, appearing to admire very much the new suit, and, inspecting the lower part of his coat, he remarked, "how very considerate," loud enough for his spouse to hear, and then left the house accompanied by the candidate. The next day the clothing was closely examined, and before the close of the week there were few of the lady acquaintances, whose husbands were known to be Masons, who did not see those pantaloons. It must not be supposed there were no secret conversations in relation to making Masons after retiring at night, between the good host and his better half. She, good soul, serious and moralizing. He unable to contain his laughter, and striving to prevent giving offense. The circumstance gave occasion for much talk among the good wives in the neighborhood. In due time the piece of cloth which had created no little excitement was removed, and the young man remained in ignorance of the practical joke; the subject being of a delicate nature, could not be communicated to him by those who believed him to have been a victim to some cruel ceremony. It was this circumstance which gave such extensive currency to the belief that a heated gridiron was a necessary implement in masonic initiation.—*Noel.*

Orpheon Mysteries.—The mysteries of which Orpheus was the author are so called, which were of high moral tone, and exercised a great influence on the intellectual development of mankind. Orpheus is said to have obtained them from the Idacan Dactyli. On the union of the mysteries with Bacchanalian they fell into disrepute.

Osiris.—Chief of the Egyptian divinities. He introduced a knowledge of religion, laws, arts, science. He visited Europe to promulgate the doctrine, and on his return was assassinated by his brother Typhon. Osiris judged the dead and ruled over the kingdom into which the souls of good

210

O'SULLIVAN.

men were admitted. After being introduced into Rome, they practiced the most licentious habits, that it was finally prohibited by law. Osiris was venerated under the sacred bulls Apis and Minerva. Plutarch's treatise gives a brilliant account of this mystery.

O'Sullivan, Anthony.—Born in the County of Kerry, Ireland, on the 29th of November, 1808. He emigrated to America about the year 1838, and lived in New York City until the next year, when he removed to New Orleans, where he was married to Miss Mary Drake, January 30th, 1841. In that year he moved to Missouri, and settled in Arrow Rock, Saline County, March 17th, 1841. In that place he was initiated in Arrow Rock Lodge, No. 55, on the 9th of May, 1846; passed June 6th, and raised June 20th, same year. He was exalted a Royal Arch Mason in Boonville Chapter, No. 5, Boonville, Cooper County, in the year 1849, and received the degrees of Royal and Select Master in the same Chapter. He was created a Knight Templar on the 1st of August, 1852, in St. Louis Commandery, No. 1. He received the degrees of the Scottish Rite in the southern jurisdiction in 1859, at a meeting called in Chicago, Illinois, of that year. He was then made a 33d and Sov. Grand Inspector General of Missouri and bordering States.

In 1852, he removed to St. Louis, where he resided until 1860, when he moved to Springfield, Mo., and remained until 1863, when he returned to St. Louis, and remained until the close of his life. On Wednesday, May 5th, 1852, he was elected Grand Secretary of Grand Lodge; on Friday, April 7th, 1854, he was elected Grand Secretary of Grand Chapter; on Tuesday, May 19th, 1863, he was elected Grand Recorder of the Grand Commandery; and on May 19th, 1864, he was elected Grand Puissant of Grand Council, and from the organization of the Order of High Priesthood, he was its Secretary. All of the above

OVERSEER.

offices he filled until death came to summon him from his labors.

Of the subordinate bodies of which he was an active member in the latter years of his life, we find the following:

In 1851, he became a member of Missouri Lodge, No. 1, and, in 1852, he affiliated with Meridian Lodge, No. 2. May 21st, 1852, he was elected a member of St. Louis Chapter, No. 8, and by his indefatigable labors he raised it from a precarious existence to be one of the first Chapters in the West. He was its High Priest in 1853, 4, 5, 6, 7, 8, and 9. He was first Thi. Ill. G. Master of St. Louis Council, No. 7, during its charter from Illinois, and remained such after the formation of the Grand Council of Missouri, and was considered one of the best authorities in Cryptic Masonry in the United States. He remained a member of St. Louis Commandery, in which he filled the office of Eminent Commander during the years 1855 and 1857. For fourteen years as Grand Secretary of the Grand Lodge of Missouri, he ever displayed those rare qualities which peculiarly belong to that office, and without any disparagement to his illustrious predecessors, we doubt whether there ever was a more faithful and laborious officer. He served under fourteen Grand Masters and received the cordial approval of all, and was fourteen times re-elected, without scarcely any opposition; and in the last two elections, he was chosen by acclamation.

Overseer.—An officer of the Mark Master's degree.

212   *PALLADIUM—PASSWORD.*

P.

Palladium.—A wooden statue of Minerva, said to have fallen from the skies as a sign to Illus, the founder of Troy, to convince him that he was under the guidance of Jupiter. On its preservation depended the safety of Troy. Accordingly Ulysses and Dimeral were commissioned to steal it, and performed the enterprise. A society of this name in France admitted both sexes into its mysteries. It had for its motto, *Je sois armei,* "I know how to love." It did not exist very long.

Pantheistic Brotherhood.—A sect with masonic form in England.

Parallel Lines.—The parallel lines that inclose the point within the circle are considered as the representations of St. John the Evangelist and St. John the Baptist. They are the two great patron saints to whom Lodges are dedicated.

Park, John.—A native of Delaware, born 1740. Col. Park was a revolutionary officer, and served under Washington as a colonel. He was one of the most active members of the American Union Lodge, organized, February 15th, 1776, by charter from the Grand Lodge of Mass. He was a Past Master of this Lodge. In 1779, he became a Knight Templar.

Paschalis Rite.—In 1754, organized by M. Paschalis, in Portugal. It was composed of nine degrees: E. A. P., F. C., M., Grand Elect, E. A. P. Cohen, F. C. Cohen, Master Cohen, Grand Architect, Grand Commander. The object was to establish beings in the spiritual and divine powers.

Passed.—A term used in the Fellow Craft degree.

Password.—A word that must be given before a per-

PAST—PENNSYLVANIA. 213

son is allowed to pass. A countersign to detect impostors or enemies, and enjoin discipline.

Past Master.—A Master who has served over a Lodge is styled a Past Master. The degree is often conferred by dispensation.

Patmos Knight.—This order was conferred by the Scottish Templars. It is commemorative of St. John's exile on the Isle of Patmos.

Pectoral.—A habit worn by the Jewish High Priests, and termed a breastplate.

Pedestal.—The lowest part that sustains a column. It has three parts: base, die, and cornice. The altar of the Lodge is called a pedestal, and upon it rests the Holy Bible, compasses, and square. The Bible is given as a rule to guide our faith, the compasses to keep us in bounds with all men and Masons, and the square to square our actions.

Penal Sign.—A sign that denotes that a punishment is attached to it. If the sinner does not receive the grace as offered in the gospel, he must expect to receive stripes for his transgressions.

Pennsylvania.—The exact date of the introduction of Freemasonry into Pennsylvania is not known, neither at what time the first Lodge was established at Philadelphia. In the newspapers of that day we find that in 1732, William Allen was Grand Master, and that *Tun Lodge* met at "Tun Tavern." In 1732, Franklin was S. Warden under Wm. Allen. In 1731, the G. L. of England appointed Franklin Provincial G. Master of Penna. On June 24th, 1734, St. John's Lodge, Boston, warranted a Lodge in Philadelphia, and of this Lodge Franklin was appointed Master. This warrant was received on St. John's day, while the brethren were engaged in a celebration under their old organization. They immediately accepted the authority, and ratified the appointment. On July 10th,

214   PENNSYLVANIA.

1749, Franklin received an appointment for Thomas H. Ward, Prov. G. M. of New York, which superseded the Boston authority. In March, 1750, Wm. Allen was appointed Prov. G. M. of Pa., by G. L. of England. In 1758, Lodge No. 2 was organized by warrant from G. L. of Ancient York Masons, of England. In 1764, a warrant for a Prov. G. Lodge was received from England. The archives of this Lodge were destroyed during the revolutionary war. On December 20th, 1777, a convention was held in Philadelphia, to reorganize the order. On September 13th, 1786, the Grand Lodge severed its connection with the Grand Lodge of England.

The first Royal Arch Chapter in America was instituted at Philadelphia, about 1758, and known as No. 3, and recognized by Military Lodge, No. 35, under warrant of G. L. of England. In 1795, Molan made an attempt to introduce innovations into the R. Arch degree, and to form an independent Grand Lodge, under warrants Nos. 19, 52, and 67, and, as he pretended, by authority of the G. Lodge of Maryland and Georgia. The Chapter working under warrant No. 3 made inquiry into the proceedings, and declared them irregular and contrary to the established custom of the craft. The Grand Lodge, upon complaint, suspended Nos. 19, 52, and 67, and appointed a committee to investigate the matter. This committee reported, and resolved "that all masonic jurisdiction in the State of Pa. is vested in the Grand Lodge of Pa., and that the officers of the different Lodges of the State are constitutional members of the Grand Lodge, that it is the right of all regular Lodges to make Masons in the higher degrees, and that the work of the Royal Arch Masons of No. 3 had met the approbation of visiting Royal Arch Masons from all parts of the globe, and that it was the prevailing wish for an establishment of a Grand Chapter." Accordingly, on November 23d, 1795, the Grand Chapter was formed. In 1797,

PENNSYLVANIA. 215

a convention of Chapters was held in Boston to form a General Grand Chapter for the U. S. The Grand Lodge of Penna. condemned this organization, as it introduced various innovations upon the ancient and established work of Royal Arch Masons. After the General Grand Chapter was formed in 1798, it was deemed advisable to adopt a regular form of work, which was done in 1810. Taking the Ancient York Rite as a standard, they selected from the Scottish Rite those things that approximated to the former, and thus formed the present system of Royal Arch Masonry. The Pennsylvania Chapters, however, still adhered to the Ancient York Rite, but have admitted the degrees of Excellent and Mark Master into the system. On December 17th, 1810, a committee was appointed by the Grand Hiram Royal Arch Chapter, to review the By-Laws, which was done, and adopted December 21st, 1812. The preamble declares "that Ancient Masonry consists of four degrees, viz., Apprentice, Fellow Craft, Master, and the Holy Royal Arch Chapter." On July 16th, 1824, the Grand Royal Arch Chapter was made independent of the Grand Lodge of Masons. On December 23d, 1828, a new series of regulations were adopted. In 1855, a change was made in the constitution of 1824, which added to its members "all High Priests, Scribes, and Kings, under its jurisdiction." In 18—, a separate Mark Lodge was opened, under warrant of Concordia, No. 67, of Philadelphia, and worked until 1824, when it obtained a warrant from the Grand Chapter.

The first Grand Encampment in the United States was constituted at Philadelphia, May 12th, 1797. The convention was composed of Nos 1 and 2, of Philadelphia, No. 3, Harrisburg, and No. 4, of Carlisle. On February 16th, 1812, Nos. 1 and 2 of Philadelphia, having united as No. 1 with No. 2 of Pittsburg, No. 1 of New York, No. 1 of Wilmington, Del., and No. 1 of Baltimore, Md., formed

216 *PENNSYLVANIA.*

the second Grand Encampment, which existed up to June 10th, 1824. In 1816, a convention was held in Philadelphia, when much discussion was had in reference to the order of conferring the degrees as practiced in the New England States; the Pennsylvania delegation objecting to the Mark and Excellent Master belonging to the system. A separation then took place by the New England delegation withdrawing and calling a convention in New York, on June 20th, 1816. This convention met, and formed the present Grand Encampment of the U. S. In May, 1852, St. John's, No. 4, Philadelphia, No. 5, Union, No. 6, and De Molay, Reading, organized a third Grand Encampment, under the alleged authority of the Grand Lodge of Pennsylvania, but that body resolved on February 16th, 1857, that it had no authority over the Templar system. A union was then permanently effected.

The Grand Council of Royal Select Masters was organized October 24th, 1847, in Pittsburg. The first of these subordinate Councils were, No. 1, at Washington, No. 2, at Pittsburg, and No. 3, Washington, Texas.

During 1849, some of the Illustrious Companions of the Grand Council having received the "Ineffable degrees," entertained doubts whether the Royal and Select Master's degrees did not actually belong to the Ancient and Accepted Rite. Various committees were appointed, time and again, to report thereupon, and the Grand Council languished until the 3d day of February, 1854, when the officers of the Grand Council, without consulting the subordinates, surrendered their authority over these degrees to the Grand Council of the Princes of Jerusalem, who, on that evening, issued a Charter for a Council of Royal and Select Masters, to be known by the name of Van Rensellear Council, No. 1, to be held in the City of Pittsburg. This Council afterward surrendered her Charter to the Princes of Jerusalem, and her members generally became affiliated

PENNSYLVANIA. **217**

with Mount Moriah, No. 2. The subordinate Councils of the State, not recognizing the act of the Grand Officers, called a meeting, December 30th, 1854, and forthwith proceeded to elect officers—since which period it has been steadily increasing in numbers and influence, and ranks, for talents and zeal, second to no Grand Council in the United States.

In 1858, the M. P. Grand M. Alfred Creigh reported a manual, which was adopted by the Grand Council as the true work of Cryptic Masonry.

June 10, 1863.—The Grand Council of Royal and Select Masters held its seventeenth annual Assembly, in Greensburg, Westmoreland County, Penna., sixteen Councils being represented.

M. P. Grand Master Creigh submitted an interesting correspondence between Illustrious Companion E. B. Moore, Chairman of the Committee on Foreign Correspondence of the Grand Council of Massachusetts, and himself, on the subject of incorporating the degree of Super Excellent Master as a regular degree of Cryptic Masonry. The Grand Master was instructed to continue the correspondence as being calculated to elicit much valuable information on Cryptic Masonry.

The M. P. Grand Master Creigh, in his annual address, suggested the propriety of dividing the State of Pennsylvania into nine districts, over each of which districts three Ghiblimites should be appointed, whose duty it shall be to make themselves acquainted with the mysteries of the S. V., and impart instruction in our rites and ceremonies to the Councils in their respective arches—these arches never to be increased or diminished—but shall always be composed of the mysterious number nine—hence the full number of Ghiblimites scattered throughout the State, to assist the Grand Officers in the diffusion of our sublime principles, would be limited to the mystic number twenty-seven.

19

218   *PENNY — PERFECT.*

This important question was postponed until the next annual assembly, for the consideration of the Grand Council, when it was adopted.

Penny.—A Roman coin. It was the hire of a laborer for a day's work. Reference is made to it in the Mark degree.

Pentalpha.—A double interlacing triangle in which the name of God is placed, form a symbol in the masonic system. The early Christians used it to denote the God-Man, or the two natures of God, *i.e.* God and man. It is formed in this manner, ⛤.

Perfect Ashler.—A stone squared that can only be tried by the compasses and square.

Perfection, Order of.—A system originated in France, in 1753, by De Bonneville, consisting of 25 degrees, to wit:

1. Entered Apprentice.	15. Knight of Sword.
2. Fellow Craft.	16. Prince of Jerusalem.
3. Master Mason.	17. Knights of E. and W.
4. Secret Master.	18. Rose Croix.
5. Perfect "	19. Grand Pontiff.
6. Most Int. Secretary.	20. " Patriarch.
7. Intendant of Buildings.	21. " Master of Keys of
8. Provost and Judge.	Masonry.
9. Elect of Nine.	22. Prince Libanus.
10. " of Fifteen.	23. Sov. Prince Adept.
11. Illustrious Elect.	24. Ill. Knight of White and
12. Gr. Master Architect.	Black Eagles.
13. Royal Arch.	25. Sub. Com. of Royal Se-
14. Grand Elect.	cret.

Perfect Union.—This order was introduced into France in 1700, and classified as follows:

1. Apprentice.	5. Elect of Fifteen.
2. Fellow Craft.	6. Elect Master.
3. Master.	7. Master Architect.
4. Elect of Nine.	8. 2d Architect.

PERJURY—PERSECUTIONS. 219

9. Grand Architect. 12. Knight Adepts.
10. Knight of the East. 13. Elect of Truth.
11. Rose Croix.

Perjury.—No crime is so abominated by a true Mason as perjury. A Mason convicted of such an offense is expelled from the order. He is not considered a fit associate for men and Masons.

Perpendiculars.—In geometry, a straight line is said to be perpendicular to another straight line when the adjacent angles formed by their intersection are equal, and consequently each is at a right angle. It is symbolical in Freemasonry.

Persecutions.—Freemasonry has ever had bitter enemies, who vainly sought to wrest the secrets and mysteries from the order. Annexed we give some extracts of these persecutions in different portions of the world, which we copy from the "*National Freemason.*"

Italy.—Freemasonry has never recovered from its persecutions in Italy. In 1737, John Gaston, Duke of Tuscany, instituted stringent enactments against the order, but only lasted a short time. In 1800, the order had gained some influence in Naples. In 1751, Charles III. of Spain, Governor of Naples, revived the persecution against the order, but shortly afterwards retracted it. The order obtained encouragement from this, and opened a Grand Lodge 27th Feb. 1764. Caroline, daughter of Francis I. of Germany, defended the order, and the civil edicts were annulled. But the priests were not idle, and in 1785 they succeeded in getting an enactment against the order. Thus matters rested until Joseph Bonaparte succeeded in re-establishing the order. In 1809, Murat was installed in the Grand Lodge. In 1816, the persecutions again were revived. At present the order has little power in Italy.

Switzerland.—There are two masonic histories in Switzerland. One party was controlled by Protestants, and

220   *PERSECUTIONS.*

the other by Catholics.   In 1745, the Council of Berne
enacted laws against the order.   In 1786, Geneva formed
a Grand Lodge.   During the French Revolution, Masonry
ceased its functions, but in 1803, revived under Grand
Master Glayre.   The Protestant order has moved along
quietly in spite of the exertions of the Catholic Masons,
who have only kept alive, to persecute and overthrow the
genuine order of Freemasons.

Sweden.—Freemasonry was interdicted here by Frederick I.   So bitter were his persecutions, that many of the
craft suffered death.   The order, however, found a protector in Gustavus III., who acted as its Grand Master,
and succeeded in placing it in a flourishing condition.

Portugal.—Fanaticism and ignorance made their influence felt upon the order in this land.   We have specimens
in the cases of John Coustos and Moulton, two diamond
cutters and polishers.   They were arrested in 1743, and
thrown into the subterranean dungeons of the Inquisition,
enduring the severest punishment, accused of not obeying
the Pope's Bull, which declared Freemasonry heresy.
Coustos suffered the most excruciating tortures; was
racked nine times in three months, and sentenced to four
years' work as a galley-slave.   As late as 1776, two Masons, Major Dalincourt and Don Oyres de Ornelles Par-
acao, a nobleman, remained incarcerated fourteen months.
In 1802, Don Costa, the masonic naturalist, was arrested.
The Jesuits banished, the Grand Lodge began to flourish
under the guidance of Egaz Moniz, M.·. W.·. G.·. M.·.
March 30th, 1818, King John promulgated from Brazil his
edict against Freemasonry, and a severer one was issued
from Lisbon, 1823.   The punishment of death was reduced
in a few years to fine and transportation to Africa, and this
has gradually become a dead letter.   Masonry is becoming
more confident daily, and will become a public institution.
She has been retiring and sensitive.   Here no mercenary

PERSECUTIONS.   221

motive has operated to add one Mason to the order. The Masonic Society is pure and earnest in Portugal.

Spain.—Freemasonry was known earlier in Spain than in Portugal. * * * 1737, Pope Clement XII. issued his decree against Masonry, and followed by the edict of Cardinal Firrao, the punishment of its practice was death and confiscation. Philip V., 1740, after a long confinement in the prisons of the Inquisition, sentenced the Masons arrested to the galleys for life, or punishment of death with torture. This inhuman treatment did not extirpate Masonry. Numerous Lodges continued their work, but very secretly as to the place of meeting, and no town but what had Masons of the martyr spirit. Peter Torrubia, the Inquisitor of Spain, having first made confession, and having received absolution, entered the order for the purpose of betraying it, and of handing to the executioner the members. As accuser, witness, and judge, and *without any pretext*, he named members of 97 Lodges for punishment. This great number of Masons were tortured on the rack. 1751, Benedict XIV., supposed to have been a Freemason, received the bull of Clement without putting it in force, but Ferdinand VI. declared Freemasonry high treason, and punishable with death, instigated by threats of Torrubia. So secret were the places and proceedings of the craft that we know little of them until 1807, when Napoleon took possession of Spain. Joseph Bonaparte had been Grand Master of French Freemasons, and under his sway many new Lodges were formed, and the *Grand Lodge of Madrid met in the hall previously occupied by the enemies of the Inquisition.* 1811, Joseph Bonaparte ordained a Superior Chapter for the high degrees. With the fall of Napoleon, and the restoration of Ferdinand VII., came the restitution of the Jesuits, the reorganization of the Inquisition, and the exterminating process against Freemasons. Pope - Pius VII. issued his decree against the Masons, August

19*

222

PERSECUTIONS.

7th, 1914, and at once 25 Masons were dragged in chains to confinement; but the number subsequently became so great that no correct account of their fate can be given. 1818, March 30th, Ferdinand dictated the punishment of Freemasons to be death, transportation to India, confiscation of estates, etc. March, 1820, General Ballasteros, by order of the Cortes and Provisional Government, ordered the release of the Freemasons, and fresh Lodges were warranted and previous Lodges reinstated. August, 1824, a law was issued commanding all Masons to declare themselves, and deliver up their papers and documents, or be declared traitors. 16th of October, every Freemason was declared outlawed. 1827, seven members of a Lodge in Granada *were executed.* At the death of Ferdinand civil war ensued, and the abandonment of the kingdom by Don Carlos enabled Mendigabel, a Freemason, to protect the craft.

Russia.—So secret were the meetings of the Lodges in Russia, that one Lodge existed for thirty-one years, without any one out of the order knowing it. The Empress Catherine II., hearing of the order, instituted rigid inquiries, and finally made herself their protector, and the Lodge Clio, in Mascon, received her especial favor. Masonry flourished. Every Russian nobleman was a member of the order. When the Emperor Paul succeeded to the throne, his love of the order was open and earnest. When Alexander ascended to the Czar's place, he was quite opposed to the order, but changed in his disposition and was initiated. Two Grand Lodges arose from a division concerning the Swedish work. One was organized August 30th, 1815, with the name of Astraa. Its four fundamental rites were: 1st. Admission of all known systems. 2d. Every Lodge to have an equal representation in Grand Lodges. 3. An annual uncontrolled election of every officer. 4th. The non-interference of Grand Lodge with the highest orders.

PERSECUTIONS.

223

August 12th, 1822, Alexander suddenly ordered the suspension of Masonry, without any reason given or motive alleged, even to the present.

Syria.—A writer from Syria states: I am fully satisfied that the order in Syria have unwittingly been subjected to persecution and great neglect and wrong, by Christians. They have been termed Shemsiyel, or worshipers of the Sun, because they study astronomy; Komariyel, or worshipers of the Moon, for the same rsason; Kelbiyel, worshipers of the day, because of their humanity; and others. They preserve the most profound secret about their origin and customs. They are noted as being free from intolerance, and full of charity, and hence are called dissemblers. For fifty years have persistent and cautious efforts been made to penetrate their mysteries and assemblies, but with no success. Mr. Barker, the British ex-consul general, who has lived among them more than half a century, and whose domestics have been mostly from this sect, declares that, on the subject of their religion, no power can unseal their lips. Our own consul at Lâdakieh informed one or our missionaries, a few years since, that even the governor of the city, a Turk, tried every art to wring the secret out of them to no purpose. He took a poor man into his employ, gradually raised him from step to step, and sought to gain his affection and confidence; and, at length, began to sound him on the matter of religion. Finding all his efforts in this way useless, he imprisoned, beat, and nearly killed him, but with no better success. The poor man finally told him that, if he should actually beat him to death, he would not disclose anything. "But," said he, "you have a slave; commit him to me for forty days; I will take him to the mountains, where he will be initiated into our mysteries; and then, as he is your slave, you may do what you please with him." But the slave, when he returned, was as stubbornly silent as the other, and actually died a martyr to his secret.

224 PERSEVERANCE—PERU.

France.—The persecutions in France would fill a volume. Masonry has ever been antagonistic in its teachings to Catholicism, and hence the bitterness with which the priesthood sought to overthrow it. In the exeeution of Jacques de Molay, we see to what an extent they sought to overthrow the order. Striking at the Grand Head of Templars, it was thought the order would languish and die, without its leader. The martyrdom of Molay, however, only proved an incentive to the order, and thousands flocked to its embrace.

In Germany, Ireland, and other states, the order met with much opposition in its infancy. But as intelligence and literature spread over these countries, the opposition grows less, and time is not far distant when Freemasonry will be acknowledged in every section of the globe.

The United States did not escape this contagious spirit of persecution. The order had many enemies who had and have sought every subterfuge to bring it into disrepute. Christianity has its enemies, and why should not that association that is wedded to its influences, feel the heel of the oppressor? To our articles upon Anti-Masonry, U. S. Anti-Masonic Convention, and Life of Bro. Dallas, we refer the reader for a history of the persecutions in the United States.

Perseverance.—This order was founded by the Countess Potoska, a Polish lady, in 1771, while residing in France, and admitted both sexes.

Persian Rite.—Instituted in 1819 at Paris, and contained seven degrees:

1. Listening Apprentice.
2. Companion Adept.
3. Master of the Sun.
4. Architect of All Rite.
5. Knight of Electicism.
6. Grand Shepherd.
7. Venerable Grand Elu.

Peru.—Freemasonry was introduced here in 1807, during the French invasion of Spain. In 1825, the Gr. Orient of Columbia granted warrants for holding Lodges. On the 2d Nov. 1830, the Supreme Council A. and A. Rite was organized. On the 23d June, 1831, the Grand Lodge was organized. On the 30th Jan. 1849, the Supreme Council was reopened. On the 13th July, 1852, the Grand Lodge was reorganized. In 1852, the Grand Chapter of Scotland granted a charter for a Chapter at Callao.

Petition.—An application for a Lodge, for membership, for dispensation, etc., is termed a petition, as it sets forth the desire of the applicant.

Phi Beta Kappa.—Thomas Jefferson was the author of this order. It was first introduced in William and Mary's College, Virginia, and now found in most colleges in America. It was devoted to philosophy. The jewel of the order is a small metal piece, and on the one side engraved six small stars, and the Greek initials Φ., B., K., and a hand pointed toward it. On the reverse, S., P., Dec. 5th, 1776. The Greek initials signify "Philosophy, the rule and guide of life ;" S. P., Societas Philosophines—Philosophic Society.

Philadelphians.—The Rite of Narbonne was practiced in a Lodge of this name at Narbonne, France.

Philaletheans (*Lovers of Truth*).—Originated in France, and composed of twelve degrees.

Philochoreites.—An order of Adoptive Masonry, instituted in Spain in 1806.

Philosophic Scotch Order.—This order was adopted by the Grand Lodge of France in 1776, and had twelve degrees:

1. Knights of Black Eagle.
2. 1st " " Rose Croix.
3. 2d " " "
4. " " Phœnix.
5. " " Sun.
6. " " Iris.
7. Freemason.
8. Knights of Argonauts.
9. " " Golden Fleece.
10. Grand Inspector.
11. Grand Scotch Mason.
12. Sub. Master of Luminous Ring.

226   PHRASES—PORTUGAL.

Phrases of Admission.—Initiated, passed, raised, congratulated, presided, marked, acknowledged, received, exalted.

Pickaxe.—It is used symbolically in the R. A. degree.

Pillars.—The pillars of the Lodge are Wisdom, Strength, and Beauty.

Pillars of the Porch of Solomon.—These pillars were named Jachin and Boaz,—Jachin representing the pillar of a cloud, and Boaz that of fire, which guided the Israelites through the wilderness.

Point within a Circle.—That point which we should not overstep, is never to go beyond the bound of reason. By guarding our actions, and being consistent in our walk and conversation as Christians and Masons, we may hope for goodly life and joy hereafter.

Poland.—In 1736, Freemasonry began to appear in Poland, but was soon interdicted. In 1742 to 1766, the order flourished. In 1780, the Grand Lodge of England organized a Lodge. In 1784, the Grand Lodge was organized at Warsaw. In 1822, the Emperor Alexander interdicted the order, and has never been removed, although several Lodges still continue to work.

Politics.—Are forbidden in all masonic Lodges. This all Freemasons know, that anything that relates to politics is never ventured upon by the brethren. The institution is social, and has all political classes within its folds.

Pomegranate.—Is a native of Asia and a kind of an apple. It was cultivated in Egypt, and hence the Israelites complained that the desert was no place for seeds, figs, vines, or the pomegranate. It was an emblem of plenty, and as such Solomon ornamented the two pillars of his porch with rows of artificial pomegranates.

Portugal.—In 1735, the Grand Lodge of England introduced Masonry at Lisbon, but did not make any headway on account of the Inquisition. In 1805, the Grand

POT—PRIEST. 227

Lodge was formed. In 1837, Freemasonry was again persecuted in Portugal, but now is privileged. The Grand Lodge is located at Lisbon.

Pot of Incense.—A pot into which were put sweet spices and frankincense. It was regarded as a pure and holy emblem.

Preparation and Prepared.—A candidate for Masonry is prepared according to masonic ceremonics. There are three preparations in the Blue Lodge, to wit: that of the E. A. P., F. C., and M. M.

Prerequisites.—Are being free-born, mature age, good report and sound, as a man of good sense.

Price, Henry.—Born in London, in 1697, and came to America in 1723. In 1733, April 30th, the Grand Lodge of England appointed him Prov. Grand Master of New England. From this deputation sprung the first Lodges of America. He settled in Boston and organized a Lodge, and appointed Andrew Belcher, son of the governor of Massachusetts, his Deputy, 30th July, 1733. In 1734, the Grand Lodge of England extended his jurisdiction over North America, and under this authority he established Lodges at Philadelphia and Portsmouth. On the 25th December, 1735, he warranted a Lodge at Charleston, S. C. In 1737, Robt. Tomlinson succeeded him as Prov. Grand Master, who was succeeded, after seven years, by Thomas Oxnord, who held the position until his death, ten years afterward. Price filled the vacancy until October, 1755, when Jeremiah Gildesk was installed. Gildesk died September, 1767, and Price resumed the office until 25th November, 1768, when John Ronce took the post. In 1738, he established a Master's Lodge at Boston, and acted as Master until 1744. In 1749, he was again the Master. He died at Townsend, Mass., 20th May, 1780, aged 83.

Priest.—The second officer in R. A. C.

228   *PRIMITIVE — PROCLAMATION.*

Primitive Scotch Rite.—Was founded at Castle Kilwinning, and contained 33 degrees.

Prince of Jerusalem.—Of the A. and A. Rite, 16th degree. It is historical of incidents that occurred during the building of the second Temple. The jewel, a balance suspended by a hand, and a sword with five stars, with the letters D. and Z., being the initials of Darius and Zerubbabel.

Prince Rose Croix.—18th degree A. and A. R. Instituted by Templars of Palestine.

Princess of the Crown—A system of Androgynel Masonry, practiced in 1777, in Saxony.

Printed Works, Masonic.—At the initiation the candidate promises he will not betray the secrets of Masonry by writing or printing. The real secrets of Masonry have never yet been betrayed by any one. As yet, no ritual has ever given the secrets of the order. The secrets are retained in the memory, and handed down orally from one generation to another. The Anti-Masons contend that the expositions of so-called Masons contain the secrets of the order. Every Mason knows this to be a great error. The matter of such works are the fictitious suppositions of diseased minds, and no secret or mystery can be found in them. The standard theological works, dictionaries, and encyclopædias contain all the symbols of the order, and the study of these works will place any one in knowledge of the masonic practices.

Printing.—The Constitutions forbid the publishing of the proceedings of meetings without proper direction.

Processions.—Masonic processions are not obligatory, but are given upon all proper occasions.

Proclamation.—Official notice given to the public. The Jews returned to Jerusalem after the proclamation of Cyrus. They were conducted by Zerubbabel, accompanied by the High Priest Joshua, and the prophet Haggai, and

PROCTOR — PROSCRIPTION. 229

the Scribe Ezra. Permission was also given by Cyrus to hew timber in Lebanon, and float it to Joppa. Zerubbabel laid the foundation of the second Temple in the second year after their return.

Proctor, Thomas.— A revolutionary officer, and member of Lodge No. 2, Philadelphia. He first brought to the notice of Prest. Mifflin, by letters of 3d February, 1790, the propriety of celebrating the birthday of General Washington. He received all the degrees, to that of Templar, in Philadelphia Lodge, No. 2. On the 18th May, 1779, the Grand Lodge of Pennsylvania issued a warrant for a Lodge to be held in 1st Pa. Regt. Art., and Proctor was made the Master. He was one of the committee to notify Washington of the design of making him Grand Master of the U. S. Lodge No. 2 is now known as Montgomery, No. 19, of Philadelphia. He died 16th March, 1807, aged 67, and buried at St. Paul's Episcopal grave-yard, on Third Street, below Walnut, Philadelphia.

Profane.—A term applied to those who are not initiated into the order.

Pro. Grand Master.—Is an officer of the G. L. of England, existing only where a prince of blood is G. M. This office originated with the Duke of Sussex, when G. M., who wished in his absence not a deputy, but an actual G. M. When the G. M. is present, the Pro. G. M. is without authority or position, but in his absence or death he is the actual Grand Master.

Pro. Grand Officers.—Are elected annually. To be a Warden of the Pro. G. L., the brother must have been an actual Master of a Lodge. No Deacon unless he has acted as a Warden of a Lodge. (Eng. Const.)

Prophet.—The third officer of the Chapter.

Proscription.—When a member is proscribed, notice is to be given to all Lodges, and he is thus prevented from affiliation until the proscription is removed.

20

230 PROVINCIAL—PUTNAM.

Provincial Grand Lodge.—This Lodge assembles at the call of the Provincial Grand Master, once in each year, for the transaction of business. (See Eng. Con.)

Provincial Grand Master.—The Provincial Grand Master is appointed to govern the craft in large districts, and derives his authority from the Grand Master. (Eng. Con.)

Prussia.—Frederick the Great has the honor of introducing the order into Prussia. He organized a Lodge at Reimsburg. In 1740, June 20th, on his assuming the reins of the government, he conducted the work at Charlotsburg. On 13th September, 1740, he organized a Lodge at Berlin, which occupied the protectorate of all Lodges in the kingdom, and was styled the Royal Grand Lodge. Frederick was G. Master of this Lodge. In 1747, he appointed as Vice-Grand Master the Duke of Holstenback. In 1765, Zinzendorf was elected Grand Master. In 1770, Zinzendorf organized the National Grand Lodge of Germany. In 1798, an edict was issued restraining the assemblage of any Lodges but the three Grand Lodges and those under their jurisdiction.

Punishment.—Masonic punishments are suspension, proscription, and exclusion.

Pursuivant.—A Messenger of the Lodge.

Putnam, Rufus.—Born in Sutton, Mass., 9th April, 1758. He was made a Mason in the "American Military Lodge," near West Point, in 1779. On the 26th July, 1779, was passed as a Fellow Craft, and raised a Master Mason on 6th September, 1779. After the war, the "American Union Lodge" convened at Marietta, Ohio, and Putnam acted as Junior Warden. In 1808, at the organization of the G. L. of Ohio, he was chosen as its first Grand Master. He died May 1st, 1824. His services rendered in the revolutionary war are known to all Amercans, and few patriots have as bright a page in history as Rufus Putnam.

QUADRANGULAR—QUEEN. 231

Q-

Quadrangular Diagram.—On the old Royal Arch floor-cloths the quadrangular diagram was found. It symbolized the seven pillars that upheld the Temple or the private entrance; seven steps of advancement, or seven seats.

Quarries of Tyre.—These quarries were extensive. They had small entrances, and were fashioned somewhat after the manner of our mines.

Quarterly Communications.—Held by the Grand Lodge in March, June, September, and December, on the first Wednesday.

Queen Elizabeth.—Being jealous of the secrets of Free-masonry,. attempted to disperse the organization. Accordingly, when the Grand Lodge had assembled on St. John's day, 27th December, 1561, an armed force, headed by the queen's officers, proceeded to the Lodge. Sir Thomas Lockville, then acting as Grand Master, received the deputation, and convinced them of the practices of Masonry. They then informed the queen that they were of immense benefit to her kingdom, as it cultivated morality, science, and religion. This satisfied Elizabeth, and the order was not again troubled during her reign.

Queen of Sheba.—When the Queen of Sheba had heard of the fame of Solomon, concerning the name of the Lord, she came to prove him with hard questions. On beholding the form of Solomon she was overpowered with astonishment. She came from the southern part of Arabia, and when she beheld the magnificent edifice glittering with gold, she raised her hands in the attitude of admiration, and exclaimed, Rabboni, which means most Excellent Master. This visit took place thirteen years after the dedication of the Temple.

232 QUEER.

Queer Documents.—Among the queer ancient documents of Masonry, the following have more than ordinary interest. In 1720, the following was destroyed in England by some brethren who were opposed to the publication of any masonic documents:

"St. Albans loved Masons well, and cherished them much, and made their pay right good, for he gave them 2 shillings per week, and 3d. to their cheer; whereas, before that time, in all the land, a Mason had but a penny a day and his meat, until St. Albans mended itt, and he got them a charter from the King and his counsell, and gave it the name of assemblie. Thereat he was himselfe and did helpe to make Masons, and made them good cheer."

In the reign of Edward III., the Grand Master ordered the following :

"That for the future, at the making of a brother, the Constitutions and Charges shall be reade by ye Masters or ye Wardens. That such as are to be admitted Masons or Masters of Works, should be examined if they be able to serve their Lords, as well the lowest as the highest, to the honor and worship of the aforesaid art, and to the profit of their Lord and Master, for they be their Lords and Masters that employ them and pay them for their service and travel."

The following is the Ancient Charge :

"Ye shall be true to the King, and the master you serve. Ye shall be true to love eider odher. Ye shall calle eider odher Brother or Fellowe, not slave or anye unkind name. Ye shall ordain the wisest to be master of the work, and neither for love nor lineage, riches nor favor, set one over the work who hath but little knowledge, whereby the Master would be evil served, and ye ashamed, and also ye shall call the governour of the work master in the time of working with him, and ye shall truly deserve your reward of the master ye serve." "All the Freres (Brothers) shall treat the peculiarities of eider odher with gentleness, decencie, and forbearance he thinks due to his owne. Ye shall have a reasonable pay and live honestlie."

In the time of James II., the Ancient Charges at the constitution of a Lodge embraced

"Every man that is a Mason take heed to these charges (we pray), that if any man find himselfe guiltie of anye of these charges, that he amende himselfe, or principally for dread of God, you that be charged to take good heede that you keepe all these charges well, for it is a great evil for a man to forsweare himselfe upon a book.

"That ye shall be true men to God and the holy church, and to use no error or heresie; allso,

"That ye true liege men to the King of England without treason or any falsehood, and ye shall know no treason or treachery, but ye shall give knowledge thereof to the King or his Counselle, also ye shall be true to one another, that is to say, every Mason of the Craft, that is a Mason allowed, yee shall doe to him as yee would be done unto yourselfe.

"That yee shall keepe truly all the counselle that ought to be kept in the way of Masonhood, etc.

"That yee shall call all Masons your Fellowes, etc.

"Yee shall not take your fellow's wife in villany, nor deflower his daughter or servant, nor put him to disworship.

"Yee shall truly pay for your meat or drinke wheresovere ye goe, to table or bord, etc.

"These be the charges general to every true Mason, both Masters and Fellowes."

R.

Rabboni.—Teacher or Master.

Rainbow.—An arch formed by the refraction and reflection of rain or light, drops of vapor appearing in the part of the hemisphere opposite the sun. It was an emblem of religious mystery in all creeds.

Raised.—A term used in the 3d degree of Masonry.

Ramsey, Andrew Michael.—Born at Ayr, Scotland, June 9th, 1686. His father was a baker, and sent his son to the Edinburgh University. Here he met Brother Porrit, who first inculcated into his mind the mystic doctrine. In 1710 he met Archbishop Fenelon of Canterbury, and persuaded by him to become a Catholic. At this time he was made a Knight of the Order of Lazarus, and soon after attached himself to the masonic fraternity. He was a strong adherent of James the Pretender. He endeavored to unite the Stuart faction with the masonic fraternity. In 1740, he delivered an address on Masonry in Paris. In 1728, he endeavored to reform the order in England. The Grand Lodge of England, however, rejected his propositions, which carried to France and organized them there into what is now termed Scottish Rite He died at St. Germaine-de-Loge, May 6th, 1743.

Ramsey, David.—An eminent Mason, who was wounded in July, 1863, while engaging with the Federal forces at Ft. Wayne, Morris Island, S. C., and died from the wound August 4th following. He was initiated Sept. 20th, 1855, in Union Kilwinning Lodge, No. 4, Charleston, S. C. In 1859 he was appointed Grand Pursuivant of the Grand Lodge. In January, 1860, he helped to open Franklin Lodge, No. 96, of which he was appointed Master. In Nov. 1860, he was elected Deputy Grand Master. In 1861 he was elected Grand Master. He was re elected to the same position. He became a Royal Arch Mason in Zerubbabel Chapter, No. 11, in 1856, a Knight Templar in South Carolina Commandery the same year, and completed the York Rite by receiving the degrees of the Royal and Select Master at the hands of the Sovereign Inspector of the 33d degree. In 1857 he was elected High Priest of his Chapter. In 1859, he was elected Grand Scribe of the Grand Chapter. In 1861, the Grand Chapter of Scotland appointed him Representative near the Grand Chapter of S. C. In 1856, he was received into the Ancient and Accepted Rite, in Pelican Chapter of Rose Croix, Charleston, and soon after elected presiding officer. In 1861, he was elected to fill a vacancy in the Supreme Council, then in session at New Orleans, which he filled until his death.

Randall, Josiah.—The only son of Matthew and Mary Robarts Randall, was born at Devizes, Wiltshire, England, on the 21st day of July, 1789.

He died in Philadelphia, on the morning of the 10th of September, 1866, in the 78th year of his age.

His father came to this country in 1793, and his mother and the family (himself and five sisters) followed in 1794 to this city. Mr. Randall, Senior, became embarrassed. in business, and was compelled to go as supercargo to the Isle of France in the year 1801. Mrs. Randall, with her son and daughters, then removed to Burlington, New Jersey, where, under the superintendence of one of the best and most pious of women, his mother, Brother Randall received his education, which was completed under the Rev. Dr. Staughton, the eminent Baptist clergyman, who was remarkable for the eloquence and force of his preaching, and who was then one of our most popular divines.

At the early age of fourteen years, being well grounded in the classics, and with a complete English education, Brother Randall entered the office of Joseph Reed, Esq., a leading member of the bar, and afterward Recorder of Philadelphia, as a student of law, where he remained for three years, and when only eighteen was admitted to practice, on the 8th of March, 1808.

One of the first appointments made by Simon Snyder, who was elected Governor of Pennsylvania in that year, was that of Brother Randall as clerk of the Mayor's Court of the city, which position he held until 1812. This appointment brought Brother Randall early into public life, from which it may be said he was never after entirely withdrawn.

Brother Randall served in the war of 1812. He marched to Camp Bloomfield as a sergeant in the volunteer corps

236 RANDALL.

of the Junior Artillerists, commanded by Captain Cash, and was subsequently promoted to be a commissioned officer, serving during the whole of the campaign of 1814, and returning with the troops to the city at the close of the year. He was appointed and commissioned by Governor Snyder as colonel of the first of the ten regiments Pennsylvania offered to the general government, just before the close of the war. Brother Randall tendered these regiments to President Madison, and while in the act of doing so, the news of the signing of the Treaty of Ghent was received by the President, the brightest day, he was accustomed to declare, that he ever saw in the history of his country.

Brother Randall was also a member of the State Legislature in 1819, '20.

Brother Randall was married in January, A.D. 1820, to Ann Worrell, the daughter of Joseph Worrell, Esq., a well-known and highly respected citizen of Philadelphia. He left one daughter and several sons, one of whom, the Hon. Samuel J. Randall, now represents the first district in the Congress of the United States; another of them, Robert E. Randall, Esq., represented the city in the State Legislature, and is now a member of the Philadelphia bar.

Brother Randall was initiated in Masonry in Montgomery Lodge, No. 19, on the 3d day of January, 1811, and was subsequently passed and raised to the sublime degree of a Master Mason in that Lodge. He resigned his membership then, and, with others from that Lodge, applied for a charter for Industry Lodge, No. 131, on the 21st day of June, A.D. 1811. This Lodge was constituted on the twenty-second day of that month, and its first meeting held on the 1st of July, 1811. He was elected its Junior Warden on the 9th of December, 1812, its Worshipful Master on the 10th June, 1813, and again its Worshipful Master on the 8th June, 1815, and December 12th,

1822. He remained with that Lodge until May 13th, 1824, when he resigned. He appears to have been quite an active member during the whole time, was frequently appointed on committees of various kinds, to whom was intrusted the important business of the Lodge.

He was elected Right Worshipful Junior Grand Warden of the Right Worshipful Grand Lodge, on the 7th December, A.D. 1818; Senior Grand Warden, on the 6th day of December, 1819; re-elected to the same station on the 4th December, 1820. On the 3d December, 1821, he was elected Right Worshipful Grand Master over Brother Thomas Elliott, Deputy Grand Master, and re-elected Right Worshipful Grand Master on the 2d December, 1822.

He was one of the many prominent Masons summoned with others to Harrisburg, by the Inquisitorial Committee appointed by the Legislature of the State, in January, 1836 to investigate what they were pleased to term the evils of Masonry. When called before them at their first meeting, he admitted "that he had been a Freemason for twenty years. He avowed that he had never known any infraction of the laws of this Commonwealth, or of the rights of conscience committed by any Lodge, Grand or Subordinate, or by any body of Masons, or by any individuals acting as such. He had never known a political vote given in committees, caucus, convention, at the polls or elsewhere, that was governed by masonic considerations; nor did he know of any selection or appointment to office, either popular, legislative, executive, or judicial, which he had any reason to believe was influenced by any such considerations. He had never known Masonry to interfere in any manner with the administration of justice. He had been concerned in law cases where one of the parties was a Mason, and the other not a Mason, and he solemnly avowed that he had never known a judge, arbitrator, juror,

238

RANDALL.

or witness, selected, preferred, or avoided, because he was or was not a Mason. Nor did he ever know of a judicial decision being made which he had the slightest reason to believe was governed or influenced by masonic feeling, fellowship, or connection."

He protested against the authority of the committee in the premises, and refused to take the oath which they required of him. Other distinguished members of the order, dragged before the same committee, refused to be sworn, and they were ordered into the custody of the sergeant-at-arms. The same course was pursued by other brethren at the second meeting of the committee, in consequence of which the action of the House of Representatives was invoked in the shape of a resolution presented by the committee, that all the protestants should be taken into custody by the sergeant-at-arms, and be brought before the House to answer for contempt.

Brother Randall visited England several times. In 1853, he was invited to the Grand Lodge in London, and upon one occasion requested to point out the difference in the mode of working in England and that in Pennsylvania. Explaining this, he mentioned in the course of his remarks that he had shaken hands with every President of the United States. After he had taken his seat, the Grand Master, believed to have been the Duke of Argyle, proposed that the brethren present should pass around the hall in regular order, and shake hands with the brother who had shaken hands with the great, good, and pious Brother, George Washington. There were some two hundred Masons present, who carried out the suggestion, headed by their Grand Master, to their great gratification.

Brother Randall was appointed on the Committee on Landmarks in December, 1858, and from that time until his decease continued a member of it.

Past Grand Master Chandler, in writing, says: "Mr.

RANDOLPH—RECHABITES. 239

Randall, though not much older than I, received his masonic honors very early, and was not much in the habit of visiting the Grand Lodge while I was an active member. He was an earnest Mason, and in his earlier years gave much time to the craft."

Randolph, Edmund.—Nephew of Peyton Randolph. It is not known when he was made a Mason. In 1774, he assisted in organizing a Lodge at Williamsburg, Va. In 1784, he was elected Deputy Grand Master. On October 27th, 1786, he was elected Grand Master, being the third G. M. of G. L. of Virginia. He granted the warrant for the Lodge at Alexandria, Va., which had Washington as its Master. He died September 12th, 1813, in Frederick Co.

Randolph, Peyton.—Was born in Virginia in 1723. The King appointed him his attorney in 1748. He was President of the Constitutional Congress that met in Philadelphia, in 1774. In 1773, he was commissioned Master of a Lodge at Williamsburg, by Lord Petre, G. M. of England, and acted as Prov. G. M. in 1774. He died October 22d, 1775.

Raymond, Edward Asa.—Grand Treasurer of the Grand Encampment of Knights Templar of the U. S., in 1863, died in Brookline, Mass., August 1st, 1864, aged 73. He was a man of note in the order, and devoted more than forty years to the service of Freemasonry, during which he held the office of Grand Master of Mass., Grand Master of the Encampment of that State, Grand High Priest of the Grand Chapter, Grand Master of the Supreme Council of the Scottish Rite for the northern jurisdiction of the U. S., Grand Treasurer of the Grand Encampment, and Grand Chapter of the U. S.

Rechabites.—A religious order, instituted by Jonedab, a Jew. His mother's name was Rechab, from whence cometh the name. The principal doctrines were abstinence from building, planting vines, and using wine.

240   *RECOGNITIONS — RED.*

Recognitions. — One Mason is entitled to recognize another by signs, grips, and tokens.

Recorder.—An officer in Commandery of K. T.

Red Jacket (*The Indian Craftsman*). — Parker was the grandson of the famous Indian Chief Red Jacket, a pure-blooded Indian, intelligent and educated, a gentleman and Mason: we believe Master of a Lodge in Galena, Illinois. At the banquet in Chicago, at the triennial meeting there, Bro. Parker was "called out" and made a speech worthy of preservation. He spoke of himself as almost a lone remnant of what was once a noble race; of his struggles in coming forward to manhood, and seeing his race thus disappearing as dew before the morning sun. As he found his race thus wasting away, he asked himself:

"Where shall I go when the last of my race shall have gone forever? Where shall I find home and sympathy when our last council-fire is extinguished? I said, I will knock at the door of Masonry, and see if the white race will recognize me, as they had my ancestors, when we were strong and the white men weak. I knocked at the door of the *Blue Lodge*, and found brotherhood around its altar; I knelt before the Great Light in the Chapter, and found companionship beneath the Royal Arch. I entered the Encampment, and found a valiant Sir Knight willing to shield me there without regard to race or nation. I went further. I knelt at the cross of my Saviour, and found Christian brotherhood, the crowning charity of the masonic tie. I feel assured that when my glass is run out, and I shall follow the footsteps of my departed race, masonic sympathizers will cluster round my coffin, and drop in my lonely grave the ever-green acacia, sweet emblem of a better meeting! If my race shall disappear from this continent, I have the consoling hope that our memory will not perish. If the deeds of my ancestors shall not live in story, their memories will remain in the names of your lakes and rivers, your towns and cities, and will call up memories otherwise forgotten."

After giving utterance in these eloquent and touching words to the exuberance of his heart, he sat down "amid

RED. 241

the solemn silence and deep emotion of the guests." His words had found a lodgment, and awakened an echo in every heart present. Tears flowed from "eyes unused to weep," for who could withhold the tribute of a tear to such touching thoughts and moving words? Silence—the silence of profound emotion, ensued, while the Chief sat a few moments subdued under the power of his own reflections. At length he rose again, and resumed his remarks:

"I have omitted one thing which I ought to have said. I have in my possession a memento which I highly prize—I wear it near my heart. It came from my ancestors to me, as their successor in office. It was a present from Washington to my grandfather, Red Jacket, when your nation was in its infancy. You will all be glad to see and handle it, and I should do wrong were I not to give you the opportunity."

As he spoke thus, he removed the wampum from his neck, and drew from his bosom a large massive medal, in oval form, some seven inches by five, and it passed from hand to hand along the tables. On one side of this medal was engraved, in full length, the figure of the two chiefs: Red Jacket, in costume, presenting the pipe of peace, and Washington, with right hand extending, as in the act of receiving it. On the other side were the masonic emblems, with the date 1792.

Such incidents are rare, even in this country where singular events are not unfrequent. An Indian Chief, descended from an illustrious ancestry of forest kings, and of one of the proudest nations among the aboriginals of this continent, sitting at a masonic festival, himself a brother, and clinging to the brotherhood as the last and most enduring refuge of his race! The descendant of Red Jacket is a noble specimen of manhood, refined and educated, a civil engineer elevated in the enjoyment of civilized and refined society. His great ancestor, the renowned Red Jacket, was in the favor, and in alliance with the great

21

242 RED—REGULATIONS.

Washington. His grandson is now an educated gentleman, a devoted and well instructed Mason, a Christian— *"I knelt at the cross of my Saviour!"* Remodeled earth: changed humanity!—*National Freemason.*

Red Sea.—It is supposed the name arose from the fact that the inhabitants bordering on it called it *Yam Edom*, Edom meaning red, and the Greeks supposing it to be the name, styled it Red Sea. At the point where the Children of Israel are supposed to have passed, the water is about 16 fathoms deep. Could a natural agent divide these waters? It is not supposable; hence the all-powerful agency of God must be recognized in this miracle.

Reformed Rite of Observance.—In 1754, this was organized by withdrawing from the Knights Templar, and was composed as follows:

Apprentice.	Knight of Holy City.
Fellow Craft.	Novice.
Master.	Professed Bro. and Knight.
Scotch Master.	

Refreshments.—The Lodge is called off from labor to refreshments, which signifies *rest.* Some Lodges, however, take it literally, and partake occasionally of a light collation. The practice is not general.

Regalia.—The proper dress worn in a Lodge room by Masons. No one is admitted unless properly clothed.

Regeneration.—The triple form of a cross is an emblem in the Royal Arch degree. The cross is looked upon as an agent in man's regeneration.

Registrar.—The Grand Officer in charge of the Seals of the G. L.

Regular Lodge.—A Lodge that works under a warrant from the Grand Lodge, composed of a requisite number of Masons, with the Bible, Warrant, and Constitution.

Regulations.—The regulations are ancient, strict, and universally enforced.

Reinstatement.—The Grand Master has power to order the reinstatement of an expelled, suspended, or removed Mason, if unjustly and harshly dealt with.

Rejection of Candidates.—A rejection implies a dissent among the brethren. In order that no improper persons obtain an admission into a Lodge, it requires the *unanimous consent* of all members present when a ballot is had. A rejection does not imply that his petition may not be renewed, which may be done as often as desired, but *always* in the Lodge where he has been rejected.

Relief, Masonic.—Is to aid the poor, feed the hungry, clothe the naked, and administer unto the sick.

Religion.—The religious belief of a Mason must be in a Divine Being. Those who deny the divinity of Christ Jesus should not be admitted as Masons. This was the practice of ancient Masons, although Jews have been admitted in some sections.

Remarkable Occurrences in Masonry.—Henry Price appointed Pro. G. Master of Mass., by G. L. of England, April 30th, 1733.

St. John's Lodge, Boston, organized July 30th, 1733.

First masonic publication in America was Benjamin Franklin's reprint of Anderson's Constitutions, 1734.

George Washington initiated in Fredericksburg Lodge, Va., November 4th, 1752.

The Prov. G. L. of Scotland appointed Joseph Warren Prov. G. M. of the Continent of America, June 24th, 1769.

American Union Lodge established in American army, at Roxbury, Ct., 1776. The minutes from 1776 to 1779 are in the hands of Robt. Morris, Ky.

The number of masonic Lodges in the United States in 1804 was 527.

"Freemasons' Magazine," Phila.: Lewis & Weaver. First masonic periodical in the United States, published in 1811.

244   REMARKABLE.

Grand Encampment of the United States organized at New York, 20th January, 1816.

General Lafayette assists in laying the corner-stones of monuments to *Greene* and *Pulaski*, July 16th, 1825.

The disappearance of Wm. Morgan, September 12th, 1826.

The "U. S. Anti-Masonic Convention" assemble at Philadelphia, September 11th, 1830.

The Legislature of Pennsylvania summon George M. Dallas and others, to testify concerning Freemasonry, January, 1836.

Grand Lodge of Pa. proposes General Washington for Gen. G. M. of U. S., 13th January, 1780.

The corner-stone of Washington Monument, Washington, D. C., laid July 4th, 1848.

Foreign Remarkable Occurrences in Masonry. — St. Alban formed the first Grand Lodge in Britain, A.D. 287.

King Athelstane granted a charter to Freemasons, 926.

Prince Edwin formed a Grand Lodge at York, 926.

Edward III. revised the Constitutions, 1358.

Masons' Assemblies prohibited by Parliament, 1425.

Henry VI. initiated, 1450.

Inigo Jones constituted several Lodges, 1607.

Earl of St. Albans regulated the Lodges, 1637.

St. Paul's begun by Freemasons, 1675.

William III. initiated, 1690.

St. Paul's completed by Freemasons, 1710.

Grand Lodge revived, Anthony Sayer, Esq., G. M. 1717.

Valuable MSS. burnt by scrupulous brethren, 1720.

Office of D. G. M. revived, 1720.

Book of Constitutions published, 1723.

Grand Secretary first appointed, 1723.

Grand Treasurer first appointed, 1724.

Com. of Charity established, 1725.

REMARKABLE. **245**

Provincial Grand Masters first appointed, 1726.

Twelve Grand Stewards first appointed, 1728.

Lord Kingston gave valuable presents to the Grand Lodge, 1729.

Duke of Norfolk, ditto, 1731.

Emperor of Germany initiated, 1735.

Fred., Prince of Wales, initiated, 1737.

The Crown Prince of Prussia (Frederick the Great) initiated, 1738.

Public Processions on Feast Days discontinued, 1747.

Their R. H., the Dukes of York and Gloster, initiated, 1766.

Registering Regulations commenced 28th October, 1768.

Hall Committee appointed, 1773.

The King of Prussia sanctioned the Grand Lodge at Berlin, 1774.

First stone of Freemasons' Hall laid, 1785.

Office of Grand Chaplain rev., 1775.

Freemasons' Hall dedicated, 1776.

Freemasons' Calendar published by authority of the G. L., 1777.

H. R. H. Henry Fred., Duke of Cumberland, elected G. M., 1781.

H. R. H. Prince of Wales (late King George IV.) initiated, 1787.

H. R. H. Duke of York initiated, 1787.

H. R. H. Duke of Clarence (late King William IV.) initiated, 1787.

Female school instituted, 1788.

H. R. H. Duke of Kent initiated, 1790.

The Prince of Wales elected G. M., 1790.

H. R. H. Prince William of Gloucester initiated, 1795.

H. R. H. Duke of Cumberland (late King of Hanover) initiated, 1796.

21*

246

REMARKABLE.

H. R. H. Duke of Sussex initiated, 1798.

Boys' Institution established, 1798.

Liquidation Fund established, 1798.

Act of Parliament passed, containing enactments respecting the society, 1799.

Foundation-stone of Covent Garden Theater laid by the Prince of Wales as G. M., 1808.

A G. M.'s Jewel, composed of brilliants (value £1000), purchased by voluntary subscription of Lodges and brethren, presented to the Earl of Moira on his quitting England, as Gov.-Gen. of India, 1813.

H. R. H. the Duke of Sussex elected G. M. on resignation of H. R. H. the Prince Regent, who took the title of G. Pat. 1813.*

Reunion of all the Freemasons of England under H. R. H. the Duke of Sussex as G. M., 27th December, 1813.

Constitutions of the United Grand Lodge published, 1815.

Brother Wm. Preston, of Lodge of Antiquity, gave, by will, £500 consols to Fund of Benevolence; £500 consols to Girls' School; £300 consols for Prestonian Lecture, 1819.

George IV. signified his pleasure to continue Patron, 1820.

H. R. H. the Duke of Sussex, G. M., gave five superb carved and gilt chairs, with velvet cushions, to Grand Lodge, 1820.

H. R. H. the Duke of York laid foundation-stone of Eton and Windsor Bridge, 1822.

H. R. H. the Duke of Sussex gave to the Grand Chapter a splendid carpet with masonic devices, 1825.

The foundation-stones of the following structures were laid by H. R. H. the Duke of Sussex, M. W. G. M., accompanied by His Grace, the Duke of Leinster, G. M. of Ireland, viz.: The Suspension Bridge, Hammersmith, 1825.

RENUNCIATION—RESURRECTION. 247

The London University and the Caledonian Asylum, 1827. The Licensed Vic. Do., 1828. The Charing-Cross Hospital, 1831.

Charity Medal, instituted as an honorary distinction to brethren who have served as Stewards for the Girls' School and Boys' School, 1829.

King William IV. declared himself Patron of the order, 1830.

The Masonic Temple built, 1830.

Her Majesty Queen Adelaide became Patroness of the Female School, 1831.

Sir John Soane gave £500 to the Fund of Gen. Purp., 1832.

H. R. H. the Duke of Sussex gave a marble bust of his Majesty King William IV., also the three gilt trowels with which II. R. H. laid the foundation-stones of the London University, the Licensed Victuallers' Asylum, and the Charing-Cross Hospital, 1833.

A piece of plate, weighing 1800 ozs., purchased by the voluntary subscription of Lodges and brethren, was presented to H. R. H. the Duke of Sussex, on completing 25 years as Grand Master, 1838.

H. R. H. the Duke of Sussex died 21st April, 1843.

The Earl of Zetland, Pro. G. M., elected and installed as Grand Master, 1844.

Renunciation.—The ancient Israelitish custom was to renounce a contract by handing the shoe to the party to whom he transferred the right. It was the custom to take off the shoe on holy ground.

Representative.—The Master and Wardens of a Lodge are the representatives of the Grand Lodge.

Resignation.—When a member desires to leave a Lodge, he hands in his application for resignation to the Lodge. He is then given a certificate commonly called a demit.

Resurrection.—After our Lord completed the work of

248

RETURNS—ROMAN.

redemption, by death upon the cross, he arose victorious from the grave, and became the Prince of life.

Returns.—Annual returns of the lists of members, initiations, passing and raising of brethren, must be made by every Lodge to the Grand Lodge.

Rhode Island.—Freemasonry was introduced into this State about 1746. On the 27th Dec. 1749, St. John's Lodge, Boston, granted a warrant for a Lodge at Newport. On the 18th Jan. 1757, a Lodge was organized at Providence. On the 3d Nov. 1790, the Grand Chapter organized. In 1805, the Grand Commandery was organized. In 1860, 30th Oct., the Grand Council was formed.

Ribbon of the Eagle.—An order of knighthood devised by Emperor Maximilian. Maximilian was executed by the Juarez Government of Mexico, in 1867, as an usurper.

Rights.—Passed and raised are a Mason's rights.

Ritual, Masonic.—Quite a number of rituals are in use. They are to instruct the young Mason in the duties of Freemasonry. They contain the work and lectures of the order. "MACOY'S TRUE MASONIC GUIDE" possesses great advantages, and perhaps is the best ritual in use.

Rivers of Eden. — Pison, Gihon, Hiddekel. and Euphrates.

Rod of Moses.—When Moses asked liberty of Pharaoh for the Hebrews to go a day's journey into the wilderness to offer solemn sacrifices to God, he refused; but God encouraged Moses with a sign, to cast his rod before Pharaoh, and it was turned into a serpent. Pharaoh still refused, and Moses and Aaron returned. The magicians were then brought to confront them. Aaron then flung down his rod and it became a living serpent, as did also the magicians', but Aaron's rod, in token of superiority, swallowed up theirs. It was held as a sign of divine authority, and the pride of Pharaoh was humbled.

Roman Eagle.—A Lodge founded in Edinburgh, Scot-

ROSAIC — RUSSIA. 249

land, by J. Brown, in 1785, in which the work was all conducted in the Latin language.

Rosaic Rite.—Instituted by Rev. Rosa in Germany.

Rossy Cross Brothers.—Instituted in Europe in 1700. Its doctrines were the study of philosophy, science, a reform in law, religion, and persons. A German named Rosenkrentz was the reputed author of the Rite. It had nine degrees:

1. Zelator.	6. Adeptus Major.
2. Thericus.	7. Adeptus Exemptus.
3. Practicus.	8. Magister.
4. Philosophus.	9. Magus.
5. Adeptus Junior.	

Rough Ashler.—A stone taken from the quarries in its crude state.

Royal Arch Captain.—An officer in the R. A. degree.

Royal Arch Degree.—The summit of ancient Freemasonry. It impresses more fully our belief in a Divine Being, and admonishes us to venerate and respect that great name.

Royal Lodge.—On the return of the captives from bondage, the Royal Lodge was opened in Jerusalem. It was presided over by Zerubbabel, Joshua, and Haggai.

Royal Master.—First degree of Council in the Secret System.

Royal Order of Scotland.—The Herodem and Rosy Cross, included in the two degrees of this order, composed the Royal Order of Scotland.

Ruammi.—Means "my people" and "obtained mercy."

Rundlett, Thomas.—Past Grand Master of the Grand Lodge of New Hampshire. Died Sept. 10th, 1864, aged 74. He was esteemed as an excellent brother.

Russia.—Freemasonry was introduced in this kingdom by the Grand Lodge of England establishing a Lodge at St. Petersburg in 1731. In 1771, Peter III. conducted the

250

SABBATH—SAINT.

order. In 1783, the Grand Lodge was formed. In 1822, Alexander interdicted the order on account of the political disturbances admitted into the order. Shortly afterwards the system again flourished. In answer to our inquiries as to Masonry in Russia, Hon. C. M. Clay, Minister of U. S. at St. Petersburg, under date of August 24th, 1867, says: "There are no Masons in Russia." Whether Mr. Clay means by this the Lodges, he does not state, but this is certainly the idea he means to convey; for there is no doubt whatever as to individual Masons living in Russia.

S.

Sabbath.—The original word signifies rest. It was a memorial of the creation, as God rested on the seventh day and hallowed it.

Sacred Lodge of Masons.—The officers who presided over the Sacred Lodges were Solomon, Hiram, King of Tyre, and Hiram Abiff, the widow's son, and instituted on Mount Moriah under the Holy of Holies.

Sacred Name (*Jehovah*).—The Jews, to express the divine essence, used this word. To express Omnipotence, El, Elah, and Eloah. For excellency, Elion. For mercy, Elchamon.

Sage, Col. Henry.—Was born in New York, and settled in Circleville, Ohio, July 4th, 1818. He was initiated into Pickaway Lodge, No. 23, of Circleville, Jan. 1820, and remained a member until his death, April 18th, 1865. He was P. G. S. Warden of the G. L. of Ohio.

Saint John, Knights of.—A military order of religious persons. They derived their name from the monastery dedicated to St. John at Jerusalem about 1048, from merchants of the Amalfi, the brotherhood of its members being devoted to taking care of poor and sick pilgrims. The

SAMARITANS—SAXONY.
251

order was instituted as a military one by Raymond du Puy, in the 12th century. It was divided into three ranks, Knights, Captains, and Servitors, and in its military capacity bound to defend the church against infidels. Being driven from Palestine in the 13th century, they fixed their headquarters at Cyprus, and afterwards Rhodes, where they remained from 1309 to 1522, when the island was captured by Solyman II. After several changes, Charles V. fixed the headquarters at Malta, in 1536, whence they took the name Knights of Malta. Here they maintained themselves until the island was taken by Napoleon in 1798. The sect was then fixed at Ferrara. Before the French Revolution they numbered 3000. Their lands and possessions were controlled by the Grand Master, who was controlled by eight governors in Provence, Auvergne, France, Italy, Aragon, Germany, Castile, and England. The lands were divided into priories, commanderies, and baillage. The spiritual power was exercised by the chapter, consisting of eight balliri conventuales. The Knights were under the rules of the Order of St. Augustine, but Protestants were not bound to celibacy. The Scottish Rite has appropriated much of their forms and symbols. The Knights Templar have incorporated the Knights of Malta in their system.

Samaritans.—An order of Adoptive Masonry, founded on the parable of the Good Samaritan, and conferred upon the wives of Royal Arch Masons.

Sanctum Sanctorum.—*Holy of Holies.*

Sanhedrim.—A Council of 72 Senators among the Jews, who advised upon the affairs of the nation.

Sash.—An Arabic word, signifying bond. It is used in the Royal Arch degree.

Saxony.—In 1738, a Lodge was opened at Dresden. In 1741, a Lodge was opened at Leipsic. In 1742, a Lodge was opened at Altenberg. In 1805, the Grand Lodge was formed.

252   *SCANDINAVIAN — SCOTTISH.*

Scandinavian Mysteries.—Sigge, a priest, is the reputed author of this system. It was a representation of a contest between Good and Evil, or Truth and Error.

Scepter.—A Staff of Wood. Among the ancients it was an insignia of honor. It is used in Royal Arch degree.

Schamir.—The Jewish rabbins contend that Solomon obtained a secret from an evil spirit, Asmodeus, by which he was enabled to complete the Temple without using the hammer or axe. It is contended that this secret was a stone called schamir, that could be used as a diamond.

School, Masonic.—In 1788, a Royal Freemason's School was established in London to educate and maintain children of deceased brethren. A second was established in 1798.

Schroeder's Rite.—Schroeder, as early as 1776, organized a Chapter of the Rose Croix, at Marburgh. The Grand Lodge at Hamburg acknowledged its legitimate Freemasonry.

Scientific Masonry.—A knowledge of Arts and Sciences.

Scotland.— Freemasonry was introduced here in the 15th century. In 1430, James I. was Grand Master. In 1441, James II. appointed Wm. St. Clair Grand Master, and made it hereditary to his heirs. St. Clair was the Baron of Roslin. Kilwinning was the seat of the Grand Lodge. In 1736, the Grand Master resigned his hereditary right, and asked the Lodge to elect a new Grand Master, which they did, October 15th, 1736, by electing Wm. St. Clair Grand Master. In 1807, Kilwinning Lodge surrendered her authority to the Grand Lodge, and her Master was appointed Provincial Grand Master of Ayrshire.

Scottish Rite (*or Ancient and Accepted Scottish Rite*).— This rite is composed of thirty-three degrees, and are given herewith as practiced in the United States:

SCOTTISH. **253**

Symbolic.
1. Apprentice.
2. Fellow Craft.
8. Master.

Perfection.
4. Secret Master.
5. Perfect Master.
6. Intimate Secretary.
7. Provost and Judge.
8. Intendant of the Building.
9. Elect of Nine.
10. Elect of Fifteen.
11. Sublime Knights Elected of the Twelve.
12. Grand Master Architect.
13. Knights of the Ninth Arch, or Royal Arch of King Solomon.
14. Grand Elect, Perfect and Sublime Master.

Prince of Jerusalem.
15. Knight of the Sword, of the East and Eagle.
16. Prince of Jerusalem.

Rose Croix.
17. Knight of East and West.
18. Knight of the Eagle, Pelican, or Sovereign Prince of Rose Croix.

Prince of the Royal Secret.
19. Grand Pontiff, or Sublime Ecossais.
20. Venerable Grand Master of all Symbolic degrees.
21. Noachite, or Prussian Knight.
22. Knight of the Royal Axe, or Prince of Libanus.
23. Chief of the Tabernacle.
24. Prince of the Tabernacle.
25. Knight of the Brazen Serpent.
26. Prince of Mercy, or Scottish Trinitarian.
27. Sovereign Commander of the Temple.
28. Knight of the Sun, or Prince Adept.
29. Grand Scottish Knight of St. Andrew, or Patriarch of the Crusades.
30. Knight Kadosh.
81. Grand Inquiring Commander.
82. Sublime Prince of the Royal Secret.

Supreme Council.
83. Sovereign Grand Inspector-General.

Scottish Templars.—This rite is five degrees, divided into two divisions. The masonic symbolic degrees are used in it. The first division consists of Novice and Esquire and Knights Templar. The second division, Knights of Priories, Knights Commanders, and Knights Grand Crosses. The Grand Conclave meet quarterly. The officers are Grand Master, Past Grand Master, Grand Sentinel, Pre-

22

254
SEABURY— SEDITION.

cepter and Grand Prior of Scotland, Grand Constable, Grand Admiral, Grand Almoner, Grand Treasurer, Grand Chancellor, Grand Secretary, Grand Provôst, Grand Standard Bearer, Grand Prelate, Grand Chamberlain, Grand Steward, Grand Bearer of the Vexillum Belli, and Grand Aids-de-Camp.

Seabury, Samuel.—Was born in New London, Connecticut, in 1728. His father was an Episcopal rector at Hempstead, Long Island, and had his son appointed an assistant in 1748. In 1754, after his return to America, he was rector of the New Brunswick church, In 1757, he changed to Jamaica, Long Island. In 1766, was made rector of St. Peter's, Westchester, N. Y. He was entered a Mason in a British Military Lodge about 1776. He delivered an address to the Prov. G. Lodge of New York in 1782, 27th December. In 1783, a warrant was obtained for the "Loyal American Regiment" for a Military Lodge. He was Chaplain of this regiment, and a member of the Lodge. To be consecrated, he went to Europe in 1784, and returned shortly afterward. He died at New London in 1796, February 25th, aged 68.

Seal.—A Lodge must be supplied with a seal; without it being affixed to documents they must be illegal.

Seal of Solomon.—It consisted in a double Triangle. It is stated that by virtue of this seal he held the evil genii fast until the Temple was completed, and also compelled it to assist. This is the legend of Moslems.

Second Degree.—The Fellow Craft.

Secretary.—An officer of the Lodge whose duty is to commit to writing the business of the Lodge.

Secret Monitor.—A side degree of Masonry deduced from the history of David and Jonathan, as found in 20th chapter 1st Samuel.

Sedition Act.—Parliament enacted the following in relation to Freemasonry: "Whereas certain societies holden in this kingdom, known as Freemasons, the meetings whereof are charitable, etc., be it enacted that nothing in this act shall extend to such meetings," etc. This was during the minority reign of Henry VI., in 1425. This Parliament received the name of *Bat Parliament* from the fact that the servants and followers of the peers came armed with stones and clubs. Henry Beaufort, Bishop of Winchester, desired to destroy these meetings of Masons on account of the secrecy observed in them. The Parliament was influenced by ignorant clergy who had arrayed themselves against the order, as they did not fully understand architecture, and were thought unfit for the brotherhood. Thinking they had the right to know all secrets by virtue of auricular confessions, and the Masons not conferring anything thereof, the clergy were offended, and thus represented them as wicked and dangerous to the State, and thus succeeded in making an act that might seem to reflect dishonor upon the fraternity.

Senior Warden.—2d officer of a M. Mason's Lodge.

Sentinel.—Guard of the R. A. C.

Serpent and Cross.—As a punishment for the idolatry of the Israelites they were bitten by serpents, from which they died. Moses, however, made a brazen serpent, and set it up, and he that looked upon it, lived. The cross from thenceforth became an emblem of life, and afterwards was introduced into Freemasonry as an emblem of life and salvation.

Seven.—An important number among Masons. Anciently the craft were required to cultivate the seven liberal arts. By joining two triangles we form a six-pointed star, and if we inclose this star with a circle, we have seven points. With this sign the ancients represented the seven subordinate powers of nature.

Seven Stars.—Denote that seven Masons are required to form a perfect Lodge.

256
SHADDAI--SHIBBOLETH.

Shaddai.—A name applied to Jehovah. The term is used in the Secret Master's deg.

Shekinah.—The visible symbol of Divine glory which dwelt in the Tabernacle and Temple. It was a concentrated glowing brightness, a preternatural splendor, an effulgent something expressed by the word glory.

Shem.—Second son of Noah, who assisted to cover his father's nakedness, for which he blessed him, and predicted in his posterity the Church of God should long remain. Referred to in the Templar System.

Shem, Ham, and Japhet.—They constructed the Ark under the superintendence of Noah, in which, as a tabernacle of repose and refuge, the chosen family took refuge until the subsidence of the deluge.

Shesh-Bazzar.—This was another name given to Zerubbabel; a common occurrence among the Jews, signifying gold and fine linen. Zerubbabel signified misery.

Shethar-boznai.—See Tatnai and Shether-boznai.

Shew-Bread.—Twelve loaves of unleavened bread, styled the presence bread on account of its always being in the presence of Jehovah.

Shibboleth.—When the Ephraimites came out of Egypt they numbered 40,500, but decreased 8000 in the wilderness. When Joshua became the leader and conquered Canaan, he assigned his own tribe the very heart of the promised land. The Amorites and Manasseh remonstrated about the narrowness of the territory, and encouraged them to expel the Canaanites from the hill country. This they did, and took Bethel. When Deborah judged Israel, she levied war against Jabin, and a body of Ephraimites were sent to attack Amalekites, who were ravaging the south of Israel. When Gideon defeated the Midians, the Ephraimites upbraided him because they had not been called to their assistance. Hence, when Jephthah marched against the Amorites, he invited them to join them, but they refused. When without their aid he defeated the enemy, great numbers of them crossed over Jordan and abused his troops as a set of vagabonds. Provoked with this ungenerous abuse, he and his troops fell upon them and put them to flight, and securing the passages of Jordan before them, they killed all they could discover to be Ephraimites by the pronunciation of *Sibboleth* instead of *Shibboleth*, as they could not frame to pronounce it otherwise. There fell that day of the Ephraimites forty and two thousand.

Shovel.—An instrument used to put away the rubbish and loose earth.

Shrine.—Depository of the R. A. Secrets.

Sic Transit Gloria Mundi (*So passeth away earthly glory*).—The symbol adopted by the Knights of the Garter.

Signet of Zerubbabel, or Signet of Truth.—The signet or private seal was frequently used among the ancients in the form of a ring, and given in place of a written instruction or testimonial as token of some authority.

Sign of Distress.—A society formed to assist each other are expected to have some sign whereby, when distressed, they can make known their condition.

Signs, Words, and Tokens.—These are characteristics of Freemasonry, and are simply indexes to the system they serve to unlock, which opens up to us the beauty and glory of the institution.

Skull and Bones.—Emblematical of mortality. It is a solemn lesson to the Mason when he knows that death must end his labors, but he is encouraged by the promises of the gospel of a better life.

Snap Dragon.—On February 3d, 1737, the petition of John Remington, attorney-at-law, was presented to the Council at Philadelphia for their action. The petitioner sets forth "that he was unfortunately deluded and drawn into the idle Diversion of performing the Ceremony of making a

258

SNAP.

Free-Mason, in order to which a Sport called Snap Dragon was prepared, at which the Petitioner was perswaded to be present; that unhappily some of the burning Spirit used in this Sport was thrown or spilled on the Breast of one Daniel Rees, which so burnt or scalded him that in a few days afterwards the said Daniel dyed. That Doctor Evan Jones had been indicted as the Principal for the murder of the said Daniel Rees, and by a Jury of the County was found guilty of manslaughter. That the Petitioner was also indicted as aiding and abetting the said Evan Jones, and altho' no Evidence did or could appear to prove that the Petitioner had any hand in the spilling or throwing the said Liquor on the Body of the said Daniel, or was privy to any Design or Intention of doing harm to the said Daniel, or to any other Person: yet the same Jury had bro't in a verdict of manslaughter likewise against the Petitioner, which if put in Execution would tend to the utter ruin of the Petitioner, his Wife, and two small children, and, therefore, humbly prayed the Prest. and Council would be pleased to grant him a Pardon: Whereupon the Board are of Opinion that the Petitioner should be pardoned the manslaughter aforesaid, and the burning in the hand which by reason thereof he ought to suffer; but it being observed in the Tryal that a certain wicked and irreligious Paper had been produced and read, which appeared to have been composed by the said Remington, who had made the aforesaid Daniel Rees repeat the same, or part of the form to be gone thro' on initiating him as a Free-Mason; the Board thereupon agreed that the Pardon should be so restricted as that it might not be pleaded in Bar of any Prosecution that should hereafter be commenced against the said Remington on account of the said scandalous paper." The perpetrators of this farce appear not to have been Masons. They conducted Rees to a dark cellar, where one of the party exhibited himself as the devil in a

SOCIAL — SOLOMON. 259

bull's hide; others were engaged in picking raisins from a dish of burning fluid. When the bandage was taken from Rees's eyes, one of the party thoughtlessly threw the dish of burning fluid upon Rees, who had been witnessing the proceeding with quaking fear. Franklin, the Grand Master, investigated the affair, and Thos. Hopkinson, G. M., Wm. Plumstead, D. G. M., Jos. Shippen and Henry Pratt, Wardens, testified that the perpetrators of this outrage did not belong to any society of Free and Accepted Masons; dated Philadelphia, June 10th, 1737.

Social Contract.—A union of Lodges in Paris, in 1776.

Sodalities.—Societies of congenial spirits. In early days, when protection could not be obtained from the laws, they banded together in such associations, so that they could assist one another.

Sojourners.—A term applied to those who have been exalted as Royal Arch Masons, but not elected to membership. The prophets incited many sojourners from Babylon to assist the glorious work of building the Temple.

Solomon.—Was the son of David, by his favorite Bathsheba. Solomon overpowered his brother Adonijah, and was anointed by the Prophet Nathan as King. His reign was remarkable for his traffic and wealth, his buildings, his ecclesiastical arrangements, his administration, his seraglio, and his enemies. He was the first Grand Master of Masons in Judea.

Solomon's Temple.—The Temple that Solomon builded has been often described. It was an immense building, and served as a dwelling-place for the priests, and a safe retreat for the Ark. The foundation was laid in the year of the world 2993. Solomon employed the best of architects that could be found. Hiram, King of Tyre, sent him Hiram Abiff, the widow's son, an illustrious and skillful architect: 180,000 men were employed in building the Temple. It was erected on Mt. Moriah. It was seven

260
SORROW.

years in building. Into the Temple were entrances from every side. The southwest gate was called Shallecheth, the east gate Sur, the south gate Asuppin. Into the outer court the Hebrews entered; in the middle the priests and Levites, where the brazen altar stood. The Temple stood east to west. On each side of the entrance stood a pillar, adorned with chapiters and pomegranates, one called *Jachin*, stability, the other, *Boaz*, strength. Passing this porch the Holy of Holies came, in which stood the golden candlestick, the ten tables of shew bread, and the altar of incense. Then came the sanctuary of the oracle, or *most holy place*, in which stood the Ark overstretched by the cherubim. Eleven months after the Temple was finished the Ark was placed in it, and the Shekinah or cloud of Divine glory entered it ,and rested over the Ark. It was dedicated by Solomon by seven days of prayer and feast offerings. The Jewish Temple remained about 30 years in its glory, when Shisak carried off its treasures. It fell into decay under Jeharon, Ahaziah, and Altholiah. Jehoida and Joash repaired it in A.M. 3150. Soon after, Joash robbed it of its treasures. Ahaz shut up the Temple after robbing it. Hezekiah repaired it, and afterward took its treasures and gave them to Sennacherib. Monnareth restored the true worship of God in the Temple. Josiah placed the Ark in it. A.M. 3398, Nebuchadnezzar carried its treasures to Babylon. In 3416, he destroyed it entirely. A.M. 3469, by the order of Cyrus, King of Persia, it began to be rebuilt. The second Temple was built under the direction of Zerubbabel and Joshua, the high priests. A.M. 3837, Antiochus profaned, but 39 years after, Judas Maccabeus purified it. A.M. 3987, Herod rebuilt it, and 70 years after, Titus burned it. At present a mock Temple, used by the Mohammedans, now stands upon the site.

Sorrow Lodges.—These Lodges are quite common in

SOUTH. **261**

Europe. On the death of a brother, his body is conveyed to the Lodge-room, which is appropriately prepared by being dressed in black. The appropriate ceremonies are there performed, the addresses made, and the body taken to its last resting-place.

South.—The position of the Senior Warden. He is symbolized as the sun at the meridian.

South Carolina.—Masonry was first introduced in South Carolina about 1736. Lord Weymouth, G. M. of England, granted a warrant October 28th, 1736, for Solomon's Lodge, No. 45, to be held at Charleston. This Lodge worked until 1811, and revived again in 1817, and worked until 1838, and revived again in 1841. In 1736, the Grand Lodge of England appointed John Hammerton Provincial G. M. In 1737, James Grome was appointed to the position. In 1754, the French government appointed Peter Leigh Chief Justice, and he reorganized the Provincial G. L., which had remained inactive for several years. In 1761, Benj. Smith was appointed Provincial G. M., which held to 1767. In 1769, the Grand Lodge of England appointed as Provisional G. M. Egerton Leigh. In 1777, Bernard Elliott was elected G. M. of the State, being the time of its independent organization, although it is stated as occurring in 1787. In 1787, the G. L. of A. Y. Masons organized. In 1808, the two Grand Lodges united. In 1809, the G. L. of A. Y. Masons reorganized, and it was not until 1817 that a complete union was effected.

The Royal Arch Chapter.—This body was organized May 29th, 1812, at Charleston. The first Grand High Priest elected was William Young.

The Ancient and Accepted Rite.—Was introduced 1783, at Charleston, but it was not fully organized until 1860. The first Most Puissant Grand Master was Albert G. Mackey, who from his masonic writings has become one of the brightest stars in American Masonry.

262

SOV.—STAVES.

Knights Templar.—This system was introduced into South Carolina about 1780 or 1782.

Sov. Grand Inspector General.—33d° A. and A. R. This degree was organized by the King of Prussia. The motto, *Deus meumque jus,* "God and my right."

Spain. — Freemasonry was introduced by the Grand Lodge of England into Spain, by chartering a Lodge at Gibraltar, in 1727. In 1728, a Lodge was opened at Madrid. In 1739, one at Andalusia. In 1740, Freemasonry was interdicted by Philip V. Persecutions were continued against the order until 1807. In 1809, a Grand Lodge was organized at Madrid. In 1811, the King organized a Grand Chapter. Ferdinand VIII. restored the Inquisition, which continued until 1814. In 1850, or about that time, a Grand Lodge was formed. Notwithstanding the persecutions of these vicious devils of Popery, the order still continues to flourish.

Square.—One of the immovable jewels of the Lodge. Operative masons use it to prove their work. Speculative Masons symbolize it, that their actions may prove upright to all men and Masons.

Standard Bearer.—An officer in the Templar system and Grand Lodge.

Star.—This was designated on certain. cases to mean God. Hence, as Balaam prophesied that a star would spring out of Jacob and a scepter out of Israel, it meant Shiloh.

Staves. — The Biblical history relates that as Moses tended the flocks of Jethro, Jehovah commanded him to go and deliver his brethren from bondage. But Moses said, "They will not believe me." And the Lord said unto him, "What is in thy hand?" And he said, "A rod." And he said, "Cast it on the ground." And he cast it on the ground, and it became a living serpent. And the Lord commanded him, "Put forth thy hand and take it by the

STATISTICS.

tail." And he put forth his hand and caught it, and it became a rod in his hand. This stave is used as symbolical in the Royal Arch degrees.

Statistics.—Number of Lodges in the various States, from 1816. In 1816, many of the Grand Lodges were not formed, and hence no returns.

	Year.	No. of Lodges.	Year.	No. of Lodges.	Year.	No. of Lodges.	Year.	No. of Lodges.	1866. Members.	Initiated.
Alabama	1816	......	1822	14	1859	255	1867	334	10,904	1,037
Arkansas	......	......	......	......	1859	128	1867	204	6,134	637
Canada	1816	23	1822	32	1859	179	1867	183	6,263	833
California	......	......	......	......	1859	138	1867	......	7,020	816
Colorado	......	......	......	......	......	......	1867	12	380	89
Connecticut	1816	54	1822	61	1859	85	1867	103	9,939	1,092
Delaware	1816	9	1822	5	1859	20	1867	24	778	......
Dist. Columbia	......	......	1822	7	1859	16	......	......	1,978	485
Florida	......	......	......	......	1859	50	1867	57	*1,495	341
Georgia	1816	14	1822	20	1859	329	......	......	†19,923	2,373
Illinois	......	......	1822	21	1859	306	1867	......	23,158	4,490
Indiana	......	......	......	......	1859	271	1867	363	16,254	3,222
Iowa	......	......	......	......	1859	137	1867	216	7,586	1,426
Kansas	......	......	......	......	1859	9	1867	50	1,470	339
Kentucky	1816	28	1822	73	1859	365	......	439	15,157	2,494
Louisiana	1816	5	1822	22	1859	160	......	196	6,171	1,616
Maine	......	......	1822	40	1859	97	1867	141	10,075	1,608
Maryland	1816	10	1822	26	1859	109	......	......	3,869	249
Montana	......	......	......	......	......	......	......	......	239	......
Massachusetts	1816	99	1822	87	1859	105	......	......	16,000	2,311
Michigan	......	......	......	......	1859	117	1867	226	13,154	2,679
Minnesota	......	......	......	......	1859	28	1867	31	......	......
Mississippi	......	......	......	......	1859	239	......	......	......	......
Missouri	......	......	......	......	1859	191	1867	275	9,558	1,415
Nevada	......	......	......	......	......	......	......	......	610	126
Nebraska	......	......	......	......	......	6	......	......	475	135
N. Hampshire	1816	21	1822	37	1859	65	1867	84	4,712	709
New Jersey	1816	27	1822	51	1859	52	1867	80	5,055	......
New York	1816	158	1822	310	1859	491	1867	661	50,200	10,889
N. Carolina	1816	29	1822	77	1859	232	1867	260	12,002	1,136
Ohio	1816	29	1822	44	1859	333	1867	372	19,750	2,600
Oregon	......	......	......	......	1859	24	......	......	1,120	153
Pennsylvania	1816	69	1822	98	1859	335	......	......	17,625	2,708
Rhode Island	1816	13	1822	14	1859	21	......	......	2,350	233
S. Carolina	1816	13	1822	51	1859	93	1867	131	......	......
Tennessee	1816	8	1822	34	1859	275	1867	236	......	......
Texas	......	......	......	......	1859	238	......	......	10,025	750
Vermont	1816	34	1822	51	1859	49	......	......	5,473	954
Virginia	1816	93	1822	67	1859	180	......	......	‡7,000	......
Wash. Ter	......	......	......	......	1859	4	......	......	347	30
Wisconsin	......	......	......	......	1859	118	1867	169	6,341	1,362
West Virginia	......	......	......	......	......	......	1867	26	1,061	259

Note.—It has been impossible to complete all the Lodge statistics.

* 30 Lodges out of 54.　　　　† 162 Lodges out of 250.　　　　‡ Partial.

264   STEWARDS—STEWART.

Stewards.—Officers in charge of the banquet, etc.

Steward's Lodge.—Originated in England in 1735. It was founded by Lord Weymouth, Grand Master.

Stewart, Edward.—Was born in the County of Morris, N. J., on the 27th day of April, 1799. He removed to Newark in the year 1835, and made that city his permanent residence. His masonic life commenced in the year 1840, at which time he connected himself with St. John's Lodge, No. 1. At the time of the institution of Newark Lodge, No. 7, being anxious to encourage that Lodge in its infancy and weakness, he affiliated with it. With a similar purpose he afterward joined his fortunes with those of Eureka Lodge, No. 39, and died in the fellowship of that Lodge. He occupied the position of Deputy Grand Master in the years 1848 and 1849. In 1850, he was elected Grand Master of the Grand Lodge of New Jersey, and was re-elected to that office for six consecutive years, having been succeeded in 1856 by Brother Babbitt.

In the honorable positions which Bro. Stewart occupied he served the Grand Lodge with zeal and fidelity. Much of the prosperity of the masonic institution in that jurisdiction is attributable to his labors. He took charge of the craft at a time of great despondency and gloom, and by his energy and enthusiasm infused new life and ambition in the brethren. He devoted a large portion of his time to the discharge of the important duties of visitation and instruction. After his retirement from office he continued his devotion and attachment to the fraternity, so long as his health permitted him to mingle in the affairs of the craft. The latter part of his life was shrouded in deep gloom and affliction. After a long and distressing illness, he was gathered to his fathers on the 29th day of January, in the year 1866, at the age of sixty-seven years.

ST. GEORGE—STORY.

St. George, Order.—See Order of Garter.

St. John, Baptist.—John denotes grace or favor. He was the forerunner of Christ, and son of Zechariah, the high priest. He made his public appearance in the fifteenth year of the reign of Tiberius. His raiment was camel's hair, and his food locusts and wild honey. When Jesus heard of John, he came unto him to be baptized. The manner of John's death is well known. He was beheaded 29th August, in the thirty-third year of his life. This was the reward for reproving a tyrant of his heinous crimes. The 24th June, his birthday, is held sacred throughout Christendom.

St. John, Evangelist.—The son of Zebedee, and one of Christ's apostles. After the ascension of Christ, John abode at Jerusalem. He was exiled to Patmos by the Roman emperor, where he wrote the Apocalypse. Dominitian had him forcibly taken to Rome and cast into a cask of oil, but he miraculously escaped. He died at Ephesus in the reign of Trajan. The Gospel of St. John is especially endeared to Masons, as therein are contained all the doctrines of the order. The 27th December, his birthday, is celebrated by Freemasons.

St. John's Masonry.—After the Scottish Rite degrees, the Blue Lodge degrees were anciently termed "St. John's Masonry."

Stone-squarers.—A society of architects, who were well known before the building of the Temple. The Temple of Hercules, at Tyre, was erected by them.

Story, Robert.—First Grand Minister of State of the Most Puissant Sov. Consistory, S. P. R. S. 32d degree, of Kentucky, was born in Slesford, Lincolnshire, England. He died at Louisville, Kentucky, Jan. 24th, 1858. He was much esteemed by the craft as a sound, well-posted Mason.

266 STRIKING OFF—SULLIVAN.

Striking Off.—A Lodge is stricken off when the Grand Master forbids its assemblage.

String of Hiram.—It was the custom of Hiram Abiff to repair at High Twelve to the Holy of Holies. The Ark had not yet been placed there, as that occurred at the dedication, after which no one was permitted to enter except the high priest, and he only once a year, on the day of expiation. It is said he always wore a string around his body, which reached into the court of the Tabernacle, so that he could be drawn out in case of death, which might come upon him while engaged in the services of the Sanctum Sanctorum.

Sublime Grand' Lodge.—A Perfection Lodge.

Substitute Grand Master.—An officer existing in Scotland, similar to that of the Pro. Grand Master of England, which see.

Succoth.—A town on the east of Jordan, belonging to the tribe of Gad. The name is derived from Jacob having tarried there on his return from Padanaram, and made *booths* for his cattle. In preparing the material for the Temple, it was prepared in the valley of Succoth, which lies between Succoth and Zarthan.

Sullivan, John.—Was born in Berwick, Maine, in 1740, February 17th. He was a lawyer by profession. In 1774, he was a delegate to the Continental Congress from New Hampshire. He was returned to Congress in 1775, and commissioned a brigadier-general the same year. In 1776, he was commissioned a major-general, and put in command of the troops of Canada. He was afterward relieved, and joined the army of Washington at New York. He was in command at the battle of Brooklyn, where he was made a prisoner. After his exchange, he was placed in command of the troops in Rhode Island. While stationed here, in 1778, he was permitted to participate in the festival of St. John's day, December 28th, held in Providence. In 1796, the Grand Lodge of Pennsylvania granted a warrant for Lodge No. 70, to be opened at Fort Sullivan. In 1780, he was again delegate to Congress from New Hampshire. In 1783, he was Attorney-General of Rhode Island. In 1786, he was elected Governor. In 1789, he was elected Grand Master of Masons of Rhode Island, and acted as Master of a Lodge in Portsmouth at the same time. He resigned the office of Grand Master in 1790. He died Jan. 23d, 1795, aged fifty-six.

Sun.—The central body of the solar system. It rises in the east and sets in the west. The Master of the Lodge is looked upon as the central point, from whence spring all wise and good influence exerted for the benefit of the craft and mankind.

Super Excellent Master.—A degree of the R. A. The presiding officer represents Zedekiah, last king of Israel.

Superintendent of Work.—The adviser of the Board of General Purposes, on plans of edifices, etc.

Sussex, Duke of.—Augustus Frederick was the ninth son of George III. He was made a Mason in Royal York Lodge, Berlin, in 1798. On the 12th February, 1812, he was appointed Deputy Grand Master of England. He occupied this position until his death, in April, 1843. In reply to an address, the duke says: "In 1798, he was made a Mason in Berlin, and then served as Warden and Representative of G. L. of England. In 1813, '14, at the union of the two London orders, he was elected Grand Master." He was a most ardent and devoted Christian and Mason, and during the long period that he acted as Grand Master he endeared himself to the fraternity by his candid, upright, manly course of action.

Sweden.—The Grand Orient of France granted a warrant to Count Sponea, in 1735. In 1738, the Lodge was closed by a decree, which was removed in 1740. In 1762, the king, Adolphus Frederick, assumed the protectorate

268   *SWEDENBORG — SWITZERLAND.*

of Freemasonry in Sweden. In 1765, the Grand Lodge of England deputed Charles Fallman to establish a Provincial Grand Lodge at Stockholm. In 1799, the Grand Lodge of Sweden and England were united. On the 27th May, 1811, Charles, of Sweden, founded the order of "Charles the XIII." Freemasonry in Sweden enjoys the protection of the government.

Swedenborg, Emanuel.—The celebrated mystic of the eighteenth century was born at Stockholm, in 1688. He was a student of theology, philosophy, mathematics, and natural sciences. His father, Joseph Swedenborg, Bishop of West Gothland, educated him in the severe doctrine of Lutheranism. In 1719, Queen Ulrica raised him to the rank of nobility, and gave his name as Swedenborg instead of Swedeberg. He was respected as a man of profound learning and an acute thinker. The masonic rite of Swedenborg is still practiced in some parts of Sweden.

Swedenborg Rite.—It consists of six degrees:

1. Apprentice.
2. Fellow Craft.
3. Master Theosophite.
4. Illuminated Theosophite.
5. Blue Brother.
6. Red   "

In 1783, Marquis de Thome modified and revised the work, and organized what is now termed the Rite of Swedenborg.

Swedish Rite.—Established by King Gustavus III. It was composed of twelve degrees:

1. 2, and 3. Blue Lodge degrees.
2. E. A. P. and F. C. of St. Andrew.
3. Master of St. Andrew.
4. Brother Stuart.
5. Favorite Bro. of Solomon.
6. Favorite Bro. of St. John, or White Ribbon.
7. Favorite Bro. of St. Andrew, or Violet Ribbon.
8. Member of Chapter.
9. Dignatory of Chapter.
10. Reigning Grand Master.

Switzerland.—In 1737, the Grand Lodge of England appointed Sir George Hamilton Provincial Grand Master,

SWORD — TABERNACLE. 269

with authority to establish a Lodge at Geneva. In 1739, the G. L. of England warranted a Lodge at Lausanne. Shortly afterward, it was interdicted, and remained so for about twenty-eight years, when the order was revived. Upon the cession of Geneva to France, the G. L. of France exercised jurisdiction over Swedish Lodges. In 1822, a reconciliation was effected between the Prov. Grand Lodge and the Grand Orient, by entitling the Provincial Grand Lodge as the Grand Lodge of Switzerland. In 1844, the Grand Lodge was reorganized at Zurich, and is now known as "Alpina."

Sword Bearer.—The Grand Master appoints annually the Grand Sword Bearer on the day he is installed.

Swords.—The sword is used as a symbol of protection. However, our ancient brethren were compelled to arm themselves, in case they were attacked while assembled in Lodge. It is a symbol of K. T.

Symbolism of the Veils.—*Blue* is emblematical of universal friendship and benevolence. *Purple* is to remind us of the intimate connection between symbolic Masonry and the Royal Arch. *Scarlet* is emblematic of fervency and zeal. *White* is emblematical of purity of life.

T.

Tabernacle.—Literally tent of assembly. The three tabernacles are stated as the Ante-Sinaitic, Sinaitic, and Davidic. The Ante-Sinaitic was placed by the camp of the Israelites in the desert to transact business. The Ante-Sinaitic, which was in use from the exodus, was superseded by the Sinaitic as a portable mansion-house, etc. The Davidic was erected by David in Jerusalem for the reception of the Ark. The second of these Moses was commanded by Jehovah to have erected in the desert, and carried by the Israelites until after the conquest of Canaan.

23*

270 — TALMUD — TATNAI.

Talmud.—The Talmud (תלמוד, *doctrine*, from לסד, *to learn*) is the book which embodies the civil and canonical law of the Jews. It contains the rules and regulations by which, in addition to the Old Testament, the conduct of the nation is regulated. The law was divided into the *written* and *unwritten*. The former contained in the Pentateuch, and the latter handed down orally. Moses received both at Mt Sinai. He imparted it to Joshua, and he to the 70 elders, from whom it was received by the prophets, the last of whom was Simon the Just. After the second destruction of Jerusalem, lest the sacred oral traditions should be lost, they were committed to writing. Rabbi Judah Hakkadosh recorded them about 120 or 150 from the destruction of the Temple, A.D. 190 or 220. This is said to be the origin of *Mishnu* or text.

Tatnai and Shethar-Boznai.—Were governors or rulers of the Jews, under the authority of Darius of Babylon. It appears that when the Jews returned from Babylon, the Samaritans did all in their power to oppose the rebuilding the Temple, and bribed some of the counselors of Cyrus to do what they could to stop it. Ahasuerus had no sooner ascended to the throne, than they wrote him a petition to that effect, accusing the Jews of disloyal designs. In the short reign of Artaxerxes, Magnus, Bishlam, Mithrebath, and Tubeel wrote to him to stop the work. About the same time Rehmn, the chancellor, Shimshai, the scribe, and companions, wrote him a letter, in which the Jews were represented as a rebellious people, who, if permitted to build their cities and Temple, would seize on the king's territories west of the Euphrates, and begged them to be stopped, as the records would show them a rebellious people. Search was made, and it was found that powerful kings ruled among the Jews, and the work was ordered to be discontinued. Soon after Tatnai and Shethar-Boznai informed Darius that they had done what they could to stop the building of the Temple, and the Jews had pretended an edict from Cyrus appointing them to build it. Upon search being made, the edict was found, and Darius ratified it, and ordered the Samaritans to give the Jews no further trouble. This history, and the names of these two governors, are in use in the Templar system.

Tau Cross.—The symbol of the R. A. Masons, distinct from the jewel. Placed in the center of a triangle, and also of a circle, it was thus a type of the great name.

Tecumseh, the Indian Chief.—Brother Robert G. Scott, Past Grand Master of Virginia, in an address delivered before the Grand Lodge of that State, in 1845, related the following anecdote, which, he says, "is well authenticated, and vouched for by several witnesses now living:"

During the last war between this country and England, a large detachment of the Northwestern army, under the command of General Winchester, was attacked at the River Raisin, and, after a sanguinary engagement, was overcome by a superior English and Indian force. The ammunition of the Americans being nearly expended, and all expectations of succor vain, they surrendered, on the assurance of their conquerors that the prisoners should be treated with humanity. But they had scarcely laid down their arms, when the Indians commenced stripping them of their clothing, and beat and insulted all who ventured to complain of such treatment. At length the passions of the Indians becoming excited, many of the Americans were tomahawked and scalped. "It was," says Brother Scott, "in the midst of such an exciting scene that an Indian chief with a lofty bearing, and the expression of gratification and vengeance marked on his countenance, looked on this work of carnage and blood. Many of his best warriors had fallen by the sure fire of the Kentucky riflemen. He was chafed and maddened by the recent hot contest. In such a frame of mind he discouraged not the bloody

272   TEN—TENNESSEE.

tragedy.   But behold now this red man of the forest.
What superhuman influence has wrought such a change?
Whither has gone that vengeful, that demon exultation?
It is the cry of a Mason and a brother which had reached
him, a cry asking for mercy, and speaking in a language
which he comprehends and obeys.   He springs from the
cannon on which he is resting, and with the swiftness of
the deer of his native forest he bounds among his followers
and warriors, his tomahawk uplifted, and with a look and
gesture which was never disregarded by his savage soldiers,
utters the life-saving command—'Let the slaughter cease;
kill no more white men.'   This was Tecumseh, a Mason,
who, with two other distinguished chiefs of his tribe, had
years before been united to our order while on a visit to
Philadelphia."

The Percy anecdotes record another instance of the attention of Tecumseh to his masonic obligations:

An officer, in a skirmish with a party of British and
Indians, in the late war, was severely wounded, and unable to rise; two Indians rushed toward him to secure his
scalp as their prey; one appeared to be a chief warrior,
and was clothed in British uniform.   The hatchet was
uplifted to give the fatal blow; the thought passed in his
mind that some of the chiefs were Masons, and with this
hope he gave a masonic sign; it stayed the arm of the
savage warrior—the hatchet fell harmless to the ground—
the Indian sprang forward, caught him in his arms, and
the endearing title of brother fell from his lips.   That
Indian was Tecumseh.

Ten.—Perfect number.

Tennessee. — Freemasonry was introduced into this
State by the Grand Lodge of North Carolina.   In 1811,
a convention was held at Knoxville to form a Grand
Lodge, but it was not until 27th December, 1813, that it
was formed.

TESTS—TEXAS. 273

Tests.—As the entire system of Freemasonry is found in the Bible, it became necessary to adopt tests, to distinguish the true brother from the impostor.

Tesselated Border.—The margin of masonic floor-cloths.

Tetragrammation.—Among several ancient nations, the name of the mystic number four, which was often symbolized to represent the Deity, whose name was expressed in several languages by four letters : the Assyrian, Adad ; Egyptian, Aman; Persian, Syre; Greek, $\theta \varepsilon o \varsigma$; Latin, Deus, German, Gott. The Jews know full well that the true pronunciation of this word is lost, and look for its revelation when the Messiah appears.

Teutonic Order.—It was founded in 1190, by Frederick, Duke of Swabia, and intended for Germans of noble rank only. Its rules were the same as those of Templars, and its object to perform service against the infidels of Palestine. It was dedicated to the Virgin Mary. After the conquest of Jerusalem by the Saracens, the G. Master removed to Venice and afterward to Marbourg. The Prussians were subdued by this order, and forced to embrace Christianity. In 1237, it was united with the Brethren of the Order of Sword of Livonia. Its conquests elevated it to a sovereign power in Europe. The G. Master during its domination resided at Marienburg, Prussia. Its dominions extended from the Odessa to the Gulf of Finland, and the population under its government reached two and a half millions. Its dominion was gradually lost by revolt and conquest. The seat of the G. Master was afterward at Mergenthenia, Swabia. By peace of Presburg, in 1805, the rights and revenues of the G. Master were obtained by the Emperor of Austria, but the order was abolished by Napoleon in 1809. The Teutonic cross is used in the 27th degree A. and A. Rite.

Texas.—The G. L. of Louisiana granted the first warrant for a Lodge in Texas. This Lodge was held at

274   *THIRD— TRIANGLE.*

Brazoria, under date of 17th December, 1835. During the Mexican war the Lodge ceased to work, and in October, 1837, it was reopened at Houston. In 1837, the Grand Lodge was opened at Houston.

Third Degree of Masonry.—Master Mason. It is a reward for merit, historical of the order, and illustrates certain emblems and inculcates many useful lessons.

Three. — Sacredly regarded by Freemasons, as their labors commence and terminate with three.

Three Globes, Rite of.—In 1740, 23d September, this order was instituted at Berlin. In 1744, 24th June, it assumed the name of Grand Mother Lodge of Three Globes. It practices the symbolic degrees and French Rite.

Three Grand Offerings. — The offering of Isaac, the prayer of David for staying the wrath of God when pestilence raged among the people, and those of Solomon at the dedication of the Temple, were all made upon Mount Moriah.

Traitor.—Despised of all men, trusted by none. The first traitor to Freemasonry is yet to be known. Many expositions of Freemasonry have been given to the public, but not one of these so-called Secret Workings of Freemasons contains any of the secrets of the order. This is not a mere idle assertion, but one that every Freemason knows to be *true.*

Treasurer.—Keeper of jewels and valuables.

Trestle-Board.—Used by the Master to draw designs upon.

Triangle.—In geometry, one of the 48 constellations of Hipparchus. The Egyptians declared the origin of everything with it. They expressed the merciful God by the water triangle; the angry God, by the fire triangle; the perfect Godhead, by uniting the two triangles as a star, and by putting around it a circle and the sacred number seven.

Trinidad.—In 1830, the Prov. Grand Master of England organized a Lodge at Trinidad, W. I. In 1798, the Grand Lodge of France granted a warrant, which the G. L. of Pennsylvania renewed in 1799. In 1814, during the revolution, this Lodge was protected by the Grand Lodge of Scotland, and is still under its jurisdiction. In 1814, a warrant was granted by the Grand Conclave of Scotland for a Grand Encampment of Knights Templar. In ——, a Chapter of Royal Arch Masons was organized.

Trinosophists.—A Lodge of Masons in Paris, that adhered strictly to the ancient landmarks, and the most influential of its day. It practiced the Entered Apprentice, Fellow Craft, Master, Rose Croix, and Grand Elect of Nine, as its only degrees.

Triple Cross Knights.—Organized in 1080, at the instance of Pierre Clements, who had returned from Jerusalem with letters from the Patriarch Surion, urging a crusade to drive the infidel from the Holy Land. The officers are G. R. Commander, Sublime Knights, G. R. Squires, and Knights. Jewel, three Crosses on a Square.

Triple Tau.—The figure forms two right angles on the exterior lines, and another by union at the center. This triplified, illustrates the jewel of the R. Arch.

Triple Triangle.—The Druids sacredly regarded the mysterious agency of medicine, and used the symbol of a triple triangle. The Pythagoreans as a symbol of health, while the Arabians and Cabalistic Jews held the same.

Trowel.—Working tool of the W. M. The operative mason uses it to spread the cement which unites the materials, and the speculative Mason to bind together in peace and unity.

Trowel and Sword, Order.—See "Brother of Bridge."

Trowel, Order.—Organized in 1792, at Berlin. The trowel was the emblem of the order, and the patron saint, St. Andrew.

276 — TRUE—TWENTY.

True Masons.—In 1778, organized by Boileau at Montpellier. It had six degrees: True Mason, True Mason in the Right Way, Knight of the Golden Key, Knight of the Rainbow, Knight of the Argonauts, and Knight of the Golden Fleece.

True Patriots.—Organized in 1787, at Frankford. It endeavored to unite all classes together in a common bond of unity through the agency of Freemasonry.

Tubal Cain.—It is stated that prior to the Deluge lived Lamech, who had two wives, Adah and Zillah. Adah bore him two sons, Jabel and Jubal. Zillah bore him two children, Tubal and a daughter Mahmah. These persons are the founders of all crafts in the world. Jabel discovered geometry, Jubal invented music, Tubal the working of all metals, and was the founder of smithery.

Turkey.—The introduction of Freemasonry into Turkey occurred in 1830, but having encountered much opposition it ceased until 1859, when the English Lodge revived it. The Oriental Lodge at Constantinople, and Homer Lodge, Smyrna, were for a long time the only two Lodges. Sir Henry Bulwer, P. G. M., and Hyde Parke, Dep. G. M., secured it position through their protection. In 1800, a German Lodge was opened at Smyrna, of which George Tren was Master, and called " Germania and Golden Horn." In 1800, the Grand Orient of France warranted a Lodge at Constantinople. In 1833 to 1840, the Grand Lodge of Scotland opened a Lodge at Beyrout.

Tuscan.—An order of architecture.

Twenty - four - inch Gauge.—An instrument used by operative masons to lay out their work. Free and Accepted Masons use it for a more glorious and noble purpose, that of dividing their time. The twenty-four parts are emblematical of the 24 hours of the day, which we are taught to divide into three parts, whereby we have one portion for God's service and relief of a worthy brother, a portion for useful avocations, and a portion for refreshment and sleep.

Tyler.—A guard of the Lodge.

Tyle.—The Tyler is required to see that no one enters the Lodge but a Mason properly clothed.

Tyre.—A city on the eastern shore of the Mediterranean. Hiram ruled both Tyre and Sidon. The inhabitants of these cities were skilled in the arts and sciences. The Israelites were not manufacturers, but agriculturists, and hence the necessity of Solomon forming an alliance with the King of Tyre.

Tyrians.—These people were known for their skill in arts. Solomon, on requesting the assistance of Hiram in building the Temple, says: "Thou knowest there is not among us any that can skill to hew timber like unto the Sidonians." He also sent and brought out of Tyre Hiram Abiff, a widow's son, skilled in all the works of brass. In subsequent years every king coveted a Tyrian robe of purple. Ezekiel speaks of its emeralds, fine linen, coral, and agate.

Tyron, Frank B.—Past Grand Engineer of the Most Puissant G. Consistory of Kentucky, was born in New York, March 13th, 1829, and died from wounds received at the battle of Stone River, Tennessee, Jan. 9th, 1863.

U.

United States Anti-Masonic Convention.—This convention assembled at Philadelphia, 11th September, 1830. It was the first formidable attempt of a national combination in opposition to Freemasonry. There were 96 members, representing Massachusetts, Connecticut, New York, Pennsylvania, Vermont, Rhode Island, Ohio, New Jersey, Michigan, Maryland, and Delaware. At that time but few

UNITED STATES.

persons of eminence were among the delegates, but several of them, attaching themselves to other "issues," and abandoning political anti-masonry, subsequently became known. Among them were Francis Granger, Henry Dana Ward, Frederick Whittlesey, Wm. H. Seward, N. Y., and Pliny Merrick, Mass. The cement that bound such minds to men like David Bernard, Moses Thatcher, Thaddeus Stevens, and Joseph Ritner, must have possessed powerful magnetism. Francis Granger was made Prest., seconded by six Vice-Presidents. A remarkable fact is, that no State west of Ohio or south of Maryland had a delegate. Maine and New Hampshire refused the part assigned them, and sent no delegate. Fourteen committees were appointed, and the questions relative to masonic rituals, history, and jurisprudence were divided among them. Mr. Seward was to report resolutions expressive of the sentiments of the Convention. A proposition to inquire into the pecuniary circumstances of the widow and children of William Morgan was rejected, as "that was not the purpose for which they had assembled." Three gentlemen of North Carolina took their seats as honorary members. The committee "on the effects of masonic ties and obligations *on commerce and revenue of the U. S.*," were discharged without a report. In the report of the influence of Masonry upon the public press, it was reported that between 1826 and 1830 there had been 124 anti-masonic papers established, to wit: Pennsylvania, 53; New York, 46; Connecticut, 2; Rhode Island, 1; Massachusetts, 5; Vermont, 4; New Jersey, 2; Ohio, 9; Indiana, 1; Michigan, 1. A number of these journals simply kept quiet to see what the mountain would bring forth, and when they found it to be a mouse, tacked about and retired from the sinking anti-masonic vessel. The summing up of these profound deliberations were: 1. That the expositions of masonic secrets are true. 2. That Freemasonry originated early in the 18th century. 3. That its oaths are not obligatory. 4. That adhering Masons are disqualified for public officers. 5. Masonry and its principles are inconsistent with the genius of American Institutions. 6. That Masonry should be extinguished at the ballot-box. 7. That Masonry is a political institution. 8. That its effects upon the public Press are evil. The Convention adjourned to meet at Baltimore, Sept. 26th, 1831, to nominate candidates for President and Vice-President. The Convention nominated Wm. Wirt and Amos Ellmaker for their standard-bearers. These renowned champions went forth to battle, and brought as trophies from the field the electoral vote of Vermont. But the dog was now dead; and the leading fanatical spirits discarded it, as it ever was a worthless hotchpotch of the villainies of broken-down political tricksters.

Universal Language.—Among Freemasons, language is said to be universal. The universal principles of the art, unity, men of all nations and tenets, and the fixed usages of the order, so renders a universal language a necessity.

Universal Order of Harmony.—A military and commercial order, founded in France in 1806, and composed of twenty-five degrees.

Universi terrarum orbis architectorris ad glorioris ingentis.—To the Glory of the Grand Architect of the Universe; the caption of the A. and A. R. documents.

Upper Chamber.—The ancient Masons met on high hills or deep valleys, so that they might observe the approach of intruders. But the institution has now become so well known that no necessity exists for out-door meetings. The Lodge-rooms are now mostly found in the upper rooms of buildings.

Urim and Thummim.—The explanation of the *Urim* and *Thummim*, the lights and perfections, and of the breastplate of Aaron, is remarkable. The initial letters of the

280   *URUGUAY—VERMONT.*

Hebrew names of the twelve stones in that breastplate, and also of the twelve tribes (by the application of a key discovered by Lanci), conveyed a meaning which the *exegesis* of a learned linguist would never have reached. The explanation of the *Urim* is, "I will cause the oracular spirit to rise at my will;" of the *Thummim*, "And of the Seers it will manifest the secret:" and by putting the first two letters in Hebrew together, the ineffable name is made out.

Uruguay.—Freemasonry was introduced here by the Grand Lodge of France in 1827. The Grand Lodge and Supreme Council were organized in 1855.

V.

Van White, Lewis.—First Grand Chancellor of the Most Puissant Grand Consistory, S. P. R. S., 32d of Kentucky, was born in Pennsylvania, and died at Louisville, Ky., Dec. 20th, 1860.

Vaults.—It is common to find vaults in every country, and yet no regularity appears to exist in their formation.

Vaulted Passage.—In order to secrete the Ark in case of misfortune to the Temple, Solomon constructed a passage. The pot of manna, Ark, holy oil, and Aaron's Rod were no doubt concealed here by Josiah.

Veils, Master of.—An officer in charge of the veils of the R. A. Chapter. There are three veils, 1st, 2d, and 3d.

Vermont.—In 1781, the Grand Lodge of Massachusetts granted a warrant for a Lodge at Cornish, dated Nov. 8th. On the 17th Jan. 1785, the Grand Lodge of Mass. granted a warrant for a Lodge at Manchester. On the 19th Oct. 1794, the Grand Lodge was organized. On the 20th Dec. 1804, the Grand Chapter. In 1825, the Grand Commandery; and on January 14th, 1852, reorganized. In 1854, the Grand Council of Select Masters was organized.

VIRGINIA — VOLTAIRE. 281

Virginia.—The first Lodge in this State was held at Norfolk under warrant from G. L. of England, and dated December 22d, 1733. The Grand Lodge of Scotland warranted a Lodge at Port Royal, in 1755. In 1757, the G. L. for Petersburg was chartered by the G. L. of Scotland. On the 21st July, 1758, the G. L. of Massachusetts granted a charter for a Lodge at Fredericksburg. On the 6th November, 1773, the G. L. of England chartered a Lodge at Gloucester. On the 5th April, 1775, the G. L. of Scotland chartered a Lodge at Cabin Point. On the 1st August, 1755, the G. L. of England chartered a Lodge at Yorktown, and one at Falmouth. On the 6th May, 1777, a convention was called at Williamsburg to take measures for opening a Grand Lodge, and adjourned to elect a Grand Master on the 23d June. This convention assembled, and suggested that his Ex. Gen. George Washington should have the preference for G. M., which he declined. The convention then adjourned to 13th October, 1778, when they unanimously elected John Blair, of Williamsburg Lodge, Grand Master. The Grand Chapter was organized 1st May, 1808. In 1823, the Grand Encampment was organized, but ceased to exist in a few years. In 1845, a new Grand Encampment was formed, under the jurisdiction of the Grand Encampment of the U. S. In 1861, it cut loose from the Grand Encampment of the U. S., and in 1866, renewed its allegiance to that body.

Visiting Brothers.—A Mason in good and regular standing has a right to visit any Lodge. It is an inherent right, which inures to every Mason. The charge written in the reign of James II., between 1685-8, recognizes this right in the welcome it orders to be given to every strange Mason.

Voltaire.—In Klof's Masonic History of France, we find the following:

"The Lodge *des Neuf Sœurs* (Nine Sisters, or Nine Muses),

24*

282

VOLTAIRE.

in Paris, February 7th, 1778, enjoyed the distinction of initiating the philosopher Voltaire. Benjamin Franklin had prevailed (?) upon him to request an initiation. The Chevalier de Cubières, who survived the event forty-two years (he died in 1820), was an eye-witness of the solemn act, and became its historian.

"The sponsor, or proposer of Voltaire, was the Abbé Cordièr de Saint Firmin. After the ballot had been spread, he entered the Lodge, leaning on the arms of Franklin and Count de Gèbelin. All the tests applied were moral ones, and the usual forms of initiation (which, by the French method, are numerous and arduous) were omitted. It is said that the examining committee themselves received more instruction than they imparted to him. It was not necessary, indeed, to examine Voltaire; sixty years devoted to genius and virtue had made him sufficiently known.

"His initiation, according to the description of the chevalier, was a triumph to him, and inestimable to all who witnessed it. Immediately upon its consummation, he was conducted to the East, where the M. W. Master Lalande saluted him, and the brethren, La Dixmeric, Garnier, and Grouvelle, honored him with addresses.

"Some time before this, the widow of Helvetius had presented to the Lodge the masonic regalia of her late consort. The apron of this brother was given to Voltaire, who, before binding it upon himself, kissed it, in token of his esteem and remembrance of one of the most eminent philosophers and illustrious Masons of France. When he received the lady's gloves—which, according to the custom in the French Lodges, were presented to him as a newly-initiated brother—he turned to the Marquis de Villétte, and said: 'As these gloves are designed for a person toward whom I confess an honest, tender, and well-deserved attachment, I beg leave to present them to that beautiful and virtuous lady, *your wife*.'

"Voltaire died May 30th, of the same year. The Lodge held a Sorrow Lodge, of a very solemn character, on the 28th of the subsequent November, in commemoration of his decease. In this, Lalande acted as W. Master; Benjamin Franklin and Stroganoff, as Wardens; Lechangeaux, orator. Visiting brethren, to the number of two hundred, entered the room, two by two, in profoundest silence. The first artists in the city performed the musical portion of the ceremonies. Mrs. Denis, Voltaire's

VOUCH. 283

niece, and the Marchioness de Villétte were the only ladies admitted. The room was draped heavily with black cloth, and lighted dimly by lamps. The walls exhibited passages selected from the prose and poetry of the talented dead. The mausoleum was placed in the background of the Lodge. After some introductory remarks by the W. Master, the orator, Bro. Lechangeaux, and Bro. Coron, addressed the assembly, and Bro. La Dixmeric pronounced a eulogy upon Voltaire. During its delivery, and upon a given signal, the mausoleum disappeared, and a representation of the apotheosis of Voltaire came in view. Bro. Roucher then recited a poem, one passage of which, 'Ou reposé un grand homme un dieu doit habiter,' caused such emotion as to demand the repetition of the entire poem. When, during the ceremonials of this Sorrow Lodge, it was required to deposit the mystic sprig upon the cenolaphium, Franklin stepped forward and laid the wreath, which the Marchioness de Villétte upon a former occasion had given to Voltaire, in the name of the Lodge, in token of his fraternal sorrow. An agape (love-feast) concluded the whole."

The above is held as correct in substance by the friends of Voltaire, yet it does not bury the fact that *he was rejected* by a legally warranted Lodge. Masonry in those days was subjected to bitter animosity and persecution. *Rejected* applicants, and *suspended* and *cited* Masons, organized Lodges that had no legal authority whatever, and hence were "clandestine Lodges." Lodge *des Neuf Sœurs* was in disrepute, and its name was held as a departure from the ancient usages of the craft. Again, Franklin never did depart from the usages of the order, and was a great enemy upon innovations. Is it probable, then, that Franklin would "prevail upon to request initiation?" His knowledge of the laws of Masonry and his own judgment would discard such an innovation.

Vouch.—To call to witness, to affirm. A visiting brother may take his seat in the Lodge if a brother present can vouch that he has "sat with him in a Lodge;" otherwise, he must be regularly examined by a committee.

W.

Wages Due.—The workman is worthy of his hire. Solomon paid them at their Lodges with shekels. There were two standards of shekels, the *sanctuary* shekel, and the *royal* shekel. The former was used in all religious places, and the other for civil purposes.

Walworth, Reuben Hyde.—Born at Bozrah, Connecticut, October 26th, 1789. He read law with Joseph Russell, Esq., of Troy. After his admission to the bar, he was appointed Master of Chancery and Associate Judge of Clinton County. In 1811, he was made a Mason at Plattsburg. In 1812, he was exalted a Royal Arch Mason at St. Albans, Vermont, and was the High Priest of the Chapter at that place several terms. He also received orders of Knighthood at this place. In 1821, he was chosen as member of Congress. In 1823, he was appointed Circuit Judge. In 1828, he was appointed Chancellor of New York State, and held the position until the office was abolished by law. In 1853, he was elected as Grand Master of the Grand Lodge of New York. He closed a useful career, 28th November, 1867.

Wands, Royal Arch.—Denote the kingly, prophetic, and sacerdotal ranks.

Wardens.—There are two wardens in a Lodge of M. M.

Warder.—An officer in a Commandery of K. T.

Warrant.—The potent authority under which a Lodge works.

Warren, Joseph.—Born at Roxbury, Mass., in 1741, and fell at the battle of Bunker Hill, June 17th, 1775, one of the first martyrs of liberty. He was a graduate of Harvard University, and at 23 commenced the practice of law in Boston. In 1768, he was a member of the association in opposition to British tyranny. On the 5th March, 1770,

WASHINGTON. 285

a British officer dispersed a crowd by force of arms, and hence styled the "Boston Massacre." On the 5th March, 1775, it was determined to have an oration in defense of the Colonial rights. It was the custom of the English officers to attend these assemblies, and overawe and threaten the speaker and people. Warren solicited the position, and at the appointed time walked into the crowded church, filled with troops and citizens, and delivered his address. Shortly after this he was elected President of the Committee of Safety and the Provincial Congress. On the 18th April, 1775, gave notice of the intended move of the British to Concord and Lexington. The British received a warm welcome from the stone walls, where the hero patriots stationed themselves, and poured into them a destructive fire. On the 14th June, 1775, he was elected a major-general by the Prov. Congress, and three days afterward fell a martyr on Bunker Hill. General Warren was made a Mason in St. Andrew's Lodge, Boston, 10th Sept. 1761, and passed 2d Nov. following, and raised 28th Nov. 1765. On the 30th May, 1769, Earl Dalhousie, Grand Master of Scotland, appointed him Prov. Grand Master of Boston. Dalhousie was succeeded by Earl of Dumfries, and he appointed Warren "Grand Master of the American Continent," 7th March, 1772. He was a zealous Mason, and had the confidence of the craft. In 1792, a monument of wood was erected by King Solomon's Lodge, Charlestown, on Bunker Hill, to his memory.

Washington. — Freemasonry was introduced into this State in or about 1855. On the 6th Dec. 1858, the Grand Lodge was organized at Olympia.

Washington, Gen. George. — Born in Virginia, Feb. 22d, 1732. In 1752, a short time before he was 21 years of age, he was a candidate for the mysteries of Masonry, in Fredericksburg Lodge, Virginia. This Lodge was warranted by the Prov. G. Master, Thomas Ormond,

286 *WASHINGTON.*

Boston. On the 6th Nov. 1752, he was entered as an Apprentice. On the 3d March, 1753, he was passed; and raised a Master Mason, 4th Aug. 1753. It is claimed by the English Masons that Washington was made a Mason in Military Lodge, No. 227, that worked in America during the French war. This error no doubt arose from the fact that the American Lodges worked under the authority of the Grand Lodge of England, while the Military Lodges were warranted by the Grand Lodges of Scotland and Ireland, and Washington on his visit to Philadelphia, in 1756, may have been re-made or healed on a visit to No. 227, in order that he might have masonic intercourse with Lodges under the jurisdiction of other Grand Lodges. During the revolutionary war quite a number of Military Lodges worked in the Colonial army. The *American Union Lodge* was warranted by John Rowe, Grand Master of Mass., 15th Feb. 1776, and constituted while the Colonial army lay at Roxbury, near Boston. Washington attended these meetings of the brethren, and while at Valley Forge had constant intercourse with the Lodges held among that glorious band of patriots. In Dec. 1776, Washington took part in the festival of St. John, which was celebrated by the Grand Lodge of Pennsylvania, at Philadelphia; Congress being in session at this time. Washington was honored with the chief place in the procession. Rev. Wm. Smith, Grand Sec. of G. L. of Pa., preached the sermon at Christ's Church, and alluding, in prophetic language, to Washington as being the Cincinnatus of America, thus closed: "Such, too, if we divine aright, will future ages pronounce the name of a ——; but you anticipate me in a name which delicacy forbids me on this occasion to mention. Honored with his presence as a brother, you will seek to derive virtue from his example." This sermon was afterward published, and dedicated to Washington, by order of

WASHINGTON.

287

the Grand Lodge. On the 23d June, 1779, the army was at New Windsor, on the Hudson. The American Union Lodge met at Nelson Point to celebrate the festival of St. John the Baptist. In the celebration they were joined by Washington and his family. Soon after this, brethren from Massachusetts obtained a warrant to hold a Military Lodge, dated Oct. 6th, 1779, called Washington Lodge. The officers were Gen. John Patterson, Master, and Col. Benjamin Tupper, and Maj. Wm. Hall, Wardens. About the close of 1779, the headquarters of Washington were again established at Warrenton, N. J. The American Union Lodge celebrated the 27th Dec., St. John's Day. At this meeting a petition was circulated by members of various Grand Lodges, to the appeal that a Grand Master should be appointed over all the States, "that the principles of Masonry may be correctly established and the abuses corrected," etc. On the 13th Jan. 1780, before the address of the army reached the Grand Lodge of Pennsylvania, that body met to consider the propriety of appointing a General Grand Master over all Grand Lodges in the United States, and upon agreeing as to the good to be derived from such a measure, a ballot was had, and *George Washington* was unanimously chosen. To this election all the Grand Lodges of the United States acquiesced, and Washington became the first Grand Master of Masons in America, *in fact*, although the Grand Lodge was not then constituted, and consequently the position and title was purely an honorary one. In 1786, he was solicited to grant a warrant as Grand Master of America, to be held at Cape Francoise. Washington transferred this request to the Grand Lodge of Pa., which granted the warrant. In 1797, a masonic medal was struck, which had upon one side the bust of Washington, with the inscription, "Geo. Washington, Prest., 1797," on the other side, "*Amor Honor et Justicia*, G. W., G. G. M." In

288 *WASHINGTON.*

1781, Nov. 22d, the Grand Lodge of Penna. dedicated Smith's Ahīman Rezon, with the Mason's coat of arms as a frontispiece, and Washington's coat of arms attached, "To his Ex. Geo. Washington, Esq," a copy of which was found among the books of Washington's library. During the great struggle for American liberty, the books and jewels of Lodge No. 227 fell into the hands of the Americans. A request was made to Washington to return them, which he did, by directing a guard of honor to convey them to the British regiment. While the Americans lay in New Jersey, the Master's apron and Templar's sash of Sergt. Kelly, of the British army, were captured in a skirmish, and carried to Washington, who directed them to be kept and returned to the owner. Sergt. Kelly bequeathed these relics to Montgomery Lodge, of New York, in 1838. Immediately after the surrender of Lord Cornwallis, Lodge No. 9 met in Yorktown, and Washington, La Fayette, Nelson, Marshall, and others were present. In or about 1781, Washington was made the recipient of a masonic sash and apron, manufactured at Nantes, France, from the finest satin, bearing the French and American flags, and a galaxy of masonic emblems. The work was forwarded by Watson & Cassoule, both Masons, who desired to testify to the virtue of so great a man and Mason. Washington acknowledged the receipt 10th Jan. 1782. His sash and apron are claimed to be in the possession of brethren of Lodge No. 22, Alexandria, Va. In 1783, May 13th, the Society of Cincinnatus was established by the American masonic officers of the Revolution, to perpetuate their friendship, and Washington was chosen the president, and remained as such until his death. In July, 1790, Rev. Bro. Wm. Smith in an address claimed the honor of the name of that society, as in 1778 he referred, in his sermon to the G. L. of Pa., to Washington as being the Cincinnatus of America. About this period a programme was published of a new

WASHINGTON. 289

order of "American Knighthood," that would be established 4th July, inst. The Grand Master was to be Washington; Chancellor, Franklin; Prelate, Dr. Witherspoon, etc. This order it appears was not constituted. On 29th Dec. 1783, Washington resigned his commission as commander of the armies, at Annapolis. On his return, he was invited by Lodge No. 37, of Alexandria, to attend the festival of St. John, 24th Dec., to which he sent his regrets, not being able to attend. However, in June he attended the festival of St. John. In the latter part of 1784, Gen. La Fayette came upon a visit to see Washington, and brought with him a beautiful white satin masonic apron, upon which the masonic emblems were beautifully worked by Madame La Fayette, the wife of Gen. La Fayette, it being her gift, while the general tendered a beautiful rosewood box. This apron is now in possession of the Grand Lodge of Pennsylvania. In 1785, the G. L. of N. Y. dedicated its Book of Constitutions to Washington. In 1788, the Lodge of Alexandria was taken under the jurisdiction of G. L. of Va., and on 29th May, 1788, the G. L. of Pa. recommended Washington as the Master of this Lodge, which request was granted. After the death of Washington, the Lodge was called *Washington Lodge*, No. 22. In 1789, 6th March, the Holland Lodge, No. 9, elected Washington an honorary member. On the 30th April, 1789, he was sworn into office as President of the U. S. by Grand Master Robert Livingston. The Bible used on this occasion belonged to St. John's Lodge, No. 9, in whose possession it still remains. In 1790, King David's Lodge, Newport, addressed him upon the subject of Freemasonry. In 1791, the G. L. of South Carolina addressed him, through Gen. Mordecai Girt, G. M. In 1795, the G. L. of Va. dedicated its Ahiman Rezon to Washington. In Dec. 1791, the G. L. of Pa. addressed renewals of respect, etc. In 1792, the G. L. of Mass. dedicated

25

WASHINGTON.

its Book of Constitutions to him. About 1790, Frederick the Great, of Prussia, then a distinguished Mason, presented him with a handsome sword. About 1782, the Earl of Buchan, G. M. of Scotland, presented him with a box made from the wood of a tree under which Sir Wm. Wallace rested after the battle of Falkirk. On the 4th March, 1793, Washington was inaugurated President of the U. S. for the second term. On the 18th Sept. 1793, he laid the corner-stone of the Capitol; Lodges Nos. 9, 22, and 15 conducted the ceremonies, and the following is the record placed in the stone:

"This S. W. corner-stone of the Capitol of the U. S. of America, in the City of Washington, was laid 18th Sept. 1793, in the 13th year of American Independence, 1st year of 2d term of the presidency of Gen. Washington, whose virtue in civil government of his country has been as conspicuous and beneficial as his military valor and prudence have been useful in establishing her liberties; and in the year of Masonry, 5793, by the President of the U. S., in concert with the G. L. of Maryland and Lodges under its jurisdiction, and Lodge No. 22, Alexandria, Va., Thomas Johnson, David Stewart, Cornly, Commissioners; Joseph Clark, R. W. G. M.; James Hoban and Stephen Hallate, Architects; Collin Williams, M. M."

Washington appeared in the procession on this occasion in the full dress of a Master Mason. On Sept. 18th, 1794, Mr. Williams presented Lodge No. 22, Alexandria, with a life-sized portrait of Washington in full masonic regalia, at his age of 64. In 1796, he prepared his Farewell Address. It is well known that at this period Europe was convulsed by the operations of secret political societies, and the allusion "beware of secret societies," was in direct reference to these political societies, and not in denunciation of Masonry, as the enemies of the order would have it. So thoroughly does Washington refute this construction, in his reply to the G. L. of Penna., who apprised him of their purpose to address him on his retirement from

WASHINGTON. **291**

public life, and presented to him the 27th Dec. 1796, that we give it place:

"Fellow-citizens and brothers of the G. L. of Pa., I have received your address with all the feelings of brotherly affection, mingled with the sentiment of the society, which it was calculated to excite. To have been in any degree an instrument in the hands of Providence to promote order and union, and erect upon a solid foundation the true principles of government, is only to have shared, with many others, in a labor, the results of which, let us hope, will prove through all ages a sanctuary for brethren and a lodge for the virtues. Permit me to reciprocate your prayers for my temporal happiness, and to supplicate that we may all meet hereafter, in that eternal temple, whose builder is the Great Architect of the Universe.

"GEO. WASHINGTON."

Washington had now given himself to the privacy of his estate, yet still he received greetings from all quarters from his masonic friends, to all of which he responded. On March 28th, 1779, the Lodges at Alexandria asked him to name the time and place to meet them, as they contemplated tendering him a dinner. He named the following Saturday. Accordingly, No. 22 met at Albert's tavern, where the repast was served. The 10th toast on this occasion was by Bro. Washington: "The Lodge at Alexandria, and all Masons throughout the World." On 22d Aug. 1798, a clergyman of Fredericksburg, named Snyder, sent him a work, "Proofs of Conspiracies against all Religious Governments," etc., by "the Freemasons, Illuminati," etc. The order of Illuminati originated in France. The author of these diabolical pamphlets was a Papist, who found that the order of Freemasons practiced benevolence, Christianity, and morality, and thus endeavored to bring it into disrepute. (Has Catholicism ever been found encouraging any Christian or moral institution?) In Washington's reply to Snyder, 25th Sept 1798, he says: "I believe, notwithstanding, that *none* of the Lodges

WEAPONS—WEBB.

of this country are contaminated with the principles ascribed to the Society of the Illuminati." Again, in reply to Snyder, 24th Oct. 1798: "I did not believe that the Lodges of Masons in this country had, as societies, endeavored to propagate the diabolical tenets of the 'Illuminati,' or the pernicious influence of the 'Jacobinites,' if they are capable of separation." On the 12th Dec. 1799, Washington took sick, and died on the 14th. The funeral ceremonies were under the direction of Lodge No. 22, of Alexandria, and he was buried on the 18th. Cols. Gilpin, Marstellar, Tuttle, Simes, Ramsey, and Payne, all members of his Lodge, were the pall-bearers. The G. Lodges throughout the country met and passed letters of condolence, and sent them to Mrs. Washington. What heartfelt thanks must these tokens of friendship have awakened within the bosom of that deserted partner of the great patriot!

Weapons.—Many Lodges repudiate the use of the drawn sword in Lodges. Among these are the Athol Masons.

Webb, Thomas Smith.—Was the son of Samuel and Margaret Webb, and was born in Boston, Mass., 30th Oct. 1771. He early evinced a great desire for learning, and was educated in Boston. He learned the printing business, and removed to Keene, New Hampshire, where he followed the trade. While in this place, he was made a Mason in Rising Sun Lodge, under warrant from G. L. of Mass., in 1784. In 1797, he married, and removed to Albany, N. Y., and opened a book store. At this period, Albany was the great masonic center, and Webb assisted in organizing a Chapter and Encampment. He had taken all the higher degrees of Freemasonry in Philadelphia prior to this date. The Ancient and Accepted Rite being practiced then, Webb no doubt received these degrees here. He saw the necessity of rearranging the Prestonian lectures, and accordingly, in 1797, published the first edition of his "Freemasons' Monitor." The first three de-

WEBB—WEIRHAUPT. 293

grees were arranged from Preston's Illustrations. As to the compilation of the degrees of the Chapter and Encampment, they were no doubt arranged by Webb, Henry Fouse, and Dr. Bentley in Boston, and, although the ideas are taken from the Scotch and French Rites, are American. About 1800, Webb removed to Providence, R. I., and was elected Grand Master of Masons in this State in 1813. While Webb was acting Grand Master, the troubles with England had led to an invasion of the Continent, and at a session of the Grand Lodge, 27th Sept. 1814, that body tendered its services to the Committee of Defense to erect fortifications, etc. Their services were accepted, and on the 3d October, Webb headed the procession from the Lodge, about 300 members, and moved to Fox Point and erected a fort. At sunset they completed their labors, and a procession was formed, marching several times round, and G. M. Webb, in the name of the G. L. of R. I., named it "Fort Hiram," which name the Governor sanctioned. On the 6th of May, 1805, a convention of Knights Templar met in Providence, R. I , to organize a "Gen. G. Encampment of the U. S.," which they did on the 13th, and elected Webb the first Gen. Grand Commander. In 1798, a convention of Companions met in Hartford, Conn., and organized a "Gen. Grand Royal Arch Chapter," and Webb was elected one of the principal officers. At a meeting in New York he was elected its presiding officer, but declined in favor of De Witt Clinton. On the 10th of June, 1819, Webb started on a tour west, and reached Cleveland, Ohio, 5th July, where he took sick and died the following Tuesday. His remains were buried in Cleveland, where they remained until the Grand Lodge of Rhode Island removed them to Providence, reinterred them 9th Nov. 1819, in accordance with Mr. Webb's request.

Weirhaupt, Adam.—The founder of the order of Illuminati. Born in Ingolstadt, February 6th, 1748, died in Gotha,

294 WEST—WHITNEY.

November 18th, 1830. He became an extraordinary professor of law in 1772, and in 1775, professor of national and common law. The latter appointment aroused the jealousy of the Jesuits, as after the suppression of their order he became their bitterest enemy. The order of Illuminati, under his leadership, became powerful. In 1785, he was obliged to leave Ingolstadt, and retired to Gotha, where he was Chancellor of the State by the duke.

West.—The position in Lodge of the S. W.

West Virginia.—The territory of West Virginia being embraced in Virginia up to 1862, its modern masonic history only dates from the organization of its Grand Lodge, 12th April, 1865, at Fairmount.

White Stone.—An emblem of purity.

Whitney, Hon. Geo. C.—Born in Fauquier, Va., December 29th, 1816, died at Washington, September 4th, 1867. At the time of his death, he was Commissioner of Pensions and acting Secretary of the Interior, and Grand Master of the district. He was a member of the B. B. French Lodge, Columbia Chapter, and Washington Commandery, and filled nearly every station in each of their bodies, and for several terms Grand Master of the district.

Whitney, William.—Past Grand Master, was born in Princeton, Massachusetts, on the 10th day of February, 1799, and died in Philadelphia, on the 11th day of March, 1865. He came to Philadelphia in 1818, and was for some years a clerk in the well-known house of Wiggin & Whitney, merchants. He went to Manchester, England, in the autumn of 1824, where he remained until 1828-29. He then returned to Philadelphia, and here took up his permanent residence.

Brother Whitney was initiated in Rising Star Lodge, No. 126, in November, 1823, Crafted in January, 1824, and raised to the sublime degree of a Master Mason in March, 1824. He continued with the Lodge until April, 1831, when he resigned. The Lodge surrendered its warrant on the 28th of January, 1834, and was not revived until the 5th day of April, 1848. It is now in a flourishing and prosperous condition.

Brother Whitney did not long remain from membership in the order, for in January, 1833, he joined Lodge No. 51, and remained with it up to the day of his lamented decease. He was elected its Senior Warden in 1836; Worshipful Master in 1837–38, and again its Senior Warden in 1844, and Worshipful Master in 1845, showing in this retreading of the path he had gone before, his earnest desire to aid Masonry, by not hesitating in the discharge of any duty that might give it strength and increase its usefulness.

Wingate, Henry.—Was initiated in Hiram Lodge, Frankfort, Ky., Nov. 22d, 1815, passed Jan. 5th, 1816, and raised Feb. 1st, 1816. He was Grand Master of the Grand Lodge in 1842. He was held in high esteem by the fraternity.

Wintersmith, Charles G.—Born in Elizabeth, Ky., July 15th, 1812. He was a graduate of Miami University, Oxford, Ohio, in 1831, and began the study of law in Frankfort in 1833. Possessed of an acute memory, he eagerly gathered all the right fruits, and was admitted with marked honor in 1837. He represented his native county four terms in the Legislature, and was Speaker during the sessions of 1853–4. A forcible writer and eminent statesman, his life has been one of usefulness and honor.

Wisconsin.—Freemasonry was introduced into this State by warrants from the Grand Lodges of Missouri, in Jan. 1843, for Lodges at Mineral Point, Plattsville, and Milwaukee. The Grand Lodge was organized 18th Dec 1843, at Madison. On 13th Feb. 1850, the Grand Chapter was organized. On the 20th Oct. 1859, the Grand Commandery was organized. In 1857, the Grand Council of Royal and Select Masters was organized.

296   *WOOSTER — WREN.*

Wooster, David.—Born in Strafford, Conn., March 2d, 1710. He became a Mason in England. Thomas Axnard, Prov. G. M. of Massachusetts, granted him a warrant to open a Lodge at New Haven, 12th November, 1750. He died from a wound received by repelling the British invader at Ridgeville, on April 27th, 1777, at Danbury, 2d of May, aged 67.

Wooster, Thomas. — Son of Gen. David, was made a Mason in Hiram Lodge, Massachusetts, 14th April, 1777. He was also an active patriot in the revolutionary war.

Worshipful Master.—The title of the presiding officer of a Lodge. The third degree is called Master's. When once the F. C. has received this privilege, he has a voice in all the consultations of the Lodge.

Wren, Sir Christopher.—An English architect, born in East Kewyle, Wiltshire, England, October 20th, 1632, and died in 1717. On the 27th December, 1663, a general assembly of Masons was held in London, and Henry Jennyn, Earl of Albans, was elected Grand Master. He appointed Sir Christopher Wren and John Webb his Wardens. In 1666, Wren was appointed Dep. G. M., under G. M. Earl of Rivers. In 1685, Wren was elected G. M. In 1703, there existed but four Lodges in London, and, notwithstanding the zeal of the G. M., the members decreased, the annual feasts were neglected, and the Lodges deserted. Under these circumstances, the Lodge of St. Paul's, now Antiquity, with the object of giving importance to the order, "*Resolved*, That the privileges of Masonry shall no longer be confined to operative masons, but be free to all men of all professions, provided that they are regularly approved and initiated into the fraternity." This changed the entire face of the society, and transformed it into what we find it to-day. Sir Christopher, however, did not approve of this innovation, and it was not until after his death that the four Lodges felt it their privilege to assemble themselves and elect a Grand Master, and put into practical operation the resolution passed by St. Paul's Lodge in 1703.

Wright, Dan. S.—Senior G. Warden of the G. L. of New York, in 1850–51–52; died 31st January, 1867, aged 65.

Y.

Year of Masonry.—To learn the masonic year, we add 4000 to the birth of Christ, and this gives us the year of Masonry.

York Masons.—Prince Edwin, brother of King Athelstane, being a Master Mason, purchased from his brother a free charter for Masons. Observing a correction among themselves, they amended anything that was transacted amiss, and held annual communications. Accordingly, Prince Edwin assembled all Freemasons in the realm to convene in York, and they instituted a Grand Lodge, of which he became the Grand Master. They framed a Constitution and charges from all the old masonic manuscripts that could be collected. These laws were made to be binding in all times to come, and after a full consent it became the English Lodge, and was recognized in all its functions.

York Rite.—This Rite practices the following degrees:

1. Apprentice.	6. Most Excellent Master.
2. Fellow Craft.	7. Holy Royal Arch.
3. Master Mason.	8. Royal Master.
4. Mark Master.	9. Super Excellent Master.
5. Past Master.	10. Select Master.

Z.

Zabud.—The principal officer in King Solomon's household. Used in Select Master's degree.

ZEREDATHA—ZINZENDORF.

Zeredatha.—The ground used by Solomon in preparing materials for the Temple. The brass work and the great pillars were cast in the clay near this place.

Zeretta or Zaradatha.—A place in Jordan in which the water stood in heaps as Joshua passed below with the Israelites. Near to this place are the plains of Jericho, and almost over against Succoth, where the vessels of the Temple were cast of metal.

Zerubbabel.—The son of Shealthief, of royal descent. As Sheshbazzar is said to have built the second Temple and was prince of the Jews, it seems he is the same Zerubbabel—that being his Jewish name, and the other the Chaldean. Cyrus, King of Persia, delivered into his hands the sacred vessels that had been conveyed to Babylon, amounting to 5400, and made him governor of the returning captives of Judah, amounting to 42,360, and 7337 servants, with whom he laid the foundation of the Temple and restored the worship of the true God. Notwithstanding the obstruction by the Samaritans, Zerubbabel, together with Joshua, the high priest, fiished the Temple.

Zinzendorf, Nikalous Fridrig.—Count of Zinzendorf and Pattendorf, a descendant of noble family of Austria, founder of the Moravian sect, born in Dresden, Saxony, May 26th, 1700; died at Herrnhut, May 9th, 1760. In 1741, he came to the United States and commenced preaching at Germantown. At Shekomeco, he established the first Indian Moravian congregation in America. His entire life was marked and brilliant. He modified Swedenborgian rites of Freemasonry; in 1737, he promulgated the Rite of Zinzendorf in Germany.

Zinzendorf Rite. — Originated by Count Zinzendorf. I. *Blue Masonry:* Apprentice, Fellow Craft, and Master. II. *Red Masonry:* Scotch Apprentice and Fellow Craft, Scotch Master. III. *Capitular Masonry:* Favorite of St. John, Elected Brother.

LIST OF LODGES, GRAND CHAPTERS, ENCAMPMENTS, ETC.

IN THE

UNITED STATES AND CANADA.

(299)

LIST OF LODGES.

ALABAMA.

Jurisdiction of the Grand Lodge of Alabama.

1. Helion, Huntsville.
3. Alabama, Claiborne.
4. Rising Virtue, Tuscaloosa.
5. Halo, Cahaba.
6. Walker, Moulton.
7. Macon, Grove Hill.
8. Farrar, Elyton.
9. Gilead, Butler.
10. Royal White Hart, Clayton.
11. Montgomery, Montgomery.
12. Marion, Suggsville.
14. Florence, Florence.
16. Athens, Athens.
18. Limestone, Mooresville.
22. Saint Alban's, Linden.
24. George Washington, Clinton.
25. Dale, Camden.
26. Lafayette, Greensboro'.
27. Selma Fraternal, Selma.
28. Marengo, Dayton.
29. Rising Sun, Decatur.
31. Autauga, Autaugaville.
33. Lowndes, Hayneville.
34. Perry, Marion.
36. Washington, Tuscumbia.
37. Courtland, Courtland.
39. Wetumpka, Wetumpka.
40. Mobile, Mobile.
41. Livingston, Livingston.
42. Hiram, Jacksonville.
43. Leighton, Leighton.
45. Jackson, Gainesville.
46. Harmony, Eufaula.
47. Warren, Kingston.
48. Vienna, Pleasant Ridge.
49. Demopolis, Demopolis.
50. Union, Uniontown.
51. Jefferson, Cedar Bluff.
52. New Market, New Market.
53. Greening, Evergreen.
54. Amity, Eutaw.
55. Mount Moriah, Pickensville.
56. Troy, Troy.
57. Tuskegee, Tuskegee.
59. Benton, Benton.
61. Tompkinsville, Tompkinsville.
62. Saint John's, Union Springs.

63. Social, Enon.
64. Eureka, Greenville.
65. Liberty, Liberty Hill.
67. Hampden Sidney, Robinson's Springs
68. Holsey, Glennville.
69. Howard, Mobile.
70. Central, Montevallo.
71. Tehopeka, Dadeville.
72. Widow's Son, Snow Hill.
73. Acacia, Lowndesboro'.
74. Solomon's, Lafayette.
76. Auburn, Auburn.
77. Uchee, Uchee.
78. Crozier, White Plains.
79. Fredonia, Fredonia.
80. Wilcox, Allenton.
82. Bellefonte, Bellefonte.
83. Friendship, Centreville.
84. Erophotic, Bragg.
88. Meridian Sun, Pleasant Hill.
89. Prattville, Prattville.
90. Pfister, McKinley.
91. Henry, Abbeville.
92. Triana, Triana.
93. Sawyer, Wedowee.
94. Philodorian, Cusseta.
95. Danville, Danville.
96. Tuckabatchee, Crawford.
97. Lozahatchee, Goshen.
98. Fulton, Orrville.
100. Bridgeville, Bridgeville.
101. Hartwell, Oxford.
102. Newbern, Newbern.
103. Benson, Mechanicsville.
104. Good Samaritan, Dudleyville.
105. Shiloh, Hampden.
106. Hermon, Sumterville.
107. Choctaw, Pushmataha.
108. Oak Bowery, Oak Bowery.
110. Forest Hill, Pleasant Grove.
111. Sylvan, Foster's.
112. Dean, Brooklyn.
115. Warrior Stand, Warrior Stand.
116. DeKalb, Lebanon.
117. Perryville, Perryville.
119. Notasulga, Notasulga.
120. Waverly, Waverly.

LIST OF LODGES.

122. Coffeeville, Coffeeville.
124. Felix, Midway.
125. Herndon, Union.
126. Tallapoosa, Rock Spring.
127. Bolivar, Stevenson.
128. Ridge Grove, Ridge Grove.
129. Geneva, Geneva.
131. Yorkville, Yorkville.
132. Roanoke, Roanoke.
133. Loachapoka, Loachapoka
134. Wiley, Farrierville.
136. Unity, Lower Pine-tree.
137. Rockford, Rockford.
138. Bradford, Bradford.
139. Chilton, La Place.
140. Shelby, Columbiana.
141. Bethel, Arbacoochee.
142. Baldwin, Stockton.
143. Burleson, Burleson.
144. Daleville, Daleville.
145. Fraternity, Blountsville.
146. Missouri, Ferote.
147. Rodgersville, Rodgersville.
150. Etam, Hamburg.
151. Bladon Springs, Bladon Springs.
152. Mount Jefferson, Rough and Ready.
153. Monroeville, Monroeville.
154. Nixburg, Nixburg.
155. Eastaboga, Eastaboga.
157. Somerville, Somerville.
158. Maysville, Maysville.
160. Mitchel, Turkey Town.
161. Penick, Central Institute.
162. Hendrix, Dublin.
163. F. Authentic, Fayetteville.
166. Sumter, Gaston.
168. Mount Hope, Mount Hope.
169. Buena Vista, Sardis Church.
170. Elba, Elba.
171. Clopton, Barnes's Cross Roads.
173. Andrew Jackson, Montgomery.
176. Davie, Indian Creek.
177. Orion, Orion.
178. Desotoville, Desotoville.
179. Ashland, Mount Sterling.
180. Mount Hilliard, Mount Hilliard.
181. Aberfoil, Aberfoil.
184. Brundidge, Brundidge.
186. Catawla, Ashville.
188. Haw Ridge, Clintonville.
189. Delta, Kizer Hill.
190. Tombigbee, Jefferson.
191. Brush Creek, Brush Creek.
192. Chattahoochee, Berlin.
193. High Log, Greenwood.
195. Opelika, Opelika.
197. Hillabee, Pinkneyville.
200. Sylacauga, Sylacauga.
201. Helicon, Helicon.
202. Pine Level, Pine Level.
205. Gainestown, Gainestown.
207. Pettusville, Pettusville.
208. Alexandria, Alexandria.
212. Putnam, Louina.
213. Euclid, Fort Browder.
214. Carrollton, Carrollton.
2 5. Builders, Planters' Institute.
217. Spring Hill, Spring Hill.

218. Sam Dixon, Centre.
219. Lineville, Lineville.
220. Pine Grove, Pine Grove.
221. Tensaw, Tensaw.
222. Western Star, Cuba.
223. Sandy Ridge, Sandy Ridge.
224. Newton, Newton.
225. Louisville, Louisville.
226. Santa Fe, Jackson.
227. James Penn, Clopton.
229. Lebanon, Marion.
230. Bexar, Bexar.
231. Duck Spring, Duck Spring.
235. Harpersville, Harpersville.
236. Gadsden, Gadsden.
237. Tallassee, Tallassee.
238. Fairmount, Fairmount.
239. Andalusia, Andalusia.
241. Bowen, Whistler.
242. Coosa, Buyckville.
243. Ramah, Ramah.
244. Dawson, Oakey Streak.
246. Harrison, Henderson.
247. Cropwell, Cropwell.
248. Lawrence, Lawrenceville.
249. Toluca, Toluca.
250. Amand, Chestnut Creek.
251. Camp Creek, Camp Creek.
252. North Port, North Port.
253. Rose Hill, Rose Hill.
254. Quitman, East Georgia.
258. Randolph, Randolph.
259. Magnolia, Mobile.
260. Bellville, Bellville.
261. Talladega, Talladega.
262. Highland, Highland.
264. Walnut Grove, Walnut Grove.
265. Meridian, Meridianville.
266. Mount Pleasant, Mount Pleasant
267. Wind Creek, Wind Creek.
270. Butler Springs, Monterey.
271. Pea River, New Hope.
272. Clifton, Clifton.
274. Paint Rock, Paint Rock.
275. Frankfort, Frankfort.
276. Bullock, Bullock.
277. Larkinsville, Larkinsville
278. Northern, Vienna.
279. Flat Creek, Pineville.
280. Springville, Springville.
281. C. Baskerville, Fayetteville.
282. Richmond, Richmond
285. Georgiana, Georgiana.
288. Hickory Flat. Hickory Flat.
289. Weeobulga, Weeobulga.
290. Gillespie, Handy.
291. Fort Deposit, Fort Deposit.
301. Norris, Pollard.
304. Zion, Aston's Store.
305. Central City, Selma.
308. New Delta, Delta.
315. Jonesboro', Jonesboro'
317. New Lexington, New Lexington.
319. Cluttsville, Cluttsville.
320. Warrenton, Warrenton.
323. Holly Grove, Holly Grove.
324. Viola, Cross Roads.
326. Youngsville, Youngsville.

LIST OF LODGES.

303

327. Andrew Chapel, Andrew Chapel.
328. Sycamore, Garland.
329. Madison Station, Madison Station.
330. Forkland, Forkland.

331. Charity, Six Mile.
332. Blue Eye, Lincoln.
334. Oliver, Choctaw Corner.

ARKANSAS.

Jurisdiction of the Grand Lodge of Arkansas.

1. Washington, Fayetteville.
2. Western Star, Little Rock.
3. Morning Star, Red Fork.
4. Mt. Horeb, Washington.
5. Liberty, Mt. Zion Church.
6. Van Buren, Van Buren.
7. Key, Lindsey's Prairie.
8. Rock Spring, ———.
9. Franklin, Clarksville.
10. Mt. Zion, Batesville.
11. Camden, Camden.
12. Mt. Carmel, Magnolia.
13. Eldorado, Eldorado.
14. Lewisville, Lewisville.
15. Woodlawn, Woodlawn.
16. Manchester, Manchester.
17. Dover, Dover.
18. Mt. Moriah, Lisbon.
19. Arkadelphia, Arkadelphia.
20. Belle Point, Fort Smith.
21. Cherokee, Tolegnah.
22. Holly Springs, Holly Springs.
23. Concord, Eudora.
24. West Point, West Point.
25. Tulip, Tulip.
26. Polk, Killsboro'.
27. Princeton, Princeton.
29. Smithville, Smithville.
30. Pleasant Valley, Nashville.
31. Pool, Jacksonport.
32. Dardanelle, Dardanelle.
33. Warren, Warren.
34. Benton, Benton.
35. Ft. Gibson, Ft. Gibson.
36. North Western, Maysville.
37. White River, Des Arc.
38. St. John's, Holly Springs.
39. English, Chambersville.
40. Eureka, Montecello.
41. Danville, Danville.
43. Oakville, Oakville.
44. Adeon, Huntsville.
45. Augusta, Augusta.
46. Lacy, Lacy.
48. Hyperian, Longrien.
49. Searcy, Searcy.
50. Calhoun, Calhoun.
51. Brownsville, Brownsville.
52. Choctaw, Daaksville.
53. South Star, Hampton.
54. Evening Star, Norristown.
55. Rome, Rome.
56. Bentonville, Bentonville.

57. Cone Hill, Booneboro'.
58. Rockport, Rockport.
59. Vernon, Mt. Vernon.
60. Magnolia, Little Rock.
61. Hamburg, Hamburg.
62. Hot Springs, Hot Springs.
63. Strict Observance, Plum Bayou.
64. Yell, Carrollton.
66. Ashley, Berryville.
67. Falcon, Falcon.
68. Champagnate, Champagnate.
69. Pine Bluff, Pine Bluff.
70. Aberdeen, Aberdeen.
71. Randolph, Pocahontas.
72. Powhatan, Powhatan.
73. Pariclifta, Pariclifta.
74. Flint, Flint.
75. Oak Bluff, Gainsville.
76. Mill Ridge, Wittsburg.
77. Mitchell, South Bend.
78. Henry, New Edinburgh.
79. Ozark, Ozark.
80. Moscow, Moscow.
81. Byers, Grand Glaize.
82. Columbia, Magnolia.
83. Merrick, Roseville.
84. Bayless, Seminary.
85. Elizabeth, Elizabeth.
86. St. Charles, St. Charles.
87. Centre Point, Centre Point.
88. Cache, Clarendon.
89. Gainsborough, Gainsborough.
90. Lamartine, Lamartine.
91. Pike, Murfreesboro'.
92. Quitman, Lost Creek.
93. Muscogee, Creek Agency.
94. Richmond, Richmond.
95. Hickory Plains, Hickory Plains.
96. Moore, Mount Elba.
97. Lebanon, Trenton.
98. Pigeon Hill, Wilmington.
99. Mount Pleasant. Saundersville.
100. Sulphur Springs, Amity.
101. Leake, Leake's Store.
102. Cincinnati, Cincinnati.
103. Bluff Springs, Marshall Prairie.
104. Carouse, Lone Grove.
105. Lewisburg, Lewisburg.
106. Rob Morris, Okalona.
107. Green Grove, East Fork.
108. Shady Grove, Shady Grove.
109. Palestine, Johnsville.
110. Hamilton, Duvall's Bluff.

304

LIST OF LODGES.

111. Paterson, Clinton.
112. Scottville, Scottville.
113. Bronson, Florence.
114. Centre Hill, Centre Hill.
115. Campbell, Burrowsville.
116. Washita, Orion.
117. Yellville, Yellville.
118. Spring Hill, Spring Hill.
119. Pea Ridge, Pea Ridge.
120. Pleasant Grove, D'Armand's Springs.
121. Fremont, Fremont.
122. White Sulphur, White Sulphur Springs.
123. Bluffton, Bluffton.
124. Lake Bluff, Lake Bluff.
125. Brushy Woods, Como.
126. Bayou Data, Sulphur Rock.
127. Springfield, Springfield.
128. Dallas, Dallas.
130. Euclid, Mt. Adams.
131. Greenwood, Greenwood.
132. Waldron, Waldron.
133. Napoleon, Napoleon.
134. Atlanta, Atlanta.
135. Crooked Creek, Crooked Creek.
136. Olive Branch, Spring Branch.
137. Walnut Plains, Walnut Plains.
138. Lucy, Van Buren.
139. Ebenezer, Graves.
140. Mount Ida, Mount Ida.
141. Lunenburg, Rocky Bayou.
142. Crescent, Portland.
143. Evening Shade, Evening Shade.
144. Curia, Curia.
145. Wooten, Stony Point.
146. Abraham, Rondo.
147. Henderson, Harold.
148. Caledonia, Morgan's Store.
149. Pitman, Pitman.
150. Providence, Mount Moriah.
151. Lanark, Lanark.
152. Sardis, Gravel Ridge.
153. Harrisburg, Harrisburg.
154. Elm Springs, Elm Springs.
155. Charleston, Charleston.
156. Accacia, Richland.
157. De Witt, De Witt.

158. Holland, Quitman.
159. Ash Flats, Ash Flats.
160. Jacob Brump, Pine Bluff.
161. Wise, Palestine.
162. Montongo, Montongo.
163. Reid, Hodges Prairie.
164. Adams, Pleasant Run.
165. Belle Font, Belle Font.
166. Mt. Holly, Mt. Holly.
167. Madison, Madison.
168. Gainesville, Gainesville.
169. Dooley's Ferry, Dooley's Ferry.
170. St. Mary's, Lexington.
171. Mariana, Mariana.
172. Galley Rock, Galley Rock.
173. Lucy Brandon, Rocky Comfort.
174. Red River, Richmond.
175. Evergreen, Oak Grove.
176. Reed's Creek, Reed's Creek.
177. Tyro, Tyro.
178. Mill Creek, Connersville.
179. Mine Creek, Greenville.
180. Magness, Big Bottom.
181. Barren Fork, Barren Fork.
182. Poe, Sulphur Springs.
183. Arcadia, Cleburne.
184. Poinsett, Harrisburg.
185. Cedar Grove, Cedar Grove.
186. Culpepper, Lehi.
187. South Fork, South Fork Church.
188. Walnut Hills, Walnut Hills.
189. Lafayette, Helena.
190. Colony, Colony.
191. Jacksouport, Jacksonport.
192. Kirkpatrick, Elgin.
193. Walnut Grove, Jones Creek Settlement.
194. Arlington, Camden.
195. Kerr, Forrest Home.
196. Kingston, Kingston.
197. Siloam, McElrath's Mill.
198. Jordan, New Bethel Church.
199. Beech Creek, Beech Creek.
200. Spring Creek, Edwardsburg.
201. New Boston, Cass.
202. Blue Mountain, Riggsville.

CALIFORNIA (1859).

Jurisdiction of the Grand Lodge of California.

1. California, San Francisco.
2. Western Star, Shasta.
3. Tehoma, Sacramento.
5. Benecia, Benecia.
8. Tuolumne, Sonora.
9. Marysville, Marysville.
10. San Jose, San Jose.
12. Yount, Napa.
13. Nevada, Nevada.
14. Temple, Sonora.
16. Eureka, Auburn.
17. Parfaite Union, San Francisco.

18. Mountain Shade, Downieville.
19. San Joaquin Stockton.
20. Washington, Sacramento.
21. Hawaiian, Honolulu.
22. Occidental, San Francisco.
23. Madison, Grass Valley.
24. Mariposa, Mariposa.
25. Georgetown, Georgetown.
26. Eldorado, Placerville.
27. Trinity, Weaverville.
28. Columbia, Columbia.
29. Diamond, Diamond Springs.

LIST OF LODGES.

305

30. Golden Gate, San Francisco.
31. Makelumne, Makelumne.
32. Golden Hill, Gold Hill.
33. Ophir, Murphey's Company.
34. Santa Clara, Santa Clara.
35. San Diego, San Diego.
36. Butte, Bidewell's Bar.
37. St. John's, Yreka.
38. Santa Cruz, Santa Cruz.
39. Yuba, Marysville.
40. Sacramento, Sacramento.
41. Martinez, Martinez.
42. Los Angelos, Los Angelos.
43. Hiram, El Dorado.
44. Mt. Moriah, San Francisco.
45. Crescent, Crescent City.
46. Texas, San Juan.
47. Michigan City, Michigan City.
49. Lebanon, San Francisco.
50. Forbestown, Forbestown.
51. Illinoistown, Illinoistown.
52. Rough and Ready, Rough and Ready.
54. St. James, Jamestown.
55. Sinsun, Sinsun.
56. Volcano, Volcano.
57. Santa Rosa, Santa Rosa.
58. Union, Sacramento.
59. Gravel Range, Camptonville.
60. Plumas, Quincy.
61. Live Oak, Oakland.
62. Geo. Washington, Chinese.
63. Iowa Hill, Iowa Hill.
64. Natoma, Mormon Island.
65. Amador, Jackson.
66. Forrest, Forrest City.
67. Minnesota, Minnesota.
68. Morning Star, Stockton.
69. Corinthian, Marysville.
70. Enterprise, Yuba City.
71. Nebraska, Michigan Bar.
72. Ekkan, Nevada.
73. Tyro, Drytown.
74. Wisconsin Hills, Wisconsin Hills.
75. Mountain Forest, Eurekaworth.
76. Bear Mt., Angel's Camp.
77. Petaluma, Petaluma.
78. Caleneras, San Andreas.
79. Humboldt, Bucksport.
80. Ione, Ione Valley.
81. Yolo, Yolo.
82. Mountain, Don Pedro's Bar.
83. Rising Star, Todd's Valley.
84. Vesper, Red Bluffs.

85. Indian Diggings, Indian Diggings.
86. St. Louis, St. Louis.
87. Naval, Vallejo.
88. Quitman, Orleans Flat.
89. Rore's Bar, Rore's Bar.
90. Polar Star, Poorman's Creek.
91. North Star, Indian Creek.
92. Acacia, Colomo.
93. Caymus, Yountville.
94. Mt. Herman, Elizabethtown.
95. Henry Clay, Sutta Creek.
96. Howard, Yreka.
97. Jefferson, Rabbit Creek.
98. Quartzburg, Quartzburg.
99. La Grange, La Grange.
100. Campo Seco, Campo Seco.
101. Clay, Dutch Flat.
102. Mansanita, San Juan.
103. Aroville, Aroville.
104. Lexington, Lexington.
105. Siskiyoa, Cottonwood.
106. Arcata, Union.
107. Mt. Jefferson, Gorrotte.
108. Owen, Johnson's Bar.
109. Dibble, Alpha.
110. Pajaro, Watsonville.
111. Chico, Chico.
112. Summit, Knight's Ferry.
113. Eden, San Leandro
114. Mt. Zion, Grizzly Flat.
115. St. Mark's, Fiddletown.
116. Windsor, Windsor.
117. Concord, Sacramento.
118. Vallecito, Vallecito.
119. Clinton, Horsetown.
120. Fidelity, San Francisco.
121. Ionic, Iowa Hill.
122. Alamo, Alamo.
123. Sotozomi, Healetsburg.
124. Tible Mountain, Oreville.
125. Progress, San Francisco.
126. Lafayette, Badega.
127. Harmon, San Francisco.
128. Visalia, Visalia.
129. Nicolaus, Nicolaus.
130. Minty, San Bernardins.
131. Woodbridge, Wood's Ferry.
132. Sincerity, Rich Bar.
133. Yosenate, Coultersville.
134. Vacaville, Vacaville.
135. Valley, Foreman's Ranche.
136. Napa City, Napa City.
137. Pacific, San Francisco.

COLORADO.

Jurisdiction of the Grand Lodge of Colorado.

1. Golden City, Golden City.
4. Nevada, Golden City.
5. Denver, Denver.
6. Chivington, Central City
7. Union, Denver.

8. Empire, Empire.
9. Montana, Virginia City.
10. Helena City, Helena City, N. T.
U. D. Black Hawk, Black Hawk.
U. D. El Paso, Colorado City.

26*

306 LIST OF LODGES.

CONNECTICUT.

Jurisdiction of the Grand Lodge of Connecticut.

1. Hiram, New Haven.
2. St. John's, Middletown.
3. St. John's, Bridgeport.
4. St. John's, Hartford.
5. Union, Stamford.
6. St. John's, Norwalk.
7. King Solomon's, Woodburn,
8. St. John's, Stratford.
9. Compoo, Wallingford.
10. Wooster, Colchester.
11. St. Paul's, Litchfield.
12. King Hiram, Derby.
13. Montgomery, Falls Village.
14. Frederick, Plainville.
15. Moriah, W. Killingly.
16. Temple, Cheshire.
17. Federal, Watertown.
18. Hiram, Newtown.
20. Harmony, New Britain.
21. St. Peter's, New Milford.
24. Unity, Mansfield.
25. Columbia, S. Glastenburg,
26. Columbia, E. Haddon.
27. Rising Star, Washington.
28. Morning Star, Warehouse Point.
29. Village, Collinsville.
31. Union, N. London.
33. Friendship, Southington.
34. Somerset, Norwich,
36. St. Mark's, Tariffville.
37. Western Star, Norfolk.
38. St. Alban's, Guilford.
40. Union, Danbury.
42. Harmony, Waterbury.
43. Trinity, Chester.
44. Eastern Star, Willimantic.
46. Putnam, Woodstock.
47. Morning Star, Seymour.
48. St. Luke's, Kent.
49. Jerusalem, Ridgefield.
50. Warren, S. Coventry.
51. Warren, Portland.
52. Mt. Olive, Essex

53. Widow's Son, N. Stonington.
55. Seneca, Wolcottsville.
56. Franklin, Bristol.
57. Asylum, Stonington.
58. N. Star, New Hartford.
59. Apollo, Suffield.
60. Wolcott, Staffordville.
62. Orient, E. Hartford.
63. Adelphia, Fair Haven.
64. St. Andrew's, West Winsted
65. Temple, Westport.
66. Widow's Son, Branford.
67. Harmony, New Canaan.
68. Charity, Mystic Bridge.
69. Fayette, Rockville.
70. Washington, Windsor.
73. Manchester, Manchester.
77. Meridian, Meridian.
78. Shepherd's, Naugatuck.
79. Wooster, New Haven.
81. Washington, Cromwell.
82. Geo. Washington, Ansonia.
83. Eureka, Bethel.
84. Olive Branch, Westville.
85. Acacia, Greenwich.
86. Daskom, Glastenbury.
87. Madison, Madison.
88. Hartford, Hartford.
89. Ansantowae, Milford.
90. Pawcatuck, Stonington.
91. St. Mark's, Granby.
92. Connecticut Rock, New Haven.
93. Monroe, Monroe.
94. Doric, Enfield.
95. Jephtha, Clinton.
96. Union, Plymouth.
97. Centre, Meridian.
98. Hiram, Bloomfield.
99. Wylly's, West Hartford.
100. La Fayette, Hartford.
101. Evening Star, Unionville,
102. Brainard, New London.
103. Corinthian, North Branford.

DELAWARE.

Jurisdiction of the Grand Lodge of Delaware.

1. Washington, Wilmington.
2. St. John's, New Castle.
4. Hope, Laurel.
5. Union, Middletown.
7. Union, Dover.
9. Temple, Milford.
11. Temple, Wilmington.
12. Franklin, Georgetown.
14. Lafayette, Wilmington.

15. Jefferson, Lewes.
17. Endeavor, Milton.
19. Jackson, Delaware City.
20. Corinthian, Wilmington.
21. Hiram, Seaford.
U. D. Smyrna, Smyrna.
 " Felton, Felton.
 " Eureka, Wilmington.

LIST OF LODGES.

307

DISTRICT OF COLUMBIA (1859).

Jurisdiction of the Grand Lodge of District of Columbia.

1. Federal.
4. Washington Nord.
5. Potomac.
7. Lebanon.
9. New Jerusalem.
10. Hiram.

11. St. John's.
12. National.
14. Washington Continental.
15. Benj. B. French.
16. Dawson.

FLORIDA.

Jurisdiction of the Grand Lodge of Florida.

1. Jackson, Tallahassee,
2. Washington, Quincy.
3. Harmony, Marianna.
4. Coe, ———
5. Hiram, Monticello.
6. Franklin, Apalachicola.
7. Jeff. Davis, Ancilla.
9. Bartow, Bartow.
10. Waldo, Waldo.
11. Madison, Madison.
12. Cherry Hill, Cherry Hill.
13. Welborn, Welborn.
14. Dade, Key West.
15. Escambia, Pensacola.
16. Santa Rosa, Milton.
17. Ucheeanna, Ucheeanna.
19. Marion, Ocala.
20. Solomon, Jacksonville.
21. Gee, Chattahooche.
22. Withlacoochee, Bellville.
23. Crawfordville, Crawfordville.
24. Naval, Warrington.
25. Hillsborough, Tampa.
26. Alachua, Neunansville.
28. Concordia, Concord.
29. Micanopy, Micanopy.
30. Suwannee, Suwannee Shoals.

31. Manatee, Manatee.
32. De Soto, Brooksville.
33. Jefferson, Waukeenah.
34. Palatka, Palatka.
35. Mount Moriah, Adamsville.
36. Orange, Orlando.
37. Orient, Jasper.
38. Chipola, Greenwood.
39. Mackey, Live Oak.
40. Orion, Orange Hill.
41. Gainesville, Gainesville.
43. Stephens, Moseley Hall.
44. Miccosukie, Miccosukie.
45 True Brotherhood, Flemington.
46. Providence, Providence.
47. Amelia, Fernandina.
48. Douglass, White Spring.
49. Marston, Silver Spring.
50. Shiloh, Hamburg.
51. Brown, Leoyville.
52. Lake Butler, Lake Butler.
53. Friendship, St. John's Church.
54. Orange Creek, Orange Creek.
55. St. John's, St. Augustine.
56. Orange Spring, Orange Spring.
57. Campbellton, Campbellton.

GEORGIA (1859).

Jurisdiction of the Grand Lodge of Georgia.

0. Solomon's, Savannah.
1. Social, Augusta.
2. Stith, Sparta.
4. Rising Sun.
5. Macon, Macon.
6 Golden Fleece, Covington.
7. Columbia, Columbia.

8. Orion, Bainbridge.
9. Mt. Hope, Hawkinsville.
10. Olive, Talbolton.
11. Franklin, Warrenton.
12. Cross, Lumpkin.
13. Americus, Americus.
14. Marion, Tazewell.

LIST OF LODGES.

15. Zerubbabel, Savannah.
16. Hamilton, Hamilton.
17. Darley, Ft. Gaines.
18. Monroe, Forsythe.
19. Washington. Cuthbert.
20. Rising Sun, Reidsville.
21. Hiram, Florence.
22. Mt. Vernon, Athens.
23. Lafayette, Washington.
24. General Warren, Monroe. Albany, Albany.
25. Philomathean, Elberton.
26. Meridian Sun, Griffin.
27. Morning Star, Thomaston.
28 Union, La Grange.
29. Madison, Madison.
30. Amity, Walkinsville.
31. Montgomery, Zebulon.
32. St. Patrick, Danville.
33. Keneson, Marietta.
34. San Marino, Greensboro'.
35. Houston, Perry.
36. Unity, Jefferson.
37. Fraternal, McDonough.
38. Blue Mountain, Dahlonega.
39. Newborn, Newborn.
40. Ebenezer, Ebenezer.
41. Pythagoras, Decatur.
42. Concord, Concord.
43. West Point, West Point.
44. Lafayette, Cumming.
45. St. John's, Jackson.
46. Washington. Pondtown.
47. Oglethorpe, Columbus.
48. Jackson, Hickory Grove.
49. St. Thomas, Thomsonville.
50. Jasper, Monticello.
51 .Hiram, Danbury.
52. St. Patrick, Louisville.
53. Mt. Moriah, Fayettesville.
54. Clinton, Savannah.
55. Knoxville,,Knoxville.
56. Burns, Lamir.
57. Greeneville, Greeneville.
58. Hamilton, Soudersville.
59. Atlanta, Atlanta.
60. Cowela, Newnan.
61. Chatahootche, Franklin.
62. Randolph, Pumpkintown.
63. Georgetown, Georgetown.
64. Mt. Moriah, Woodstock.
65. Traveler's Rest, Traveler's Rest.
66. Coosa, Rome.
67. Dawson, Crawfordville.
68. Dawson, Social Circle.
69. Carroll, Carrollton.
70. Erin, Erin.
71. Oxford, Oxford.
72. Villa Rica, Villa Rica.
73. Aleova, Newton Factory.
74. Unity, Palmetto.
75. Laurens, Dublin.
76. Campbellton, Campbellton.
77 Canton, Canton.
78. Lincoln, Lincolnton.
79. Tien, Buena Vista.
80. Weston, Weston ⋈ Roads.
81. Oak Brewery, Elizor.

82. W. P. Arnold, Wrightsboro'.
83. Zaradotha, Lexington.
84. Lithoma, Lithoma.
85. Daniel, Island Creek.
86. Magnolia, Blakely.
87. Jonesboro', Jonesboro'.
88. Pinta, Barnesville.
89. Eldorado, Plattsburg.
90. Ringold, Colbert's Mills
91. Western, La Fayette.
92. Carten, Pleasant Hill.
93. St. Mark's, Gold Hill.
94. New River, Corinth.
95. Eureka, Starkville.
96. Liberty Union, Taylor's Creek.
97. Euharlee, Van Wert.
98. Houston, Houston.
99. Siloam, Snapping Shoals.
100. St. John, Raysville.
101. Cartersville, Cartersville.
102. Rose, Whitesville.
103. Pleasant Ridge, Pleasant Ridge.
104. Montpelier, Montpelier.
105. Dalton, Dalton.
106. Quitman, Ringgold.
107. Thurmond, Hillsboro'.
108. Chapel, Lumpkin.
109. Summerville, Summerville.
110. Ft. Valley, Ft. Valley.
111. Stone Mountain. Stone Mountain.
112. Walton, Shady Dale.
113. Tallapoosa, Buchanan.
114. Allegheny, Blairsville.
115. Troup Factory, Troup Factory.
116. Woruam, Clinton.
117. Farmer's, Vienna.
118. Kiubrough, Columbus.
119. McIntosh, Indian Springs.
120. Mackey, Cove Spring.
121. Caledonia, Cedartown.
122. Williamsville, Williamsville.
123. Baker, White Plains.
124. Furlon, Bobtsville.
125. Jabon Burr, Mountville.
126. St. Mary's, St. Mary's.
127. Ancient York, Sandy Ridge.
128. Union, Quito.
129. Fickling, Butler.
130. Salem, Culloden.
131. Lawrenceville, Lawrenceville.
132. Long Cone, Long Cone.
133. Mt. Hickory, Easterling.
135. Fergus. Buncombe.
136. Cassville, Cassville.
137. Malloryville, Malloryville.
138. Howard, Maxey's Depot.
139. King David, King's Chapel.
140. Claremont, Liberty Hill.
141. Charity, Petersburgh.
142. Haralson, Haralson
143. South Western, Oglethorpe
144. Ellerslie, Ellerslie.
145. Cohultah, Spring Place.
146. Kirlin, Mulberry Grove.
147. Sulphur Springs,White Sulphur Spgs.
148. Phi Delta, Phi Delta.
149. Woodbury, Woodbury.
150. Carmel, Irwington.

LIST OF LODGES. 309

151. Wellington, Wellington.
152. Sharon Grove, White Water.
153. Springville, Powder Springs.
154. Otheologa, Calhoun.
155. Chandler, Jamestown.
156. Harmony, McLendon's Store.
157. Oakland, Ferris Bridge.
158. Irving, Chickasawahatchee.
159. Bowenville, Bowenville.
160. Harmony, Appling.
161. Tallulah, Clarksville.
162. Joppa, Pt. Peter.
163. Star in the East, Millhaven.
164. Triggs, Marion.
165. Rosswell, Rosswell.
166. Webbs', Augusta.
167. Floyd Springs.
168. Adairsville, Adairsville.
169. Mt. Ebal, Fayettsville.
170. Emory, St. Cloud.
171. Philadelphus, Penfield.
172. Ocopilco, Ocopilco.
173. Patrick Henry, Drayton.
174. Holt, Quebec.
175. Zabud, New-Market.
176. Acworth, Acworth.
177. Pine Grove, Pine Grove.
179. Trenton, Trenton.
180. Fairburn, Fairburn.
181. Milford, Milford.
182. Dallas, Dallas.
183. High Falls, Cross Ridge.
184. St. John Baptist, Troupville.
185. Cool Spring, Cool Springs.
186. Carnersville, Carnersville.
187. Centre, Union.
188. Marshal, Preston.
189. Herman, Hartwell.
190. Baker, Newton.
191. Rockwell, Mulberry.

192. Rehoboth, Nockway.
193. Coffee, Jacksonville.
194. Worth, Isabella.
195. Holmesville, Holmesville.
196. Trader's Hill, Trader's Hil
197. Wells, Calaparchee.
198. Milwood, Milwood.
199. Lumber City, Lumber City.
200. Eastern Light, Copeland.
201. Ococee, Morganton.
202. Tunnel Hill, Tunnel Hill.
203. Ashler, Concord.
204. Miller, Thomson.
205. Hickory Flat, Hickory Flat.
206. Bowden, Bowden.
207. Armonia, Duncansville.
208. Hudson, Glades ⋈ Rond.
209. Alopaha, Troublesome.
210. Brookline, Brookline.
211. Butler, Alopaha.
212. Irwin, Irwinville.
213. Ogechee, Ogechee.
214. Ocean, Brunswick.
215. Goulding, Dublin.
216. Fulton, Atlanta.
217. Waresborough, Waresborough.
218. Halt, Colginth.
219. Gainesville, Gainesville.
220. Picken's Star, Jasper.
221. Sonora, Sonora.
222. Etowah, Dawsonville.
223. Smith, Red Hill.
224. Magnolia, Magnolia.
225. Attapulgus, Attapulgus.
226. Ft. Early, Warwick.
227. Altamaha, Johnson.
228. Yellow River, Gwinnett.
229. Schley, Dawson.
230. Mineral Spring, Plains of Dura.

ILLINOIS (1859).

Jurisdiction of the Grand Lodge of Illinois.

1. Bodley, Quincy.
2. Equality, Equality.
3. Harmony, Jacksonville.
4. Springfield, Springfield.
7. Friendship, Dixon.
8. Macon, Decatur.
9. Rustville, Rustville.
13. St. John's, Peru.
14. Warren, Shawneetown.
15. Peoria, Peoria.
16. Temperance, Vandalia.
17. Macomb, Macomb.
18. Lafayette, Chicago.
19. Clinton, Petersburg.
20. Hancock, Carthage.
23. Casa, Beardstown.
24. St. Clair, Belleville.

25. Franklin, Upper Alton.
26. Hiram, Henderson.
27. Piara, Alton.
28. Monroe, Waterloo.
29. Pekin, Pekin.
30. Morning Star, Canton.
31. Mount Vernon, Mount Vernon.
33. Oriental, Chicago.
34. Barry, Barry.
35. Charleston, Charleston.
36. Kavanagh, Elizabeth.
37. Monmouth, Monmouth.
38. Olive Branch, Danville.
39. Herman, Quincy.
40. Occidental, Ottawa.
42. Mount Joliet, Joliet.
43. Bloomington, Bloomington

LIST OF LODGES.

44. Hardin, Mount Sterling.
45. Griggsville, Griggsville.
46. Temple, Peoria.
47. Caledonia, N. Caledonia.
48. Unity, St. Charles.
49. Cambridge, Cambridge.
50. Carlton, Carrollton.
51. Mount Moriah, Hillsborough.
52. Benevolent, Meredosia.
53. Jackson, Shelbyville.
54. Reclamation, Nauvoo.
55. Washington, Nashville.
56. Pittsfield, Pittsfield.
57. Trio, Rock Island.
58. Fraternal, Monticello.
59. New Boston, New Boston.
60. Belvidere, Belvidere.
61. Lacon, Lacon.
63. St. Mark's, Woodstock.
64. Benton, Benton.
65. Euclid, Naperville.
66. Knoxville, Knoxville.
67. Acacia, La Salle.
68. Naples, Naples.
69. Eureka, Camden Mills.
70. Social, Hennepin.
71. Central, Springfield.
72. Chester, Chester.
73. Batavia, Batavia.
74. Rockton, Rockton.
75. Roscoe, Roscoe.
76. Mount Nebo, Carlinville.
77. Prairie, Paris.
78. Union, Waukegon.
79. Scott, Carlyle.
80. Whitehall, Whitehall.
81. Vitrurius, Wheeling.
82. Metamora, Metamora.
83. Iroquois, Middleport.
84. DeWitt, Clinton.
85. Mitchell, Pinckneyville.
86. Kaskaskia, Kaskaskia.
87. Mount Pulaski, Mount Pulaski.
88. Havana, Havana.
89. Fellowship, Marion,
90. Jerusalem Temple, Aurora.
91. Metropolis, Metropolis.
92. Stewart, Genesee.
93. Toulon, Toulon.
94. Morning Sun, Jerseyville.
95. Perry, Perry.
96. Davis, Mount Morris.
97. Excelsior, Freeport.
98. Taylor, Washington.
99. Edwardsville, Edwardsville.
100. Astoria, Astoria.
101. Madison, Upper Alton.
102. Rockford, Rockford.
103. Magnolia, Magnolia.
104. Lewistown, Lewistown.
105. Winchester, Winchester.
106. Lancaster, Lancaster.
107. Fayette, Fayette.
108. Versailles, Versailles.
109. Sharon, Sharon.
110. Lebanon, Lebanon.
111. Jonesboro', Jonesboro'.
112. Bureon, Princeton.

113. Burns, Keithburg.
114. Marcelline, Marcelline.
115. Rising Sun, Hainesville.
116. Vermont, Vermont.
117. Elgin, Elgin.
118. Waverly, Waverly.
119. Henry, Henry.
120. Jacksonville, Jacksonville.
122. Mound, Taylorville.
123. Oquaka, Oquaka.
124. Cedar, Morris.
125. Greenup, Greenup.
126. Empire, Pekin.
127. Antioch, Antioch.
128. Raleigh, Raleigh.
129. Greenfield, Greenfield.
130. Marion, Salem.
131. Golconda, Golconda.
132. Mackinaw, Mackinaw.
133. Marshall, Marshall.
134. Sycamore, Sycamore.
135. Lima, Lima.
136. Hutsonville, Hutsonville.
137. Polk, McLeanesboro'.
138. Marengo, Marengo.
139. Geneva, Geneva.
140. Olney, Olney.
141. Garden City, Chicago.
142. Ames, Sheffield.
143. Richmond, Richmond.
144. DeKalb, DeKalb.
145. Rawson, Pecatonica.
146. Lee Centre, Lee Centre.
147. Clayton, Clayton.
148. Bloomfield, Bloomfield.
149. Ewington, Ewington.
150. Vienna, Vienna.
151. Bunker Hill, Bunker Hill.
152. Fidelity, Fidelity.
153. Clay, Richview.
154. Russell, Georgetown.
155. Alpha, Galesburg.
156. Delavan, Delavan
157. Urbana, Urbana.
158. McHenry, McHenry.
159. Wethersfield, Wethersfield.
160. Wabouria, Chicago.
161. Virdon, Virden.
162. Hope, Sparta.
163. Westfield, Westfield.
164. Lawrenceville, Lawrenceville.
165. Atlanta, Atlanta.
166. Star in the East, Rockford.
167. Oswego, Oswego.
168. Milford, Milford.
169. Nunda, Nunda.
170. Evergreen, Freeport.
171. Girard, Girard.
172. Wayne, Waynesville.
173. Cherry Valley, Cherry Valley.
174. Lena, Lena.
175. Matteson, Joliet.
176. Mendota, Mendota.
177. Stanton, Stanton.
178. Illinois Central, Amboy.
179. Wabash, Paradise.
180. Moweagna, Moweagna.
181. Moultrie, Sullivan.

LIST OF LODGES.

311

182. Germania, Chicago.
183. Meridian, Earlville.
185. Abingdon, Abingdon.
186. Fort Armstrong, Rock Island
187. Mystic Tie, Palo.
188. Cyrus, Mount Carroll.
189. Fulton City, Fulton City.
190. Dundee, Dundee.
191. Xenia, Xenia.
192. Farmington, Farmington.
193. Herrick, Pontosne.
194. Freedom, Freedom.
195. La Harpe, La Harpe.
196. Louisville, Louisville.
197. King Solomon, Kane.
198. Grandview, Grandview.
199. Homer, Homer.
200. Sheba, Grayville.
201. Centralia, Centralia.
202. Sterling, Sterling.
203. Lovely, Williamsville.
204. Flora, Flora.
205. Corinthian, West Paw Paw.
206. Fairfield, Fairfield.
207. Tamarawa, Tamarawa.
208. Wilmington, Wilmington.
209. Warren, Chicago.
210. Lincoln, Lincoln.
211. Cleveland, Chicago.
212. Shipman, Shipman.
213. Ipava, Ipava.
214. Gillespie, Gillespie.
215. Weir, Six Miles.
216. Newton, Newton.
217. Mason, Mason.
218. New Salem, New Salem.
219. Oakland, Oakland.
220. Mahomet, Middletown.
221. Le Roy, Le Roy.
222. General Washington, Chillicothe.
223. Keeney, Gelington.
224. Mount Pleasant, Santa Anna.
225. Awisco, Kankakee.
226. Pana, Pana.
227. Columbus, Columbus.
228. Lovington, Lovington.
229. Manchester, Manchester.
230. New Haven, New Haven.
231. Wyanett, Wyanett.
232. Farmers', Tindall Valley.
233. Blandensville, Blandensville.
234. Dugnoin, Dugnoin.
235. Dallas City, Dallas City.
236. Charter Oak, Litchfield.
237. Cairo, Cairo.
238. Black Hawk, Hamilton.
239. Mt. Carmel, Mt. Carmel.
240. Western Star, West Urbana.
241. Shekinah, Carbondale.

242. Aegis, Annawan.
243. Salva, Salva.
244. Horicon, Lane.
245. Greenville, Greenville.
246. Panola, Panola.
247. Robert Morris, Minork.
248. Golden Gate, Prairie City.
249. Hubbard, Brighton.
250. Robinson, Robinson.
251. Keyworth, Keyworth.
252. Aledo, Aledo.
253. Avon Harmony, Avon.
254. Aurora, West Aurora.
255. Donaldson, Donaldson.
256. Algonquin, Algonquin.
257. Warsaw, Warsaw.
258. Bowers, Bowers.
259. New Berlin, Berlin.
260. Mattoon, Mattoon.
261. Aurora, De Witt.
262. Channahon, Channahon.
263. Illinois, Peoria.
264. Franklin Grove, Franklin Grove.
265. Vermillion, Dallas.
266. Kingston, Kingston.
267. Laprairie, Laprairie.
268. Paris, Paris.
269. Wheaton, Wheaton.
270. Levi Lusk, Arlington
271. Blaney, Chicago.
272. Carmi, Carmi.
273. Miners', Galena.
274. Byron, Byron.
275. Milton, Milton.
276. Elizabeth, Elizabeth Town.
277. Accordia, Chicago.
278. Daviess, Warren.
279. Neoga, Neoga.
280. Kansas, Kansas.
281. Martinsville, Martinsville.
282. Brooklyn, Brooklyn.
283. Meteor, Sandwich.
284. Alton, Alton.
290. Cache, Mound City.
291. Wetago, Wetago.
292. Windsor, Windsor.
293. Chenon, Chenon.
294. Prophetstown, Prophetstown.
295. Pontiac, Pontiac.
296. Dills, Breckenridge.
297. Quincy, Quincy.
298. Benjamin, Camp Point.
299. Wancondia, Wancondia.
300. Mechanicsburg, Mechanicsburg.
301. Ingersoll, Ingersoll.
302. Hanover, Hanover.
303. Durand, Durand.
304. Raven, Oswego.
305. Cement, Utica.

312

LIST OF LODGES.

INDIANA.

Jurisdiction of the Grand Lodge of Indiana.

1. Vincennes, Vincennes.
2. Union, Madison.
3. Carlisle, Carlisle.
4. Lawrenceburg, Lawrenceburg.
5. Cambridge, Cambridge City.
6. Rising Sun, Rising Sun.
7. Versailles, Versailles.
8. Parke, Rockville.
9. Boone, Lebanon.
10. Napoleon, Napoleon.
11. Harmony, Brookville.
12. Goshen, Goshen.
13. Washington, Brownstown.
14. Bedford, Bedford.
15. Warren, Connersville.
16. Golden Rule, Knightstown.
17. Harrison, Bright.
18. Attica, Attica.
19. Terra Haute, Terre Haute.
20. St. John, Columbus.
21. Salem, Salem.
22. Monroe, Bloomington.
23. Centre, Indianapolis.
24. Webb, Richmond.
25. Wayne, Fort Wayne.
26. Western Star, Danville.
27. Florence, Florence.
28. Shelby, Shelbyville.
29. Laurel, Laurel.
30. Charity, Washington.
31. Milan, South Milan.
32. Pisgah, Corydon.
33. Tipton, Logansport.
34. Manilla, Manilla.
35. Marion, Indianapolis.
36. Greensburg, Greensburg.
37. Perry, Lafayette.
38. Williamsport, Williamsport.
39. New Albany, New Albany.
40. Clark, Jeffersonville.
41. Laporte, Laporte.
42. Hiram, Centreville.
43. Springfield, Mt. Carmel.
44. Madison, Pendleton.
45. St. Joseph, South Bend.
46. Delaware, Muncie.
47. Temple, Greencastle.
48. Mt. Olive, Delphi.
49. Hagerstown, Hagerstown.
50. Montgomery Crawfordsville.
51. Aurora, Aurora.
52. Westport, Westport.
53. Chesterfield, Chesterfield.
54. Clinton, Frankfort.
55. Burns, Manchester.
56. Winchester, Winchester.
57. Noblesville, Noblesville.
58. Liberty, Liberty.
59. Jenuings, Vernon.
60. Fountain, Covington.
61. Hanna, Wabash.
62. Phœnix, Rushville.

63. Ashler, Pleasant Hill.
64. Evansville, Evansville.
65. Belleville, Belleville.
66. Brookston, Brookston.
67. Miami, Peru.
68. Friendship, Hart's Mills.
69. Worthington, Worthington.
70. Brownsville, Brownsville.
71. Solomon, Hardingsburg.
72. Lewisville, Lewisville.
73. Warsaw, Warsaw.
74. Martinsville, Martinsville.
75. Bainbridge, Bainbridge.
76. Meridian Sun, Lagrange.
77. Mt. Moriah, Anderson.
78. Mooresville, Mooresville.
79. Fulton, Rochester.
80. Hopewell, Dillsborough.
81. Allensville, Enterprise.
82. Russiaville, Russiaville.
83. Michigan City, Michigan City.
84. Bloomfield, Bloomfield.
85. Clay, Bowling Green.
86. Social, Terra Haute.
87. Jay, Jay.
88. Deming, North Manchester.
89. Montezuma, Montezuma.
90. Portland, Portland Mills.
91. Newcastle, Newcastle.
92. Gosport, Gosport.
93. Kokomo, Kokomo.
94. Milford, Clifty.
95. Spencer, Spencer.
96. Andersonville, Andersonville.
97. Albion, Albion.
98. Fairfield, Fairfield.
99. Jerusalem, Clinton.
100. Edinburg, Edinburg.
101. Hancock, Greenfield.
102. Economy, Economy.
103. Dayton, Dayton.
104. Jefferson, New Albany.
105. Grant, Marion.
106. Blackford, Hartford City.
107. Franklin, Franklin.
108. Milton, Milton.
109. Jonesboro', Jonesboro'.
110. Mystic, Huntington.
111. Burlington, Burlington.
112. Rockport, Rockport.
113. Thorntown, Thorntown.
114. Anderson, Anderson.
115. Westfield, Westfield.
116. Leatherwood, Hiltonville.
117. Deerfield, Deerfield.
118. Clarksville, Clarksville.
119. Paoli, Paoli.
120. Scott, Austin.
121. Pike, Petersburg.
122. Switzerland, Vevay.
123. Lafayette, Lafayette.
124. Clarksburg, Clarksburg.

LIST OF LODGES. 313

125. Prairie, Rensellaer.
126. Millersville, James' Switch.
127. Annapolis, Annapolis.
128. Austin, Tipton.
129. Shawnee, Shawneetown.
130. Mishawaka, Mishawaka.
131. Larrabee, Stilesville.
132. Cloverdale, Cloverdale.
133. Rome, Rome.
134. Pleasant, Acton.
135. Nashville, Nashville.
136. Vesta, Jefferson.
137. Porter, Valparaiso.
138. Saltillo, Saltilloville.
139. Milroy, Milroy.
140. Oakland, Germantown.
141. Russelville, Russelville.
142. North Salem, North Salem.
143. Tuscan, Lagro.
144. Alamo, Alamo.
145. Bluffton, Bluffton.
146. Jackson, Seymour.
147. Farmers, Winterowd's.
148. Morning Star, Patriot.
149. Plymouth, Plymouth.
150. Hope, Hope.
151. Hartford, Hartford.
152. Cannelton, Cannelton.
153. Orleans, Orleans.
154. Libanus, Monticello.
155. Applegate, Fillmore.
156. Metamora, Metamora.
157. Lake, Crown Point.
158. Wilmington, Wilmington.
159. White Water, White Water.
160. Lawrence, Briantsville.
161. Cedar, Leesville.
162. Bridgeport, Bridgeport.
163. Mount Vernon, Mount Vernon.
164. Ovid, Ovid.
165. Allen, Moore's Hill.
166. Newberry, Newberry.
167. New Washington, New Washington.
168. Mount Pleasant, Loogootee.
169. Bridgeton, Bridgeton.
170. Summit City, Fort Wayne.
171. Anthony, Albany.
172. Lodiville, Waterman.
173. Stanford, Stanford.
174. Newburg, Newburg.
175. Greensboro' Greensboro'.
176. Wooster, Everton.
177. Springville, Springville.
178. Teutonia, Indianapolis.
179. Carthage, Carthage.
180. Wolcott, Wolcott.
181. Leesburg, Leesburg.
182. Greenwood, Greenwood.
183. Kane, Elkhart.
184. Hermon, Michigantown.
185. Ligonier, Ligonier.
186. Darlington, Darlington.
187. Ladoga, Ladoga.
188. Posey, Levenworth.
189. Columbia City, Columbia City.
190. Oxford, Oxford.
191. Grandview, Grandview.
192. Westville, Westville.

193. Morristown, Morristown.
194. Excelsior, Laporte.
195. Roanoke, Roanoke.
196. Richmond, Richmond.
197. Zion, Zionsville.
198. Ripley, Rei.
199. Cicero, Cicero.
200. Hazelrigg, Jamestown.
201. Rono, Rono.
202. Alton, Alton.
203. Jerome, Jerome.
204. Terre Coupee, New Carlisle.
205. Richland Newtown.
206. Livonia, Livonia.
207. Portville, Portville.
208. Monong, Francisville.
209. Newport, Newport.
210. Northeastern, Fremont.
211. Mount Zion, Camden.
212. Pennville, Pennville.
213. Moorefield, Moorefield.
214. De Kalb, Auburn.
215. Lima, Lima.
216. Bayless, Jonesville.
217. Waldron, Conn's Creek.
218. ————.
219. Butlerville, Butlerville.
220. Advance, Delphi.
221. Paris, Paris.
222. Kingsbury, Kingsbury.
223. Lynn, Lynn.
224. Leo, Leo.
225. Star, Orland.
226. Blazing Star, Charlestown.
227. Bourbon, Bourbon.
228. Mitchell, Mitchell.
229. Whitney, New Burlington.
230. Quincy, Duck Creek.
231. Prince. Princeton.
232. Cornelius. Abbington.
233. Downey, Boston.
234. Orange, Orange.
235. Alexandria, Alexandria.
236. Angola, Angola.
237. Martinsburg, Martinsburg.
238. Taylorville, Taylorville.
239. Forest, Jarvis.
240. Strangers' Rest, Booneville.
241. Brownsburg, Brownsburg.
242. Acacia, Greensfork.
243. O'Brian, Knox.
244. Galveston, Galveston.
245. Elletsville, Elletsville.
246. King, Warren.
247. Perkinsville, Perkinsville.
248. Olive Branch, Root,
249. Elizabethtown, Elizabethtown.
250. Bethel, Bethel.
251. Keystone, Castleton.
252. Reynolds, Reynolds.
253. Sardis, Charlotsville.
254. Decatur, Decatur.
255. Newpoint, Rossburg.
256. Troy, Troy.
257. Bennington, Bennington.
258. Hudson, Reelsville.
259. Roseville, Roseville.
260. Winslow, Winslow.

314

LIST OF LODGES.

261. Monrovia, Monrovia.
262. Winamac, Winamac.
263. Sullivan, Sullivan.
264. Brazil, Brazil.
265. Mississinawa, Wheeling.
266. North Liberty, North Liberty.
267. Xenia, Xenia.
268. Miller, Clark's Hill.
269. Adams, Adams.
270. Southport, Southport.
271. Middletown, Middletown.
272. Orient, Logansport.
273. Owen, Quincy.
274. Mound, State Line.
275. Dunkirk, Dunkirk.
276. Kendalville, Kendalville.
277. Cadiz, Cadiz.
278. Due Guard, Larwill.
279. Sugar Creek, Fairland.
280. Crescent, Miami.
281. Independence, Rigdon.
282. Rob Morris, Campbellsburg.
283. New London, New London.
284. Geneva, Scipio.
285. Corinthian, Salem Centre.
286. Newland, Salem.
287. Plainfield, Plainfield.
288. Montpelier, Montpelier.
289. Merom, Merom.
290. Frankton, Frankton.
291. Rolling Prairie, Rolling Prairie.
292. Pimento, Pimento.
293. Monroeville, Monroeville.
294. South Bend, South Bend.
295. Lafontaine, Lafontaine.
296. Harlan, Harlan.
297. Ossian, Ossian.
298. Halfway, Halfway.
299. Selma, Selma.
300. Waveland, Waveland.
301. Germania, South Bend.
302. Waynetown, Waynetown.
303. Moore, Raglesville.
304. Middlefork, Middlefork.
305. Snow, Gooves.
306. Fravel, Goshen.
307. Waterloo City, Waterloo City.
308. Farmland, Farmland.
309. Fidelity, Boxley.
310. Hinkle, Deming
311. Wild Cat, Wild Cat.
312. Capital City, Indianapolis.

313. Battle Ground, Battle Ground.
314. Harveysburg, Harveysburg.
315. Rainsville, Rainsville.
316. Reed, Evansville.
317. Ninevah, Ninevah.
318. Rossville, Rossville.
319. Ancient Landmarks, Indianapolis.
320. Asbury, Toronto.
321. Hacker, Wilmot.
322. Harrodsburg, Harrodsburg.
323. Clear Spring, Mooney.
324. Rural Marklesville.
325. George Washington, Bristol.
326. William Hacker, Newville.
327. Bell River, Patriot.
328. Vallonia, Vallonia.
329. Tunnelton, Tunnelton.
330. Sandford, Sandford.
331. Blountsville, Blountsville.
332. White River, Halbert's Bluff.
333. Mt. Etna, Mt. Etna.
334. Windfall, Windfall.
335. Galeua, Laporte.
336. Vienna, Vienna.
337. Utica, Utica.
338. De-Pauw, New Albany.
339. Owensburg, Owensburg.
340. Jeffersonville, Jeffersonville.
341. Greentown, Greentown.
342. J. L. Smith, Stockwell.
343. Camon, Clifford.
344. Unity, Perryville.
345. Emmet, Bedford.
346. Lexington, Lexington.
347. Mexico, Mexico.
348. Sulphur Spring City, Sulphur Spring
349. Dublin, Dublin.
350. Lindon, Lindon.
351. Remington, Remington.
352. West Lebanon, West Lebanon.
353. Lakeville, Lakeville.
354. Gilead, Gilead.
355. Pythagoras, New Albany.
356. Walkerton, Walkerton.
357. M. L. McClelland, Hobart.
358. Morgantown, Morgantown.
359. Sol. D. Bayless, Fort Wayne.
360. W. Hacker, Shelbyville.
361. Newton, Adriance.
362. Doric, Ridgeville.
U. D. Colfax, Lowel.

IOWA.

Jurisdiction of the Grand Lodge of Iowa.

1. Des Moines, Burlington.
2. Iowa, Muscatine.
3. Dubuque, Dubuque.
4. Iowa City, Iowa City.
5. Wapello, Wapello.
6. Marion, Marion.

7. Hiram, Augusta.
8. Mt. Pleasant, Mt. Pleasant.
10. Keosauqua, Keosauqua.
11. Cedar, Tipton.
12. Eagle, Keokuk.
13. Claypoole, Ft. Madison.

LIST OF LODGES. 315

14. Franklin, Bloomfield.
15. Clinton, Fairfield.
16. Ottumwa, Ottumwa.
17. Salem, Salem.
18. Triluminar, Oskaloosa.
20. Burlington, Burlington.
21. Olive Branch, Agency City.
22. Pioneer, Des Moines.
24. Golden Rule, Rochester.
25. Crescent, Cedar Rapids.
26. Washington, Washington.
27. Mt. Moriah, Farmington.
28. New London, New London.
29. Hardin, Keokuk.
30. Hawkeye, Muscatine.
31. Zion, Iowa City.
33. Winchester, Winchester.
34. De Witt, De Witt.
36. Helion, Maquoketa.
37. Davenport, Davenport.
38. Richland, Richland.
40. Troy, Troy.
42. Jackson, Centerville.
43. Evening Star, Winterset.
44. Snow, Le Claire.
45. Crawfordsville, Crawfordsville.
46. Anamosa, Anamosa.
47. Bentonsport, Bentonsport.
48. Danville, Danville.
49. Metropolitan, Dubuque.
50. Niles, Niles.
51. Bellevue, Bellevue.
52. Lafayette, Montezuma.
53. Warren, Indianola.
55. Pella, Pella.
56. Birmingham, Birmingham.
58. Glenwood, Glenwood.
59. Newton, Newton.
60. Camanche, Camanche.
61. Oriental, Knoxville.
62. Vinton, Vinton.
63. Chariton, Chariton.
64. Brighton, Brighton.
65. Black Hawk, Cedar Falls.
66. Union Band, Frankville.
67. Constellation, Colesburg.
68. Glasgow, Glasgow.
69. West Union, West Union.
70. Clayton, Monona.
71. Bluff City, Council Bluffs.
72. Elkader, Elkader.
73. Bonaparte, Bonaparte.
74. Eddyville, Eddyville.
75. West Point, West Point.
76. Albia, Albia.
77. Osceola, Osceola.
78. Grand River, Leon.
79. Mt. Olive, Boonsboro'.
80. Adel, Adel.
81. Benton City, Shellsburg.
83. Hartford, Hartford.
84. Epworth, Epworth.
86. Jefferson, Drakeville.
87. Independence, Independence.
90. Garnavillo, Garnavillo.
91. Corydon, Corydon.
93. Lyons, Lyons.
94. Butler, Clarksville.

95. Mt. Calvary, West Liberty.
96. Richmond, Richmond. ..
99. Nevada, Nevada.
100. Western Star, Clinton.
102. Osage, Osage.
103. Sioux City, Sioux City.
104. Abingdon, Abingdon.
105. Waterloo, Waterloo.
106. Martinsburg, Martinsburg.
107. Columbus City, Columbus City.
108. Marshall, Marshalltown.
109. Decatur, Decatur.
110. Capital, Des Moines.
111. Ashlar, Ft. Dodge.
112. Mt. Vernon, Mt. Vernon.
113. Polar Star, Orford.
114. Marengo, Marengo.
115. Star, Swede Point.
116. Tyrrell, Waverly.
117. Montague, Eldora.
118. Toledo, Toledo.
119. Unionville, Unionville.
120. Adoniram, Marshall.
121. Panora, Panora.
122. Ionic, Atalissa.
123. Orange, Guthrie Center.
124. Lovilia, Lovilia.
125. Mosaic, Dubuque.
126. Magnolia, Magnolia.
127. Cascade, Cascade.
128. Pleasant, Pleasantville.
129. Bradford, Bradford.
130. Strawberry Point, Strawberry Point.
131. Equity, Jaynesville.
132. Orion, Dyersville.
133. Bellair, Bellair.
135. Bezer, McGregor.
136. Joppa, Montrose.
137. Lewis, Lewis.
138. Fontanelle, Fontanelle.
139. Springville, Springville.
140. Nodaway, Clarinda.
141. St. Charles, Charles City.
142. Vienna, Center Point.
144. Evergreen, Lansing.
145. Benevolence, Mason City.
146. Talleyrand, Talleyrand.
147. Prairie la Porte, Prairie la Porte.
148. Fairbank, Fairbank.
149. Dayton, Dayton.
150. New Oregon, New Oregon.
151. Afton, Afton.
152. Newbern, Newbern.
153. Nishnebotany, Sidney.
154. Waukon, Waukon.
155. Patmos, Mechanicsville.
156. Taylor, Bedford.
157. Adams, Quincy.
158. Wiscotta, Wiscotta.
159. Morning Star, Jefferson.
160. Clermont, Clermont.
162. Red Oak, Red Oak.
163. Bellefontaine, Bellefontaine.
164. St. Clair, Florence.
165. Manchester, Delaware.
166. St. John's, Yankton, D. T.
167. Wilton, Wilton.
168. Farmers', Foote.

316

LIST OF LODGES.

169. Resurgam, Sabula.
170. Temple, Garden Grove.
171. Doric, Morning Sun.
172. National, National.
173. Burns, Monticello.
174. Corinthian, Brooklyn.
175. Hope, Belle Plaine.
176. Acacia, Webster City.
177. Euclid, Clarence.
178. Occidental, Sac City.
179. Faith, Mt. Ayr.
180. Pythagoras, Lancaster.
181. Great Lights, Decorah.
182. Webb, Sigourney.
183. Hiram Abiff, Lineville.
184. Zeredatha, Wheatland.
185. Tyre, Gosport.
186. Amity, Oskaloosa.
187. Rising Sun, Worthington.
188. Naphthali, South English.
189. Emblems, Pleasant Plain.
190. Attentive Ear, Sandyville.
191. Anchor, Hampton.
192. Mason's Home, Iowa Falls.
193. Clay, Lewisburg.

194. Fairview, Monroe.
195. Eastern Star, Dakota.
196. Mystic Tie, Prairie Grove.
197. Charity, Carrollton.
198. Kilwinning, Batavia.
199. Lincoln, Blairstown.
200. Ancient Landmark, Walnut Fork.
201. Jephtha, Grant City.
202. York, Fairfield.
203. Hiram of Tyre, Tama City.
204. Brotherly Love, Postville.
205. Prudence, Algona.
206. Keystone, Wyoming.
207. Xenium, Mt. Pleasant.
208. Trinity, Davenport.
209. Composite, Montana.
210. King Solomon, Belmond.
211. Relief, Riceville.
212. Unity, Ottawa.
213. Truth, Forest City.
U. D. Howard, Lime Spring.
U. D. Concordia, Hopeville.
U. D. Trowel, La Porte City.
U. D. Quitman, Stilesville.
U. D. Preston, Prairie City.

KANSAS.

Jurisdiction of the Grand Lodge of Kansas.

1. Smithton, Iowa Point.
2. Leavenworth, Leavenworth.
3. Wyandotte, Wyandotte.
4. Kickapoo, Round Prairie.
5. Washington, Atchison.
6. Lawrence, Lawrence.
7. Union, Junction City,
8. Bourbon, Ft. Scott.
9. Ceased to exist.
10. King Solomon, Leavenworth.
11. Ottumwa, Ottumwa.
12. Emporia, Emporia.
13. Lecompton, revoked.
14. Oskaloosa, Oskaloosa.
15. Tecumseh, Tecumseh.
16. Lafayette, Manhattan.
17. Topeka, Topeka.
18. Franklin, Ottowa.
19. Olathe, Olathe.
20. Circleville, Circleville.
21. Grasshopper Falls, Grasshopper Falls.
22. Paris, Paris.
23. Palmyra, Baldwin City.
24. Osage, Ossowatomie.
25. High Prairie, High Prairie.

26. St. John's, ceased.
27. Neosha, LeRoy.
28. Eldorado, Mapreton.
29. Pacific, Humboldt.
30. Amburg, ceased.
31. Arcana, Doniphan.
32. Auburn, Auburn.
33. Mound City, Mound City.
34. Indianola, Indianola.
35. Hiawatha, Hiawatha.
36. Council Grove, Council Grove.
37. Paola, Paola.
38. Iola, Iola.
39. Seneca, Seneca.
40. De Soto, De Soto.
41. Blooming Grove, Blooming Grove.
42. Holton, Holton.
43. Monticello, Monticello.
44. Delphian, Garnett.
45. Easton, Easton.
46. Rising Sun, Ft. Scott.
47. Xenia, Xenia.
48. Monrovia, Monrovia.
49. Nine Mile, Delaware.
50. Cavalry, Leavenworth.

☞ There are a number under dispensation not returned.

LIST OF LODGES.

317

KENTUCKY.

Jurisdiction of the Grand Lodge of Kentucky.

1. Lexington, Lexington.
4. Hiram, Frankfort.
5. Solomon's Shelbyville.
8. Abraham, Louisville.
9. Jerusalem, Henderson.
14. Mount Vernon, Georgetown.
16. Paris Union, Paris.
17. Russellville, Russellville.
18. St. Andrews, Cynthiana.
20. Winchester, Winchester.
22. Daviess, Lexington.
23. Montgomery, Mt. Sterling.
24. Allen, Glasgow.
25. Richmond, Richmond.
37. Hopkinsville, Hopkinsville.
40. Amity, Millersburg.
41. Land Mark, Versailles.
47. Fortitude, Lagrange.
50. Springfield, Springfield.
51. Clarke, Louisville.
52. Confidence, Maysville.
53. Warren, Harrodsburg.
54. Greensburg, Greensburg.
55. Bath, Owingsville.
57. Bloomfield, Bloomfield.
58. Benevolent, Centreville, Bourbon Co.
60. Lincoln, Stanford.
61. Hart, Nicholasville.
65. Dougherty, Carlisle.
66. Morganfield, Morganfield.
67. Breckinridge, Hardinsburg.
71. Vesper, Elkton.
73. Bowlinggreen, Bowlinggreen.
76. Morrison, Elizabethtown.
78. Jonathan, Liberty.
80. Augusta, Augusta.
81. Salem, Salem.
82. Clinton, Princeton.
85. Grant, Williamstown.
86. De Witt Clinton, Clintonville.
87. Lebanon, Lebanon.
88. Green River, Munfordville.
89. Greenup, Greenupsburg.
90. Anderson, Lawrenceburg.
95. Good Faith, Florence.
96. Columbia, Columbia.
99. Duvall, Bardstown.
104. Lancaster, Lancaster.
105. Murray, Murray.
106. Mount Moriah, Louisville.
108. Tadmor, Warsaw.
110. Warren, Leesburg.
111. Somerset, Somerset.
112. Fleming, Fleminsburg.
115. Hancock, Hawesville.
116. Minerva, Minerva.
117. Sharpsburg, Sharpsburg.
118. Big Spring, Big Spring.
120. Fulton, Hickman.
121. Cadiz, Cadiz.
122. Harrison, Brandenburg.
123. Bradford, Independence.

124. Pitman, Campbellsville.
125. St. John's, Salvisa.
127. Paducah, Paducah.
128. Owen, Owenton.
129. Barker, Westpoint.
130. Owensboro' Owensboro'.
131. Hickman, Clinton.
132. B. R. Young, Hodgenville.
133. Cloverport, Cloverport.
134. Carrollton, Carollton.
136. Marion, Bradfordsville.
137. Irvine, Irvine.
138. Smithland, Smithland.
140. Paintlick, Paintlick.
142. Blandville, Blandville.
143. Madisonville, Madisonville.
144. McKee, London.
145. Trimble, Grayson.
147. Mount Zion, Louisville.
148. Providence, Providence.
150. Crittenden, Crittenden.
151. La Fayette, La Fayette.
152. Alexandria, Alexandria.
153. Holloway, Sherburne.
154. Brooksville, Brooksville.
155. Bullitt, Sheperdsville.
156. Hartford, Hartford.
157. Lovelaceville, Lovelaceville.
158. Bedford, Bedford.
159. Col. Clay, Covington.
160. Devotion, Lexington.
161. Wingate, Simpsonville.
163. Robert Burns, Newport.
164. Taylor, Colemansville.
165. Westport, Westport.
167. Joppa, Empire Iron Works, Trigg.
168. Caseyville, Caseyville.
169. Oldham, Beard's Station.
170. Milburne, Milburne.
172. Roberts, Feliciana.
173. Columbus, Columbus.
174. Good Samaritan, Lexington.
176. Oxford, Oxford.
177. Simpson Benevolent, Franklin.
178. Tomkins, Edmonton.
179. Adams' Fork, Fordsville.
180. Salt River, Mt. Washington.
182. Allensville, Allensville.
183. Madison, Kirksville.
184. Hustonville, Hustonville.
185. Rumsey, Rumsey.
186. Livermore, Livermore.
187. Mountain, Barboursville.
188. Concord, New Concord.
189. Simpson, New Castle.
190. Suwanee, Eddyville.
191. Lewis, Portland.
192. Neetsville, Neetsville.
193. Harry Hudson, Middletown.
194. Butler, Pitts' Point.
195. Apperson, Louisa.
196. Sardis, Sardis.

27*

LIST OF LODGES.

197. Bryantsvillo, Bryantsville.
198. Mayo, Flagg Spring.
199. Zerubbabel, Aaron's Run.
200. Model, Moscow.
201. Magnolia, Mackville.
202. Walton, Walton.
203. Scott, Stampingground.
204. Bethel, Trenton.
205. Benton, Benton.
206. Albany, Albany.
207. Germantown, Germantown.
208. Graham, Scottsville.
209. Harvey Maguire, Perryville.
210. Taylorsville, Taylorsville.
211. Wintersmith, Garnettsville.
212. Stephensburg, Stephensburg.
213. Proctor, Proctor.
214. Fairview, Fairview.
215. New Haven, New Haven.
216. Napoleon, Napoleon.
217. Gordonsville, Gordonsville.
218. Philip Swigert, Fisherville.
219. Union, Uniontown.
220. Demoss, Demossville
221. Roaring Spring, Roaring Spring.
222. Orion, Falmouth.
223. Compass, Louisville.
224. Willis Stewart, Louisville.
226. Mitchell, Keene.
228. Bewleyville, Bewleyville.
229. McAfee, Cornishville.
230. James Moore, New Stead.
231. Bear Wallow, Horse Cave.
232. Dycusburg, Dycusburg.
233. Red River Iron Works, Vienna.
234. Nolin, Nolin.
235. Hampton, Catlettsburg.
236. Litchfield, Litchfield.
238. Adairville, Adairville.
239. Saint George, Louisville.
240. Saint Mary's, Concord.
242. Canton, Canton.
244. Pond River, Greenville.
245. Carroll, Blue Lick Springs.
246. Hope, Flat Rock.
247. Fredonia, Fredonia.
248. Ashbysburg, Ashbysburg.
249. Henry, Campbellsburg.
251. Gradyville, Gradyville.
252. Hoffmansville, Nebo.
253. Ceralvo, Ceralvo.
254. Morse, Kingston.
255. Mt. Gilead, Adams' Mill.
256. Bigham, Marion.
258. Excelsior, Louisville.
260. Sparta, Sparta.
261. Trumbo, Wyoming.
262. Hudsonville, Hudsonville.
263. Mount Eden, Mount Eden.
264. Burlington, Burlington.
265. West Union, Little Eagle.
266. Robinson, Louisville.
267. McCorkle, Cogar's Landing.
268. Wm. B. Allen, Greensburg.
270. Rochester, Rochester.
271. Hillsboro', Hillsboro'.
272. Cassia, Logansport.
273. Zebulon, Prestonsburg.

274. Foster, Foster's Landing.
275. Ausonia. Volney.
276. Temple Hill, Shiloh.
278. Meridian, Poplar Plains.
279. Charity, Mayslick.
280. Woodbury, Woodbury.
281. Preston, Louisville.
282. Eminence, Eminence.
283. New Retreat, Viola Station.
284. Russell, Jamestown.
285. Oak Grove, Murray.
286. Newton, Bethel.
287. J. M. Bullock, Christiansburg.
288. Pembroke, Pembroke.
289. Rob Morris, Flint Island.
290. Birmingham, Birmingham.
291. Mount Olivet, Mount Olivet.
292. Dunavan, Boston.
293. Yelvington, Yelvington.
294. Johnston, Webster.
295. Cunningham, Low's Station.
296. Mullin, Rutland.
297. Hodges, Whitesville.
298. J. Speed Smith, Willisburg.
299. Raywick, Raywick.
300. Jamestown, Woodville.
301. Ion, Hanley.
302. Harmony, Mayfield.
303. Lewisport, Lewisport.
304. Boone Union, Union.
306. Garrard, Buckeye.
307. Forsythe, Ruddles Mills.
308. Forest, Beverley.
309. ———— Howe's Valley.
310. Calhoon, Calhoon.
311. Highland, West Liberty.
312. Paradise, Paradise.
313. Faithful Friend, Lockport.
314. Carlow, Carlow.
315. Kingston, Kingston.
316. Manchester, Manchester.
318. Marks, Knottsville.
319. Mark Tyler, Wallonia.
320. Jas. F. Keel, Center.
321. Tomkinsville, Tomkinsville.
322. Alma, Mt. Sterling.
323. Loving, Fountain Run.
324. Henryville, Russellville.
325. Poage, Ashland.
326. Metcalfe, Fredericktown Washingt'n.
327. L. M. Cox, Fruit Hill.
328. Waynesburg, Waynesburg.
330. Middleton, Franklin, Simpson Co.
331. T. M. Lillard, Verona.
332. Antioch, Blandville.
333. Preachersville, Lancaster.
334. Point Isabel, Somerset.
335. Beaver Creek, Camdensville.
336. Asher W. Graham, Smith's Grove.
337. Helena, Helena.
338. Waco, Waco.
339. Crotona, Moscow, Hickman Co.
340. Thomas Ware, Claysville.
341. Miles, Bitter Water.
342. Mason, Maysville.
343. Harney, Woodburn.
344. Ghent, Ghent.
345. Golden Rule, Covington.

LIST OF LODGES.

319

346. Sacramento, Sacramento.
347. Prathersville, Slaughterville.
348. Pleasant Grove, Monticello.
349. T. N. Wise, Duncansville.
350. Marrowbone, Marrowbone.
351. Wingfield, Bohan.
352. Stanton, Stanton.
354. Hamilton, Hamilton.
357. Pellville, Black Ford Creek.
358. Newport, Newport.
359. Sugar Grove, Sugar Grove.
360. Haywood, Paducah.
361. Baltimore, Wingo's Stat'n, Graves Co.
362. Wilmington, Northcutt's Store.
363. Polar Star, Vanceburg.
365. Pythagoras, Goshen.
366. Pleasant Grove, Murray.
367. Ark, Millerstown.
368. Bibb, Irvine.
369. Hinton, Mayfield.
370. Athland, Mt. Vernon.
371. Zion Hill, Westonburg.
372. Ilico, Aurora, Marshall Co.
373. Trowel, Glover's Creek.
374. Auburn, Auburn.
375. Thos. C. Cecil, Pikeville.
376. Falls City, Louisville.
377. Elijah Upton, Greencastle.
378. Melone, Jeffersontown.
379. Monsarrat. Calhoon.
380. Reliance, Keysburg.
381. Paintsville, Paintsville.
382. Farmington, Farmington.
383. Cannonsburg, Cannonsburg.
384. Olive Branch, Falls of Rough.
385. Cairo, Cairo.
386. Fox, Dover.
387. Carrsville, Carrsville.
388. Rio Verde, Canmer.
389. John J. Daviess, Owensboro'.
390. Bordley, Bordley.
391. Gasper River, Auburn.
392. Mintonville, Mintonville.
393. West McCracken, Woodville.
394. Dever, Liberty.
395. Hiram Bassett, North Fork.
396. Danville, Danville.
397. Aspen Grove, Flower Creek.
398. Dick Barnes, Bainbridge.
399. Beech Grove, Greensburg.

400. Louisville, Louisville.
401. Briensburg, Benton.
402. Shearer, Bridgeport.
403. Pleasant Valley, Henderson.
404. Union Grove, Rockfield.
405. Sullivan, Trenton.
406. Stephensport, Stephensport.
407. East McCracken, Florence Station.
408. Lynnville, Lynnville.
409. M. J. Williams, New Liberty.
410. Pleasureville, Pleasureville.
411. East Owen, Owenton.
412. Cuba, Mayfield.
413. Cumberland, Burkeville.
414. T. F. Rees, Franklington.
415. Muhlenburg, South Carrollton.
416. Long View, Long View.
417. Three Springs, Three Springs.
418. Cave City, Cave City.
419. Tampico, Cane Valley.
420. Cromwell, Cromwell.
421. Consolation, Williams' Post Office.
422. Hebardsville, Hebardsville.
423. Mason's Creek, Mason's Creek.
424. Casey, Williams' Store.
425. Booneville, Booneville.
426. Panther Creek, Curdsville.
427. Marshall, Port Royal.
428. Curdsville, Pleasant Hill.
429. Thos. Todd. Clayvillage.
430. T. W. Wash, Alliston, Boyle County.
431. Monticello, Monticello.
432. Crab Orchard, Crab Orchard.
433. Chaplin, Chaplin.
434. Oakland, Benton.
435. Southville, Southville.
U. D. Four Mile, Winchester.
U. D. Sympsonia, ———.
U. D. King, Murray.
U. D. Joseph H. Brannan, Pleasant Point.
U. D. Readyville, Green Castle, Warren.
U. D. Eldorado, McAfee.
U. D. Red Lick, Irvine.
U. D. Franklin, Danville.
U. D. Fairfield, Fairfield.
U. D. Newburg, Newburg.
U. D. East Union, Carlisle.
U. D. Athens, Athens.
U. D. Short Creek, Falls of Rough.
U. D. Corydon, Corydon.

LOUISIANA.

Jurisdiction of the Grand Lodge of Louisiana.

1. Parfaite Union, New Orleans.
2. Etoile Polaire, New Orleans.
3. Charité, New Orleans.
4. Amis Réunis, New Orleans.
5. Trinosophes, New Orleans.
6. Concorde, New Orleans.
7. Liberal, New Orleans.
8. Perseverance, New Orleans.

9. Amor Fraternal, New Orleans.
10. Disc. du Sénat Maçonnique, N. Orleans.
11. Los Amigos del Orden, New Orleans.
12. Friendship, Mobile, Alabama.
13. Reunion Frater. de Caridad, New Orleans.
14. Amigos Reunidos, New Orleans.
15. Reunion de la Virtud, Campeche.

320   *LIST OF LODGES.*

16. Etolle Flamboyante, Baton Rouge, Parish of East Baton Rouge.
17. Templo de la Divina Purlda, Matanzas, Cuba.
18. La Vérité, Donaldsonville, Ascension Parish.
19. L'Union. Natchitoches, Natchitoches Parish.
20. La Rectitude, Havana, Cuba.
21. Columbian, Alexandria, Parish of Rapides.
22. Eureka, Blakesley, Alabama.
23. Washington, Baton Rouge, Parish of East Baton Rouge.
24. Aurera de ****, Yuoatan.
25. Humble Chaumière, Opelousas, St. Landry Parish.
26. Triple Bienfaisance, New Orleans.
27. Sincère Amitié, St. Martinsville, Attakapas.
28. Mobile, Mobile, Alabama.
29. Union, Parish of St. James.
30. Western Star, Monroe, Ouachita Parish.
31. Lafayette, New Orleans.
32. Harmony, New Orleans.
33. Numantina, New Orleans.
34. St. Albans, Jackson, East Feliciana.
35. Harmony,Opelousas,St.Landry Parish.
36. Lafayette, Vermillionville, Attakapas.
37. Feliciana, St. Francisville, West Feliciana.
38. Louisiana, New Orleans.
39. Hiram, Cheneyville, Avoyelles.
40. Selected Friends, Clinton, Avoyelles.
41. Fraternité, New Orleans.
42. Holland, Brazoria, Texas.
43. Alexandria, Alexandria, Parish of Rapides.
44. Phœnix, Natchitoches.
45. Poinsett, New Orleans.
46. Milam, Nacogdoches, Texas.
47. McFarland, St. Augustine, Texas.
48. Morning Star, Arkansas Post, Arkans's.
49. Western Star, Little Rock, Arkansas.
50. Foyer Maçonnique, New Orleans.
51. Désert, Napoleonville, Assumption Parish.
52. Jackson, Greenwood, Caddo Parish.
53. Germania, New Orleans.
54. St. James, East Baton Rouge.
55. Hospitalière du Teche, St. Martinsville, Attakapas.
56. Caddo, Shreveport, Caddo Parish.
57. Providence, Lake Providence, Carroll Parish.
58. Minden. Minden, Claiborne Parish.
59. Olive, Clinton, East Feliciana.
60. Union Fraternal, Farmerville, Union Parish.
61. Mt. Gerizim, Bastrop, Morehouse Par.
62. De Soto, Mansfield, De Soto Parish.
63. Lafayette, Vernon, Jackson Parish.
64. Franklin, Franklin, St. Mary Parish.
65. Friends of Harmony, New Orleans.
66. Mt. Moriah, New Orleans.
67. Coushatta, Coushatta, Natchitoches Parish.
68. Western Star, Monroe, Ouachita Parish

69. Hermann, New Orleans.
70. Tunica, Tunica, West Feliciana.
71. Edna, Columbia, Caldwell Parish.
72. George Washington, New Orleans.
73. Dudley, New Orleans.
74. Warren, New Orleans.
75. Marion, New Orleans.
76. Crescent City, New Orleans.
77. Hiram, New Orleans.
78. Eureka, New Orleans.
79. Alpha Home, New Orleans.
80. St. John's, New Orleans.
81. Joppa, Shreveport, Caddo Parish.
82. Sabine, Fort Jessup, Sabine Parish.
83. Quitman, New Orleans.
84. Mt. Moriah, Port Hudson, Parish of East Feliciana.
85. Orleans, New Orleans.
86. St. Joseph, St. Joseph, Tensas Parish.
87. De Witt Clinton, Marion, Union Parish.
88. Iberville, Plaquemine, Iberville Parish.
89. Clinton York, Clinton, East Feliciana Parish.
90. Mt. Vernon, Logansport, De Soto Parish.
91. Oliver, Alexandria, Rapides Parish.
92. Florida, Jackson, East Feliciana Parish.
93. Pleasant Hill, Pleasant Hill, De Soto Parish.
94. Lafayette, Pattersonville, St. Mary Parish.
95. Many, Many, Sabine Parish.
96. Cypress, Collinsburg, Bossier Parish.
97. Thibodeaux Benevolent, Thibodeaux, Lafourche Interior.
98. Livonia. Livonia, Point Coupeé Parish.
99. Monticello, Monticello, Carroll Parish.
100. Le Vrais Amis, Cheniere Caminada, Barrataria.
101. Napoleon, Marion, Union Parish.
102. Bellevue, Bellevue, Bossier Parish.
103. St. Helena, Greensburg, St. Helena Parish.
104. Patmos, Richmond, Madison Parish.
105. Hermitage, New Orleans.
106. Henderson, Cotile, Rapides Parish.
107. Taylor, Homer, Claiborne Parish.
108. Franklinton, Franklinton, Washington Parish.
109. Louisiana, New Orleans.
110. Cloutierville, Cloutierville, Natchitoches Parish.
111. Mt. Lebanon, Mt. Lebanon, Bienville Parish.
112. Trinity, Trinity, Catahoula Parish.
113. Vienna, Vienna, Jackson Parish.
114. Patrick Henry, City of Jefferson, Jefferson Parish.
115. Sparta, Sparta, Bienville Parish.
116. Castor, Castor, Caldwell Parish.
117. Harrisonburg, Harrisonburg, Catahoula Parish.
118. Urim, Forksville, Ouachita Parish.
119. Bartholomew, Plantersville, Morehouse Parish.

LIST OF LODGES.

321

120. Thomas Jefferson, Spearsville, Union Parish.
121. Friendship, Woodville, Jackson Parish.
122. Shreveport, Shreveport, Caddo Parish.
123. Acacia, Plaquemine, Iberville Parish.
124. Milford, Manchac Settlement, East Baton Rouge.
125. Terryville, Quay Post-office, Claiborne Parish.
126. Constantine, Waterproof, Tensas Parish.
127. Deerfield, Deerfield, Carroll Parish.
128. Lisbon, Lisbon, Claiborne Parish.
129. Mackey, Ringgold, Bienville Parish.
130. Liberty, Keachi, De Soto Parish.
131. Kellertown, Kellertown, East Feliciana.
132. Pearl River, Line Academy (Shady Grove), Washington Parish.
133. Arcadia, Arcadia, Bienville Parish.
134. Springhill, Springhill Church, Union Cross Roads.
135. D'Arbonne, D'Arbonne, Union Parish.
136. Dawson, Scottville, Claiborne Parish.
137. Solomon, Goodrich Landing, Pecan Grove P. O., Carroll Parish.
138. Shiloh, Shiloh, Union Parish.
139. Warren, Winnsboro', Franklin Parish.
140. Gordy, Cheneyville, Rapides Parish.
141. Harry Hill, Bastrop, Morehouse Parish.
142. Plains, Plains Store, East Baton Rouge.
143. Athens, Athens, Claiborne Parish.
144. Murray, Alexandria, Rapides Parish.
145. Jeffersonian, Jefferson Mills, De Soto Parish.
146. Houma, Houma, Terrebonne Parish.
147. Cool Spring, Cool Spring Academy, Claiborne Parish.
148. Huntington, Minden, Claiborne Parish.
149. Home, New Orleans.
150. Downsville, Downsville, Union Parish.
151. Ocean, New Orleans.
152. Hope, Vermillionville, Lafayette Parish.
153. Silent Brotherhood, Coushatta Chute, Natchitoches Parish.
154. Anacoco, Anacoco, Sabine Parish.
155. Red Land, Rocky Mount, Bossier Parish.
156. Darlington, Darlington, St. Helena Parish.
157. Perkins, Donaldsonville, Ascension Parish.
158. Eastern Star, Winnfield, Winn Parish.

159. Homer, Homer, Claiborne Parish.
160. Saints John, Algiers, Parish of Orleans.
161. Fillmore, Fillmore, Bossier Parish.
162. Cherry Ridge, Cherry Ridge, Union Parish.
163. Kissatchie, Kissatchie, Natchitoches Parish.
164. Grosse Tête, Iberville Parish.
165. Rapides, Huddleston, Rapides Parish.
166. Morganza, Morganza, Point Coupée Parish.
167. Livingston, Ponchatoula, Livingston Parish.
168. Brookville, Point Jefferson, Morehouse Parish.
169. Burnsville, Shangaloo, Claiborne Parish.
170. Atchafalaya, Simmsport, Avoyelles Parish.
171. Columbia, Columbia, Caldwell Parish.
172. Lake Charles, Lake Charles, Calcasieu Parish.
173. Silencio, New Orleans.
174. Excelsior, New Orleans.
175. Linn Wood, City of New Orleans.
176. Montgomery, Montgomery, Winn Parish.
177. Haynesville, Haynesville, Claiborne Parish.
178. Orus, New Orleans.
179. Kosmos, New Orleans.
180. Union, New Orleans.
181. Orient, New Orleans.
182. Dante, New Orleans.
183. Amite City, Amite City, St. Helena Parish.
184. Perfect Harmony, New Orleans.
185. Eureka, near Woodville, Jackson Parish.
186. Tulip, Tulip Town, Claiborne Parish.
187. Caddo, Shreveport, Caddo Parish.
188. Little Flock, Godwin's Bluff, Sabine Parish.
189. Jeffersonian, Kingston, De Soto Parish.
190. Sam Todd, Sugar Town, Calcasieu Parish.
191. Longwood, Hope Mills, Caddo Parish.
192. Spring Creek, Spring Creek Church, Washington Parish.
193. Orphans' Friend, Big Cane, St. Landry Parish.
194. Kissatchie Union, U. D., Kiles Mills, Natchitoches Parish.
195. Magnolia, U. D., Washington, St. Landry Parish.
196. Flat Lick, U. D., Flat Lick, Claiborne Parish.

322   *LIST OF LODGES.*

MAINE.

Jurisdiction of the Grand Lodge of Maine.

1. Portland, Portland.
2. Warren, East Machias.
3. Lincoln, Wiscasset.
4. Hancock, Castine.
5. Kennebec, Hallowell.
6. Amity, Camden.
7. Eastern, Eastport.
8. United, Brunswick.
9. Saco, Saco.
10. Rising Virtue, Bangor.
11. Pythagorean, Fryeburg.
12. Cumberland, N. Gloucester.
13. Oriental, Bridgeton.
14. Solar, Bath.
15. Orient, Tomorton.
16. St. George, Warren.
17. Ancient Landmark, Portland.
18. Oxford, Norway.
20. Maine, Farmington.
21. Orien Star, Livermore.
22. York, Kennebeck.
23. Freeport, Freeport.
24. Phœnix, Belfast.
25. Temple, Winthrop.
26. Village, Bandanigham.
27. Adoniram, Livington.
28. North Star, North Anson
29. Tranquil, Auburn.
30. Blazing Star, Mexico.
31. Union, Union.
32. Herman, Gardiner.
33. Walterville, Walterville.
34. Somerset, Skowhegan.
35. Bethlehem, Augusta.
36. Casco, Yarmouth.
37. Washington, Lubec.
38. Harmony, Gorham.
39. Penobscot, Dexter.
40. Lygonia, Ellsworth.
42. Freedom, Limerick.
43. Alna, Damariscota.
44. Piscatuquis, Milo.
45. Central, China.
46. St. Croix, Calais.
47. Dunlap, Biddeford.
48. Pacific, Exeter.
48. Lafayette, Beadfield.
49. Mer. Splendor, Newport.
50. Aurora, Rockland.
51. St. John, S. Berwick.
52. Mosaic, Foxcrift.
53. Rural, Sidney.
54. Vassalborough, Vassalboro'.
55. Fraternal, Alfred.
56. Mt. Moriah, Denmark.
57. Benevolent, Carmel.
58. Unity, Freedom.
59. Mt. Hope, South Hope.
60. Star in the East, Oldtown.
61. King Solomon, Waldeboro'.
62. King David's, Lincolnville.
63. Richmond, Richmond.

65. Mystic, Hampden.
66. Mechanics', Orona.
67. Blue Mountain, Phillips.
68. Mariner's, Lorsport.
69. Howard, Winterport.
70. Standwish, Standwish.
71. Rising Sun, Orland.
72. Pioneer, Ashland.
73. Tyrian, Mechanics' Falls.
74. Bristol, Bristol.
75. Plymouth, Plymouth.
76. Arundale, Kennebunkport.
77. Fremont, Fremont.
78. Crescent, Pembroke.
80. Keystone, Solon.
81. Atlantic, Portland.
82. St. Paul's, Rockfort.
83. St. Andrew's, Bangor.
84. Eureka, St. George.
85. Star in the West, Unity.
86. Temple, Saccaroppa.
88. Narragus, Cherryfield.
89. Island, Isleboro'.
90. Hiram Abiff, Washington.
91. Harwood, Machias.
92. Siloam's, Kendall's Mills.
93. Horeb, Lincoln Centre.
94. Paris, S. Paris.
95. Corinthian, Hartford.
96. Monument, Houllin.
97. Bethel, Bethel.
98. Kathadin, Palten.
99. Vernon Valley, Mt. Vernon.
100. Jefferson, Bryant's Pond.
101. Neziucei, Turner.
102. Marsh River, Brooks.
103. Dresden, Dresden.
104. Dirigo, S. China.
105. Ashler, Lewistown.
106. Tuscan, Addison Point.
107. Day Spring, W. Newfield.
108. Relief, Belgrade.
109. Mt. Kineo, Abbot.
110. Monmouth, N. Monmouth.
111. Liberty, Montville.
112. E. Frontier, W. Fairfield.
113. Nessalouskee, W. Waterville.
115. Moderation, Baxter.
116. Lebanon, Norndynock.
117. Greenleaf, Cornish.
118. Drummond, W. Parsonfield.
119. Pownal, Stockton.
120. Neduncook, Friendship.
121. Acacia, Durham.
122. Marine, Deer Isle.
123. Franklin, New Sharon.
124. Olive Branch, Charleston.
125. Meridian, Pittsfield.
126. Timothy Chase, Belfast.
127. Presumpscot, Windham.
128. Eggemaggin, Sedgwick.
— Felicity, Buckstown.

LIST OF LODGES. 323

129. Quantabacook, Learsmont.
130. Trinity, Presque Isle.
131. Lookout, Calter.
132. Mt. Terin, Waterford.
133. Asylum, Wayne.
134. Trojan, Troy.
135. Riverside, Jefferson.
136. Ionic, Gardner.
137. Kenduskeag, Kenduskeag.

138. Levey's Island, Princeton.
139. Archon, E. Dixnunt.
140. Mt. Desert, Mt. Desert.
141. Augusta, Augusta.
174. Polar Star, Bath.
791. Rockland, Rockland.
U. D. Morning Star, Litchfield.
U. D. Ocean, Wells.

MARYLAND (1860).

Jurisdiction of the Grand Lodge of Maryland.

3. Washington, Baltimore.
13. Concordia, Baltimore.
25. Amicable, Baltimore.
34. St. John's, Baltimore.
44. Mt. Ararat, Bel Air.
45. Cassia, Baltimore.
48. Union, Elkton.
51. Warren, Baltimore.
53. Harmony, Port Deposit.
58. Columbia, Frederick.
60. Union, Baltimore.
61. Cumberland, Cumberland.
66. Cambridge, Cambridge.
68. King David, Baltimore.
70. Patmos, Ellicott's Mills.
84. Friendship, Williamsport.
87. Burns, Trappe.
88. Adherence, Baltimore.
89. Annapolis, Annapolis.
90. Gilman, Cumberland.

91. Wicomico, Salisbury.
92. Pocomoke, Snow Hill.
93. Corinthian, Baltimore.
94. Washington, Westminster.
95. Nottingham, Nottingham.
96. Monumental, Baltimore.
97. Ben Franklin, Baltimore.
98. Eureka, Millington.
99. Mountain, Frostsbury
100. Potomac, Cumberland
101. Howard, Elk Ridge.
102. Coots, Easton.
103. Hiram, Westernport.
104. Lebanon, Manchester.
105. Eureka, Sharpsburg.
106. Manakin, Princess Anne.
107. Hiram, Baltimore.
108. Centre, Baltimore.
109. Mystic Circle, Baltimore.

MASSACHUSETTS (1860).

Jurisdiction of the Grand Lodge of Massachusetts.

St. John's, Boston.
St. Andrew's, Boston.
Massachusetts, Boston.
Columbian, Boston.
Mt. Lebanon, Boston.
Amicable, Cambridge.
Washington, Roxbury.
King Solomon, Charleston.
Union, Dorchester.
Bathesda, Brighton.
Hiram, W. Cambridge.
Star of Bethlehem, Chelsea.
Mt. Tabor, E. Boston.
St. Paul's, S. Boston.
Baalbeal, E. Boston.
Mt. Hermon, Medford.
Putnam, E. Cambridge.
Germania, Boston.
Gate of the Temple, S. Boston.
St. Mark's, Newburyport.

Jordan, Danvers.
Warren, Amesbury.
Philanthropic, Marblehead.
Essex, Salem.
Liberty, Beverly.
Tyrian, Gloucester.
Mt. Carmel, Lynn.
Ashler, Rockport.
St. John's, Newburyport.
Corinthian, Concord.
St. Paul's, Groton.
Rentucket, Lowell.
Aurora, Fitchburg.
Grecian, Lawrence.
Ancient York, Lowell.
St. Matthew's, Andover.
Merrimac, Haverhill.
Good Samaritan, Reading.
Mt. Horeb, Woburn.
Middlesex, Framingham.

LIST OF LODGES.

Monitor, Waltham.
Meridian, Natick.
Rising Star, Stoughton.
Corner-Stone, Duxbury.
Rural, Quincy.
Plymouth, Plymouth.
Old Colony, Hingham.
Agawam, Wareham.
Norfolk Union, Randolph.
St. Alban's, Foxboro'.
Olive Branch, Webster.
Meridian Sun, Brookfield.
Mt. Zion, Hardwick.
Harris, Templeton.
Morning Star, Worcester.
Oxford, Oxford.
Doric, Southbridge.
Solomon's Temple, Uxbridge.
Eden, Ware.
Franklin, Grafton.
Montgomery, Milford.
Blackstone River, Blackstone.
Fellowship, Bridgewater.
King David, Taunton.
Star in the East, New Bedford.
Mt. Hope, Troy.
Bristol, Attleboro'.
Paul Revere, N. Bridgewater.
Fraternal, Barnestable.
Mt. Horeb, W. Warwick.
Ben Franklin, W. Dennis.

De Witt Clinton, Sandwich.
Cincinnatus, Sheffield.
Evening Star, Lee.
Mystic, Pittsfield.
Hamden, Springfield.
La Fayette, N. Adams.
Chicopee, Chicopee.
Mt. Moriah, Westfield.
Republican, Greenfield.
Harmony, Northfield.
Jerusalem, Northampton.
Mt. Tom, Holyoke.
Revere, Boston.
Pegnosette, Watertown.
Orphan's Hope, Weymouth.
Mt. Zion, Barre.
Social Harmony, Wareham.
Eureka, N. Bedford.
King Hiram, Provincetown.
Marine, Falmouth.
Union, Nantucket.
Thomas, Palmer.
Wisdom, W. Stockbridge.
Bethel, Enfield.
Berkshire, Adams.
Mountain, Shelburne.
Wyoming, Melrose.
Mt. Vernon, Malden.
John Abbott, Somerville.
Jos. Warren, Boston.
Henry Price, Charleston.

MICHIGAN.

Jurisdiction of the Grand Lodge of Michigan.

1. Zion, Detroit.
2. Detroit, Detroit.
3. Union of S. O., Detroit.
4. St. Jos. Valley, Niles.
5. Rochester, Rochester.
6. Mt. Clemens, Mt. Clemens.
7. Washington, Tekousha.
8. Trenton, Trenton.
9. Evergreen, St. Clair.
10. Dowagiac, Dowagiac.
11. Pine Grove, Port Huron.
12. Battle Creek, Battle Creek.
13. Phœnix, Ypsilanti.
14. Murat, Albion.
16. Lafayette, Jonesville.
17. Jackson, Jackson.
18. Tyre, Coldwater.
19. Adrian, Adrian.
20. St. Albans, Marshall.
21. Pontiac, Pontiac.
22. Kalamazoo, Kalamazoo.
23. Flint, Flint.
24. Mt. Hermon, Centreville.
25. Paw Paw, Paw Paw.
26. Maxson, Hudson.
27. Monroe, Monroe.
28. Union, Union City.

29. Humanity, Homer.
30. Concord, Concord.
31. Portland, Portland.
32. Fidelity, Hillsdale.
33. Lansing, Lansing.
34. Grand River, Grand Rapids.
35. Siloam, Constantine.
36. Ionia, Ionia.
37. Lyons, Lyons.
38. Howell, Howell.
39. Western Star, Berrien.
40. Franklin, Litchfield.
41. Romeo, Romeo.
44. Birmingham, Birmingham.
46. Orion, Orion.
47. Plymouth Rock, Plymouth.
48. Austin, Austin.
49. Meridian Sun, Sturgis.
50. Michigan, Jackson.
51. Almont, Almont.
52. Hastings, Hastings.
54. Lapeer, Lapeer.
55. Backus, Cassopolis.
56. Occidental, St. Joseph.
57. Three Rivers, Three Rivers.
58. Port Huron, Port Huron.
59. Climax, Climax.

LIST OF LODGES.

60. Cedar, Clarkston.
61. Lexington, Lexington.
62. S. Ward, Marine City.
63. Eaton Rapids, Eaton Rapids.
64. Macomb, Brooklyn.
65. Washtenaw, Dexter.
66. Capital of S. O., Lansing.
67. Ontonagon, Ontonagon.
68. Buchanan, Buchanan.
69. Tecumseh, Tecumseh.
70. Mason, Mason.
73. Colon, Colon.
74. Dundee, Dundee.
75. Utica, Utica.
76. Livingston, Pinckney.
77. Saginaw, E. Saginaw.
78. Otsego, Otsego.
79. Germania, Saginaw City.
80. Byron, Byron.
81. Owosso, Owosso.
82. Lake St. Clair, N. Baltimore.
83. Bellevue, Bellevue.
84 Oxford, Oxford.
85. Ann Arbor, Ann Arbor.
86. Valley City, Grand Rapids.
88. Butler, Butler.
89. Myrtle, Belleville.
90. Lowell, Lowell.
91. Ashlar, Detroit.
92. Prairie, Galesburg.
93. Star, Osseo.
94. Charity, Detroit.
95. J. Moors, Morenci.
96. Greenville, Greenville.
97. Niles, Niles.
98. Waterford, Waterford.
99. Decatur, Decatur.
100. Oakwood, Oakwood.
101. Marquette, Marquette.
102. Blanchard, Petersburg.
103. Greenly, Adrian.
104. White Pigeon, White Pigeon.
105. St. John's, St. John's.
106. St. Peter's, Edwardsburg.
107. Eureka, Monroe.
108. Rockland, Rockland.
109. Fentonville, Fentonville.
110. Hiram, Flat Rock.
111. Allegan, Allegan.
112. Wayne, Wayne.
113. Hamilton, Moscow.
114. Blissfield, Blissfield.
115. Corunna, Corunna.
116. Excelsior, Grass Lake.
117. Reading, Reading.
118. Schoolcraft, Schoolcraft.
119. Rising Sun, Lawrence.
120. Charlotte, Charlotte.
121. Commerce, Commerce.
122. Ottawa, Ottawa.
123. Ithica, Ithica.
124. Eagle, Burr Oak.
125. Fairfield, Fairfield.
126. Forest, Capac.
127. Ovid, Ovid
128. Ypsilanti, Ypsilanti.
129. Bay City, Bay City.
130. Stockbridge, Unadilla.

131. Newaygo, Newaygo.
132. Linden, Linden.
133. Saline, Saline.
134. Holly, Holly.
135. Quincy, Hancock, L. S.
136. Pokagon, Pokagon.
137. Mendon, Mendon.
138. Pt. Hope, Pt. Hope.
139. Grand Haven, Grand Haven.
140. Muskegon, Muskegon.
141. Mystic, Bronson.
142. Memphis, Memphis.
143. Harmony, Burke's Cor's.
144. Russell, Erie.
145. Maple Rapids, Maple Rapids.
146. Boston, Saranac.
147. Warren, Hudson.
148. Manchester, Manchester.
149. United, Cooper.
150. Dryden, Dryden.
151. Farmington, Farmington.
152. Redford, Redford.
153. Williamston, Williamston.
154. Saginaw Valley, Saginaw City.
155. Salina, Salina.
156. Olive, Chelsea.
157. Addison, Addison.
158. Star of Lake, South Haven.
159. Golden Rule, Ann Arbor.
160. Dansville, Dansville.
161. North Newburg, N. Newburg.
162. Coloma, Coloma.
163. Cass River, Vassar.
164. Fowlerville, Fowlerville.
165. Milford, Milford.
166. Mt. Vernon, Quincy.
167. Tracy, Deerfield.
168. Temple, Adrian.
169. Brooklyn, Brooklyn.
170. Wyandotte, Wyandotte.
171. Big Rapids, Big Rapids.
172. Dearborn, Dearborn.
173. Evening Star, Medina.
174. Genesee, Flint.
175. Clinton, Clinton.
176. Hillsdale, Hillsdale.
177. Croton, Croton.
178. Tuscan, Hubbardston.
179. Grand Ledge, Grand Ledge.
180. Pilgrim, Fremont.
181. Orangeville, Orangeville.
182. Lovel Moore, Muskegon.
183. Parma, Parma.
184. Palmyra, Palmyra.
185. Pleasant Lake, Henrietta.
186. Northville, Northville.
187. Ricomond, Beebe's Co'rs.
188. St. Louis, St. Louis.
189. Adams, N. Adams.
U. D. Portsmouth, Portsmouth.
" Houghton, Houghton.
" Richland, Yorkville.
" Unity, Holland.
" Traverse City, Traverse City.
" Summit, Buchanan.
" Dutcher, Douglass.
" Lawton, Lawton.
" Chesaning, Chesaning.

326   LIST OF LODGES.

U. D. Delta, Escanaba.
" Athens, Athens.
" Grattan, White Swan.
" Bloomingdale, Bloomingdale.
" Winfield, Winfield.
" Montague, Montague.
" Leslie, Leslie.
" Alpena, Alpena.
" Flushing, Flushing.
" Oceana, Pentwater.
" Algonac, Algonac.
" Negaunee, Negaunee.
" Palo, Palo.

U. D. Coffinbury, Bangor.
" Cato, Forestville.
" Hartland, Hartland.
" Cass, Pt. Austin.
" Vienna, Pine Run.
" Cedar Springs, Cedar Springs.
" Park, Parkville.
" Peninsula, Dowagiac.
" Bedford, Bedford.
" Brady, Brady.
" Hadley, Hadley.
" Liberty, Liberty.

MINNESOTA.

Jurisdiction of the Grand Lodge of Minnesota.

1. St. John's, Stillwater.
2. Cataract, St. Anthony.
3. Saint-Paul, Saint Paul.
4. Hennepin, Minneapolis.
5. Ancient Landmark, Saint Paul.
7. Dakota, Hastings.
8. Red Wing, Red Wing.
11. Mantorville, Mantorville.
12. Mankato, Mankato.
14. Wapahasa, Wabashaw.
16. Monticello, Monticello.
17. Hokah, Hokah.
18. Winona, Winona.
19. Minneapolis, Minneapolis.
20. Caledonia, Caledonia.
21. Rochester, Rochester.
22. Pleasant Grove, Pleasant Grove.
23. North Star, Saint Cloud.
24. Wilton, Wilton.
26. Western Star, Albert Lea.
27. Blue Earth Valley, Winnebago City.
28. Clearwater, Clearwater.
29. Morning Star, LaCrescent.
30. Anoka, Anoka.
31. King Hiram, Belle Plaine.

32. Sakatah, Waterville.
33. Star in the East, Owatonna.
34. Oriental, Cannon Falls.
35. Mount Moriah, Hastings.
36. Preston, Preston.
37. Mystic Tie, Pine Island.
38. Washington, Wasioja.
39. Fidelity, Austin.
40. Carnelian, Lake City.
41. Hermon, Zumbrota.
42. Hope, Glencoe.
43. Harmony, Utica.
44. King Solomon, Shakopee.
45. Union, LeSueur.
46. Evergreen, Troy.
47. Concord, Cleveland.
48. Social, Northfield.
49. Rising Sun, Saint Charles.
50. Watertown, Watertown.
51. Acacia, Cottage Grove.
52. Cannon River, Morristown.
53. Faribault, Faribault.
54. Nicollet, Saint Peter.
U. D. Zion, Taylor's Falls.
U. D. Merriden, Chatfield.

MISSISSIPPI (1860).

Jurisdiction of the Grand Lodge of Mississippi.

1. Harmony, Natchez.
2. Andrew Jackson, Natchez.
3. Washington, Pt. Gibson.
5. Columbus, Columbus.
16. Clinton, Clinton.
17. Leake, Benton.
18. Quitman, Georgetown.
19. Leaf, Monroe.
21. Raymond, Raymond.
23. Pearl, Jackson.

24. Lexington, Lexington.
25. Gallatin, Gallatin.
26. Vicksburg, Vicksburg.
28. Canton, Canton.
29. Coleman, Brandon.
31. Grenada, Grenada.
32. Aberdeen, Aberdeen.
33. Oxford, Oxford.
34. Olive Branch, Williamsburg.
35. Holly Springs, Holly Springs.

LIST OF LODGES.

327

36. Carrollton, Carrollton.
37. Liberty, Liberty.
39. Monroe, Monroe.
40. Macon, Macon.
41. Grand Gulf, Grand Gulf.
42. Yazoo, Yazoo.
43. Shady Grove, Line Store.
45. Salem, Salem.
47. Ripley, Ripley.
48. Pythagorean, Middletown.
49. Greensboro', Greensboro'.
51. Hernando, Hernando.
53. Lafayette, Quitman.
54. Sterting, Paulding.
55. Chulahoma, Chulahoma.
56. Mississippi, Rodney.
57. Harrison, Garlandsville.
58. Hinds, Fayette.
59. Tappan, Brownsville.
60. St. Albans, Columbia.
61. Eureka, Richland.
62. Marion, Marion.
63. Asylum, Woodville.
64. De Kalb, De Kalb.
65. Brown, Jackson.
66. Panola, Panola.
67. Houston, Houston.
68. Vanalta, Raleigh.
69. Holemsville, Holemsville.
70. Evening Star, Steen's Creek.
71. Joseph Warren, N. Albany.
72. Wilson, Enterprise.
73. Madison, Vernon.
74. Camden, Camden.
75. Louisville, Louisville.
76. Ebenezer, Tatesville.
77. Evergreen, Decatur.
78. Westville, Westville.
79. Eastern Star, Monticello.
80. Scott, Hillsboro'.
81. Pontotoc, Pontotoc.
82. Oakland, Oakland.
83. Coffeeville, Coffeeville.
84. DeWitt Clinton, Shongolo.
85. Pikeville, Pikeville.
86. Mt. Moriah, Black Hawk.
87. Prairie, Okolona.
88. Trinity, Kosciusko.
89. Albert, Starkville.
90. Belmont, Belmont.
91. United Friends, Princeton.
92. Willis, Polkville.
93. Philadelphia, Philadelphia.
94. Eastport, Eastport.
95. Emory, Lexington.
97. Richmond, Richmond.
98. Utica, Utica.
99. Mt. Pleasant, N. Mt. Pleasant.
100. De Soto, Cockrum.
101. Malone, Palo Alto.
102. Wayne, Miltonville.
103. Sharon, Sharon.
104. Coahoma, Friar's Point.
105. Pearl River, Carthage.
106. Union, Mt. Carmel.
107. Bethel, Burkettsville.
108. Carrollville, Carrollville.
109. Danville, Danville.

110. Claiborne, Rocky Spring.
111. Cook, Gainesville.
112. Bovina, Bovina.
113. Hyland, Warrenton.
114. Lowndes, Columbus.
115. Byhalia, Byhalia.
116. Farmington, Farmington.
117. Unity, Edwards' Depot.
118. Camargo, Camargo.
119. Snowsville, Bankston.
120. Magnolia, Biloxi.
121. Hill City, Vicksburg.
122. Tchula, Tchula.
123. Oak Ridge, Ingraham.
124. Thomastown, Thomastown.
125. Centre Hill, Olive Branch.
126. Solomon, Flastlin's X Roads.
127. Friendship, Sledgeville.
128. Tallaloosa, Tallaloosa.
129. Patton, Louderdale.
130. Alamutcha, Alamutcha.
131. Fulton, Fulton.
132. Water Valley, Water Valley.
133. Summerville, Summerville.
134. Lodi, Lodi.
135. Greenwood, Greenwood.
136. Charles Scott, Sondifer's Mill.
137. Falconer, Quitman.
138. Millen, Chunkeyville.
139. Castilian, Lexington.
140. Benela, Benela.
141. Waterford, Waterford.
142. Jacinto, Jacinto.
144. Lipscomb, Crawfordsville.
145. Looxahoma, Looxahoma.
146. Jefferson, Scorba.
147. Bay St. Louis, Shieldsboro'.
148. Lamar, Lamar.
149. Orizaba, Orizaba.
150. Centre Ridge, Centre Ridge.
151. Daleville, Daleville.
152. Palmetto, Palmetto.
153. Pine Bluff, Pine Bluff.
154. Polar Star, Handsboro'.
155. Hartford, Pittsboro'.
156. Hornsbury, Hornsbury.
157. Washington, Chesterton.
158. Jeremiah, Horn Lake.
159. Carmon, Columbus.
161. Ellisville, Ellisville.
162. St. John's, Spring Ridge.
163. Vinton, Vinton.
164. Carson, Snow Creek.
165. Smithville, Smithville.
166. Auburn, Auburn.
167. Bay Springs, Bay Springs.
168. Homestead, Deasonville.
169. Prairie Mount, Prairie Mount.
170. Franklin, Meadville.
171. Good Hope, Good Hope.
172. Rienzi, Rienzi.
173. Bobolu, Raysville.
174. Adelphian, Bellefonte.
175. Houry, Cooksville.
176. Sartartia, Sartartia.
177. Burns, Kilmichael.
178. Speight, Cotton Gin Port.
179. Tuscumbia, Bone Yard.

328 LIST OF LODGES.

180. Chappell, Kosciusko.
181. Concord, Union Church.
182. Theodosia, Lorepta.
183. Dawson, Winchester.
184. Eldorado, Hohenlinden.
185. Rocky Ford, Rocky Ford.
186. Sogerville, Sogerville.
187. Houry, Spring Dale.
188. Marietta, Marietta.
189. Long Creek, Long Creek.
190. Centre, Kosciusko.
191. White Plains, White Plains.
192. Livingston, Livingston.
193. S. Union, Pulaski.
194. Walnut Hill, Vicksburg.
195. Laurel Hill, Laurel Hill.
196. Bluff Springs, Bluff Springs.
197. Dover, Dover.
198. Oakbowery, Paulding.
199. Enon, Enon.
200. Hebeon, Oakohay.
201. Yockena, Rebecca.
202. Pasgagoula, Pascagoula.
203. Fair River, Monticello.
204. Big Creek, Whitfield.
205. Webster, Webster.
206. Greenville, Greenville.
207. Marshall, Holly Springs.
208. Palestine, Palestine.
209. Mitchell, French Camp.

210. Bolivar, Bolivar.
211. Vienna, Pineville.
212. Plattsburg, Pinshook.
213. Huntsville, Huntsville.
214. Sincerity, Holmesville.
215. Rising Glory, Ooyka.
216. Peach Creek, Peach Creek.
217. Mellen, Densontown.
218. Mooresville, Mooresville.
219. Canaan, Canaan.
220. Sparta, Sparta.
221. Rankin, Pelahatchie.
222. Stampley, Hamburg.
223. Sunflower, Greenwood.
224. New Hope, Fame.
225. Cooper, Old Hickory.
226. Sylvwiena, Raleigh.
227. Chapel Hill, Big Creek.
228. Campbelltown, Campbelltown.
229. Western Star, Paris.
230. Cato, Cato Springs.
231. Summit, Summit.
232. Paltona, Paltona.
233. Burnsville, Burnsville.
234. Chickasawhoy, De Soto.
235. Lackey, Lenasha.
236. Mt. Moriah, Mt. Moriah.
237. Pleasant Hill, Pleasant Hill.
238. Hillyer, Wheeling.
239. Bond, Hickory Flat.

MISSOURI.

Jurisdiction of the Grand Lodge of Missouri.

1. Missouri, St. Louis.
2. Meridian, St. Louis.
3. Beacon, St. Louis.
4. Howard, New Franklin.
5. United, Springfield.
6. Ark, Newark.
8. Williamsburg, Williamsburg.
9. Geo. Washington, St. Louis.
10. Agency, Walnut Hill.
11. Pauldingville, Millville.
12. Tyro, Caledonia.
13. Rising Sun, Barry.
14. Auburn, Auburn.
15. Western Star, Victoria.
16. Memphis, Memphis.
17. Clarksville, Clarksville.
18. Palmyra, Palmyra.
19. Paris Union, Paris.
20. St. Louis, St. Louis.
21. Greencastle, Greencastle.
22. Wellington, De Kalb.
23. Florida, Florida.
24. Wyaconda, La Grange.
25. Naphthali, St. Louis.
26. Mexico, Mexico.
27. Evergreen, New Haven.
28. St. John's, Hannibal.

29. Windsor, Windsor.
30. Huntsville, Huntsville.
31. Liberty, Liberty.
32. Lafayette, Lexington.
33. Ralls, Madisonville.
34. Troy, Troy.
35. Mercer, Princeton.
36. Cooper, Boonvile.
37. Dawson, Wellington.
38. Callao, Callao.
39. Modena, Modena.
40. Mount Moriah, St. Louis.
41. Etna, Etna.
42. Houston, Breckenridge.
43. Jefferson, Jefferson.
45. Bonhomme, Manchester.
46. Wentzville, Wentzville.
47. Fayette, Fayette.
48. Fulton, Fulton.
49. Haynesville, Haynesville.
50. Xenia, Xenia.
51. Livingston, Glasgow.
52. Wakanda, Carrolton.
53. Weston, Weston.
54. Douglass, Marthasville.
55. Arrow Rock, Arrow Rock.
56. Tipton, Tipton.

LIST OF LODGES. 329

57. Richmond, Richmond.
58. Monticello, Monticello.
60. New Bloomfield, New Bloomfield.
61. Waverly, Waverly.
63. Cambridge, Cambridge.
64. Monroe, Monroe City.
65. Pattonsburg, Pattonsburg.
66. Linn, Linn.
67. Rocheport, Rocheport.
68. Tebo, Clinton.
69. Sullivan, Sullivan.
70. Roanoke, Roanoke.
71. Savannah, Savannah.
72. Danville, Danville.
74. Warren, Keytsville.
75. Ashley, Ashley.
76. Independence, Independence.
77. Lebanon. Steelville.
78. St. Joseph, St. Joseph.
79. Polar Star, St. Louis.
80. Bridgeton, Bridgeton.
81. Hickory Grove, Hickory Grove.
82. Jackson, Linneus.
83. Laclede, Lebanon.
84. Potter, Longwood.
85. Miami, Miami.
86. Brookfield, Brookfield
87. Washington, Greenfield.
89. Friendship, Chillicothe.
90. King Solomon, St. Catharines.
91. Madison, Madison.
92. Perseverance, Louisiana.
93. St. Mark's, Cape Girardeau.
94. Evening Star, Cuba.
95. Chapman, Fort Union.
96. St. Andrew's, Shelbyville.
97. Bethany, Bethany.
98. Webster, Marshfield.
100. Canton, Canton.
101. Easton, Easton.
102. Bloomington, Bloomington.
103. West View, Millersville.
104. Heroine, Kansas City.
105. Kirksville, Kirksville.
106. Macon. Macon.
109. Montezuma, Santa Fe.
110. Marcus, Fredericktown.
111. Trenton, Trenton.
113. Plattsburg, Plattsburg.
116. Daviess, Gallatin.
117. Versailles, Versailles.
121. Erwin, St. Louis.
122. Dover, Dover.
123. Hermann, Hermann.
125. Gentryville, Gentryville.
126. Seaman, Milan.
127. Athens, Albany.
129. Constantine Charlestown.
130. West Prairie, West Prairie.
131. Potosi, Potosi.
132. Farmington, Farmington.
133. Star of the West, Ironton.
134. Pleasant Mount, Pleasant Mount.
136. Phœnix, Bowling Green.
137. Prairieville, Prairieville.
138. Lincoln, Fillmore.
139. Oregon, Oregon.
141. Middlebury, Middlebury

142. Pleasant Grove, Otterville,
143. Irondale, Irondale.
145. Rising Star, Ebenezer.
146. McGee, College Mound.
149. Lexington, Lexington.
150. Birming, Birming.
151. Milton, Milton.
153. Bloomfield, Bloomfield.
154. Concord, Concord.
155. Spring Hill, Spring Hill.
156. Ashland, Ashland.
157. North Star, Rockport.
159. Pacific, Pacific.
161. Thomasvi le, Thomasville.
162. Whitesville, Whitesville.
163. Occidental. St. Louis.
164. Joachim, Hillsboro'.
165. Maryville, Maryville.
166. Mirabile, Mirabile.
168. Colony, Colony.
170. Benevolence, Utica.
171. Hartford, Hartford.
172. Wolf Island, Wolf Island.
174. Sturgeon, Sturgeon.
176. Point Pleasant, Point Pleasant.
178. Griswold, Bear Creek.
179. Pride of the West, St. Louis.
180. Kenner, Athens.
181. Novelty, Novelty.
183. Stewartsville, Stewartsville.
183. California, California.
185. Chamois, Chamois.
187. Henry Clay, Millersburg.
188. Hannibal, Hannibal.
189. Zeredatha, St. Joseph.
198. Putnam, Newton.
191. Zerubbabel, Platte City.
192. Frankford, Frankford.
193. Angerona, Missouri City.
194. Wellsville, Wellsville.
196. Quitman, Quitman.
198. Allenville, Allenville.
199. New Hope, New Hope.
200. Somerset, Somerset.
207. Clay, Greenville.
209. Poplar Bluff, Poplar Bluff.
210. Unionville, Unionville.
213. Rolla, Rolla.
214. Forest City, Forest City.
218. Good Hope, Carondelet.
220. Kansas City, Kansas City.
221. Mystic Tie, Oak Ridge.
222. Farmer's, La Belle.
225. Salem, Salem.
226. Saline, St. Mary's.
227. Cypress, Laclede.
228. Shelbina, Shelbina.
229. Nevada, Nevada.
230. St. James, St. James.
231. Warrenton, Warrenton.
233. Bucklin, Bucklin.
234. St. Francois, Libertyville.
235. Ionic, Van Rensellear Ac'y.
236. Sedalia, Sedalia.
237. La Plata, La plata.
238. Rushville, Rushville.
239. Spencersburg, Spencersburg.
240. Granville, Granville.

28*

330 LIST OF LODGES.

241. Palestine, St. Charles.
242. Portland, Portland.
243. Keystone, St. Louis.
244. Middle Fabius, Middle Fabius.
245. Knob Knoster, Knob Knoster.
246. Montgomery City, Montgomery City.
U. D. High Hill, Montgomery.
" Dresden, Pettis.
" Aztec, Los Cruos.
" Graham, Graham.
" Twilight, Columbia.
" Pittsville, Pittsville.
" Kingston, Kingston.
" De Soto, De Soto.
" Western Star, Harrisonville.
" Warrensburg, Warrensburg.
" Live Oak, Pleasant Hill.
" Centralia, Centralia.

U. D. Modern, Humansville.
" Rochester, Rochester.
" Des Moines, Athens.
" Johnson, Greenville.
" Vincil, Cameron.
" Pleasant, West Bend.
" O'Sullivan, Walnut Grove.
" Camden Point, Camden Point
" Texas, Houston.
" Calhoun, Calhoun.
" New Boston, New Boston.
" Renick, Renick.
" Mt. Vernon, Mt. Vernon.
" Bolivar, Bolivar.
" Carthage, Carthage.
' Lindley, Lindley.
" Sonora, Sonora.

NEBRASKA (1860).

Jurisdiction of the Grand Lodge of Nebraska.

1. Nebraska, Bellevue.
2. Western Star, Nebraska City.
3. Capital, Omaha.

4. Nemeho Valley, Brownville.
5. Amadi, Amadi.
6. Plattsmouth, Plattsmouth.

NEW HAMPSHIRE.

Jurisdiction of the Grand Lodge of New Hampshire.

1. St. John's, Portsmouth.
6. Franklin, Lebanon.
7. Benevolent, Milford.
8. North Star, Lancaster.
9. Hiram, Claremont.
11. Blazing Star, Concord.
12. Faithful, Charlestown.
14. King Solomon's, Wilmot Flat.
15. Mount Vernon, Newport.
16. Olive Branch, Plymouth.
17. Morning Star, Wolfborough.
18. Charity,‡ Jaffrey.
19. Sullivan, Lee.
21. Humane, Rochester.
22. Mount Moriah,* Grafton Centre.
23. Cheshire, Cornish Flat.
24. Bethel, New Ipswich.
26. Altemont, Peterborough.
29. Strafford, Dover.
30. St. Paul's, Alstead.
31 St. Peter's, Bradford.
32. Mount Lebanon, Gilford.
37. Evening Star, Colebrook.

38. Harmony, Hillsborough.
39. Rising Sun, Nashua.
40. Phileslan.‡ Winchester.
41. Lafayette, Manchester.
42. Social Friends, Keene.
43. Aurora, Henniker.
44. St. Mark's, Derry.
46. Grafton, Haverhill.
47. Rising Star, New Market.
49. Libanus, Somersworth.
50. Social, Enfield.
52. Clinton, Wilton.
53. Columbian, Walpole.
56. St. Andrew's, Portsmouth.
57. Carroll, Freedom.
58. Charter Oak, Effingham.
59. Star in the East, Exeter.
60. Meridian, Franklin.
61. Washington, Manchester.
62. Unity, Wakefield.
63. Moosehillock, Wentworth.
64. Kane,‡ Lisbon.
65. Granite, Rollinsford.

* Revived and removed June, 1866. † Chartered June, 1866. ‡ Dues paid since June 13, 1866.

LIST OF LODGES.

331

66. Burns, Littleton.
67. Souhegan, Mason.
68. Red Mountain, Sandwich.
69. Mount Prospect, Holderness.
70. Eureka, Concord.
71. Fraternal, Farmington.
72. Horace Chase, Fisherville.
73. Gorham, Gorham.
74. Ossipee Valley, Ossipee.
75. Winnipisaukee,† Alton.

76. Rockingham,† Candia.
77. Golden Rule,† Hinsdale.
78. Doric,† Sanbornton, Br.
79. Union,† Bristol.
80. Monadnock,† Troy.
81. Kearsarge,† Andover Center.
82. Corinthian, Pittsfield.
83. Chocorua, Meredith.
84. Gideon, Kingston.

† Chartered June, 1866.

NEW JERSEY.

Jurisdiction of the Grand Lodge of New Jersey.

1. St. John's, Newark.
2. Brearley, Bridgeton.
3. Cincinnati, Morristown.
4. Tuckerton, Tuckerton.
5. Trenton, Trenton.
6. Lebanon, New Hampton.
7. Newark, Newark.
8. Clinton, Brackinridge.
9. Wash. Shrewsbury, Eatontown.
10. Franklin, Irvingtown.
11. Union, Orange.
12. Amwell, Lambertville.
13. Warren, Belvidere.
14. Mt. Holly, Mt. Holly.
15. Camden, Camden.
16. Olive Branch, Freehold.
17. Hiram, Jersey City.
18. Harmony, Toms River.
19. Union, N. Brunswick.
20. Acacia, Dover.
21. Mystic Bro., Red Bank.
22. Dogenes, Newark.
23. Harmony, Newton.
24. Prospect, Mendham.
25. Northern, Newark.
26. Jerusalem, Plainfield.
27. La Fayette, Bordentown.
29. Joppa, Paterson.
30. Cape Island, Cape Island.
31. Varick, Jersey City.
32. Burlington, Burlington.
33. Washington, Elizabeth.
34. Stewart, Clinton Station.
35. Hoboken, Hoboken.
36. Mansfield, Washington.
37. Darcy, Flemington.
38. Princeton, Princeton.
39. Eureka, Newark.
40. Bloomfield, Bloomfield.
41. Hightstown, Hightstown.

42. Independence, Hackettstown.
43. Paterson, Paterson.
44. Central, Vincentown.
45. Benevolent, Paterson.
46. Solomon's Somerville.
47. Bergen, Bergen.
48. Enterprise, Jersey City.
49. Essex, Elizabethport.
50. Mercer, Trenton.
51. Oriental, Newark.
52. Delaware, Phillipsburg.
53. Eagle, Hudson City.
54. Excelsior, Salem.
55. Kane, Newark.
56. Orion, Frenchtown.
57. Corinthian, Orange.
58. Shekinah, Millville.
59. Caldwell, Caldwell.
60. Arcona, Boonton.
61. Raritan, Perth Amboy.
62. La Frat. Francaise, Newark.
63. St. Stephen's, South Amboy.
64. Cæsarea, Keyport,
65. Star, Tuckahoe.
66. Schiller, Newark.
67. Passaic, Passaic.
68. St. Alban's, Newark.
69. Vineland, Vineland.
70. Pioneer, Hackensack.
71. Hudson, Hoboken.
72. Teutonia, Jersey City.
73. Wall, Squan Village.
74. Jersey City, Jersey City.
75. Neptune, Mauricetown.
76. Ashler, Trenton.
77. Alpine Closter, Bergen Co.
78. Long Branch, Long Branch.
79. Trinity, Absecom. Atlantic Co.
80. Highland, Hudson City.

LIST OF LODGES.

NEW YORK.

Jurisdiction of the Grand Lodge of New York.

1. St. John's, New York City.
2. Ind. Royal Arch, New York City.
3. Mt. Vernon, Albany.
4. St. Patrick's, Johnstown.
5. Masters, Albany.
6. St. George's, Schenectady.
7. Hudson, Hudson.
8. Holland, New York City.
9. Unity, New Lebanon.
10. Kingston, Kingston.
11. Lodge of Antiquity, New York City.
12. Trinity, New York City.
13. Apollo, Troy.
14. Temple, Albany.
15. Western Star, Bridgewater.
16. Prince of Orange, New York City.
17. L'Union Française, New York City.
19. Fortitude, Brooklyn.
20. Abrams, New York City.
21. Washington, New York City.
22. St. John's, Greenfield Centre.
23. Adelphi, New York City.
26. Albion, New York City.
27. Mt. Moriah, New York City.
28. Benevolent, New York City.
30. Dirigo, New York City.
31. Mechanic, New York City.
32. Warren, Schultzville.
33. Ark, Geneva.
35. Howard, New York City.
34. Columbia, New Paltz.
39. Olive Branch, Le Roy.
40. Olive Branch, Frankfort.
41. Sylvan, Moravia.
44. Evening Star, Hornelsville.
45. Union, Lima.
47. Utica, Utica.
48. Ark, Coxsackie.
49. Watertown, Watertown.
50. Concord, New York City.
51. Fidelity, Ithaca.
53. Brownville, Brownville.
54. German Union, New York City.
55. Granville, Middle Granville.
56. Hohenlinden, Brocklyn.
58. Phœnix, Lansingburg.
62. Manhattan, New York City.
63. Morton, Hempstead.
64. Lafayette, New York City.
65. Morning Star, Canisteo.
66. Richmond, Port Richmond.
67. Mariners', New York City.
68. Montgomery, New York City.
69. Naval, New York City.
70. John Hancock, New York City.
73. Lockport, Lockport.
75. Evening Star, West Troy.
79. Hamilton, Canajoharie.
82. Phœbus, New Berlin.
83. Newark, Newark.
84. Artizan, Amsterdam.
85. Washington, Albany.

86. Pythagoras, New York City
87. Schodack Union, Schodack Centre.
90. Franklin, Ballston Spa.
91. King Solomon's Primitive, Troy.
93. Military, Manlius.
94. L. of Strict Observance, N. York City
95. Union, Elmira.
96. Phœnix, Whitehall.
97. Renovation, Albion.
98. Columbia, Chatham Four Cor's.
103. Rising Sun, Saratoga Springs.
104. Lewis, Howard.
105. Hiram, Buffalo.
106. Manitou, New York City.
107. North Star, Moira.
108. Milo, Penn Yan.
109. Valley, Rochester.
110. Scipio, Aurora.
111. St. Lawrence, Canton.
112. Steuben, Bath.
113. Seneca, Waterloo.
114. Union, Ovid.
115. Phœnix, Dansville.
116. Cohoes, Cohoes.
117. Painted Post, Corning.
118. Addison Union, Addison.
119. Oasis, Prattsville.
120. Hamilton, Hamilton.
121. Glen's Falls, Glen's Falls.
122. Mount Morris, Mount Morris.
123. Dundee, Dundee.
124. St. Paul, Auburn.
126. Eastern Light, Greene.
127. Oswego, Oswego.
128. Ogdensburg.
129. Sanger, Waterville.
130. Port Byron, Port Byron.
131. Myrtle, Havana.
132. Niagara Frontier, Niagara Falls.
133. Naples, Naples.
134. Lowville, Lowville.
135. Sacket's Harbor, Sacket's Harbor.
136. Mexico, Mexico.
137. Anglo-Saxon, Brooklyn.
138. Otsego, Cooperstown.
139. Milnor, Victor.
140. Clinton, Waterford.
141. Cato, Cato.
142. Morning Sun, Port Henry.
143. Concordia, Buffalo.
144. Hiram, Fulton.
145. Mt. Moriah, Jamestown.
146. Western Union, Belfast.
147. Warren, Union Springs.
148. Sullivan, Chittenango.
149. Au Sable River, Keeseville.
150. Sauquoit, Sauquoit.
151. Sentinel, Greenwood.
152. Hanover, Forestville.
153. Friendship, Oswego.
154. Penfield Union, Penfield.
155. Clinton, Plattsburg.

LIST OF LODGES.

333

156. Ocean, New York City.
157. Trumansburg, Trumansburg.
158. Carthage, Carthage.
159. Pultneyville, Pultneyville.
160. Seneca River, Baldwinsville.
161. Erie, Buffalo.
162. Schuyler's Lake, Schuyler's Lake.
163. Yonnondio, Rochester.
164. Philanthropic, Camden.
165. Boonville, Boonville.
166. Forest, Fredonia.
167. Susquehanna, Bainbridge.
168. Montour, Painted Post.
169. Clinton, Clinton.
171. Lafargeville, Lafargeville.
172. Chaumont, Chaumont.
173. Monroe, Brockport.
174. Theresa, Theresa.
175. Oxford, Oxford.
176. Montezuma, Montezuma.
177. Binghamton, Binghamton.
178. Atlantic, New York City.
179. German Pilgrim, New York City.
180. Westchester, Sing Sing.
181. Little Falls, Little Falls.
182. Germania, New York City.
183. Farmersville, Farmersville.
184. Turin, Turin.
185. Independent, New York City.
187. Darcy, New York City.
188. Marsh, Brooklyn, E. D.
189. Cortlandt, Peekskill.
190. Munn, New York City.
191. Lebanon, New York City.
193. Ulster, Saugerties.
194. Piatt, New York City.
195. Excelsior, New York City.
196. Solomon's, Tarrytown.
197. York, New York City.
198. Silentia, New York City.
199. Harmony, New York City.
200. Sincerity, Phelps.
201. Joppa, Brooklyn.
202. Zschokke, New York City.
203. Templar, New York City.
204. Palestine, New York City.
205. Hyatt, Brooklyn, E. D.
206. Empire City, New York City.
207. United States, New York City.
208. Cyrus, New York City.
209. National, New York City.
210. Worth, New York City.
211. Pocahontas, Seneca Falls.
213. Racket River, Potsdam.
214. Geneseo, Geneseo.
216. Franklin, Westville.
217. Gouverneur, Gouverneur.
218. Hartland, Johnson's Creek.
219. Summit, Westfield.
221. Cayuga, Scipio Centre.
223. Roman, Rome.
224. Oriental, Utica.
225. Alleghany, Friendship.
226. Antwerp, Antwerp.
227. Eastern Star, New York City.
228. Enterprise, New York City.
229. Pike, Hume.
230. Scio, Wellsville.

231. Canastota, Canastota.
232. Navigator, New York City.
233. Pacific, New York City.
234. Rising Sun, Adams.
235. Keystone, New York City.
236. Philipstown, Cold Spring.
237. Champlain, Champlain.
238. Orient, Copenhagen.
239. Cattaraugus, Little Valley.
240. Washington, Buffalo.
241. Constitution, New York City.
243. Eureka, New York City.
244. Hope, New York City.
245. Polar Star, New York City.
246. Arcana, New York City.
247. Tonawanda, Tonawanda.
248. Palmyra, Palmyra.
249. Charter Oak, New York City.
250. John D. Willard, New York City.
252. Olean, Olean.
253. Old Oak, Millport.
254. Walworth, Walworth.
255. Living Stone, Colden.
256. Fort Brewerton, Brewerton.
257. Mount Neboh, New York City.
258. Macedonia, Bolivar.
259. Sisco, Whallonsburg.
260. Mount Hope, Fort Ann.
261. Evans, Angola.
262. Phœnix, Gowanda.
263. Mount Vernon, North Java.
264. Baron Steuben, Stokes.
265. Speedsville, Speedsville.
266. Poughkeepsie, Poughkeepsie.
267. Fort Edward, Fort Edward.
268. Hermann, New York City.
270. Oneida, Oneida Depot.
271. Chancellor Walworth, N. York City.
272. Mystic Tie, New York City.
273. Metropolitan, New York City.
274. Arcturus, New York City.
275. Sylvan Grove, New York City.
276. Mohawk Valley, Mohawk.
277. Henry Clay, New York City.
278. Marion, West Farms.
279. King Solomon's, New York City.
280. Doric, New York City.
281. Peru, Peru.
282. Otego Union, Otego.
283. Beacon, Matteawan.
284. Baltic, Brooklyn, E. D.
285. George Washington, New York City.
286. Montauk, Brooklyn.
287. Continental, New York City.
288. Brooklyn, Brooklyn.
289. St. Andrew's, Hobart.
290. Spencer, Spencer.
291. N. Constellation, Malone.
292. Parish, North Buffalo.
293. Cape Vincent, Cape Vincent.
294. Canandaigua, Canandaigua.
295. Cataract, Reynales Basin.
296. Clayton, Clayton.
297. Alexandria, Alexandria.
298. Fish House, Northampton.
299. Keshequa, Nunda.
300. Garoga, Rockwood.
301. Irondequoit, Dunkirk.

LIST OF LODGES.

302. Norwich, Norwich.
303. Sylvan, Sinclearville.
304. Schiller, Brooklyn, E. D.
305. Central City, Syracuse.
306. Cuba, Cuba.
307. Ellicottville, Ellicottville.
308. Seneca Lake, West Dresden.
309. Newburg, Newburg.
310. Lexington, Brooklyn.
311. Mount Zion, Troy.
312. Grass River, Madrid.
313. Stony Point, Haverstraw.
315. Wawayanda, Piermont.
316. Atlas, New York City.
317. Neptune, New York City.
318. Joseph Enos, Rushford.
319. Black Lake, Morristown.
320. Union Star, Honeoye Falls.
321. St. Nicholas, New York City.
322. Star of Bethlehem, Brooklyn.
323. Amity, New York City.
324. Freedom, Unadilla.
325. Republican, Parish.
326. Salem Town, Cayuga.
327. Acacia, New York City.
328. Port Jervis, Port Jervis.
329. Zerubbabel, New York City.
330. New York, New York City.
331. Hornellsville, Hornellsville.
332. Jefferson, Watkins.
333. Westbrook, Nichols.
334. Cherry Valley, Cherry Valley.
335. Widow's Son, Clermont.
336. Medina, Medina.
337. Greenbush, Greenbush.
338. Putnam, New York City.
339. Puritan, New York City.
340. Modestia, Buffalo.
341. Clyde, Clyde.
342. Lily, Morrisania.
343. Rondout, Rondout.
345. Lodi, Lodi.
346. Whitesville, Whitesville.
347. Hampton, Westmoreland.
348. Adelphic, New York City.
349. Peconic, Greenport.
350. Chemung Valley, Chemung.
351. Springville, Springville.
352. Homer, Homer.
353. Woodhull, Woodhull.
354. Progressive, Brooklyn, E. D.
355. Jerusalem, Lansingburg.
356. United Brothers, New York City.
357. Caneadea, Caneadea.
358. Queen City, Buffalo.
359. Elm Creek, Randolph.
360. Afton, Afton.
361. Central, Brooklyn.
362. Valatie, Valatie.
363. Evergreen, Springfield Centre.
364. Horse Heads, Horse Heads.
365. Goshen, Goshen.
367. Corner Stone, Brooklyn, E. D.
368. Croton, Croton Falls.
369. Callimachus, Phœnix.
370. Molang, Crown Point.
371. Sagamore, New York City.
372. Sandy Hill, Sandy Hill.

373. La Sincerité, New York City.
374. Monumental, Red Hook.
375. Niagara, Lockport.
376. Ontario, Wilson.
377. Rushville, Rushville.
378. Big Flatts, Big Flatts.
379. Oakland, Castile.
380. Murray, Holley.
381. Huguenot, Tottenville.
382. Long Island, Brooklyn.
383. Aurora, Fort Covington.
384. Cherry Creek, Cherry Creek.
385. Weedsport, Weedsport.
386. Jordan, Jordan.
387. La Fraternidad, New York City.
388. Upper Lisle, Upper Lisle.
389. Margaretville, Margaretville.
391. Salem, Salem.
392. Sodus, Sodus.
393. Waddington, Waddington.
394. Cobbleskill, Cobbleskill.
395. Amber, Parishville.
396. Deposit, Deposit.
397. Ivy, Elmira.
398. Home, Northumberland.
399. Maine, Maine.
400. Van Rensselaer, Hoosick Falls.
401. Suffolk, Port Jefferson.
402. Crescent, New York City.
403. Greenpoint, Brooklyn, 17 w.
406. Humanity, Lyons.
407. Waverly, Waverly.
408. City, New York City.
409. Commonwealth, Brooklyn.
410. La Clem'te Am. Cos., New York City.
411. Candor, Candor Centre.
412. Hoffman, Middletown.
413. West Star, Varysburg.
414. Scriba, Constantia.
415. Pulaski, Pulaski.
416. Wayne, Ontario.
417. Wadsworth, Albany.
418. Mosaic, New York City.
419. Arcade, China.
420. New London, New London.
421. Genoa, Kings Ferry.
422. Frontier City, Oswego.
423. Herkimer, Herkimer.
425. Warrensburg, Warrensburg.
426. Northfield, Pittsford.
427. Cascade, Oakhill.
428. High Falls, Colton.
429. Gloversville, Gloversville.
430. Star of Hope, Brooklyn, 18 w.
431. Auburn, Auburn.
432. Rhinebeck, Rhinebeck.
433. Fort Plain, Fort Plain.
434. Hiawatha, Mt. Vernon.
435. Otseningo, Binghamton.
436. Schroon Lake, Schroon Lake.
437. Wamponamon, Sag Harbor.
438. Marathon, Marathon.
439. Delhi, Delhi.
440. Vienna, Vienna.
441. L. Anc't Landmarks, Buffalo.
442. Windsor, Windsor.
444. Sherburne, Sherburne.
445. Cassia, Brooklyn, E. D.

LIST OF LODGES. 335

446. Oltmans, Brooklyn, E. D.
447. Franklin, New York City.
448. Huguenot, New Rochelle.
449. Hiram, New York City.
450. Rising Star, Yonkers.
451. Delta, Brooklyn.
452. Ancient City, Albany.
453. Clinton, New York City.
454. Kane, New York City.
455. Newport, Newport.
456. Senate, Glen's Falls.
457. Harlem, Harlem.
458. Shekomeko, Mabbettsville.
459. Urbana, Urbana.
461. Yew Tree, Brooklyn, E. D.
462. Attica, Attica.
463. Weston, Weston.
464. Downsville, Colchester.
465. Wilton, Wilton.
466. Oneonta, Oneonta.
467. Greenwich. New York City.
468. Catskill, Catskill.
470. Cortlandville, Cortland.
471. Tompkins, Stapleton.
472. Dryden, Dryden.
473. White Plains, White Plains.
474. Belmont, Belmont.
475. Batavia, Batavia.
476. Fairport, Fairport.
477. Wildwood, Edwards.
478. Dansville, Rogersville.
479. Etolian, Spencerport.
480. Webotuck, North East.
481. Cambridge Valley, Cambridge.
482. Richfield Springs, Richfield Springs.
483. Zeradatha, Brooklyn.
484. Columbian, New York City.
485. Stella, Brooklyn.
486. Ionic, New York City.
487. Tecumseh, New York City.
488. Corinthian, New York City.
489. Manahatta, New York City.
490. Pyramid, New York City.
491. Schoharie Valley, Schoharie.
492. Wyoming, Westchester.
493. South Side. Catchogue.
494. Jephtha, Huntington.
496. Groton. Groton.
497. Glendale, Pottersville.
498. De Molay, Buffalo.
499. Deer River, Lawrenceville.
500. Hermon, Hermon.
501. Syracuse, Syracuse.
503. Old Ti, Ticonderoga.
504. Montgomery, Stillwater.
505. Northern Light, West Chazy.
506. Rodman, Rodman.
507. Genesee Falls, Rochester.
508. Herschel, Hartford.
509. Lindenwald. Stuyvesant Falls.
510. Liberty, Cohocton.
511. Kings County, Flatbush.
512. Humboldt. New York, 11 w.
513. Massena, Massena.
514. Zion, East Hamburg.
515. Butternuts. Butternuts.
516. Park. New York, 22 w.
517. Frontier, Chateaugay.

518. Coventry, Coventry.
519. Architect, New York City.
520. Salt Springs. Syracuse.
521. Callicoon, Callicoon.
522. Skaneateles, Skaneateles.
523. Normal, New York City.
524. Morning Star, Marcellus.
525. Liverpool, Liverpool.
526. Henrietta, Henrietta.
527. Akron, Akron.
528. Monitor, New York City.
529. Mountain, Windham Centre.
530. Washington Heights, New York City.
531. Fultonville, Fultonville.
532. Monticello, Monticello.
533. Round Hill, Union.
534. Tioga, Smithsboro'.
535. Americus, New York City.
536. Nassau, Brooklyn.
537. Gramercy, New York City.
538. Webster, Webster.
539. Fayette, Fayette.
540. Hill Grove. Brooklyn.
541. Brasher, Brasher Falls.
542. Garibaldi, New York City.
543. Triluminar, Pike.
544. Warwick, Warwick.
545. Copernicus, Brooklyn, E. D.
546. Jamaica, Jamaica.
547. Cameron Mills, Cameron Mills.
548. Laurens, Laurens.
549. Warsaw, Warsaw.
550. Hannibal, Hannibal.
551. Ransomville, Ransomville.
552. Hancock, Hancock.
553. Farmers', Burlington.
554. Working, Jefferson.
555. Diamond, Dobb's Ferry.
556. North Bangor, Bangor.
557. James M. Austin, Greenville.
558. Andover, Andover.
559. Walton, Walton.
560. Red Creek, Red Creek.
561. Delaware, Cochocton.
562. Franklin, Franklin.
563. Cornucopia, Flushing.
564. Sandy Creek, Sandy Creek.
565. Guiding Star, Vill. of Tremont.
566. Russell, Russell.
567. Argyle, Argyle.
568. St. Cecile, New York City.
569. Greenwood, Brooklyn, 8 w.
570. Avon Springs, Avon Springs.
571. Cœur de Lion, Roxbury.
572. Mt. Hermon, Ellenburg.
573. Depeyster, Depeyster.
574. Bedford, Brooklyn, 7 or 20 ws.
575. Olive, Sherman.
576. Fessler, New York City.
577. Elk, Nicholville.
578. Fayetteville, Fayetteville.
579. Portville, Portville.
580. Glen Cove, Glen Cove.
581. Winfield, West Winfield.
582. Wawarsing, Ellenville.
583. Prattsburg, Prattsburg.
584. Ashlar, Greenwich.
585. Cosmopolitan, Brooklyn.

336 LIST OF LODGES.

586. Island City, Long Island City.
587. Ahwaga, Owego.
588. Globe, New York City.
589. Ramapo, Suffern.
590. Rose, Rose.
591. Ilion, Ilion.
592. Schenevus Valley, Schenevus.
593. Charlotte River, Davenport.
594. Alden, Alden.
595. Socrates, New York City.
596. Hopewell, Fishkill Plains.
597. Western Light, Lisle.
598. Tabernacle, New York City.
599. Kennyetto, Broadalbin.
600. Evangelist, New York City.
601. Altair, Brooklyn.
602. Adirondack, Elizabethtown.
603. Astor, New York City.
604. Perfect Ashlar, New York City.
605. Tienuderrah, Morris.
606. Masonville, Masonville.
607. Hudson River, Newburg.
608. Lessing, Brooklyn.
609. Rensselaer, Rensselaerville.
610. Ivanhoe, New York City.
611. St. Johnsville, St. Johnsville.
612. Hillsdale, Hillsdale.
613. Cleaveland, Cleaveland.
614. Newark Valley, Newark Valley.
615. Stissing, Pine Plains.
616. Cazenovia, Cazenovia.
617. Teutonia, New York City.
618. Tyrian, East New York.
619. Eagle, Richmond.
620. Clinton F. Paige, Otto.
621. Orange, Orange.
622. Central Square, Central Square.
623. Sayles, Bridgeport.

624. Sharon Springs, Sharon.
625. Fraternal, White's Corners.
626. Franklinville, Franklinville.
627. Walkill, Montgomery.
628. Citizens, New York City.
629. Goethe, New York City.
630. Gilboa, Gilboa.
631. Girard, New York City.
632. Prudence, New York City.
633. Richville, Richville.
634. Scotia, New York City.
635. Advance, Astoria.
636. Manual, Brooklyn, E. D.
637. Rising Light, Belleville.
638. Crystal Wave, Brooklyn.
639. Somerset, Somerset Corners.
640. Adytum, Brooklyn.
641. Copestone, New York City.
642. Knickerbocker, New York City.
643. Daniel Carpenter, New York City.
644. Raymond, New York City.
645. Riverhead, Riverhead.
646. Red Jacket, Lockport.
647. Mistletoe, Brooklyn.
648. Centreville, Centreville.
649. McClellan, Troupsburg.
650. Amboy, West Amboy.
651. True Craftsman's, New York City.
652. Perseverance, New York City.
653. Mamaro, Mamaroneck.
654. Emanuel, New York City.
655. Bunting, Harlem.
656. Euclid, Brooklyn.
657. Livingston, New York City.
658. Morrisville, Morrisville.
659. South Otselic, Otselic.
660. Rochester, Rochester.
661. Beethoven, New York City.

NORTH CAROLINA.

Jurisdiction of the Grand Lodge of North Carolina.

1. St. John's, Wilmington.
2. Royal White Hart, Halifax.
3. St. John's, Newbern.
5. Charity, Windsor.
7. Unanimity, Edenton.
8. Phœnix, Fayetteville.
10. Johnson Caswell, Warrenton.
17. American George, Murfreesboro'.
31. Phalanx, Charlotte.
32. Stokes, Concord.
37. William R. Davie, Lexington.
40. Hiram, Raleigh.
45. Liberty, Wilkesboro'.
56. King Solomon, Jackson.
58. Concord, Tarboro'.
59. Perseverance, Plymouth.
64. Kilwinning, Wadesboro'.
71. Eagle, Hillsboro'.
75. Widow's Son, Camden C. H.

76. Greensboro', Greensboro'.
78. Sharon, Greenville.
81. Zion, Trenton.
82. Mount Moriah, Statesville
83. La Fayette, Jacksonville.
84. Fellowship, Smithfield.
85. Morning Star, Nashville.
88. Enfield, Enfield.
90. Skewarkee, Williamston.
91. Western Star, Rutherfordton.
92. Joseph Warren, Stantonsburg.
95. Jerusalem, Hookerton.
96. St. John's, Kingston.
97. Wake Forest, Dunnsville.
98. Hiram, Clinton.
99. Fulton, Salisbury.
101. Warren, Kenansville.
102. Columbus, Pittsboro'.
103. Pasquotank, E. City.

LIST OF LODGES. 337

104. Orr, Washington.
106. Perquimans, Hertford.
107. Clinton, Yanceyville.
108. Belmont, Bear Swamp P. O.
109. Franklin, Beaufort.
111. Wentworth, Wentworth.
112. Wayne, Goldsboro'.
113. Person, Roxboro'.
114. St. Albans, Lumberton.
115. Holly Springs, Holly Springs.
117. Mt. Lebanon, Wilson.
118. Mt. Hermon, Ashville.
121. Logan, Jamestown.
122. Tuscarora, Oxford.
123. Franklinton, Franklinton.
124. Clinton, Louisburg.
125. Mill Creek, Newton Grove.
126. Gatesville, Gatesville.
127. Blackmer, Clark's Creek.
128. Hanks, Franklinsville.
129. Dan River, Madison.
131. Conoho, Hamilton.
132. Radiance, Snow Hill.
133. Alamance, Graham.
134. Mocksville, Mocksville.
135. Black Rock, Black Rock.
136. Leaksville, Leaksville.
137. Lincoln, Lincolnton.
138. King Solomon, Long Creek.
140. Mount Energy, Tranquility.
141. Carolina, Ansonville.
142. Cane Creek, Snow Camp.
143. Mount Vernon, Goldston's P. O.
144. Taylor, Belle Voir.
145. Junaluska, Franklin.
146. Cherokee, Murphy.
147. Palmyra, Averasboro'.
149. Adoniram, Young's ⋈ Roads.
150. Pee Dee, Norwood's Store.
151. Chalmers, Carbonton.
153. Mt. Carmel, Scott's Hill.
154. Scotch Ireland, Mt. Vernon.
155. White Stone, Wakefield.
156. Rolesville, Rolesville.
157. Mount Pleasant, Rogers' Store.
158. Knap of Reeds, Knap of Reeds.
159. Rocky River, Mudlick.
160. Beaumont, Beaumont.
161. Rock Rest, Hadley's Mills.
162. Yadkin, Yadkinsville.
164. Deep River, Foust's Mills.
165. Archer, Creechville.
166. St. Paul's, Beatty's Bridge.
107. Winston, Winston.
168. Pleasant Hill, Patterson's Store.
170. Blackmer, Reem's Creek.
171. Delk, Coleraine.
172. Buffalo, Buffalo P. O.
173. Union, Kernersville.
174. Geo. Washington, Lassiter's ⋈ Roads.
175. Pollocksville, Pollocksville.
177. Marlboro', Marlboro'.
178. Siloam, Harrel's Store.
179. La Fayette, Leasburg.
180. Caldwell, Chapel Hill.
181. Carthage, Carthage.
182. Townesville, Townesville.
183. Centre Grove, Summerfield.

184. Jordan, Reynoldson.
185. Sandy Creek, Laurel P. O.
186. Pine Forest, Harrington.
187. Central Cross, Peach Tree Grove.
188. Balfour, Ashboro'.
190. Fair Bluff, Fair Bluff.
191. Granite, Clayton.
192. Burnsville, Burnsville.
194. Cape Fear, Elizabethtown.
195. Mount Olivet, Brower's Mills.
196. Falkland, Falkland.
197. Cherokee, Grogansville.
198. Carey, Carey P. O.
199. High Point, High Point.
200. Pisgah, Hendersonville.
201. Eagle Rock, Eagle Rock.
202. Cleaveland, Shelby.
203. Roanoke, Weldon.
204. Berea, Berea.
205. Long Creek, Hopewell.
206. Mingo, Draughn's Store.
207. Lebanon, Whitesville.
208. Mount Olive, Mount Olive.
209. New Salem, New Salem.
210. Enoe, Durham's.
211. Ashland, Mount Airy.
212. Industrial, Company Shops.
213. Crane's Creek, Cane's Creek.
214. Richland, Thomasville.
215. New Light, New Light.
216. Rockingham, Rockingham.
217. Cawtaba Valley, Morganton.
218. W. G. Hill, Raleigh.
219. Jefferson, Jefferson.
220. Stokesburg, Walnut Cove.
222. Webster, Elevation.
223. Tabernacle, Gilmer's Store.
224. County Line, County Line.
225. Haw River, Summerfield.
226. Wilson, Olin.
227. Jonesville, Jonesville.
228. McCormick, Jonesboro'.
229. Henderson, Henderson.
230. Corinthian, Rocky Mount.
231. William T. Bain, Holland's.
232. Gunter, Haywood.
233. Lenoir, Lenoir Institute.
234. Anchor, Auburn.
235. Cokesbury, ————.
236. Mount Zion, St Lawrence.
237. Mystic Tie, Marion.
238. Atlantic, Currituck.
239. Nahunta, Nahunta.
240. Wiccacon, Harrellsville.
241. Oscilla, Tally Ho.
242. Loch Lomond, Floral College.
243. Rountree, Contentnea Neck.
244. Monroe, Monroe.
345. New Berne, New Berne.
246. Elmwood, Geensboro'.
247. Mount Hermon, Curtis' Mills.
248. Catawba, Newton.
249. Pythagoras, Smithville.
250. Shiloh, Williamsboro'.
251. Rockford, Rockford.
252. Holly Grove, Holly Grove.
253. Lee, Taylorsville.
254. Mount Bethel, Lomaxville.

29

338 LIST OF LODGES.

255. Oaks, Oaks.
256. Trinity, Trinity College.
357. J. B. Person, Beulah.

258. Harnett, Raleigh P. O.
259. Waynesville, Waynesville.
260. Centre Hill, Centre Hill.

OHIO.

Jurisdiction of the Grand Lodge of Ohio.

1. American Union, Marietta.
2. N. C. Harmony, Cincinnati.
3. Old Erie, Warren,
4. New England, Worthington.
5. Amity, Zanesville.
6. Scioto, Chillicothe.
7. Morning Dawn, Gallipolis.
8. Harmony, Urbana,
9. Mount Zion, Mount Vernon.
11. Center Star, Granville.
12. Unity, Ravenna.
13. St. John's, Dayton.
14. Franklin, Troy.
15. Cleveland City, Cleveland.
16. Belmont, St. Clairsville.
17. Washington, Hamilton.
18. Hiram, Delaware.
19. Jerusalem, Hartford.
20. Magnolia, Columbus.
21. Western Star, Youngstown.
22. Rising Sun, Ashtabula.
23. Pickaway, Circleville.
24. Warren, Piqua.
25. Paramuthea, Athens.
26. Lebanon, Lebanon.
28. Temple, Painesville.
29. Clermont Social, Williamsburg.
30. Columbus, Columbus.
33. Ebenezer, Wooster.
35. Mansfield, Mansfield.
37. Mount Moriah, Beverly.
38. Highland, Hillsboro'.
40. Northern Light, Maumee City.
43. West Union, West Union.
44. Columbia, Miamisburg.
45. Steubenville, Steubenville.
46. Miami, Cincinnati.
47. Clinton, Massillon.
48. Aurora, Portsmouth.
49. Xenia, Xenia.
50. Science, Sandusky.
52. Wilmington, Wilmington.
54. Milford, Milford.
55. Eastern Star, Franklin.
56. King Solomon, Elyria.
57. Lancaster, Lancaster.
58. Medina, Medina.
59. Tuscarawas, Canal Dover.
60. Canton, Canton.
61. Bethel, Bethel.
64. Mount Vernon, Newark.
65. New Lisbon, New Lisbon.
66. Cambridge, Cambridge.
67. Oxford, Oxford.

70. Marion, Marion.
71. Union, Ripley.
72. Georgetown, Georgetown.
73. Temperance, Sidney.
74. Seville, Seville.
76. Somerset, Somerset.
77. Sandusky, Tiffin City.
78. Leesburg, Leesburg.
79. Lafayette, Zanesville.
80. Libanus, Lewisburg.
81. Lafayette, Cincinnati.
82. Bolivar, Eaton.
83. Akron, Akron.
85. Jackson, Brownsville.
87. Salem, New Salem.
88. King Hiram, West Alexandria.
89. Friendship, Barnesville.
90. Jefferson, Middletown.
91. Western Sun, Wheelersburg.
93. Chardon, Chardon.
94. Montgomery, Montgomery.
96. Coshocton, Coshocton.
97. Newark, Newark.
98. Minerva, Miamisburg.
100. New Carlisle, New Carlisle.
101. Clark, Springfield.
102. Felicity, Felicity.
103. Dresden, Dresden.
104. Tarleton, Tarleton.
105. Moriah, Jacobsburg.
106. Fellowship, New Paris.
107. Fayette, Washington.
108. Watatomika, West Bedford.
109. Batavia, Batavia.
111. Corinthian, McConnelsville.
112. Wood County, Bowling Green.
113. Mechanicsburg, Mechanicsburg.
115. Hanover, Loudonville.
116. Hebron, Hebron.
118. Malta, Norwich.
119. Goshen, Goshen.
120. McMakin, Mt. Healthy.
121. Mercer, Mercer.
122. Moscow, Moscow.
123. Phœnix, Perrysburg.
124. Carroll, Carrollton.
126. Sparta, Millersburg.
127. Wellington, Wellington.
131. Vinton, Vinton.
132. Trowel, Jackson.
133. Cincinnati, Cincinnati.
134. Columbian, Columbia.
135. Butlerville, Butlerville.
136. Sharon, Sharon.

LIST OF LODGES.

339

137. Harrisville, Lodi.
138. Chandler, London.
139. Bucyrus, Bucyrus.
140. Cheviot, Cheviot.
141. McMillan, Cincinnati.
143. Greenville, Greenville.
144. Toledo, Toledo.
145. Valley, Malta.
147. Dayton, Dayton.
148. Mt. Olive, Chesterfield.
149. Aberdeen, Aberdeen.
150. Buckeye, New Richmond.
151. Ashland, Ashland.
152. Venus, Mansfield.
153. Farmers' Fredonia.
154. Latham, Kenton.
155. Cynthia, Cincinnati.
156. Albany Hebardsville.
157. Philodorean, Nelsonville.
158. Palestine, Marysville.
159. Camden, Camden.
160. New Vienna, New Vienna.
161. Mad River, West Liberty.
162. Yeatman, Columbia.
163. Waynesville, Waynesville.
164. Pomeroy, Pomeroy.
165. Hildreth, Republic.
166. Russelville, Russelville.
167. Hamer, Wapakonetta.
168. Covington, Covington.
169. Lithopolis, Lithopolis.
170. Thrall, Frederickstown.
171. Mingo, Logan.
172. Doric, Deavertown.
174. Tippecanoe, Hyattsville.
175. Lone Star, Newcomerstown.
176. Warpole, Upper Sandusky.
177. New Philadelphia, New Philadelphia.
178. Lynchburg, Lynchburg.
179. Superior, West Unity.
180. Wellsville, Wellsville.
181. Bridgeport, Bridgeport.
182. Smithfield, Smithfield.
184. Irville, Nashport.
185. Perry, Salem.
186. Springdale, Springdale.
187. Star, Cuyahoga Falls.
189. Monroe, Woodsfield.
190. Roscoe, Roscoe.
191. Blanchester, Blanchester.
192. Mystic Tie, Urichsville.
193. Snow, Harrison.
194. Fielding, South Charleston.
195. Tuendawie, Defiance.
196. Bainbridge, Bainbridge.
197. Kreider, Quincy.
198. Lawrence, Ironton.
199. Ohio, Bladensburg.
200. Venice, Venice.
201. Richland, Plymouth.
202. Port Washington, Port Washington.
203. Marathon, Marathon.
204. Sharonville, Sharonville.
205. Lima, Lima.
206. Gilead, Mt. Gilead.
207. Delta, McArthur.
208. Hanselmann, Cincinnati.
209. Bellefontaine, Bellefontaine.

210. Olive, Sarahsville.
211. Rushville, Rushville.
213. Summit, Twinsburg.
214. Hope, Delphos.
215. Bryan, Bryan.
216. Mt. Pleasant, Mt. Pleasant
217. Social, Lena.
218. Van Wert, Van Wert.
219. Harrison, Cadiz.
220. Hubbard, Adamsville.
221. Madison, West Jefferson.
222. Evergreen, Conneaut.
224. Plainfield, E. Plainfield.
225. Fort Stephenson, Fremont.
226. Mount Olivet, Addison.
227. Findlay, Findlay.
228. Hamer, Owensville.
229. Iris, Cleveland.
231. N. Birmingham, N. Birmingham.
232. Lockbourne, Lockbourne.
233. Eureka, Washington.
234. Meridian, Steubenville.
235. Brown, Minerva.
236. Winchester, Scott P. O.
237. Rubicon, Toledo.
238. Chester, Chesterville.
239. Erie, Milan.
240. Groveport, Groveport.
241. Celina, Celina.
243. Bigelow, Cleveland.
244. Monticello, Clyde.
245. Golden Gate, Chagrin Falls.
246. Garretsville, Garretsville.
247. E. Liberty, E. Liberty.
248. Fulton, Delta.
249. Newton, Newton.
250. New Lexington, New Lexington.
251. Hazen, Morristown.
252. Webb, Stockport.
253. Cumminsville, Cumminsville.
254. Buford, Buford.
255. Warsaw, Warsaw.
256. Napoleon, Napoleon.
257. Germantown, Germantown.
258. Emory, Loveland.
259. Mineral, Hamden.
260. Floral, Fitchville.
261. N. Fairfield, N. Fairfield.
262. Napthall, Carroll.
263. Clarington, Clarington.
264. Paddy's Run, New London.
265. Morrow, Morrow.
266. Meridian, Richfield.
267. Bellair, Bellair.
268. Blazing Star, N. Lewisburg.
269. Mount Sterling, Mount Sterling.
270. Union City, Union City.
271. Alliance, Alliance.
272. Arcadia, Crestline.
273. Bellevue, Bellevue.
274. Village, Burton.
275. Orphan's Friend, Wilksville.
276. Allen, Columbiana.
277. Rock Creek, Morgan.
278. Amesville, Amesville.
279. Central, Calais.
280. Kalida, Kalida.
281. Ward, Piqua.

340

LIST OF LODGES.

282. Pleasant Ridge, Pleasant Ridge.
283. Anchor, Duncan's Falls.
284. Relief, Pierpont.
285. Clement Amitie, Unionville.
286. Antioch, Danville.
287. Sylvania, Sylvania.
288. Fostoria, Fostoria.
289. Grand Rapids, Gilead.
290. Versailles, Versailles.
291. Licking, Utica.
292. Boggs, De Graff.
293. Bartlett, Plymouth.
294. Charter taken away, Forest.
295. Ithica, Ithica.
296. Western Phœnix, Parkman.
297. Grand River, Harpersfield.
298. Flushing, Flushing.
299. Amelia (Charter taken away), Amelia.
300. Stafford, Stafford.
301. Gibson, Birmingham.
302. Willoughby, Willoughby.
303. Mount Carmel, Richwood.
304. Rose, Monroeville.
305. Stokes, Port Jefferson.
306. Acadia, Acadia.
307. Lake Shore, Centreville.
308. Aurelius, Macksburg.
309. Frankfort, Frankfort.
310. Eden, Melmore.
311. Urania, Pleasant Valley.
312. Harveysburg, Harveysburg.
313. Sullivan, Sullivan.
314. Wyandot, McCutchensville.
315. Riddle, E. Liverpool.
316. Rockton, Franklin Mills.
317. Manchester, Manchester.
318. Greenfield, Greenfield.

319. Osborn, Osborn.
320. Tiffin, Tiffin.
321. Orient, Waverly.
322. E. Townsend, Townsend.
323. Clarksville, Clarksville.
324. Sabina, Sabina.
325. Ottawa, Buckley's P. O.
326. Center, Johnstown.
327. Fidelity, Galion.
328. Rural, N. Bloomfield.
329. Perseverance, Sandusky City
330. Caldwell, Bolivar.
331. Golden Rule, Cherry Valley.
332. Edenton, Edenton.
333. Union Port, Union Port.
334. Geneva, Geneva.
335. Antwerp, Antwerp.
336. Brainard, Fremont.
337. Coolville, Coolville.
338. New Home, Hanover.
339. Blendon, Westerville.
340. Reynoldsburg, Reynoldsburg
341. O. H. Perry, Port Clinton.
342. Tuscan, Jefferson.
343. Nevada, Nevada.
344. Ada, Ada.
345. Concordia, Cleveland.
346. North Bend, Cleves.
347. Belle Center, Belle Center.
348. Salineville, Salineville.
349. Wauseon, Wauseon.
350. Shelby, Shelby.
351. Portage, Elmore.
352. Jamestown, Jamestown.
353. Orion, Kingsville.
354. Somerton, Somerton.

OREGON

Jurisdiction of the Grand Lodge of Oregon

1. Miltonomah, Oregon.
2. Willamette, Portland.
3. Lafayette, Lafayette,
4. Salem, Salem.
6. Triality, Hillsboro'.
7. Temple, Astoria.
9. Jennings, Dallas.
10. Warren, Jacksonville.
11. Eugene, Eugene City.
12. Harmony, Portland.

13. Laurel, Roseburg.
14. Corvallis, Corvallis,
15. Wasco, Dallas.
16. Winchester, Winchester.
17. Corinthian, Albany.
18. Western Star, Kerbyville.
19. Ainsworth, Salem.
20. Bethel, Bethel.
23. Phœnix, Wait's Mills.
24. Rainier, Rainier.

LIST OF LODGES.

341

PENNSYLVANIA.

Jurisdiction of the Grand Lodge of Pennsylvania.

2. Philadelphia.
3. Philadelphia.
9. Philadelphia.
19. Montgomery, Philadelphia.
21. Perseverance, Harrisburg.
22. Perseverance, Sunbury.
25. Bristol, Bristol.
43. Lancaster.
45. Pittsburg.
51. Philadelphia.
52. Harmony, Philadelphia.
59. Washington, Philadelphia.
60. Brownsville, Brownsville.
61. Wilkesbarre.
62. Reading.
67. Concordia, Philadelphia.
70. Rural Amity, Athens.
71. Lafayette, Philadelphia.
72. Philadelphia, Philadelphia.
75. Phœnix, Phœnixville.
81. Hiram. Philadelphia, 22d Ward.
91. Columbia, Philadelphia.
106. Williamsport.
108. Union, Towanda.
114. Solomon's, Philadelphia.
115. St. John's, Philadelphia.
121. Union, Philadelphia.
125. Herman's, Philadelphia.
126. Rising Star, Philadelphia.
130. Phœnix, Philadelphia.
131. Industry, Philadelphia.
134. Franklin, Philadelphia.
135. Roxborough, Manayunk.
138. Schuylkill, Orwigsburg.
143. Geo. Washington, Chambersburg.
144. Charity Lewisburg.
152. Easton, Easton.
153. Waynesburg, Waynesburg.
155. Mt. Moriah, Philadelphia.
156. Washington, Drumore Center.
158. Meridian Sun, Philadelphia.
163. Evergreen, Monroetown.
164. Washington, Washington.
186. Eastern Star, Philadelphia.
187. Integrity, Philadelphia.
190. Charity, Norristown.
194. Lafayette, Selin's Grove.
197. Cumberland Star, Carlisle
199. Lafayette, Lock Haven.
203. Lewistown, Lewistown.
211. Kensington, Philadelphia.
216. Pulaski, Pottsville.
218. Honesdale, Honesdale.
219. St. John's, Pittsburg.
220. Portage, Hollidaysburg.
221. Franklin, Pittsburg.
222. Minersville, Schuylkill Co.
223. Allegheny, Allegheny.
224. Danville, Danville.
225. Philanthropy, Greensburg.
226. Mt. Lebanon, Lebanon.
227. Chandler, Reading.

228. Fayette, Uniontown.
229. Rochester, l'ochester.
230. Richmond (Port Richmond), Phila.
231. Solomon's, Pittsburg.
232. La Belle Valle, Jersey Shore.
233. St. John's, Pittston.
234. Crawford, Meadville.
236. Chester, Chester.
237. Chandler, Beallsville.
338. Tamaqua, Tamaqua.
239. Armstrong, Freeport.
240. Warren, Montrose.
241. North Star, Warren.
242. Carbon, Mauch Chunk.
243. Mahoning, New Castle.
244. Kittanning, Kittanning.
245. Doylestown, Doylestown.
246. Shekinah, Philadelphia.
347. Friendship, Mansfield.
248. Temple, Tunkhannock.
249. Carbondale, Carbondale.
250. Sharon, Sharon.
251. Hebron, Mercer.
252. Grummer, Fayette City.
253. Washington, Pittsburg.
254. Stichter, Pottstown.
255. Shamokin, Shamokin.
256. Milton, Milton.
258. Western Crawford, Conneautville.
260. St. John's, Carlisle.
261. Hiram, Providence.
262. Orrstown, Orrstown.
263. Franklin, Laceyville.
264. Columbus, Columbus.
265. Washington, Bloomsburg.
266. York, York.
267. Swatara, Tremont.
268. Bellefonte, Bellefonte.
269. Monongahela, Birmingham.
270. Page, Schuylkill Haven.
271. Keystone, Philadelphia.
272. Butler, Butler.
273. Cassia, Athensville.
274. Hamilton, W. Philadelphia.
275. Loyalhanna, Latrobe
276. Hobah, Brookville.
277. Clarion, Clarion.
278. Cambria, Johnstown.
279. Newcomb, Carmichael.
280. Harmony, Bradford.
281. Mountain, Altoona.
282. Juniata, Hollidaysburg
283. Bethlehem, Bethlehem.
284. Porter, Catasauqua.
285. Anthracite, St. Clair.
286. Columbia, Columbia.
287. Milnor, Pittsburg.
288. Jefferson, Allegheny.
289. Orient, Philadelphia.
290. Eureka, Greenville.
291. Union, Scranton.
292. Frankford, Frankford.

29*

LIST OF LODGES.

294. Ashland, Ashland.
295. Melita, Philadelphia.
296. Mitchell, Germantown.
297. Chartiers, Canonsburg.
298. G. W. Bartram, Media.
299. Muncy, Muncy.
300. Mt. Moriah, Huntingdon.
301. Waverly, Waverly.
302. Eureka, Mechanicsburg.
303. Oil Creek, Titusville.
304. Western Star, Albion.
305. Hawley, Hawley.
306. Trojan, Troy.
307. Williamson, Womelsdorf.
308. Washington, Ft. Washington.
309. Williamson, Downingtown.
310. Warren, Trappe.
311. Mt. Bethel, Mt. Bethel.
312. Summit, Ebensburg.
313. Indiana, Indiana.
314. Clearfield, Clearfield.
315. Cumberland, Shippensburg.
316. Myrtle, Franklin.
317. Ossea, Wellsboro'.
318. McKinley, Allegheny.
319. Adams, N. Bloomfield.
320. Bedford, Bedford.
321. Hailman, E. Liberty.
322. West Chester, W. Chester.
323. Peter Williamson, Scranton.
324. Union, Mifflintown.
325. Barger, Stroudburg.
326. Lehigh, Trexlertown.
327. Hazel, Hazelton.
328. Freedom, Jackson.
329. Craft, Greensboro'.
330. Salem, Hamlinton.
331. Ft. Ligonier, Ligonier.
332. Plymouth, Plymouth.
333. Barger, Allentown.
334. Bradford.
335. Eureka, Montoursville.
336. Good Samaritan, Gettysburg.
337. H. M. Phillips, Monongahela City.

338. Great Bend, Great Bend.
339. Hyde Park, Hyde Park.
340. Thomson, Garret's Sideing.
341. Factoryville, Factoryville.
342. Eulalia, Coudersport.
343. Skerrett, Cochransville.
344. Milford, Milford.
345. Schiller, Scranton.
346. King Solomon, Connellsville.
347. Lake Erie, Girard.
348. Patmos, Hanover.
349. Catawissa, Catawissa.
350. Blose, Blossburg.
351. Cowanesque, Knoxville.
352. L. H. Scott, Chester.
353. Oxford, Oxford.
354. Sylvania, Shickshinny.
355. Acacia, Blairsville.
356. Ten Mile, Ten Mile Village.
357. Mahanoy, Mahanoy City.
358. Somerset, Somerset.
359. Humboldt, Philadelphia.
360. Canawacta, Susquehanna Depot.
361. Big Spring, Newville.
362. Tyrian, Erie.
363. Petrolia, Oil City.
364. Susquehanna, Millersburg.
365. Corry, Corry.
366. Eureka, Union Mills.
367. Teutonia, Reading.
368. Corinthian, Philadelphia.
369. Williamson, Philadelphia.
370. Mifflinburg, Mifflinburg.
371. Lamberton, Thompsontown.
372. Spartan, Spartansburg.
373. Tioga, Tioga.
374. Davage, Manchester.
375. Alliquippa, McKeesport.
376. McVeytown, McVeytown.
377. Huguenot, Kurtztown.
378. Mt. Carmel, Mt. Carmel.
379. Elk, Ridgeway.
380. Pennsylvania, Philadelphia.

RHODE ISLAND (1860).

Jurisdiction of the Grand Lodge of Rhode Island.

1. St. John's, Newport.
2. St. John's, Providence.
3. Washington, Warren.
4. Mt. Vernon, Providence.
6. St. Albans, Bristol.
7. Friendship, Chepachet.
8. Mt. Moriah, Lime Rock.
9. Harmony, Pawtuxet

10. Union, Pawtuxet.
11. King Solomon, E. Greenwich.
12. Manchester, Coventry.
13. Morning Star, Woonsocket.
15. Hamilton, Clayville.
16. Warwick, Greenville.
20. Franklin, Westerly.
21. What Cheer, Providence.

LIST OF LODGES.

343

SOUTH CAROLINA.

Jurisdiction of the Grand Lodge of South Carolina.

1. Solomon's, Charleston.
3. Clinton, Abbeville.
4. Union Kilwinning, Charleston.
5. Washington, Charleston.
9. Friendship, Charleston.
10. St. Andrew's, Charleston.
11. Winnsboro', Winnsboro'.
14. Orange, Charleston.
15. Cheraw, Cheraw.
17. Harmony, Barnwell C. H.
18. Chester, Chester.
19. Palmetto, Laurens C. H.
21. Pythagorean, Charleston.
22. Harmony, Beaufort.
23. Independent, Due West.
24. Williamston, Williamston.
25. Friendship, Kuksey's ⋈ Roads.
26. Benton, Simmonsville.
27. Buford, Barnwell.
28. Orangeburg, Orangeburg.
29. Kershaw, Camden.
30. Ridgeway, Ridgeway.
31. Recovery, Greenville.
32. Johnson, Bennocks.
33. Aurora, Clio.
34. Pendleton, Pendleton.
35. Fraternity, Adams Run.
36. Le Candeur, Charleston.
37. Centre, Honea Path.
38. Allen, Bambery.
39. Richland, Columbia.
40. Winyah, Georgetown.
41. St. John's, Blufton.
42. Tyrian, Erwinton.
43. Eureka, Adamsville.
44. Campbell, Clinton.
45. Effingham, Effingham.
46. Kingstree, Kingstree.
47. Eureka, Ninty-six.
48. Lebanon, Leesville.
49. Wallace, Pleasant Mound.
50. Concordia, Edgefield.
52. Mackey, Hickory Grove.
53. Jackson, Lancaster.
54. St. Peter's, Manning.
55. Unity, Walterboro'.
56. Catawba, Fort Mill.
57. Mt. Willing, Mt. Willing.
58. Mt. Moriah, White Plains.
59. Butler, Clarytown.
60. Clinton, Marion.
61. Harmony, George's Station.
62. Charity, White Cane.
63. Blackville, Blackville.
64. Claremont, Sumter.
65. Horry, Conwayboro'.
66. Walhalla, Charleston.
67. Harmony, Hamburg.
68. Hiram, Anderson.
69. Oman, Cedar Falls.
70. Spartan, Spartan.

71. Eyeria, Charleston.
72. St. David, Darlington.
73. Strict Observance, Charleston.
74. Washington, Abbeville.
75. Union, Union.
76. Landmark, Charleston.
77. Mackey, Harleesville.
78. Philanthropic, Yorkville.
79. Keowee, Pickens.
80. Biscomb, Cokesbury.
81. Calhoun, Glen Springs.
82. Caldwell, Liberty Hill.
83. Little Peedee, Allon's Bridge.
84. True Brotherhood, Columbia.
85. Flint Hill, Flint Hill.
86. Roslin, Lowndesville.
87. Amity, Newberry.
88. Marlboro', Bennettsville.
89. Bascomville, Bascomville.
90. Caldwell, Calhoun's Mills.
91. Greenwood, Greenwood.
92. Blue Ridge, Walhalla.
94. Acacia, Columbia.
95. Etiwan, Mt. Pleasant.
96. Franklin, Charleston.
97. Coleman, Fensterville.
98. American, Gillisonville.
99. Star, Graniteville.
100. Monticello, Monticello.
101. Ebenezer, Marietta.
102. Reedville, Reedville.
103. Saluda, Troy Level.
104. Bishopville, Bishopville.
105. Summerton, Allendale.
106. Burnett, Piercetown.
107. Gowansville, Gowansville.
108. Columbia, Columbia.
109. Allendale, Allendale.
110. Branchville, Branchville.
111. Rockhill, Rockhill.
112. Bethel, Woodruff.
113. Scull Shoals, Scull Shoals.
114. Faust, Graham's P. O.
115. Prosperity, Troy Level.
116. Hermon, Millford's Mills.
117. Mine, Doing Greedmine.
118. Bruns, Brownsville.
119. Livingston, Livingston Mills.
120. Sumter, Sumter.
121. Amity, Florence.
122. Hope, Walker's P. O.
123. Boylston, Lexington.
124. Cross Hill, Cross Hill.
125. Stonewall, Millway.
126. Pine Grove, Fort Motte.
127. Hope, Wittiston.
128. Hopewell, Duncan Mills.
129. Campbell, Kingstree.
130. Mt. Hope, Mt. Hope.
131. Tumbling Shoals, Tumbling Shoals.

344

LIST OF LODGES.

TENNESSEE.

Jurisdiction of the Grand Lodge of Tennessee.

5. Overton, Rogersville.
7. Hiram, Franklin.
8. Cumberland, Nashville.
9. Western Star, Springfield.
13. Whitesides, Blountville.
14. Carthage, Carthage.
18. Mt. Moriah, Murfreesboro',
24. Elkton, Elkton.
31. Columbia, Columbia.
38. Union, Kingston.
44. Rising Star, Rutledge,
45. Jackson, Jackson.
47. Rhea, Jonesboro'.
50. Meridian.Sun, Athens.
54. Clinton, Bolivar.
57. Mt. Pleasant, Mt. Pleasant.
58. Brownsville, Brownsville.
59. Mt. Libanus, Knoxville.
64. Constantine, Lexington.
67. Blair, Kingsport.
68. Jackson, Fayetteville.
69. Somerville, Somerville.
77. Liberty, Smithville.
80. Tellico, Madisonville.
81. Lagrange, Lagrange.
86. Trenton, Trenton.
88. Western Sun, Troy.
89. Clarksville, Clarksville.
90. Dresden, Dresden.
93. Hess, Dyersburg.
94. King Solomon, Gallatin.
95. Germantown, Germantown.
96. Caledonia, McKenzie.
97. Charlotte, Charlotte.
98. Lebanon, Lebanon.
99. Sparta, Sparta.
100. Ripley, Durhamville.
101. Pulaski, Pulaski.
102. Savannah, Savannah.
104. Union, Mason.
105. St. James, Williamsport.
106. Huntingdon, Huntingdon.
107. Laurenceburg, Laurenceburg.
108. Paris, Paris.
109. Marshall, Cottage Grove.
111. Benton, Santa Fe.
112. Dilahunty, Lewisburg.
113. Union, Hartsville.
114. Harrison, Harrison.
115. Yorkville, Yorkville.
117. McLemoresville, McLemoresville.
118. S. Memphis, Memphis.
119. Greenville, Greenville.
120. Macon, Macon.
121. Boydsville, Boydsville.
122. Shelbyville, Shelbyville.
123. Petersburg, Petersburg.
124. Spring Hill, Spring Hill.
125. Warren, McMinnville.
126. Cornersville, Cornersville.
127. Waynesboro', Waynesboro'
128. N. Providence, Maryville.

129. Mar's Hill, Middleton.
130. Sandy Hill, Manleyville.
131. Phœnix, Nashville.
132. Purdy, Purdy.
133. Tannehill, Gainsboro'.
134. Cleveland, Cleveland.
135. Triune, Triune.
136. Oakland, Oakland.
137. Hampton, Port Royal.
138. Pleasant Grove, Pleasant Grove.
139. Vale of Tempe, Pikeville.
140. Union, Mifflin.
141. Martin, Rome.
144. Morning Sun, Ecklin's.
145. Conyersville, Conyersville.
146. Holly Springs, Macedonia.
147. Andrew Jackson, Beulah.
148. Whiteville, Whiteville.
149. Lafayette, Lafayette.
150. Dunham, Covington.
151. Hatchie, Middleburg.
152. Colliersville, Colliersville.
153. Cotton Grove, Cotton Grove.
154. Denmark, Denmark.
157. Acacia, N. Providence.
158. Cumberland, Winchester.
159. Washington, Poland Springs.
160. Chapel Hill, Chapel Hill.
161. Boon's Hill, Boon's Hill.
163. Mason's Grove, Mason's Grove.
164. Quincey, Quincey.
165. Danceyville, Danceyville.
166. Medon, Medon.
167. Bigbyville, Bigbyville.
168. Angerona, Memphis.
169. Dukedom, Dukedom.
170. Berlin, Salisbury.
172. Owen Hill, Jordan's Store.
173. Clifton, Clifton.
174. Lavina, South Carroll.
175. Alexandria, Alexandria.
176. Limestone, Georgetown.
177. Mt. Pelia, Mt. Pelia.
178. Como, Como.
179. Camden, Camden.
180. Evening Star, Tazewell.
181. Washington, Louisville.
182. Nolensville, Nolensville.
183. Polk, Centerville.
184. Harmony, Tiptonville.
185. Lymville, Lymville.
186. Morning Star, Sulphur Well.
188. McCulloch, Palmyra.
189. Hiwasse, Calhoun.
190. Brazleton, Dandridge.
191. Shady Grove, Milan Depot.
192. Merriwether, Hampshire.
193. Spring Creek, Spring Creek.
194. Bethel, Prospect.
195. Roche, Columbia.
197. Mountain Star, Sevierville.
198. Moscow, Moscow.

LIST OF LODGES. 345

199. Chattanooga, Chattanooga.
200. Pearl, Mason's Hall.
201. Bethesda, Bethesda.
202. Humboldt, Shiloh.
203. Milton, Milton.
204. Tennessee, Loudon.
206. Eaton Eaton
207. Lineport, Lineport.
208. New Portland, Magnolia.
209. Baker, Macedonia.
210. Linden, Linden.
211. Woodlawn, Bartlett.
212. Ocoee, Benton.
213. Meigs, Decatur.
214. Harmony, Manchester.
215. Sulphur Well, Antioch Ch'ch.
216. Green Mount, Houston.
217. Wilson, Pinewood.
218. Decaturville, Decaturville.
220. Hamburg, Pebble Hill.
221. Smyrna, Smyrna.
222. Pinson, Pinson Station.
223. St. James, Henryville.
224. Lanefield, Lanefield.
225. Fredonia, Fredonia.
226. Tipton, Mt. Zion.
227. Cherry Mount, Mulloy's.
228. Valley Forge, Oakwood.
229. Friendship, Jack's Creek.
230. Cuba, Cuba.
231. Morristown, Morristown.
232. Gravel Hill, Gravel Hill.
233. Salem, Salem.
234. Newport, Newport.
235. Woodbury, Woodbury.
236. Washington, Washington.
237. Laguardo, Laguardo.
238. Dashiell, Elizabethtown.
239. Hermon, Beech Grove.
240. Beech, Beech.
241. Ducktown, Ducktown.
242. Thyatira, Bradyville.
243. Taylorsville, Taylorsville.
244. Masters, Knoxville.
245. Woodville, Woodville.
246. New Market, New Market.
247. John Hart, Peacher's Mill.
248. Vesper, Big Spring.
249. N. Middleton, N. Middleton.
250. Center Point, Center Point.
251. Friendship, Friendship.
252. Bone, Rutherford Dep.
253. Chota, Concord.
254. Edgefield, Edgefield.
255. Sycamore, Sycamore Mill.
256. Bradshaw, Simpson's Store.
259. Livingston, Livingston.
260. Clarksburg, Clarksburg.
261. Mountain, Spencer.
262. Tullahoma, Tullahoma.
263. Ellen, D'ble Bridges.
264. Adams, Jenkin's Depot.

265. Farmville, Farmville.
266. Cookeville, Cookeville.
267. Saltillo, Saltillo.
268. Reliance, Bellbuckle.
269. Fuller, Ripley.
270. Phenix, Dover.
271. Tannehill, Goodletsville.
272. Burton, White Hill.
273. Caldwell, Big Bottom.
274. Johnson, Fall Branch.
275. Newcastle, Newcastle.
276. Turley, Maynardville.
277. Sneedville, Sneedville.
278. Tyre, Fremont.
279. West Point, West Point.
280. Sale Creek, Sale Creek.
281. Jamestown, Jamestown.
282. Crystal Fountain, Black Jack.
283. Union Chapel, Union Chapel.
284. Felix Grundy, Pelham.
285. Newbern, Newbern.
286. Lewis, Palestine.
287. Farmington, Farmington.
288. Marlboro', Marlboro'.
289. Leila Scott, Memphis.
290. Pleasant Ridge, Danville.
291. Pleasant Green, Pleasant Green.
292. Sweetwater, Sweetwater.
293. Claiborne, Nashville.
294. Union City, Union City.
295. Unitia, Unitia.
296. Palestine, Palestine.
297. Olive Branch, Jasper.
298. Lowreyville, Lowreyville.
299. Hamilton, Memphis.
300. Wisdom, F'rk. Well's Creek.
301. Moriah Gr'v., St'dg Rocks Creek.
302. T. McCulloch, Cedar Hill.
303. Indian Mound, Indian Mound.
304. Waverley, Waverley.
305. Pleasant Plains, Pleasant Plains.
306. Forked Deer, Bell's Station.
307. Anderson, Gladesville.
308. Libanus, Center Academy.
309. Mt. Moriah, Mt. Moriah.
310. Rhea Springs, Sulphur Springs.
311. Chas. Fuller, Lafayette Depot.
312. Manley, Manley's Church.
313. Rock Spring, Rock Spring.
314. Western Valley, Western Valley.
315. Mt. Tabor, Unionville.
316. 10 Mile Valley, 10 Mile Stand.
317. T. Hamilton, Riceville.
318. Lynchburg, Lynchburg.
319. Yellow Creek, Yellow Creek.
320. Barren Plains, Barren Plains.
321. Snodderley, Woodbourne.
322. Jacksboro', Jacksboro'.
323. Nolachucky, Rheatown.
324. Verona, L'tl Hatchie Church.
325. Perry, Lobleville.
326. Fountain Head, Fountain Head.

346

LIST OF LODGES.

TEXAS.

Jurisdiction of the Grand Lodge of Texas.

1. Holland, Houston.
2. Milam, Nacogdoches.
3. Red Land, San Augustine.
5. St. John's, Columbia.
6. Harmony, Galveston.
7. Matagorda, Matagorda.
11. Milam, Independence.
12. Austin, Austin.
13. Constantine, Bonham.
14. Trinity, Livingstone.
16. Friendship, Clarksville.
17. Orphan's Friend, Anderson.
18. Washington, Washington.
19. Forest, Huntsville.
20. Graham, Benham.
21. Lathrop, Crockett.
22. Marshall, Marshall.
23. Clinton, Henderson.
24. Red Land, Henderson.
25. Montgomery, Montgomery.
26. Olive Branch, Cincinnati.
27. Paris, Paris.
29. De Witt Clinton, Jasper.
30. Gonzales, Gonzales.
31. Palestine, Palestine.
32. Sam Houston, Shelbyville.
34. Lafayette, La Grange.
35. Jackson, Milan.
36. Lavaca, Lavaca.
37. Mt. Moriah, Cold Springs.
38. Jefferson, Jefferson.
39. Leona Union, Leona.
40. Victoria, Victoria.
41. Eagle, Bethany.
43. Douglass, Douglass.
44. Alamo, San Antonio.
45. Euclid, Rusk.
46. Florida, Round Top.
48. Liberty, Liberty.
51. St. John's, McKinsey's.
52. Touchill, Dallas.
53. St. John's, Tyler.
54. Grand Bluff, Grand Bluff.
55. Gillespie, Wheelock.
56. Warren, Caldwell.
57. Lavissa, Lavissa.
58. Bastrop, Bastrop.
59. Lockhart, Lockhart.
60. Mt. Enterprise, Mt. Enterprise.
62. Woodville, Woodville.
63. Rocky Mount, Bunker Hill.
65. Joppa, Elysian Fields.
66. Cherino, Cherino.
67. Hubert, Chapel Hill.
68. Caledonia, Columbus.
69. Boston, Boston.
70. Temple, Mt. Pleasant.
71. Mt. Vernon, Mt. Vernon.
72. Moreton, Richmond.
73. Washita, Sherman.
74. Springfield, Springfield.

75. Brazos, Hootsville.
76. Cameron, Cicero.
77. Concord, McClorty's.
78. Carthage, Carthage.
79. Oasis, Dangerville.
80. Menchison, Hallettsville.
81. Rio Grande, Brownsville.
83. Terrel, Alto.
84. Indianola, Indianola.
85. Pine Bluff, Troy.
86. Tuscalenn, Pine-tree.
87. New Salem, New Salem.
88. Jackson, Cass.
89. San Gabriel, Georgetown.
90. Waxahatchie, Waxahatchie.
91. Tarrant, Tarrant.
92. Basque, Waco.
93. Ioni, San Pedro.
94. Goliad, Goliad.
95. Sharon, Sharon.
96. Colorado, Webberville.
97. Newtern, Newbern.
98. Canton, Canton.
99. Wharton, Wharton.
100. Freedom, Fredericksburg.
101. Danville, Danville.
102. Unity, Greenville.
103. Fairfield, Fairfield.
104. Corcicana, Corcicana.
105. Kickapoo, Kickapoo.
106. San Jacinto, Danville.
107. San Andres, Cameron.
108. Jacksonville, Jacksonville.
109. Guadalope, Seguin.
110. Greenville, Greenville.
111. Burleson, Navarre.
112. Bloomfield, Kaufman.
113. Magnolia, Magnolia.
114. Prairie Lea, Prairie Lea.
115. Kaufman, Andover.
116. Red River, Pine Creek.
117. Travis, Sherman.
118. Starr, Starrville.
119. Flora, Quitman.
120. McDonald, Trim Flat.
121. Mt. Hope, Mt. Hope.
122. Quitman, Chatfield Point.
123. Texana, Texana.
124. Colleti, Yorktown.
125. Baylor, Gay Hill.
126. Madison, Madison.
127. Burns, Concord.
128. Cushney, San Marcos.
129. Brazos Union, Boonville.
130. El Paso, San Elizaria.
131. Belmont, Belmont.
132. Griffin, Griffin.
133. Retreat, Retreat.
134. Bethel, Fannin.
135. Camden, Camden.
136. Newton, Burkeville.

LIST OF LODGES. 347

137. Mt. Horeb, Gabriel Mills
138. Neill, Lexington.
139. Herschell, Coffeeville.
140. Kerchix, Centreville.
141. Castilian, Canton.
142. Bethesda, Gilmer.
143. Ochiltree, Melrose.
144. Pierce, Sterling.
145. Walnut Grove, Gordon's Stand.
146. Cypress, Wm. Sparks.
147. Plantersville, Plantersville.
148. Ft. Worth, Ft. Worth.
149. Truit, Truit's Store.
150. Jamestown, Jamestown.
151. Cabulo, Valley.
152. Marlin, Marlin.
153. Eclectic, Warren.
154. Cotton Gin, Cotton Gin.
155. Spring Hill, Spring Hill.
156. Hickory Hill, Hickory Hill.
157. East Trinity, Rockwell.
158. Taylor, Mt. Carmel.
159. McClellan, Union.
160. Lancaster, Lancaster.
161. Eureka, Palmer's.
162. Imvirol, Panola Co.
163. Sumpter, Sumpter.
164. Honey Grove, Honey Grove.
165. Athens, Athens.
166. Belton, Belton.
167. Kentucky, Kentucky.
168. Monroe, Madisonville.
169. Taylor, Ash Spring.
170. San Andres, Cameron.
171. Basque. Basque.
173. Mound Prairie, Mound Prairie.
174. Corsicana, Corsicana.
175. Valley, Hamilton.
176. Anadako, Ft. Graham.
177. St Paul, Port Sullivan.
178. Glover, Coffeeville.
179. Hardeman. Plum Creek.
180. Hopkins, Theodosia.
182. Concrete, Concrete.
183. Hopkinsville, Hopkinsville.
184. Hickory Grove, Mt. Vernon.
185. White Oak, Saratoga.
186. West Fork, Taylorsville.
187. Tyrian, Augusta.
189. Corpus Christi, Corpus Christi.

190. Refugio, Refugio.
191. Havana, Havana.
192. Cusseta, Cusseta.
193. Leon, Leon River.
194. Jack Titus, Red Oak Grove.
195. Lyons, Lyons.
196. Aquilla, Hillsboro'.
197. Gatesville, Gatesville.
198. Tyre, Tennessee Colony.
199. De Molay, Souders Chapter.
200. Alamita, Helena.
201. Denton, Louisville.
202. J. A. Baker, Walker Co.
203. Pine, Newburg.
204. Mt. Colm, Mt. Colm.
205. Walnut Creek, Littleton's Spring.
206. Frank Sexton, Pittsburg.
207. W. P. Brittain, Social, Cherokee Co.
208. McMahon, Lockhart.
209. Mantua, Mantua.
210. Gainesville, Gainesville.
211. Science Hill, Science Hill.
212. Deer Creek, Evans' Store.
213. Acton, Buchanan.
214. Farmersville, Farmersville.
215. Stedman, Newton.
216. Twin Sisters, Hodges' Mills.
217. Stanfield, Denton.
218. J. G. Craven, Dresden.
219. Millville, Millville.
220. Orion, Union School-House.
221. Bright Star, Sulphur Springs.
222. Parsons, Parson's Seminary.
223. Belleville, Belleville.
224. Miller, Hunt Co.
225. San Saba, San Saba.
226. Brohan, Bethesda.
227. Round Rock, Round Rock.
228. Newport, Newport.
229. Randolph, Randolph.
230. Ocean, Weatherford.
231. Sampson, Oak Hill.
232. Tampasas, Tampasas.
233. Eutaw, Eutaw.
234. White Rock, Walnut Grove.
235. Plano, Plano.
236. Relief, Rusk Creek.
237. Lively, Denton Co.
238. Prarieville, Prarieville.

VERMONT.

Jurisdiction of the Grand Lodge of Vermont.

1. Dorchester, Vergennes.
2. Union, Middleburg.
3. Washington, Burlington.
4. Franklin, St. Albans.
5. Morning Star, Bridgeport.
6. Lamville, Fairfax.
7. Rising Sun, Royalton.
8. Mt. Vernon, Hyde Park.

9. Missinsquoi, E. Berkshire.
10. Independence, Orwell.
11. Columbus, Allburg.
12. North Star, Williston.
13. Mt. Anthony, Bennington.
14. '76, Scranton.
15. De Witt Clinton, Northfield.
16. Masonic Union, Troy.

348

LIST OF LODGES.

17. Isle of Patmos, North Hero.
18. Vermont, Hartland.
19. Liberty, Franklin.
20. Meridian Sun, Graftsbury.
21. United Brethren, Hartford.
22. Aurora, Montpelier.
23. Blazing Star, Fayetteville.
24. Friendship, Charlotte.
25. St. Paul's, Brandon.
26. McDonough, Essex.
27. Passumpic, St. Johnsbury.
28. Phœnix, W. Randolph.
29. Rural, Rochester.
30. Lee, Castleton.
31. Woodstock, Woodstock.
32. Golden Rule, Putney.
33. Patriot, Hinesburg.

34. Center, Rutland.
35. Granite, Barre.
36. Columbia, Brattleboro'.
37. Morning Star, W. Poultney.
38. Social, Wilmington.
39. Haswell, Sheldon.
40. Seneca, Milton.
41. St. John's, Springfield.
42. Adoniram, Manchester.
43. Charity, Bradford.
44. Island Pond, Island Pond.
45. King Solomon, Bellews Falls.
46. Mt. Lebanon, S. Londonderry.
47. Libanus.
48. White Rock, Wellingford.
49. Washington, Chelsea.

VIRGINIA.

Jurisdiction of the Grand Lodge of Virginia.

1. Norfolk, Norfolk.
2. Atlantic, Norfolk.
2. Kilwinning, Pt. Royal (extinct).
3. Blanford, Petersburg.
4. Fredericksburg, Fredericksburg.
5. St. Tammany, Hampton.
6. Williamsburg, Williamsburg.
7. Blue Ridge,† Flint Hill.
7. Botetourt, Gloucester C. H.
8. Roanoke, Cluster Springs.
9. Fairmount, Fairmount.
10. Richmond, Richmond.
11. Metropolitan, Richmond.
12. Monroe,† Union.
13. Staunton, Staunton.
14. Manchester, Manchester.
15. Petersburg, Petersburg.
16. Brooklyn,† Brooklyn.
17. Chestnut Grove, Witmell.
18. Smithfield Union, Smithfield.
19. Richmond Randolph, Richmond.
20. Franklin,† Buckhannon.
21. Hiram, Winchester.
22. Alexandria Washington, Alexandria.
23. Taylor,† Salem.
24. Pittsylvania, Pittsylvania C. H.
25. Mt. Olivet.† Carrsville.
26. Weston,† Weston.
27. Rockingham, Harrisonburg.
28. Bigelow,† Philippi.
29. Corinthian, Petersburg.
30. Suffolk, Suffolk.
31. Marion, Marion.
32. George, Howardsville.
33. Warren, Pedlar Mill.
34. Solomon. Suffolk.
35. Catlett, Estillville.
36. St. John's, Richmond.
37. Marshall,† Moundsville.
38. Central,† New Market.
39. Marshall, Lynchburg.

40. Henry,† Fairfax C. H.
41. Farmville, Farmville.
42. Berlin, Berlin.
43. Fairfax, Culpoper C. H.
44. Prudence, New London.
45. Scottville, Scottville.
46. Worthington, Mt. Solon.
47. Preston, Jonesville.
48. Abingdon, Abingdon.
49. Greenbrier, Lewisburg
50. Piedmont, Stanardsville.
51. Dove, Richmond.
52. Brunswick, Lawrenceville.
53. Loge Francaise, Richmond.
54. Excelsior,† Mill Creek.
55. Palmyra, Columbia.
57. Geo. Washington,† Berryville,
58. Day, Louisa C. H.
59. Warren.† Lunenburg.
60. Widow's Son, Charlottesville.
61. Polk, Riceville.
62. Tazewell, Jeffersonville.
63. Fredericksburg Amer.,† Fredericksburg.
64. Natural Bridge, Gilmore's Mills.
65. Jefferson, Surrey C. H.
66. Friendship, Vincastle.
67. Mt. City, Lexington.
68. Powhatan, Powhatan.
69. Mackey, Campbell C. H.
70. Bonesborough, Bedford.
71. Blue Ridge, Albemarle Co.
72. James Evans, Buchanan.
73. Clinton,† Clinton.
74. Fayetteville,† Fayetteville.
75. Rocky Mount, Rocky Mount.
76. Montrose, Montrose.
77. Chuckatuck, Chuckatuck.
78. Washington,† Washington.
79. Green Spring,† Poindexter's Store.
80. Malta, Charlestown.

LIST OF LODGES. 349

81. Salem, Middlebury.
82. Wytheville, Wytheville.
83. Flat Rock, Lunenburg.
84. Acacia,† Jerusalem.
85. Astrea, Sussex C. H.
86. McDaniel,† Christiansburg.
87. Vincent Witcher, Callands.
88. Lancaster, Lancaster C. H.
89. Black Heath,† Buck Hill.
90. Starke,† Gholsonville.
91. Mt. Nebo, Shephardstown.
92. Fleetwood Harmony, Providence.
93. Morgantown Union,† Morgantown.
94. Greenway Court,† White Post.
95. Liberty, Liberty.
96. Halifax Hiram,† Halifax C. H.
97. Frankford,† Frankford.
98. Hermon, Clarksburg.
99. Somerton, Somerton.
100. Portsmouth, Portsmouth.
101. Ohio,† Wheeling.
102. Front Royal,† Rappahannock Co.
103. New Hope.† Piedmont.
104. Wetzel,† New Martinsville.
104. Kanawha,† Charleston.
105. Benevolentia,† Heathsville.
106. Giles, Pearisburg.
107. Monroe, Appomattox C. H.
108. Wellsburg,† Wellsburg.
109. Door to Virtue, New Castle.
110. Western Star,† Guyondotte.
111. Charity,† Harper's Ferry.
112. Laurel, Red House.
113. Mt. Olivet,† Parkersburg.
114. Olive Branch, Leesburg.
115. Prince George, Prince George C. H.
116. Princeton,† Princeton.
117. Triluminar, Middleway.
118. Washington Union, Clarksville.
119. Meherrin, Mecklenburg Co.
120. Andrew Jackson, Alexandria.
121. Ashton,† Ravenswood.
122. Roman Eagle, Danville.
123. Blue Stone Union, Mecklenburg Co.
124. Avon,† Summit Point.
125. Mt. Crawford, charter not lifted.
126. Linn Banks, Madison C. H.
127. Washington,† Martinsville.
128. Wheeling,† Wheeling.
129. Independence, Independence.
130. Henrico Union, Henrico Co.
131. Leitch, Jacksonville.
132. Dallas, Brucetown.
133. Mt. Carmel, Warrenton.
134. Blackwater, Isle of Wight C. H.
135. Hunter, Edinburg.
136. Equality,† Martinsburg.
137. Lafayette, Luray.
138. Independent Orange, Orange C. H.
139. Clinton,† Romney.
140. Patrick Henry, Patrick Co.
141. De Witt Clinton, Cartersville.
142. Cassia, Woodstock.
143. Buckingham, Maysville.
144. St. John's, Charlotte C. H.
145. Emory,† Emory.
146. Doric,† Cumberland C. H.
147. Kanawha,† Charleston.

148. Chandler,† Berryville.
149. Harmony, Nansemond Co.
150. Widow's Son, Hickford.
151. Franklin,† Franklin Depot.
152. Fitzwhylson, Boydton.
153. Dan River, Hyco Falls.
154. Keysville,† Keysville.
155. Staunton, Brookneal.
156. Hunters, Blacksburg.
157. Prospect Hill, Prospect Hill.
158. Mannington,† Mannington.
159. Snowville, Snowville.
160. Ripley,† Ripley.
161. Chesterfield,† Chester.
162. Shelby, Goodson.
163. Friendship, Loringston.
164. Temperance,† Windsor.
165. Henry Clay, Newbern.
166. Mt. Vernon, Portsmouth.
167. Preston,† Kingwood.
168. Ashland, Ashland.
169. Relief,† Littleton.
170. Fettermont,† Grafton.
171. Covington,† Covington.
172. Minturn,† Point Pleasant.
173. Hope,† Lebanon.
174. New Cumberland,† New Cumberland.
175. Mt. Olivet,† Whitehall.
176. Covington, Covington.
177. Virginia, Cabin Point.
178. Kanawha Valley, Buffalo.
179. Wakoma,† Summersville.
180. Cameron,† Cameron.
182. Wayne,† Wayne C. H.
183. Hill City, Lynchburg.
184. Capital, extinct.
185. McAllister. Cypress Chapel.
187. Rye Cove, Rye Cove Academy.
188. Martin's Station, Martin's Station.
189. Patmos, Upperville.
190. Lakeland, Big Lick Depot.
191. South Side, Pamplin's Depot.
192. Moorefield, Moorefield.
193. Fulton, Hillsville.
194. King Solomon's, Hillsborough.
195. Eureka, Bridgewater.
196. Stuart, Hansonville.
197. Monitor, Old Point Comfort.
198. Wakefield, Wakefield.
199. Freedom, Lovettsville.
200. Stonewall, Buckingham Institute.
201. Johnson, Stickleyville.
202. Bayley, Marysville.
203. Reedy Spring, Reedy Spring.
204. Warm Spring, Warm Springs.
205. Fancy Hill, Fancy Hill.
206. Bland, Bland C. H.
207. Meadsville, Meadsville.
208. Linville, Rockingham Co.
209. Lee, Waynesboro'.
210. Maratock, Danville.
211. Midlothian, Midlothian.
212. Tower Hill, Tower Hill.
213. Treadwell, Berryville.
214. Stella, Ruckersville.
215. Lebanon, Lebanon.
216. Cove Creek, Cove Creek.
217. Grayson, Grayson.

350

LIST OF LODGES.

218. Sinking Creek, Newport.
219. Waterman, Abingdon.
220. Mt. Moriah, Sperrysville.
221. Silentia, Ayletts.

222. Harman, Blue Stone.
223. Wilson, ———.
U. D. Virginia, Liberty Hill.
U. D. Indian Creek, Centreville.

† These Lodges not represented in Grand Lodge.

WEST VIRGINIA.

Jurisdiction of the Grand Lodge of West Virginia.

1. Ohio, Wheeling.
2. Wellsburg, Wellsburg.
3. Mt. Olivet, Parkersburg.
4. Morgantown, Morgantown.
5. Wheeling, Wheeling.
6. Herman, Clarksburg.
7. Franklin, Buckhannon.
8. Marshall, ———.
9. Fairmount, Fairmount.
10. Weston, Weston.
11. Western Star, Guyondotte.

12. Ashton, Ravenswood.
13. Minerva, Cabell.
14. Preston, Kingwood.
15. Grafton, Grafton.
16. Ripley, Jackson C. H.
17. Cameron, Marshall.
18. Wayne, Wayne Co.
19. Mudturn, Pt. Pleasant.
20. Kanawha, Charleston.
26. Liberty, West Liberty.

WASHINGTON TERRITORY.

1. Olympia, Olympia.
2. Steilacoon, Steilacoon.

3. Grand Mound, Grand Mound.
4. Washington, Vancouver.

WISCONSIN.

Jurisdiction of the Grand Lodge of Wisconsin.

1. Mineral Point, Mineral Point.
2. Melody, Platteville.
3. Milwaukee, Milwaukee.
4. Warren, Potosi.
5. Madison, Madison.
9. Jefferson County, Jefferson.
10. Morning Star, Beloit.
11. Sheboygan, Sheboygan.
13. Wisconsin, Milwaukee.
14. Western Star, Janesville.
16. Franklin, Highland.
17. Ozaukee, Ozaukee.
18. Racine, Racine.
20. Lancaster, Lancaster.
21. Washington, Green Bay.
24. St. John's, Sheboygan Falls.
25. Amicitia, Shullsburg.
26. Fountain, Fond du Lac.
27. Oshkosh, Oshkosh.
28. Burlington, Burlington.

30. Aurora, Milwaukee.
31. Smith, Monroe.
32. Union, Evansville.
33. Fort Winnebago, Portage City.
34. Baraboo, Baraboo.
36. Albany, Albany.
37. Waukesha, Waukesha.
38. Berlin, Berlin.
40. Horicon, Horicon.
41. St. James, East Troy.
43. Hazel Green, Hazel Green.
44. Geneva, Geneva.
45. Frontier, La Crosse.
46. Lake Mills, Lake Mills.
47. Kenosha, Kenosha.
48. Waupun, Waupun.
49. Watertown, Watertown.
50. Hiram, Madison.
51. Waverley, Appleton.
52. Wyocena, Wyocena.

LIST OF LODGES.

53. Kingston, Kingston.
55. Janesville, Janesville.
56. St. Croix, Mudson.
57. St. John's Whitewater.
58. Muscoda, Muscoda.
59. Markesan, Markesan.
60. Valley, Sparta.
61. Kane, Neenah.
62. Vesper, Mayville.
63. Waterloo, Waterloo.
64. Evening Star, Darlington.
65. Manitowoc, Manitowoc.
66. Richland, Richland Centre.
67. Fox Lake, Fox Lake.
68. Palmyra, Palmyra.
69. Fulton, Edgerton.
70. Orion, Orion.
71. Quincy, Friendship.
72. Dodge County, Beaver Dam.
73. Kegonsa, Stoughton.
74. Black River, Black River Falls.
75. Columbus, Columbus.
76. Plover, Plover.
78. Dells, Delton.
79. Ironton, Ironton.
80. Independence, Milwaukee.
81. Northern Light, Mauston.
82. Weyauwega, Weyauwega.
83. Concordia, Madison.
84. La Belle, Viroqua.
85. Des Peres, Depere.
86. Solomon, Juneau.
89. Pepin, Pepin.
90. Waucoma, Cooksville.
91. Oxford, Oxford.
92. Belle City, Racine.
93. Evergreen, Stevens Point.
94. Bicknell, Brodhead.
95. Ripon, Ripon.
96. Temple, Waterford.
97. Crescent, Mazomanie.
98. Bryan, Menasha.
99. Lodi Valley, Lodi.
100. Fairfield, Fairfield,
102. Marquette, Marquette.
103. Juneau, New Lisbon.
104. Astrea, Cedarburg.
105. North Western, Prescott.
106. Prairie du Chien, Prairie du Chien.
107. Tracy, Manitowoc.
108. Neosho, Neosho.
109. River Falls, River Falls
110. Lowell, Lowell.
111. Rosendale, Rosendale.
112. Eau Claire, Eau Claire.
113. Eureka, Prairie du Sac.

114. Palestine, Lone Rock.
115. Robert Morris, Eagle.
117. Trempeleau, Trempeleau.
118. Warden, Wiota.
119. Dodgeville, Dodgeville.
120. Hartford, Hartford.
121. Delavan, Delavan.
122. Bark River, Hartland.
123. Waupaca, Waupaca.
124. Columbia, Kilbourn City.
125. Salem, West Salem.
126. Darien, Darien.
127. Lebanon, Juda.
128. Grand Rapids, Grand Rapids.
129. Jamestown, Jamestown.
130. Forest, Wausau.
131. New London, New London.
132. Tomah, Tomah.
133. Ellsworth, Oconomowoc.
134. Oceola, Oceola.
135. Good Samaritan, Shopiere.
136. Springfield, Springfield.
137. Footville, Footville.
138. West Bend, West Bend.
139. Billings, Fort Atkinson.
140. Fond du Lac, Fond du Lac.
141. Montello, Montello.
142. Harmony, Milwaukee.
143. Sun Prairie, Sun Prairie.
144. Brandon, Brandon.
145. Washburn, Bristol.
146. Beetown, Beetown.
147. Green Lake, Dartford.
147. Wautoma, Wautoma.
149. Durand, Durand.
150. Burnett, Burnett.
151. Oregon, Oregon.
152. Cambria, Cambria.
153. Mifflin, Mifflin.
154. Chilton, Chilton.
155. Monticello Union, Monticello.
156. Corinthian, Union Grove.
157. Reedsburg, Reedsburg.
158. Oakfield, Oakfield.
159. Zerah, Necedah.
160. Bloomfield, Bloomfield.
161. Milton, Milton.
162. West Eau Claire, West Eau Claire.
163. Neillsville, Neillsville.
164. Menomonee, Menomonee.
165. Ferrin, Montford.
166. Princeton, Princeton.
167. Cassia, Greenbush.
168. Omro, Omro.
169. Grant, Boscobel.

352

LIST OF LODGES.

CANADA.

Jurisdiction of the Grand Lodge of Canada.

Antiquity, Montreal.
1. Provost, Dunham.
2. Niagara, Niagara.
3. St. John's, Kingston.
4. Dorchester, St. John's.
5. Sussex, Rockville.
6. Barton, Hamilton.
7. Union, Grimsby.
8. Nelson, Henryville.
9. Union, Nepanee.
10. Norfolk, Simcoe.
11. Moira, Belleville.
12. Golden Rule, Stanstead.
13. Western Light, Belton.
14. True Britons, Perth.
15. St. George, St. Catherines.
16. St. Andrew, Toronto.
17. St. John's, Cobourg.
18. Prince Edward, Picton.
19. St. George, Montreal.
20. St. John's, London.
21. Zetland, Montreal.
22. King Solomon's, Toronto.
23. Richmond, Richmond Hill.
24. St. Francis, Smith's Falls.
25. Ionic, Toronto.
26. Ontario, Port Hope.
27. Strict Observance, Hamilton.
28. Mt. Zion, Kemptville.
29. United, Brighton.
30. Composite, Whitby.
31. Jerusalem, Bournonville.
32. Amity, Dunville.
34. Thistle, Amherstsburg.
35. St. John's, Cayuga.
36. Welland, Fonthill.
37. King Hiram, Ingersoll.
38. Trent, Trenton.
39. Mt. Zion, Brooklyn.
40. St. John's, Hamilton.
41. St. George, Kingsville.
42. St. George, London.
43. Solomon's, Woodstock.
44. St. Thomas, St. Thomas.
45. Brant, Brantford.
46. Wellington, Chatham.
47. Great Western, Windsor.
48. Madock, Madock.
49. Harrington, Quebec.
50. Consecon, Consecon.
51. Corinthian, Grahamsville.
53. Shefford, Waterloo.
54. Vaughan, Maple.
55. Merickville, Merickville.
56. Victoria, Sarnia.
57. Harmony, Binbrook.
58. Doric, Ottawa.
59. Corinthian, Ottawa.
60. Hoyle, La Calle.
61. Acacia, Hamilton.
62. St. Andrew's, Caledonia.
64. Kilwinning, London.

66. Durham, Newcastle.
67. St. Thomas, Richmond.
68. St. John's, Ingersoll.
69. Sterling, Sterling.
71. Victoria, Sherbrooke.
72. Alma, Galt.
73. St. James, St. Mary's.
74. St. James, Maitland.
75. St. John's, Toronto.
76. Oxford, Woodstock.
78. King Hiram, Tillsonbury.
79. Simcoe, Bradford.
80. Albion, Newburg.
81. St. John's, Delowne.
82. St. John's, Paris.
83. Beaver, Strathroy.
84. Clinton, Clinton.
85. Rising Sun, Parmersville.
86. Wilson, Toronto.
87. Union, Markham.
88. St. George, Owen Sound.
90. Marito, Collingwood.
91. Colborne, Colborne.
92. Cataraqui, Kingston.
93. Northern Light, Kincardine
94. St. Mark's, Pt. Stanley.
95. Rideout, Allenville.
96. Corinthian, Barrie.
97. Sharon, Sharon.
98. True Blue, Albion.
99. Tuscan, New Market.
100. Valley, Dundas.
101. Corinthian, Peterboro'.
103. Maple Leaf, St. Catherines.
104. St. John's, Norwichville.
105. St. Mark, Drummondville.
106. Burford, Burford.
107. St. Paul, Lambeth.
108. Blenheim, Drumbo.
109. Albion, Harrowsmith.
110. Central, Prescott.
111. Maitland, Goderich.
113. Wilson, Waterford.
115. Ivy, Smithville.
116. Cassia, Sylvan.
117. Stanbridge, Stanbridge.
118. Union, Loyaltown.
119. Maple Leaf, Bath.
120. Warren, Fingal.
121. Doric, Brantford.
122. Renfrew, Renfrew.
123. The Belleville, Belleville.
124. Mount Kilwinning, Montreal.
125. Cornwall, Cornwall.
126. Golden Rule, Campbleford.
127. Franc, Frankford.
128. Pembroke, Pembroke.
129. The Rising Sun, Aurora.
130. Yamaska, Granby.
131. St. Lawrence, Southampton.
133. Lebanon Forest, Francestown.
134. Shonenegan, Three Rivers.

LIST OF LODGES.

135. St. Clair, Milton.
136. Richardson, Stouffville.
137. Pythagoras, Newford.
138. Aylmer, Aylmer.
139. Lebanon, Ashawa.
140. Malahide, Aylmer.
141 Tudor, Mitchell.
142. Excelsior, Morrisburg.
143. Friendly Bros., Iroquois.
144. Tecumseh, Stratford.
145. J. B. Hall, Millbrook.
146. Prince of Wales, Newburgh.
147. Mississippi, Almonte.
148. Civil Service, Ottawa.
149. Erie, Port Dover.
150. Hastings, Hastings.
151. The Grand River, Berlin.
152. Clarenceville, Clarenceville.
153. Burns, Wyoming.
154. Irving, Tucon.
155. Peterborough, Peterborough.
156. York, Eglington.
157. Simpson, Delta.
158. Alexandria, Oil Springs.
159. Goodwood, Richmond.

160. Quebec Garrison, Quebec.
161. Percy, Workworth.
162. Forest, Waseter.
163. Browne, Adamsville.
164. Star in the East, Wellington.
165. Burlington, Wellington Square.
166. Wentworth, Stony Creek.
167. Royal Albert, Montreal,
168. Merritt, Welland.
169. Macriale, Port Colborne.
170. Brittania, Seaforth.
171. Prince of Wales, Iona.
172. Ayr, Ayr.
173. Victoria, Montreal.
174. Walsingham, Port Rowan.
175. St. John's, South Patton.
176. Spartan, Sparta.
177. The Builder's, Ottawa.
178. Plattville, Plattville.
179. Bothwell, Bothwell.
180. Speed, Guelp.
U. D. Oriental, Port Burwell.
U. D. Petrolia, Petrolia.
U. D. Tuscan, Lewis.

CANADA EAST.

Jurisdiction of the Grand Lodge of England.

17. Albion, Quebec.
68. Quebec, Quebec.
214. St. John's, Quebec.
512. Union, Montreal.
513. Provost, Freligsburg.
514. St. Paul, Montreal.
515. Nelson, Clarenceville.
516. St. Andrew, St. Andrew's.
517. Golden Rule, Stanstead.
518. Wellington, Montreal.
519. Columbia, Hull.

520. Odell, Odelltown.
531. Sussex, Quebec.
643. St. George, Montreal.
731. Zetland, Montreal.
775. Dorchester, St. John's.
776. Prevost, Dunham.
923. St. Lawrence, Montreal.
931. Alma, Quebec.
934. Shefford, Waterloo.
938. Halye, La Colle.

Jurisdiction of the Grand Lodge of Ireland.

159. Hawksburg.
211. Port Stanley.
222. Toronto.
226. Ingersoll.
227. Montreal.
231. Hamilton.

232. St. Thomas.
237. Quebec.
286. York.
358. Benbrook.
359. Stratford.

Jurisdiction of the Grand Lodge of Scotland.

348. Elgin, Montreal.

356. St. Andrew, Quebec.

30*

854 LIST OF LODGES.

CANADA WEST.

Jurisdiction of the Grand Lodge of England.

488. Dalhousie, Niagara.
489. Sussex, Brockville.
490. Niagara, Niagara.
492. Fredsburg, Fredsburg.
493. Addington, Earnestown.
494. Union, Grimsby.
495. Toronto, Toronto.
498. King Hiram's, Oxford.
501. St. George, St. Catharines.
503. Union, Ancostia.
506. Mt. Moriah, Westminster.
720. Goderick Union, Goderick.

733. Barton, Hamilton.
779. St. John's, York.
789. Zetland, Toronto.
790. Richmond, Richmond Hill.
796. St. John's, Castle Place.
797. St. Francis, Smith Falls.
799. Unity, Whitby.
834. Corinthian, Petersboro'
835. Dalhousie, Ottawa.
848. Wellington, Guelph.
895. St. George, London.

LIST OF GRAND CHAPTERS.

MEM.—These are arranged under months, having January, etc., as sub-heads, under which Grand Chapters are arranged.

JANUARY.—FLORIDA.—Organized at Tallahassee, January 11th, 1847.

G. H. P.—1847, Thos. Douglass; 1848, John P. Duval; 1849, Isaac H. Brunson; 1850, Harry R. Taylor; 1851, Thomas Brown; 1852, R. A. Shino; 1853, Samuel Boardman; 1854-5, J. Wayles Baker; 1856, Thos. Hayward; 1857, Gad Humphreys; 1858, Thomas Hayward; 1859, D. P. Holland; 1860, Dr. Thos. G. Henrey, Quincey; 1861-4, Geo. F. Baltzell, Greenwood; 1865, David Jones, Columbia.

Grand Secretary.—J. B. Taylor, from organization until death; 1864-5, Hugh A. Corley, Tallahassee.

Subordinates.—No. 1. Tallahassee; 3. Apalachicola; 5. Monticello; 7. Quincy; 8. Madison; 9. Lake City; 15. Greenwood; 16. Micanopy; 17. Tampa.

MICHIGAN.—Organized 1849.

Grand High Priests.—E. Smith Lee; 1851, Czar Jones; 1852, Jeremiah Moore, Detroit; 1853-4, Michael Shoemaker, Jackson; 1855, Wm. L. Greenly, Adrian; 1859, Salathiel C. Coffinberry, Constantine; 1860, Wm. P. Innes, Grand Rapids; 1861-4, Benj. Porter, Jackson; 1865, Ebenezer Sprague, Battle Creek.

Grand Secretaries.—1851-2, Wm. J. Ives, Detroit—died in 1852, A. C. Smith, appointed; 1853-9, R. S. Cheney, Jackson (in which year R. S. C—— came under censure of the G. L.), J. Eastman Johnston, Centreville, appointed and continues in office 1865.

Subordinates.—No. 1. Detroit; 2. Niles; 3. Jackson; 4. Marshall; 5. Pontiac; 6. Ann Arbor; 7. Grand Rapids; 8. Jonesville; 9. Lansing; 10. Adrian; 11. Centreville; 12. St. Clair; 13. Kalamazoo; 14. Ionia; 15. Flint; 16. Detroit; 17. Romeo; 18. Hillsdale; 19. Battle Creek; 20. Rockland; 21. Coldwater; 22. Monroe; 23. Three Rivers; 24. Eaton Rapids; 25. Ypsilanti; 26. Sturgis; 27. Port Huron; 28. Hudson; 29. Fentonville; 30. Howell; 31. East Saginaw; 32. Albion; 33. Corunna; 34. Paw Paw; 35. Dowagian; 36. Newaygo.

MISSISSIPPI.—Organized at Vicksburg, May 18th, 1846. No. 3. Vicksburg; 4. Columbia; 5. Holly Springs; 6. Jackson.

Grand High Priests.—1846-7, Benj. S. Tappan; 1848, Walter Brooks, Lexington; 1849, W. H. Stevens; 1850, T. C. Tupper; 1851, Charles Scott; 1852, C. S. Spann; 1853, Abner V. Rowe, Lexington; 1854, Wm. S. Patton; 1855, Wm. R. Cannon, Columbus; 1856, Wm. Cothran; 1857, J. M. Houry; 1858, A. R. Johnson; 1859, M. S. Ward; 1860, Giles M. Hillyer, Natchez.

Grand Secretaries.—1846, Wm. Wing, Jackson; 1847, James H. Campbell; 1849-53, David N. Barrows, Jackson; 1854, Richmond McInnis; 1855-60, Robert W. T. Daniel, Jackson.

Subordinates.—No. 1. Natchez; 2. Port Gibson; 3. Vicksburg; 4. Columbus; 5. Holly Springs; 6. Jackson; 7. Brownsville; 8. Yazoo City; 9. Lexington; 10. Canton; 11. Macon; 12. Grenada; 13. Aberdeen; 14. Fayette; 15. Carrollton; 16. Woodville; 17. Gallatin; 18. Pontotoc; 20. Kosciusko; 21. Hernando; 22. Raymond; 23. Houston; 28. Como; 29. Cayuga; 30. Vaiden Station; 31. Decatur; 33. Oxford; 34. Philadelphia; 36. Louisville; 37. Richmond; 40. Mt. Pleasant; 42. Amite; 44. Charleston; 45. Enterprise; 46. Carthage; 48. Ripley; 49. New Albany; 50. Mt. Carmel; 51. Chulahoma; 52. Lauderdale Springs; 53. Palo Alto; 54. Handsboro'; 55. Palmer's Springs; 56. Flewellin's Cross Roads; 57. Carrollville; 58. Clinton; 59. Quitman; 60. Panola; 61. Richland; 62. Looxahoma; 63. Jeremiah Hall; 64. Dover; 65. Hohenlinden; 66. Jacinto; 67. Cockrum; 68. Byhalia; 69. Brandon; 70. Scooba; 71. Bavaria; 72. Satartia; 73. Senatobia.

(355)

356   LIST OF GRAND CHAPTERS.

NEW YORK.—Organized at Albany, March 1798.
Subordinates.—No. 1. New York; 2. New York; 5. Albany; 6. Hudson; 8. N. York·
13. N. Lebanon; 22. Waterville; 23. Ballston Spa; 24. Pottsdam; 25. Whitehall; 26.
Cooperstown; 28. Malone; 30. Moravia; 34. Auburn; 35. Batavia; 36. Geneva; 39,
Plattsburg; 42. Elmira; 47. Owego; 48. Troy; 50. Hamilton; 54. Canajoharie; 55.
Glen's.Falls; 57. Atica; 58. Ithica; 59. Watertown; 62. Rochester; 63. Ogdensburg; 64.
Aurora; 67. Jamestown; 68. Sackett's Harbor; 70. Syracuse; 71. Buffalo; 72. Manlius;
75. Kingston; 76. Fredonia; 77. Trumansburg; 78. Johnstown; 79. Palmyra; 80. Af-
ton; 88. Lockport; 91. Dansville; 92. Ovid; 95. Bath; 96. Cape Vincent; 100. Penn
Yan; 101. Hornelville; 103. Greenfield; 106. Greene; 107. Lima; 109. Brooklyn; 116.
Northampton; 117. Newark; 131. Saratoga Springs; 132. Canton; 133. Lansingburg;
135. Mexico; 136. Gowanda; 137. Mt. Morris; 138. N. York; 139. Binghamton; 140
N.York; 141. N. York; 142. Williamsburg; 143. Wellsville; 144. Camden; 145. Booneville; 146. Addison; 147. New York; 148. Brooklyn; 149. Theresa; 150. Olean; 151.
Norwich; 152. Belfast; 153. Rome; 155. Nunda; 156. Pt. Byron; 157. Schenectady.
158. New York; 159. New York; 160. New York; 161. Little Falls; 163. Buffalo; 164.
Canandaigua; 165. Oswego; 166. Little Valley; 167. Fulton; 168. Watervliet; 169.
Waterford; 170. New York; 171. Ft. Edward; 172. Poughkeepsie; 173. Seneca Falls;
174. Sing Sing; 175. Albion.
    Grand High Priests.—1823–4, Ezra Ames; 1852–3–4. John L. Lewis, jun., Penn Yan;
1855. John S. Perry, Troy; 1856, Chas. L. Church; 1858, Peter P. Murphy, Royalton;
1859, James M. Austin; 1861, Geo. H. Thatcher, Albany; 1864, D. A. Ogden; 1865,
Horace S. Taylor. N. York.
    Grand Secretary.—John O. Cole, Albany.
    FEBRUARY.—SOUTH CAROLINA.—Organized Charleston, 13th and 22d March and 29th
May, 1812, by Chapter No. 15, Charleston; 3. Beaufort; 5. Charleston.
    Grand High Priests.—1812–14, Wm. Young, Charleston; 1815, Edward Hughes;
1816–20, Wm. Young; 1821–4, Joel R. Poinsett; 1826, John L. Wilson; Albert G. Mackey, Charleston. (List incomplete.)
    Grand Secretaries.—1812, John Hanmer, Beaufort; 1813–14, John Izard Wright;
1815, C. S. Tucker; 1816, James Drummond; 1817, Wm. Waller; 1818, John Roche;
1819–22, Richard Maynard; 1823, H. G. Street; 1826, James.England.
    LOUISIANA.—Files incomplete.
    Grand High Priests.—1824 to 1835, John Henry Holland, New Orleans (died March
29th, 1864); 1848, Thos. H. Lewis; 1849, Wm. H. Howard—went to California; 1850–1,
Thos. H. Lewis; 1852, James R. Hartsock; 1853–4, Thos. H. Lewis; 1855–6, Amos
Adams; 1857–8, Dr. Robert F. McGuire (died at Monroe, La., 1862); 1859, John Q. A.
Fellows; 1860, Abel J. Norwood, Clinton; 1861, A. S. Washburn, Bastrop; 1862–5,
Henry R. Swasey, New Orleans.
    Grand Secretaries.—1860–1, Samuel G. Risk, New Orleans (died at Memphis, Tenn.);
1862–5, Samuel M. Todd, N. Orleans.
    Subordinates.—No. 1. New Orleans; 2. New Orleans; 3. New Orleans; 4. Clinton;
6. Baton Rouge; 8. Lake Providence; 9. Farmersville; 10. Shreveport; 11. St. Francisville; 12. Franklin; 14. Mansfield; 15. New Orleans; 16. Bastrop; 17. Minden; 18.
Monroe; 21. New Orleans; 24. Homer; 25. Union Cross Roads.
    WISCONSIN.—Organized February 13th, 1850.
    No. 1. Milwaukee; 2. Plattsville; 3. Southport.
    Grand High Priests.—1850–52, Dwight F. Lawton; 1853, Geo. Whitman Cobb, Min-
eral Point; 1854, Luther M. Tracy, Milwaukee; 1855, Henry S. Baird, Green Bay;
1856, Rufus Dela Pulford, Mineral Point; 1857, Daniel Howell, Jefferson; 1858–9,
Henry L. Palmer; 1860, Erastus Lewis, Janesville; 1861, John H. Rountrell, Plattsville; 1862, Montgomery M. Cothren, Mineral Point; 1863, Alvin B. Alden, Portage
City; 1864, Melvin L. Youngs, Milwaukee.
    Grand Secretaries.—1850–7, Wm. Rudolph Smith, Mineral Point; 1858–9, John W.
Hunt, Madison (died in 1859); 1860–5, Wm. T. Palmer, Milwaukee.
    Subordinates.—No. 1. Milwaukee; 2. Platteville; 3. Kenosha; 4. Madison; 5. Janes-
ville; 6. Mineral Point; 7. Milwaukee; 8. Green Bay; 9. Beloit; 10. Sheboygan Falls;
11. Watertown; 12. Racine; 13. La Crosse; 14. Portage City; 15. Osh,Kosh; 17. Elk-
horn; 18. Berlin; 19. Sparta; 20. Fond du Lac; 21. Monroe; 22. Waterloo.
    RHODE ISLAND.—Organized March 12th, 1798, under Gr. Chapter Northern States of
America, formed at Hartford January preceding.
    D. Grand High Priest.—Highest office—1798, Seth Wheaton; 1799, Moses Dix,
G. H. P., Newport; 1804 to 1814, Thos. Smith Webb (died Cleveland, O., July 6th,
1819); 1819, John Carlisle; 1820, Wm. Wilkinson; 1822–3, Caleb Earle; 1824–5; Sam-
uel Jackson; 1826, Peter Grinnell; 1827, Asa Bosworth; 1828–9, Caleb Drown; 1831,
Joseph Tomkins; 1832, Barney Merry; 1833–7, Moses Richardson; 1838–9, James
Salsbury; 1840–1, Wm. C. Barker; 1842–3, Cyrus Fisher; 1844–5, Wm. Field; 1846,
Alvin Jencks; 1847, Roger W. Potter; 1848–51, Thomas Whitaker; 1852–3, James

LIST OF GRAND CHAPTERS. 357

Hutchinson; 1854–5, Cyrus B. Manchester; 1856, Samuel Lewis; 1857, John Eldred; 1858, John Eldred; 1859, Joseph Belcher, Prov.; 1860, Oliver Johnson, Prov.; 1861, Ariel Ballou, Woonsocket; 1862, Lyman Klapp, Providence; 1863, Nathan H. Gould, Newport.

Grand Secretaries.—1798 to 1800, B. Wheeler; 1801, Wm. F. Magee; 1802–3, Amos T. Jenckes; 1804, M. Richardson; 1805–10, Otis Ammidon; 1811–15, Moses Richardson; 1816, John Snow; 1817, M. Richardson; 1818 to 1832, Sylvanus Tingley; 1833–9, Roger W. Potter; 1840–1, C. M. Nestell; 1842–6, C. B. Manchester; 1847–8, James Hutchinson; 1849 to 1859, Wm. C. Barker; 1860–5, Samuel B. Swan, Providence.

Subordinates.—No. 1. Providence, organized 1793, 303 members; 2. Newport, organized 1811, 34 members; 3. Warren, 1819, 38 members; 4. Pawtucket, 1820, 111 members; 5. Woonsocket. 1858, 43 members. Total members in State in 1863, 530.

APRIL.—GEORGIA.—Organized Feb. 23d, 1821, Louisville and Augusta represented; subsequently approval and vote of officers forwarded by Chapters at Lexington, Eastonton and Milledgeville—files in my possession imperfect.

Grand High Priests.—1822, Gov. William Schley, Louisville (died Nov. 20th, 1858); 1848, Wm. T. Gould, Augusta; 1854–9. Philip T. Schley, Savannah.

Grand Secretaries.—1823, Daniel Hook, Louisville; 1848, W. H. Kitchen, Augusta; 1854 to 1860, Benjamin B. Russell, Augusta.

Subordinates.—No. 1. Athens; 2. Augusta; 3. Savannah; 4. Macon; 5. Forsyth; 6. Milledgeville; 7. Columbus; 8. Talbotton; 9. Washington; 10. Griffin; 11. La Grange; 12. Ft. Gaines; 13. Marietta; 14. Newbern; 15. Albany; 16. Atalanta; 17. Lumpkin; 18. Fort Valley; 20. Eatonton; 21. Warrenton; 22. Carrollton; 23. Ellaville; 24. Dalton; 25. Elberton; 26. Rome; 27. Greensboro'; 28. McDonough; 30. Hamilton; 31. Cuthbert; 32. Lithonia; 33. Sandersville; 34. Newnan; 35. Zebulon; Cartersville; . 37. Fayetteville; 38. Franklin; 39. Lawrenceville; 40. Monroe; 41. Cedar Town; 42. Americus; 43. Covington; 44. Thomasville; 45. Blakely.

MAY.—CONNECTICUT.—Organized at Hartford, 17th of May, 1798.

Subordinates in 1865.—No. 1 was Newtown; 2. N. Haven, 265 members; 3. Derby; 4. Norwich, 164 members; 5 was Colchester; 6. Middletown; 7. N. London, 154 members; 8 was Reading; 9 was Windham, now at Willimantic; 10. Woodbury; 11. Stamford; 12 was Woodstock, now at Killingly; 13. Bridgeport; 14 was Kent; 15 was Canaan; 16. Litchfield; 17. Hartford, 314 members; 18 was Tolland, now at Rockville; 19. Ridgefield; 20. Granby; 21. Stonington; 22 was at Oxford, now at Waterbury, 102 members; 23. Danbury; 24. Norwalk; 25. New Britain; 26. Fair Haven; 27. West Meriden; 28. Pawtucket. List of officers not at hand.

Grand High Priests.—1847, Benonia Shepherd; 1848, Wm. E. Sanford; 1852, George Giddings; 1853–4, Cyrus Goodell; 1855–6, Isaac H. Coe, Killingly; 1858, David Clark, Hartford; 1860, Fred'k J. Calhoun, N. Haven; 1861–2, Nathan Dikeman, jun., Waterbury; 1863–4, Asa Smith, Norwalk; 1865, Luke A. Lockwood, Greenwich.

Grand Secretaries.—Eliphalet G. Storer served until 1864; 1865, William E. Sanford, New Haven.

MAINE.—Organized 1821.

Grand High Priests.—1823–5, Robert P. Dunlap; 1826–9, Nathaniel Coffin, Wiscassett (died at Watauga, Ill., April 7th, 1864); 1846, James C. Churchhill; 1847, Freeman Bradford; 1853, Abner B. Thompson, Brunswick; 1854, Timothy Chase, Belfast; 1855–6, Abner B. Thompson; 1857–8, Jos. C. Stevens, Bangor; 1860, Moses Dodge, Portland; 1861, Edward P. Burnham, Saco; 1862–3, John J. Bell, Carmel; 1864–5, Andrew J. Fuller, Bath.

Grand Secretaries.—1853, Allen Haines; Ira Berry, Portland, since 1854. [Arthur Shirley, Grand Secretary 1830–48, died at Portland, January 20th, 1864, aged 80 years. He was a faithful servant and reliable strength when anti-masonic persecution was hottest.]

Subordinates.—No. 1. Portland; 2. Bath; 3. Wiscassett; 4. Hallowell; 5. Saco; 6. Bangor; 7. Belfast; 8. Rockland; 9. Lewiston; 10. Eastport; 11. Saccarappa; 12. China; 13. Portland; 14. Brunswick; 15. Skowhegan.

JUNE.—NEW HAMPSHIRE.—Organized 1819.

Grand High Priests.—1819–20, John Harris; 1821, Thomas S. Bowles; 1822, Jonathan Nye; 1823, Thomas W. Colby; 1824–6, Samuel Cushman; 1827–9, Frederick A. Sumner; 1830–1, Andrew Pierce; 1832, Jonathan Nye; 1833, Robert Smith; 1834–6, B. L. Greenough; 1837–8, Robert Smith; 1830–40, Weare Tappan; 1841–3, Daniel Chase; 1844–5, David Parker; 1846–7, Philemon Tolles; 1848–9, John Knowlton; 1850, John J. Prentis; 1851–2, Daniel Balch; 1853–4, Albert R. Hatch; 1855–6, John Christie; 1857–9, Theodore T. Abbott, 1860, Moses Paul; 1861, Jonas Livingston; 1862, Samuel L. Wilcox; 1864, John R. Holbrook, Portsmouth.

Grand Secretaries.—1819–22, Thomas W. Colby; 1823–5, Timothy Kenrick; 1826 to 1843, Albe Cady; 1844–8, Hosea Fessenden; 1849 to 1865, Horace Chase, Hopkinton.

358 LIST OF GRAND CHAPTERS.

Subordinates.—No. 1 was Lebanon; 2. Concord; 3. Portsmouth; 4. Keene; 5. Lisbon; 6 Claremont; 7 was Sandbolton; 8. Dover; 9. Nashua (was at Dunstable); 11. Manchester.

TEXAS.—Grand High Priests.—1850, Samuel M. Williams; 1851, E. B. Nichols; 1852, G. M. Patrick; 1853, W. M. Taylor; 1854. H. R. Cartmell, Washington; 1855, Joseph C. Harrison, Linwood; 1859, Andrew Neill; 1860, W. T. Austin, Galveston.
Grand Secretaries.—1850-1, A. S. Ruthven; 1852-5, James M. Hall, Crockett; 1856-60, A. S. Ruthven, Galveston.
Subordinates.—No. 1. Galveston; 2. Houston; 3. Anderson; 4. Crockett; 5. Brenham; 6. Austin; 7. Huntsville; 8. Washington; 9. San Augustine; 10. Palestine; 11. Rusk; 12. Henderson; 14. Wheelock; 15. Clarksville; 18. La Grange; 19. Marshall; 21. Burleson; 22. Larissa; 24. Tyler; 25. Shelbyville; 27. Lockhart; 29. Mt. Enterprise; 30. Leona; 32. Jefferson; 33. Montgomery; 34. Columbia; 36. Matagorda; 37. Elysian Fields; 38. Cold Springs; 39. Moscow; 41. Corsicana; 42. Fairfield; 43. Hallettsville; 44. Richmond; 46. Columbus; 47. Dallas; 48. Paris; 49. Gilmer; 51. Gonzales; 52. Bonham; 53. McKinney; 54.Goliad; 55. Athens; 56. Seguin; 57.Gabriel Mills; 58. Fort Worth; 59. Jasper; 60. Douglasville; 61. Wharton; 62. Sherman; 63. Tarrant; 65. Lexington; 66. Cameron; 67. Hempstead; 68. Decatur; 69. Kaufman; 70. Sabine Pass; 71. Port Sullivan; 72. Texana; 78. Waxahachie; 74. Woodville; 75. Belton; 76. Veal's Station.

IOWA.—Organized at Mt. Pleasant, June 8th, 1854.
Grand High Priests.—1854, Theo. S. Parvin; 1855-6, J. R. Hartsock, Iowa City; 1857-9, E. W. Eastman, Oskaloosa; 1860, Kimball Porter; 1861, C. Stewart Ells, Davenport; 1862, Caleb Lamb, Newton; 1863, W. E. Woodward, Burlington.
Grand Secretaries.—1854, J. H. Wallace, Muscatine; 1855-6, Theo. L. Parvin; 1857, D. S. Warren; 1858-65, W. B. Langridge, Muscatine.
Subordinates.—No. 1. Burlington; 2. Iowa City; 3. Dubuque; 4. Muscatine; 5. Fairfield; 6. Oskaloosa; 7. Keokuk; 8.,Mt. Pleasant; 11. Winterset; 12. Newton; 13. Washington; 14. Des Moines; 15. Vinton; 18. Knoxville; 20. Cedar Falls; 23. Keosanqua; 25. Bloomfield; 26. Sioux City; 27. McGregor; 27. Fort Madison.

MISSOURI.—Imperfect reports.
Grand High Priests.—1852, John F. Ryland; 1853, Thornton Grimsley; 1854, P. H. McBride; 1855, Thos. S. Miller, Hannibal; 1862, James Carr; 1865, Thomas E. Garrett, St. Louis.
Grand Secretaries.—1854, John D. Taylor; 1865, Anthony O'Sullivan, St. Louis.

NORTH CAROLINA.—Organized in 1822 by representatives of Mount Ararat, No. 4, Murfreesboro'; Roanoke, No. 14; Halifax, No. 16, Raleigh; Cyrus, No. 17, Milton; Concord, No. 18. Tarboro'. Files imperfect.
Grand High Priests.—1852-4, Robert G. Rankin, Wilmington; 1855-6, Peter Custis, Newbern.
Grand Secretaries.—1824, Robt. Strange; 1825, Simmons J. Baker, Tarboro'; John Cruso; George Anderson, Halifax; 1852-3, Henry P. Russell, Wilmington; 1855-6, Thos. B. Carr, Wilmington.
Subordinates.—No. 1. Wilmington; 2. Fayetteville; 3. Murfreesboro'; 4. Halifax; 5. Tarboro'; 7. Newbern; 8. Oxford; 9. Warrenton; 10. Raleigh; 11. Hillsboro'; 13. Greensboro'; 14. Hartford; 17. Duplin; 18. Roxboro'; 19. Plymouth; 20. Salisbury; 22. Lincolnton; 23. Montgomery; 24. Stokes; 25. Buncombe; 26. Edgcombe; 27. Wilson; 28. Graham.

AUGUST.—VERMONT.—Organized Dec. 20th, 1804.
Grand High Priests.—1804, Jonathan Wells; 1805-8, Cephas Smith; 1809, Isaac Tichenor; 1810-12, Ozias Fuller; 1813-15, John Chipman; 1816-17, Charles K. William; 1818-21, John H. Cotton; 1822-4, Samuel Whitney; 1825-26, John H. Cotton, Windsor; 1827-9, Joel Clapp, Shelburne; 1830, Silas Bowen; 1831-9, Nathan B. Haswell (no officers elected until reorganization, July 18th,1849); 1849-51, N. B. Haswell; 1852-7, Philip C. Tucker, Vergennes; 1858, John S. Webster, Winooski; 1859, Thos. H. Campbell, St. Albans; 1860-2, Barzillai Davenport, Brandon; 1863-4, Gamaliel Washburn; 1865, Leverett B. Englesby, Burlington.
Grand Secretaries.—1804, Cephas Smith; 1805, Nicholas Goddard; 1806, R. Washburn; 1807-11, Nicholas Goddard; 1812-13, William Page; 1814-1816, Levi Lawton; 1817, Lemuel Whitney; 1818-34, Joel Green (no activity until reorganization in 1849); 1849-51, Philip C. Tucker, Jr.; 1852-4, Leverett B. Englesby; 1855-65, John B. Hollenbeck, Burlington.
Subordinates.—No. 1. St. Albans; 2. Vergennes; 3. Burlington; 4. East Berkshire; 5. Royalton; 6. Windsor; 7. Montpelier; 8. Bennington; 9. Rutland; 10. Poultney; 11. St. Johnsbury; 12. Brattleboro'; 13. Bradford.

SEPTEMBER.—MASSACHUSETTS.—Organized by two Chapters: St. Andrews, Boston, and King Cyrus, Newburyport, March 13th, 1798. Highest officer, a Deputy Grand High Priest, the presiding officer of the Grand Royal Arch Chapter of the Northern

LIST OF GRAND CHAPTERS.

359

States of America being then the head of all the State Grand Chapters allied with it; altered next year.

1798, Deputy Grand High Priest, Benj. Hurd, Jr., Charlestown; Grand High Priest, 1799–1800, Benj. Hurd, Jr.; 1801–2, Dudley Atkins Tyng; 1803–05, Timothy Bigelow; 1806–8, Isaiah Thomas, Worcester; 1809, Oliver Prescott; 1810–12, James Dean Hopkins; 1813–15, John Abbott; 1816–17, Andrew Sigourney; 1818–19, James Prescott; 1820–2, Jonathan Gage; 1823–5, Rev. Paul Dean; 1826–8, Daniel Lewis Gibbons; 1829–31, Rev. Samuel Clarke, Princeton; 1832–3, Josiah J. Fiske; 1834–6, Edward A. Raymond; 1837–9, Simon W. Robinson; 1840, John B. Hammatt; 1841–3, Elijah Atherton; 1844–5, Thos. Tolman; 1846–8, Charles Wheelock Moore; 1849–51, Benj. Huntoon, Canton; 1852–4, Rev. Stephen Lovell; 1855–6, Daniel Harwood; 1857, Wendell Thornton Davis; 1858, John McClellan; 1859–61, James Kimball, Salem; 1862–4, Solon Thornton.

Grand Secretaries.— List incomplete. 1800, Wm. Woart; 1823, John J. Loring; 1824–31, Samuel Howe; 1840–64, Thos. Waterman, Boston.

Subordinates.—No. 1. St. Andrews. This Royal Arch Lodge—then so called—James Brown, Master, met in Boston, 28th August, 1769. The degrees conferred therein were Excellent, Super Excellent, and Royal Arch. On 14th May, 1770, Joseph Warren (afterward a martyr in battle of Bunker Hill, 1775) was made a Royal Arch Mason in this Lodge. This was in the Hall of St. Andrew's Lodge, Green Dragon Tavern, Union Street. (Mem.: Benj. Hurd, Jr., was Secretary in 1789.) 1793, Mark degree conferred; 1794, Royal Arch Chapter used as title for the first time. Members in 1864, 291.

3d Chapter at Groton, Sept. 1803; closed during anti-masonic excitement—charter renewed Sept. 12th, 1848 (1805, Disp. of Mt. Vernon Chapter, Portland, Me.); 1805, Charlton; 1811, Salem; 1815, Greenwich; 1816, Attleboro'—then Taunton, 1845, revived at New Bedford; 1817, Springfield; 1817, Greenfield—surrendered 1836, renewed 1853; 1818, Nantucket; December, 1818, St. Paul's, Boston—1865, 330 members; 1820, Mt. Zion, Stoughton; 1821, Princeton, and in 1847 changed location to Fitchburg; 1823, Worcester, suspended 1830 and revived 1846; 1824, Modway, New Milford; 1825, Brookfield; 1825, Northampton (suspended and renewed, 1848); 1826, Concord, Framingham; 1826, Bethlehem, N. Bedford—afterward extinct; 1826, Lowell; 1826, Mt. Zion, Sutton (this Chapter, with St. Andrew and St. Paul, Boston, did not suspend their organization during the anti-masonic excitement); 1854, St. John's, East Boston, 70 members; 1855, Chelsea; 1856, Hyannis; 1856, Haverhill; 1858, Pittsfield; 1858, Enfield; 1860, Foxboro'; 1860, Lawrence; 1862, Abington; 1863, Melrose; 1863, South Boston; 1863, Palmer; 1863, Medford; 1863, Lynn; 1864, Fall River, Cambridge, Waltham, Taunton.

NEW JERSEY.—Organized at Burlington, Dec. 30th, 1856.

Grand High Priests.—1856–7, William H. Doggett, Jersey City; 1858, George A. Tator; 1859, Wm. W. Goodwin, Berkley; 1860–1, Dr. Thomas J. Carson, Trenton; 1862, George B. Edwards, Bergen; 1863, John Sheville, Hudson City; 1864, Dr. Chas. M. Zeh, Newark; 1865, Dr. J. C. G. Robertson, Patterson.

Grand Secretaries.—1856–7, Ferdinand Brother, New Brunswick; 1858, Frank Corlies, Eatontown; 1859–65, Dr. John Wolverton, Trenton.

Subordinates.—No. 1. Eatontown; 2. Jersey City; 3. Burlington; 4. New Brunswick; 5. Trenton; 6. Bridgeton; 7. Newark; 8. Bergen; 9. Newark; 10. Patterson; 11. Hoboken; 12. Phillipsburg, since to Washington; 13. Lambertville; 14. Keyport.

OCTOBER.—OHIO.—Organized 1816.

Grand High Priests.—1816, Samuel Hoyt, Marietta; 1817, Chester Griswold, Delaware; 1817–19, John Snow (was Grand Secretary of Grand Chapter of Rhode Island, year before); 1820, Davis Embree, Cincinnati; 1821–2, Phineas Ross, Lebanon; 1823, Joseph S. Hughes, Delaware; 1824, Edward King, Chillicothe; 1825, John Cotton, Marietta; 1826, Edward King; 1827–8, Charles Rogers Sherman, Lancaster; 1829, Irwin McDowell, Columbus; 1830, James Gates, Lancaster; 1831, Wm. R. Foster, Cincinnati; 1832, Samuel Stokeley, Steubenville; 1833, William James Reese, Lancaster; 1834, Henry Sage, Circleville; 1835, Wm. B. Thrall, Circleville; 1836–8, W. J. Reese; 1839, Wm. B. Thrall; 1840–1, Oliver M. Spencer, Cincinnati; 1842–6, Wm. B. Hubbard, Columbus; 1847, George D. Hine, Massillon; 1848–50, Jacob Graff, Cincinnati; 1851–2, Jacob B. Brown, Mt. Vernon; 1853–56, Horace M. Stokes, Lebanon; 1857–9, George, Rex, Wooster; 1860, Harvey Vinal, Springfield; 1861–2, John M. Parks, Cincinnati; 1863–4, Thomas Jefferson Larsh, Eaton; 1865, George Rox, Wooster.

Grand Secretaries.—1816–17, R. Kercheval, Chillicothe; 1818–19. B. Gardner, Columbus; 1820–4, A. J. McDowell; 1825, Henry Brown, Columbus; 1826–9, Bela Latham; 1830, John Lyne Starling, Columbus; 1832, Bela Latham; 1834–6, John C. Broderick, Lancaster; 1837–43, James D. Caldwell; 1844–50, Benj. F. Smith; 1851–65, John D. Caldwell, Cincinnati.

Subordinates.—No. 1. Marietta; 2. Cincinnati; 3. Worthington; 4. Chillicothe; 5.

360   LIST OF GRAND CHAPTERS.

Lebanon; 6. Newark; 7. Norwalk; 9. Zanesville; 11. Lancaster; 12. Columbus; 14. Cleveland; 15. Steubenville; 16. Dayton; 17. St. Clairsville; 18. Delaware; 19. McMillan, Cincinnati; 21. Hamilton; 22. Eaton; 23. Portsmouth; 24. Troy; 25. Akron; 26. Mt. Vernon; 27. Wooster; 28. Mansfield; 29. Toledo; 30. Medina; 31. Piqua; 33. Republic; 34. Urbana; 35. Milford; 36. Xenia; 37. McConnellsville; 38. New Philadelphia; 39. Athens; 40. Hillsboro'; 41. Felicity; 42. Tiffin; 44. Miamisburg; 45. Bryan; 46. Painesville; 47. Elyria; 48. Springfield; 49. Lima; 50. Coshocton; 51. St. Mary's; 52. Georgetown; 53. Cambridge; 54. Delaware; 55. Wellsville; 56. Vinton; 57. New Carlisle; 58. Findlay; 59. Gilead; 60. Bellefontaine; 61. Somerset; 62. Marion; 63. Wilmington; 64. Fremont; 65. Ashtabula; 66. Warren; 67. Ashland; 68. Ironton; 69. Barnesville; 70. Jackson; 71. Van Wert; 72. Sandusky City; 73. London; 74. Twinsburg; 75. Logan; 76. Conneaut; 77. Greenville; 78. Moscow; 79. Gallipolis; 80. Pomeroy; 81. Smithfield; 82. Ripley; 83. Alliance; 84. Canton; 85. Woodfield; 86. Millersburg; 87. Middletown; 88. Crestline; 89. Defiance; 90. Clyde; 91. Ravenna; 92. New Lisbon.

TENNESSEE.—Organized in 1825. Imperfect record in our archives.
Grand High Priests.—1827, Wm. Gibbes Hunt; 1828, Moses Stevens; 1829, Wilkins Tannehill; 1838, Benj. S. Tappan. Franklin; 1849, Charles A. Fuller, Nashville; 1850, Archelaus M. Hughes, Columbia; ——, Edward M. Kenney; 1856. Solomon W. Cochran; 1857, Robert J. Chester, Jackson; 1858-9, Robert S. Moore, Clarkesville; Masslon, Whitten,[Yorkville.
Grand Secretaries.—1827-31, Joseph Norvell, Nashville; 1838, Moses Stevens; 1849-50, John S. Dashiell, Nashville; 1856-65, Chas. A. Fuller, Nashville.
Subordinates.—No. 1. Nashville; 2. Franklin; 3. Clarksville; 4. Columbia; 5. Jackson; 6. Knoxville; 8. Washington; 9. Clinton; 10. Tuscumbia; 11. Lafayette; 15. Caledonia; 16. Yorkville; 17. Dresden; 18. Union; 19. Good Will; 20. Pulaski; 21. Washington; 22. Penn; 23. Pythagoras; 24. Pearl; 25. Lebanon; 26. Warren; 27. Eureka; 28. Haywood; 29. Raleigh, charter returned; 30. Trinne; 31. Trenton; 32. Quincey; 33. Obion; 34. Bolivar; 35. Wesley; 36. Morning Sun; 37. Lexington; 38. Hunting; ton; 39. Cleveland; 40. Tannehill; 41. Hughes; 42. Dyersburg; 43. Berlin; 44. Denmark; 45. Mt. Zion; 46. Lewisburg; 47. Springfield; 48. Gallatin; 49. Hamilton; 50. Alexandria; 51. Winchester.

ILLINOIS.—Organized 1850.
Past Grand High Priests.—1850, Wm. B. Warren, John J. Holton, J. V. Z. Blaney; 1851-2, Levi Lusk, Rushville; 1853, M. J. Noyes, Pittsfield; 1854, Louis Watson, Quincy; Ira A. W. Buck, Aurora; E. M. M. Clarke, James H. Hibbard, Alton; 1858-59, Nelson D. Elwood, Joliet; 1861, W. W. Mitchell; 1862-3, Hiram W. Hubbard, Bloomington; 1864, Wiley M. Egan, Chicago.
Grand Secretary.—Harman G. Reynolds, Springfield, from early day even until now.
Subordinates.—No. 1. Springfield; 2. Chicago; 3. Jacksonville; 4. Henderson; 5. Quincy; 6. Shawneetown; 7. Peoria; 8. Alton; 9. Rushville; 10. Pittsfield; 13. Naperville; 14. St. Charles; 15. Upper Alton; 16. Hennepin; 17. Keithsburg; 19. Macomb; 20. Vermont; 21. Decatur; 22. Aurora; 23. Freeport; 24. Rockport; 22. Pekin; 26. Bloomington; 27. Joliet; 28 Princeton: 29. Beardstown; 30. Monmonth; 31. Morris; 32. Edgar; 33. Carthage; 34. McHenry; 35. Harmony; 36. Woodstock; 37. Ottawa; 38. Olney; 40. Hutsonville; 41. Waukegan; 42. Lacon; 43. Chicago; 44. Duquoin; 45. Jonesboro'; 46. Galesburg; 47. Kewanee; 48. Monticello; 49. Sycamore; 50. Champaign; 51. Galena; 52. De Kalb; 54. Charleston; 56. Dixon; 57. Sterling; 58. Utica; 59. Clinton; 60. Peru; 61. Polo; 62. Lebanon; 63. Hillsboro'; Tuscola, Salem, Bement, Canton.

CALIFORNIA.—Organized July 28th, 1854.
Grand High Priests.—1854, Chas. M. Radcliff; 1855, John D. Creigh; 1856, Orange H. Dibble; 1857, Wm. W. Traylor; 1858, Thos. H. Caswell; 1859, Whiting G. West; 1860-1. Henry Hare Hartley; 1862. Adolphus Hollub; 1863, Ezra H. Van Decar; 1864, Isaac Davis.
Past Grand Secretaries.—George J. N. Monell, Sacramento; L. C. Owen, San Francisco, 1864.
Subordinates.—No. 1. San Francisco; 2. Sonora; 3. Sacramento; 4. Diamond Springs; 5. San Francisco; 6. Nevada; 7. Benicia; 8. Columbia; 9. Shasta; 10. Forest City; 11. Sutter Creek; 12. Murphy; 13. Marysville; 14. San Jose; 15. Yreka; 16. Placerville; 17. Iowa Hill; 18. Grass Valley; 19. Weaverville; 20. Oroville; 21. Downieville; 22. Petaluma; 23. Todd's Valley; 24. Camptonville; 25. Georgetown; 26. Oakland; 27. Auburn; 28. Stockton; 29. North San Juan; 30. Napa City; 31. Martinez; 32. Quincy; 33. Los Angelos; 34. La Porte.

KENTUCKY.—Organized 1817. Reports on file are incomplete.
Grand High Priests.—1820-1, David Graham Cowan; 1822, William G. Hunt; 1823, John McKinney, Jr., Versailles; 1824, Thomas McLauahan—died 1825, at Louisville; 1825, James M. Pike, Lexington; 1826, Robert Johnston, Frankfort; 1827, Thomas H.

LIST OF GRAND CHAPTERS.

361

Bradford; 1828, Henry Wingate; 1829, Levi Tyler; 1830, And. M. January, Maysville; 1831, Warham P. Loomis, Frankfort; 1841, Derrick Warner; 1842, Abner Cunningham; 1845, Herman Bowman, Jr.; 1846, Dempsey Carroll, Maysville; 1847, Willis Stewart, Louisville; 1848, Humphrey Jones, Richmond; 1849, James II. Daviess; 1850, C. G. Wintersmith; 1851, Thomas Ware, Cynthiana; 1852, Isaac Cunningham, Winchester; 1853, John M. S. McCorkle, Greensburg (now at Louisville); 1854, John D. McClure, Owenton; 1855, Harvey T. Wilson, Sherburne; 1862, Thomas Sadler, Paris (now Cincinnati); 1863, Samuel D. McCullough, Lexington; 1864. Wm. E. Robinson; 1865, Harry Hudson, Louisville.

Grand Secretaries.—1820, J. H. Crane; 1821, John McKinney, Jr., Versailles; 1822-65, Philip Swigert, Frankfort.

Subordinates.—No. 1. Lexington; 2. Shelbyville; 3. Frankfort; 5. Louisville; 6. Versailles; 8. Russellville; 9. Maysville; 12. Winchester; 13. Georgetown; 14. Hopkinsville; 15. Paris; 16. Richmond; 17. Cynthiana; 18. Louisville; 19. Lexington; 20. Hardinsburg; 21. Mt. Sterling; 22. Danville; 23. Owenton; 24. Lafayette; 25. Somerset; 26. N. Middletown; 27. Springfield; 28. Princeton; 29. Harrodsburg; 30. Paducah; 31. Bardstown; 32. Owensboro'; 34. Elizabethtown; 35. Covington; 36. Greensburg; 38. Bowling Green; 40. Cadiz; 41. Carlisle; 42. Irvine; 43. Mumfordsville; 44. Shepherdsville; 45. Glasgow; 46. Millersburg; 47. Sherburne; 48. Crittenden; 49. Hickman; 50. Newton; 51. Napoleon; 53. Bloomfield; 54. Morganfield; 55. Carrollton; 56. Lancaster; 57. Albany; 58. Brandenburg; 59. Stanford; 60. N. Liberty; 61. Eddyville; 62. Owingsville; 63. Union; 64. Columbus; 65. Henderson; 66. Paint Lick; .67. Hawesville; 68. Mt. Eden; 69. Mayfield; 70. Marion; 71. Flemingsburg; 72. Providence; 73. Concord; 74. Concord; 75. Fairview; 75. Newport.

NOVEMBER.—PENNSYLVANIA.—Royal Arch Masonry, as claimed by Masons of this State, was started in Philadelphia, under a Provincial Grand Lodge, as early as 1758. The Grand Lodge of Pennsylvania founded the first Grand Chapter of Pennsylvania, November, 1795—its Grand Master being all the while Grand High Priest. 1824, Grand Chapter became independent. Reports on file incomplete.

Past Grand High Priests.—Daniel Thompson, James Simpson, David C. Sterrett, Edward P. Lascure, Harman Baugh, John C. Smith, Benjamin Parke, Harman Yerkes.

Grand Secretary.—William H. Adams, Philadelphia.

Subordinates.—No. 1. Philadelphia; 21. Harrisburg; 43. Lancaster; 52. Philadelphia; 91. Philadelphia; 150. Washington; 153. Reading; 159. Minersville; 161. Towanda; 162. Pittsburg; 163. Lock Haven; 164. Brownsville; 166. Hollidaysburg; 167. Rochester; 169. Philadelphia; 171. Carlisle; 172. Tunkhannock; 173. Easton; 174. Sunbury; 175 Philadelphia; 176. Chambersburg; 177. Tamaqua; 178. Catawissa; 179. Carbondale; 180. Montrose; 181. Mauch Chunk; 182. Wilkesbarre; 183. Philadelphia; 185. Scranton; 187. Conneautville; 189. Altoona; 190. Norristown; 191. Meadville; 192. Greensburg; 194. Wellsboro'; 195. Pottsville; 196. Lebanon; 197. Phœnixville.

MARYLAND AND DISTRICT COLUMBIA.—Organized 1812.

Grand High Priests.—1812, Daniel Kurtz, P. P. Eckle, J. E. Jackson; Hezekiah Niles; 1825–26, Joseph K. Stapleton. Thomas Phœnix, Grand Secretary and Grand Lecturer. 1840, J. K. Stapleton, Maryland; 1841–9, Joseph K. Stapleton; 1850–3, Benjamin B. French; 1858–61, James Gozler; 1863, John N. McJilton; 1863–4, Dr. John L. Yeates.

Grand Secretaries.—1825–6, Thomas Phenix; 1840, Chas. Gilman; 1841–59, Joseph Robinson, Baltimore; 1860–5, William Morris Smith, Washington City, D. O.

ARKANSAS.—Record incomplete.

Grand High Priests.—1852, Thos. D. Merrick; 1853–4, Albert Pike, Little Rock; 1859, Thos. D. Merrick.

Grand Secretaries.—1852–3, Luke E. Barber, Little Rock; 1854, John E. Reardon, Little Rock; 1859, Jno. H. Newbern, Little Rock.

Subordinates.—No. 1. Fayetteville; 2. Little Rock; 3. El Dorado; 4. Camden; 5. Union Springs; 7. Pine Bluff; 8. Fort Smith; 9. Batesville; 10. Woodlawn.

DECEMBER.—VIRGINIA.—The M. Ex. Supreme Gr. R. A. Chapter organized May 1st, 1808, at Norfolk. R. A. Masonry was introduced into Virginia under the auspices of Joseph Myers, who was an Inspector General of the Ancient and Accepted Scotch Rite—of Southern jurisdiction—of Charleston, S. C. From efforts of Comp. Jas. Cushman, H. P., Franklin Chapter, No. 4, Connecticut, who exemplified the work of the Gen'l Gr. Chapter U. S., in 1820, to Grand Chapter of Virginia, which Virginia agreed to adopt, and so instructed the subordinates to use its work. An effort was made to unite under General Grand Chapter, but the matter was deferred, and alliance was finally declined by Grand Chapter of Virginia. Files are imperfect.

Grand High Priests.—1820, James Penn; 1823, George Cabell; 1824, Rev. Wm. Hart; ——, James Collins, 1827, John G. Williams; 1828, George C. Dromgoole, Lawrenceville; 1830, Seth L. Stevenson; 1836–7, Blair Bolling; 1840, J. Worthington Smith, Staunton; 1841, Charles A. Grice, Portsmouth; 1841–7, James Points; 1851-2,

31

362   *LIST OF GRAND CHAPTERS.*

Morgan Nelson; 1853, John R. McDaniel, Lynchburg; 1855, Lewis B. Williams Orange C. H.

Grand Secretary.—1820–65, John Dove, Richmond—a servant of great service to Masonry. Honor to the Veteran!

ALABAMA.—Grand High Priests.—1823, Dugald McFarlane, Tuscaloosa; 1824–5, Governor Israel Pickens; 1826, Nimrod E. Benson; 1827–8, John Murphy; 1829–30, Thomas B. Creagh. (No meeting until 1837.) 1837–9, John C. Hicks, Leighton; 1840, A. B. Dawson, Wetumpka; 1841–3, David Moore; 1844, James Penn, Huntsville; 1845–6, Felix G. Norman, Tuscumbia; 1847–9, Wm. Hendrix, Marion; 1850, Rufus Greene, Mobile; 1851–2, Wm. P. Chilton, Tuskegee; 1853–5, W. A. Ferrell, Hollow Square; 1856–8, David Clopton, Tuskegee; 1859–60, S. A. M. Wood, Florence.

Grand Secretaries.—1823–4, John B. Hogan, Mobile; 1825–7, Wm. D. Stone, Pickensville; 1828–30, John G. Aikin; 1837–8, Doric. S. Ball, Tuscaloosa; 1839–56, Amand P. Pfister, Montgomery (died 3d Dec. 1856); 1856–61, Daniel Sayre, Montgomery.

Subordinates.—No. 1. Tuscaloosa; 4. Claiborne; 5. Huntsville; 6. Florence; 10. Tuscumbia; 11. Greensboro'; 12. Marion; 17. Wetumpka; 18. Warsaw; 19. Clinton; 21. Mobile; 22. Montgomery; 24. Eufala; 25. Courtland; 26. Uniontown; 28. Selma; 30. Jacksonville; 31. Benton; 32. Orrville; 33. Autaugaville; 34. Union Springs; 35. Glennville; 36. Pickensville; 37. Lafayette; 40. Camden; 41. Summerfield; 44. Butler; 49. Bridgeville; 50. Gainesville; 52. Allentown; 53. Uchee; 54. Troy; 55. Suggsville; 56. Waverly; 57. Lebanon; 58. Cahaba; 60. Braggs; 61. Society Hill; 62. Rockford; 63. Clayton; 64. Montevallo; 65. Stevenson; 66. Mobile; 67. Farriorville; 68. Centre; 69. Lower P. Tree; 70. Choctaw Corner; 71. Barnes Cross Roads; 72. Midway.

OREGON.—(Meets in September.)—Organized at Salem, Sept. 18th, 1860.

Grand High Priests.—1860, Albert W. Ferguson, Salem; 1861–2, John McCracken, Portland

Grand Secretary.—T. McF. Patton, Salem.

Subordinates.—No. 1. Salem; 2. Oregon City; 3. Portland; 4. Jacksonville; 5. Corvallis.

MINNESOTA.—(Meets in October.)—Organized 1860.

Grand High Priests.—Alfred E. Ames, Minneapolis; R. S. Alden; Geo. W. Prescott, St. Paul.

Grand Secretary.—Azariah T. C. Pierson, St. Paul.

Subordinates.—No. 1. St. Paul; 2. Vermillion; 3. St. Anthony; 4. Red Wing.

CANADA.—Organized at Canada West, 19th January, 1857. Chapters had, previously, authority under Grand Lodge.

1. Anc. Frontenac, Kingston; 2. The Hiram, Hamilton; 4. St. Andrew's, Toronto; 5. St. George's, London; 6. St. John's, Hamilton; 7. Moira, Belleville; 8. King Solomon's, Toronto; 9. Golden Rule, Stanstead; 10. Catasaqui, Kingston; 13. Stadaconia, Quebec; 14. Bedford Dist. Dunham; 15. Wawanosh, Sarnia; 16. Castleton, Ottawa; 17. Dorchester, Waterloo; 18. Oxford, Woodstock; 19. Mt. Moriah, St. Catherine; 20. Mt. Horeb, Brantford; 21. Carnarvon, Montreal; 22. Grenville; Prescott; 23. Ezra, Simcoe; 24. Tecumseh, Shatford; 25. Mt. Horeb, Montreal; 26. St. Mark's, Trenton; 27. Maniton, Collingwood.

Gr. H. Z.—1857, William Mercer Wilson, Simcoe; 1858, Thompson Wilson, London; 1859–64, Thos. Douglas Harrington.

Grand Secretary, or Scribe Ezra.—Thomas B. Harris, Hamilton.

Subordinates.—At Kingston, Hamilton, London, Toronto, Batterville, Stanstedt, Windsor.

SUBORDINATE ENCAMPMENTS.

Organized under Authority of the Grand Encampment of the U. S., or recognized by it, since its formation, on first day of June, 1816.

Ohio.—Mount Vernon, at Worthington, June, 1818; chartered Sept. 1st, 1819, re-organized, 1841; Miami, at Lebanon, March 4th, 1826; Lancaster, at Lancaster, 1835; Cincinnati, at Cincinnati, November, 1839–41; Massillon, at Massillon, July 5th, 1843–44; Clinton, at Mt. Vernon, July 22d, 1843–44. Grand Encampment of Ohio, organized at Lancaster, O., Oct. 24th, 1843; Mt. Vernon Encampment, No. 1, now at Columbus, O.

Connecticut. — Recognized Encampment at Colchester, September, 1819; New Haven, at New Haven, disp. Nov. 5th, chartered September, 1826. Grand Encampment of Connecticut, organized Sept. 13th, 1827.

Vermont.—Vermont, at Windsor, chartered Feb. 23d, 1821; Green Mountain, at Rutland, March 12th, 1823; Mt. Calvary, at Middlebury, Feb. 20th, 1824; revived in 1850; Burlington, at Burlington, June 28th, 1849; Sept. 17th, 1850; Lafayette, at Berkshire, revived Nov. 9th, 1850. State Grand Encampment, formed Aug. 14th, 1851.

North Carolina.—Fayetteville, at Fayetteville, Dec. 21st, 1821. Dormant several years; charter lost by fire. In 1850, authorized to resume labor at Wilmington and Fayetteville. State Grand Encampment formed.

Virginia.—Richmond, at Richmond, May 5th, 1823; Warren, at Harper's Ferry, July 4th, 1824 (recognized); Winchester, at Winchester, July 4th, 1824 (recognized); Wheeling, at Wheeling, 1838. Grand Encampment of Virginia represented in Grand Encampment of the U. S. in 1826. Soon extinct. Formed new Grand Encampment in 1845, without approval of Grand Encampment U. S.; and the above Encampments, except Wheeling, were erased from register of Grand Encampment U. S. 1847, Grand Encampment of Virginia relinquished her allegiance. On the 22d Jan., 1851, Virginia again united with Grand Encampment U. S., but seceded again in 1861.

Georgia.—Georgia, at Augusta, May 5th, 1823; St. Omer, at Macon, 26th July, and September, 1848; St. Aldemar, at Columbus, December, 1857; Jan. 24, 1860; Comy. Cœur de Lion, at Atlanta, May 14th, 1859; September 17th, 1859. Grand Encampment formed, April 25th, 1860.

New Hampshire.—Trinity, at Hanover, March 24th, 1824. Rechartered, Sept. 19th, 1853, at Manchester; De Witt Clinton, at Portsmouth, January, 1826; Mt. Horeb, at Hopkinton, May 1st, 1826; North Star, at Lancaster, May 2d, 1857; September, 1859; St. Paul's, at Dover, Nov. 7th, 1857; Sept. 16th, 1859; Mt. Horeb, at Concord, May 31st, 1859.

District of Columbia. — Washington, at Washington, Jan. 14th, 1825; revived, 1847; Columbia, at Washington, Dec. 8th, 1862; chartered September, 1865.

South Carolina.—Lafayette, at Georgetown, March, 1825; Columbia, at Columbia, Jan. 24th, 1824 (recognized); South Carolina, at Charleston, Sept. 23d, 1823; charter lost by fire, disp. May 17th, 1843; ch. 1844 (recognized). Grand Encampment of S. C. was represented in Grand Encampment U. S. 1826.

Kentucky.—Webb, at Lexington, Jan. 1st, 1826; revived, 1841; Louisville, at Louisville, Jan. 2d, 1840–41; Versailles, at Versailles, April 26th, 1842–44; Frankfort, at Frankfort, April, 1844–47; Montgomery, at Mt. Sterling, 1844–47.

Louisiana.—Invincibles, at New Orleans, 1828; Indivisible Friends, at New Orleans —jurisdiction from N. Y., 1838; revived, 1844 (this Encampment was chartered by Grand Encampment of New York, in May, 1816, before organization of the Grand Encampment of U. S.); Jacques De Molay, at New Orleans, April 15th, 1850; April 25th,

(363)

364 SUBORDINATE ENCAMPMENTS.

1851; Orleans, at New Orleans, May 19th, 1860; Sept. 4th, 1862. Grand Commandery of Louisiana, formed February, 1864.

MARYLAND.—Maryland, at Baltimore (revived, 1848); Baltimore, at Baltimore, June 17th, 1859; Sept. 10th, 1859.

TEXAS.—San Felipe de Austin, at Galveston (then a State of the Republic of Mexico), 1835; Ruthven, at Houston, Feb. 2d, 1848; Sept. 17th, 1853; Palestine, at Palestine, May 16th, 1853; Sept. 20th, 1853. Grand Encampment, formed Jan. 19th, 1855.

ALABAMA.—(There was a Barker Encampment in Alabama in 1829.) Marion, at Marion, 1844; Washington, at Marion (perhaps same), 1846; Barker, at Claiborne, chartered 1847; Mobile, at Mobile, April 7th, 1848; March 18th, 1851; Tuscumbia, at Tuscumbia, Aug. 1st, 1848; Oct. 12th, 1850; Montgomery, at Montgomery, Oct. 17th, 1850: Sept. 19th, 1853; Selma, at Selma, May 13th, 1858; Sept. 16th, 1859. State Grand Commandery, formed Nov. 29th, 1860; 1st election, Dec. 1st, 1860.

MISSISSIPPI.— Mississippi, at Jackson, July 5th, 1844; ——, 1844; Magnolia, at Vicksburg, Oct. 2d, 1850; Jan. 4th, 1854; Lexington, at Lexington, July 22d, 1856; Sept. 11th, 1856. State Grand Commandery, formed Jan. 22d, 1857.

MAINE.—Portland, at Portland, 1845–1847; Maine, at Portland; St. John's, at Bangor, Feb. 18th, 1850; Sept. 17th, 1850. State Grand Commandery, organized May 5th, 1852.

PENNSYLVANIA.—As early as May 12th, 1797, a Grand Encampment of Knights Templar of Pa. was formed. 1812, Dec. 27th—Encampment No. 1 and 2; originally under its constitution organized as No. 1. 1814, Feb. 15 and 16—delegates attended at Philadelphia, hoping to establish a governing body of Templars for the United States. The Encampments in the Eastern States not favoring the basis in Pennsylvania, which was to have the Encampments under subordination to the Grand Lodge of Pennsylvania, did not unite in the Philadelphia movement, but subsequently organized the Gen. Gr. Enc. U. S. Some delegates from Encampments in Pennsylvania, New York, Delaware, and Maryland organized Gr. Enc. of Pennsylvania. In April, 1814, charters were issued by the Pennsylvania organization to Rising Sun Enc., at New York; to No. 1, at Philadelphia; to No. 2, at Pittsburg. 2d of May, at Baltimore, Maryland, No. 3, 16th Feb., 1816, at Philadelphia, 9th June, 1819, and No. 4, at Philadelphia. This Gr. Enc. became dormant. In 1826, De Witt Clinton, for Gr. Enc. U. S., issued a disp. to Enc. at Harrisburg. July 26th, 1826—Enc. at Elmira, N. Y., divided itself and granted authority to Towanda Encampment, at Bradford, Pa. (the Pennsylvania record of which is), "We were in union with them, as a branch, so long as they proceeded agreeable to ancient usages to confer the Order of K. Templar, Knights of Malta, and of the Mediterranean Pass and of the Red Cross." The following were chartered by G. Enc. U. S.: Pittsburg, at Pittsburg, May 13th, 1847; Jaques De Molay, Washington, Sept. 12th, 1849; Oct. 24th, 1850; St. Omers, Uniontown, chartered Nov. 17th, 1853; Hubbard, Waynesburg, Nov. 10th, 1851; reorganized 5th Dec. 1853; chartered Sept. 1856. A State Grand Commandery was organized April 12th, 1854. On the 12th Feb., 1857 (by a two-thirds vote of fifteen Commanderies), union of it with the Gr. Enc. under Gr. Lodge of Pennsylvania.

TENNESSEE.—Disp. by W. G. Hunt, Jan. 1829—efforts to reinstate in 1842; Nashville, at Nashville, new disp. 1844; Yorkville, at Yorkville, July 10th, 1857; Sept. 17th, 1859; De Molay, at Columbia, Dec. 19th, 1858; Sept. 16th, 1859; Cyrene, at Memphis, March 27th, 1859; Sept. 16th, 1859. Tennessee Grand Commandery, organized Oct. 12th, 1859.

ILLINOIS.—Appollo, at Chicago, 1845, chartered 1847; Belvidere, at Alton, March 25th, 1853, Nov. 1st, 1853; Central, at Decatur, July and October, 1856; Peoria, at Peoria, July 25th, 1856, Sept. 15th, 1856; Freeport, at Freeport, June 10th, 1857, Sept. 16th, 1859. Grand Commandery of Illinois, organized Oct. 27th, 1857.

MISSOURI.—St. Louis, at St. Louis, chartered 1847; Weston, at Weston, March 4th, 1853, Sept. 19th, 1853; Lexington, at Lexington, Sept. 30th, 1853, Sept. 10th, 1856; St. Joseph, at St. Joseph, Nov. 9th, 1859. Grand Commandery of Missouri, organized May 22d, 1860.

MICHIGAN.—Detroit, at Detroit, Nov. 1st, 1850, Sept. 19th, 1853; Pontiac, at Pontiac, March 25th, 1852, Oct. 7th, 1853; Eureka, at Hillsdale, Feb. 13th, 1854; Sept. 10th, 1856; Peninsula, at Kalamazoo, March 3d, 1856, Sept. 10th, 1856; Monroe, at Monroe, March 29th, 1856, Sept. 12th, 1856; De Molay, at Grand Rapids, May 9th, 1856, Sept. 10th, 1856. Grand Commandery, Michigan, organized Jan. 15th, 1857, election April 7th, 1857; Peninsular Commandery united with it in 1859.

WISCONSIN.—Wisconsin, at Milwaukee, June 12th, 1850, Oct. 28th, 1851; Janesville, at Janesville, June 24th, 1856, Sept. 11th, 1856; Robert Macoy, at Madison, Jan. 29th, 1859, Sept. 16th, 1859. Grand Commandery, organized Oct. 20th, 1859.

FLORIDA.—De Molay, at Quincy, March 17th, 1851, continued to 1853; Hall burned down 31st Dec. 1851, Disp. to hold at Tallahassee.

IOWA.—De Molay, at Muscatine, March 14th, 1855, Sept. 10th, 1856; Palestine, at

CPSIA information can be obtained
at www.ICGtesting.com
Printed in the USA
BVHW082045200622
640215BV00001B/184